# DARKWELL

The patron god of any who would slay another of his kind, Bhaal found plentiful worshipers among the humans and other creatures of the many worlds. Foremost among them were the people of the Forgotten Realms.

It was in the Realms that the eagle flew, and died, and it was in the Realms that Bhaal's most powerful minions had been fought and bested by these humans who called themselves the Ffolk. Now Bhaal focused his entire baneful nature on the land claimed by these humans. Now one servant, a cleric of great power and even greater evil, still remained to do his bidding.

Slowly Bhaal's vengeance took form. The humans who obsessed him would die, but only after everything they loved had died before them. He himself would see to that. No longer would he trust his revenge to the talents of his minions.

To this end, Bhaal fostered the Darkwell. . . .

# THE MOONSHAE TRILOGY

Book One: Darkwalker on Moonshae
Book Two: Black Wizards
Book Three: Darkwell

# DARKWELL

## by Douglas Niles

### Cover Art by
### JEFF EASLEY

**TSR, Inc.**
PRODUCTS OF YOUR IMAGINATION™

# DARKWELL

Distributed to the book trade in the United States by Random House, Inc., and in Canada by Random House of Canada, Ltd.

Distributed in the United Kingdom by TSR Ltd.

Distributed to the toy and hobby trade by regional distributors.

FORGOTTEN REALMS, PRODUCTS OF YOUR IMAGINATION, AD&D, and the TSR logo are trademarks owned by TSR, Inc.

First Printing: February, 1989
Printed in the United States of America.
Library of Congress Catalog Card Number: 88-51722

9 8 7 6 5 4 3 2 1

ISBN: 0-88038-717-3

TSR, Inc.
P.O. Box 756
Lake Geneva,
WI 53147 U.S.A.

TSR Ltd.
120 Church End, Cherry Hinton
Cambridge CB1 3LB
United Kingdom

To Colby Ward, Dragonslayer

# Moonshae Isles

Korinn Archipelago

Norland

Sea of Moonshae

Rogarsheim

Alaron

Oman's Isle

Iron Keep

Strait of Oman

Moray

Myrloch Vale

Gwynneth

Strait of the Leviathan

Myrloch

N

Corwell Firth

Corwell Town

Flamsterd

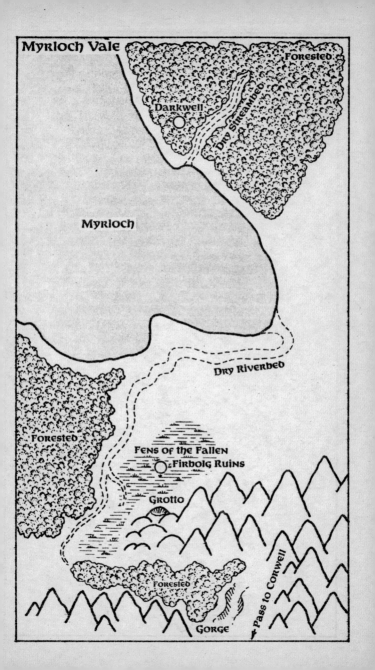

# What has
# gone before . . .

Tristan Kendrick, Prince of Corwell, stood upon the brink of manhood when the Beast, Kazgoroth, emerged from its fetid pool to savage the land. The insidious monster, often disguised in the flesh of a man, engaged the help of firbolg giants and savage northmen to attack the Ffolk of Corwell.

The prince came of age during this, the Darkwalker War. He returned a lost artifact, the Sword of Cymrych Hugh, to his people. He led them to ultimate victory against the Beast. And he found his life's love in the person of Robyn, a maiden who had been raised with him as the king's ward.

Also during the war, Robyn discovered her own deep powers as a druid, harnessing the forces of the earth to work magic and miracles. She loved the prince but faced a deeper calling after the war. She journeyed to pastoral Myrloch Vale to study the ways of her order under the Great Druid of the isles, Genna Moonsinger.

But there she found that the influence of Kazgoroth was not altogether banished. An unnatural army of corpses invaded the vale, and Robyn alone of the druids escaped. The others were imprisoned as stone statues around the scene of their last stand, and as Robyn departed, the vale was turned into a wasteland behind her.

His father murdered, Tristan journeyed to the neighboring island of Callidyrr to confront the High King of all the Ffolk. Caught in a rebellion and finally joined by Robyn, Tristan found himself once more victorious, receiving the royal Crown of the Isles. He was crowned High King by the Ffolk, then prepared to return to Corwell.

But still the evil lurked in Myrloch Vale. . . .

# Prelude

The goddess Earthmother wept, her wound a gaping slash across her flesh. The cut was deep, perhaps mortal, but there was none to know her suffering.

She cried out in pain from the scar of black magic, where her body lay torn and ripped from the assault of evil. Though the last convulsion of her power had excised the rot, tearing it from herself and allowing the cool sea to wash the wound, still the pain continued.

The goddess cried out for her servants, her devoted druids. These human caretakers were trapped in a prison of the mother's own invention. They stood frozen as stone statues around the blasted scene of their final defeat. The protection of the goddess had imprisoned them thus, saving them at least from death. One druid, and one alone, had escaped petrification.

And the goddess wept for the Ffolk, her people. War ravaged their fair land relentlessly, striking each of the four kingdoms with cruel force. Many Ffolk died while resisting the attack of northman or foul beast, but still peace eluded them.

Now her grief manifested itself in the glowering clouds that hung low over the isles, and the unnatural chill that sucked the summer's warmth from the land and, though the season was but early autumn, brought a winterlike frost. Her pain sent whirlwinds exploding from her soul, twisting funnels of violence that tore at the land, unmindful of the hurt they caused.

Yet the land was not altogether without hope. For the first

time in many decades, the king of the Ffolk was a true hero, as was right and proper. And though one lone druid remained free, she was a druid of great faith and steadily growing might.

But they were both very young, and the goddess was very old. She doubted that she could live long enough to see them prevail.

Or fail.

# ❧ 1 ❧

# THE OBSCENE

Heavy breakers assaulted the stone barrier protecting Llewellyn Harbor. They crashed against the rocky rampart, sending clouds of spray through the air, roaring in frustration as the eternal power of the sea dispersed against the fundamental strength of stone.

A lone figure stood near the end of the breakwater. The man was heavily wrapped in oilskins and ignored the salty shower that doused him each time a fresh wave expended itself. If anything, he relished the bracing cold of the water.

The man was young, but he was a king of many lands. He had bested creatures foul and wizards of might, yet he felt unsure of his own strength. He held the love of a strong woman in his heart, but still his future remained a muddled blur before him.

Tristan Kendrick claimed as ancestors a long line of kings, but for two centuries the Kendricks ruled only the small, sparsely populated land of Corwell. Now, as High King of the Ffolk, King Kendrick accepted fealty also from Moray, Snowdown, and mighty Callidyrr.

The king had recently won a war, the Darkwalker War, besting a supernatural beast and its human allies. He had claimed as allies the graceful warriors of the Llewyrr and the doughty fighters of the dwarven realms. His blade, the Sword of Cymrych Hugh, girded him as ample proof of his heroism, for he had returned the weapon to the Ffolk after many decades of its absence.

Finally the man turned from the sea, walking slowly along the rocky barrier toward the welcoming lights of Llewellyn

Town. The sea had given him no answers. Nothing, it seemed, could give him the answers.

And there were so many questions.

\* \* \* \* \*

The eagle soared slowly. Its eyes, dulled by fatigue, searched the barren landscape below, seeking any morsel of lifesaving food.

But the bird saw nothing. No trace of animal, small or large, appeared across the stretches of brown marsh. Even the trees of the once-vast forests now resembled gaunt skeletons, barren of leaves and needles, surrounded by heaps of rotting compost.

The great bird swirled, confused. It sought a glimpse of the sea, or even the high coastal moor. But everywhere the view yielded scenes of rot and corruption. With a sharp squawk of despair, the eagle soared off in a new direction.

A sudden movement caught the eagle's keen eye, and it swept into a diving circle to investigate. But it pulled up short, screeching its frustration at the shambling figure on the ground. Though the creature smelled of carrion, it moved. Though it moved, it was not alive.

Growing desperate now, the eagle soared away in search of something, anything, to eat. It came upon a region of utter desolation, a place that made the past reaches of barren land seem fertile. The predator flew north, over a stagnant brown stream. It crossed a reach of dead, fallen timber.

Finally it came to a small pond. The water was surrounded by twenty stone statues, remarkably lifelike human figures in various poses of battle. The surface of the pond itself was an impenetrable black.

But what was that? The eagle saw, or imagined, motion below that flat, lightless surface. It could have been a trout, swimming complacently in the center of the pond. It could have been anything.

The bird tucked its wings and plummeted toward the shadow. The water rushed up to meet it, and the true nature of the dark shape became visible. The eagle shrieked and struck outward with its wings, slowing but not halting its descent. One claw, still extended to clutch the imagined prey, touched the surface of the black water.

A crackling hiss broke the silence, and for a moment the eagle froze, outlined in blue light. In another instant, the bird was gone, though no ripple disturbed the surface of the dark pond. A lone white feather, caught by an errant breath of wind, drifted upward and fluttered forlornly to settle upon the muddy shore of the Darkwell.

\* \* \* \* \*

Bhaal, god of murder, relished the eagle's death. Though he still dwelt in his fiery bier upon the distant and hostile plane of Gehenna, the minor snuffing of life in a place unimaginably remote was power transmitted directly to his foul essence.

Such was the power of the Darkwell. And such was the power of Bhaal.

The patron god of any who would slay another of his kind, Bhaal found plentiful worshipers among the humans and other creatures of the many worlds. Foremost among them were the people of the Forgotten Realms.

It was in the Realms that the eagle flew, and died, and it was in the Realms that Bhaal's most powerful minions had been fought and bested by these humans who called themselves the Ffolk. Now Bhaal focused his entire baneful nature on the land claimed by these humans. Now one servant, a cleric of great power and even greater evil, still remained to do his bidding.

Slowly Bhaal's vengeance took form. The humans who obsessed him would die, but only after everything they loved had died before them. He himself would see to that. No longer would he trust his revenge to the talents of his minions.

To this end, Bhaal fostered the Darkwell.

A deep laugh rumbled in his cavernous breast as he pondered the history of the pool. Only a month before, it had been a crystalline symbol of hope and purity, a Moonwell, sacred shrine of the goddess Earthmother. Her body was the earth itself, but her spirit resided primarily in pools such as this—clear, unspoiled water blessed with the benign enchantment of the goddess Earthmother.

This had been her most sacred well, but now the might of Bhaal, coupled with the deadly skills of his servant, the cleric Hobarth, had desecrated and polluted the water so that it no longer resembled its former state. Indeed, now it was a festering sore upon the land, spreading decay like a cancer through the rocks and clay and sand of the earth.

The former soul of the goddess now gave Bhaal a window into the world of man, and he liked what he saw. Slowly the god of murder moved toward the Darkwell.

He knew exactly what to do.

\*    \*    \*    \*    \*

The stag stumbled weakly against a rotten trunk. Its bedraggled flanks heaved with the effort of breathing. Its sweeping antlers swayed toward the ground, and the creature's dry, swollen tongue fell limply from its jaws. Unsteadily the huge deer lumbered away from the dead tree, past many more, through the dead forest.

Blinking in confusion and despair, the animal sought some sign of the Myrloch Vale it had known all its life. The broad valley of sun, the brilliant leaves of autumn, vast meadows of flowers swaying easily in the fresh breeze . . . all these things were gone.

The stag's ribs showed clearly through its torn pelt, for it had not eaten in many days. Yet this was not the greatest of the animal's needs.

The stag had to find water. It sensed that it could live no more than a few hours without it. The swollen tongue flopped loosely, and the wide eyes were obscured by an unnatural glaze.

A feeble breath of wind stirred the dead wood, and with it came the smell of water. Not clean water, to be sure—the scent was well mixed with those of rot and decay—but it was the scent of water nonetheless. With renewed vigor, the stag trotted toward the promising sign.

Soon the great deer came upon a black pond. The stag

ignored the unnatural stillness of the water. It paid scant notice to the twenty stone statues arrayed around the perimeter of the pool, except to ascertain that the human-like figures were indeed stone and not flesh. Even had they been living huntsmen, however, it is doubtful the deer could have turned from that compelling pond.

Bhaal watched the stag approach, willing it closer and closer. The god remembered his flash of pleasure upon the death of the eagle, and Bhaal relished the thought of the much larger body that approached.

The swollen tongue reached for the black surface. At the last moment, the stag sensed the *wrongness* of the water. It tried to pull back, to raise its broad antlers away from this awful thing. But it was too late.

The neck bent, pulled by a force far greater than the stag's own muscles, and its muzzle struck the surface of the Darkwell. A crackling blaze of blue light illuminated the stag's body, casting an intense glow across the pond for an instant.

Then the deer was gone. As with the eagle, its body had caused no ripple to mar the inky surface of the well. Only the skull remained, resting on the muddy bottom in several inches of water. Its empty eye sockets stared skyward, while overhead spread the massive rack of antlers like a ghastly tombstone.

\* \* \* \* \*

Robyn of Gwynneth lay in the hold of the lunging ship and prayed for a word from her goddess. The wooden timbers around her seemed to thrum softly with the power of her prayer, but that was all she sensed. She felt lonely and afraid, fearing for the Earthmother more than for herself.

In the darkness of the hold, she felt the touch of her spiritual mother, but it was faint and frail. She sensed a growing void between herself and her goddess, but she was at a loss to close it. "Mother, hold me, help me!" she whispered, but the unfeeling planks of the hull gave no comfort, and there was no reply. The source of her faith and her power was on the verge of extinction, and the druid could do little to help.

Strangely, even as the presence of the Earthmother faded, Robyn felt her own earthmagic growing in potency. Within the confinement of the long sea voyage, her body grew stronger daily. Her muscles were hard and wiry. Her mind was sharp and alert, to the point that she could hardly sleep. And she could feel the power growing within her.

But when she prayed, or on those rare nights when she slept deeply enough to dream, there was no word, barely the faintest image, to suggest that the mother was near.

Robyn knew of no other druid still walking free upon any of the Moonshaes. The most powerful of her order all stood frozen, locked in stone at the moment they had lost their most crucial battle. Only Robyn had escaped, and she felt pitifully inadequate for the tasks arrayed before her.

But she had no choice except to try.

\* \* \* \* \*

The fat cleric wiped a hand through his greasy hair, anxious now to reach his destination. For several days, he had explored the surrounding lands of Myrloch Vale, but his journey was nearly complete.

The entirety of Myrloch Vale was now known to him. The vast valley, in the center of the island of Gwynneth, had long been a bastion of the goddess who had watched over these isles. Now, however, it had become a land of death, a monumental wasteland in testament to the awesome power of the cleric's god.

And he had ventured to northern Gwynneth, beyond the vale and into the lands of the northmen along the fir coast. These invaders had claimed the land from the native Ffolk, establishing a number of villages and even one good-sized town, but had nothing resembling a separate state there. Bhaal had wondered about these humans, and so the cleric had investigated.

The southern land of Gwynneth, occupying nearly half the isle, was the kingdom of Corwell, of the people known as the Ffolk. This land the cleric had not visited, but that mattered little, for Corwell was already well known to the minions of Bhaal.

Now Hobarth, cleric of Bhaal, returned to the Darkwell with good news for his foul master. Decay spread rapidly across the vale. Everywhere he went, Hobarth found death and rot, as whole forests died and placid lakes shriveled into festering swamps.

The area around the well was particularly barren. The corpses of the many zombies he had raised from death were gone now, as Hobarth had ordered them into the well. Their presence, in fact, had been a prime source of the pollution that had so effectively corrupted the Moonwell. And the decay seemed to be spreading rapidly. Bhaal, Hobarth knew, would be pleased.

As he neared the Darkwell, he sensed a difference around him. It was not a difference in the land, or even the air, but a subtle presence on a deeper level. Something was here that had not been here when he left.

He saw the well before him, its slick black surface barely reflecting the white outlines of the statues. The Darkwell had, since its creation a month before, been a center of power for his god.

But now Hobarth sensed something mightier, more dynamic than the gate connecting his god's world to his own. In a flash of understanding, he understood, and as he understood he dropped to his knees.

*Bhaal was here!*

Hobarth shivered, a strange mixture of ecstasy and fear. He knelt, closed his eyes, and prayed with all his heart.

"O mighty Bhaal, Reveler in Blood, master of my destiny . . ." The cleric moaned his prayer softly, wondering at the presence of his god. Was Bhaal angry? Was he pleased? What was the purpose of this visitation?

*Approach the well.*

Hobarth froze for a moment as the god's command grasped his heart. He felt cold fingers engulf his soul, only to let it free again after a glimpse of something awesome and terrible. Numb, he stood and stepped slowly toward the Darkwell.

*The Great Druid.*

Hobarth understood the command instantly and stopped

beside the Great Druid—or rather, the statue that had been Genna Moonsinger, the mistress of Myrloch Vale and Great Druid of the isles. Now she stood frozen as a white stone sculpture, lifelike in every detail. Many times had Hobarth stood before her and cursed her defiant expression.

He saw the challenge still lurking in her eyes, and in the firm set of her jaw. Her wrinkled skin and tightly wrapped hair might have given her a grandmotherly look, but instead she looked more like a warrior.

*The Heart.*

This command brought a glimmer of defiance, for just a brief moment, to the cleric. Hobarth kept the Heart of Kazgoroth in a pouch at his side, and he was most reluctant to remove it for anyone or anything. The stone was black, shaped more like a lump of coal than a heart, but it was a talisman of great evil. In the cleric's hands, the Heart of Kazgoroth had brought death and decay to the formerly pastoral vale.

But Hobarth overcame his reluctance instantly and hastened to obey the word of his god. He removed the stone from its pouch and held it out before him. It seemed to absorb the rays of the sun, already dimmed by the pale haze. In its own shadow, the cleric reached forward to touch the heart against the cold stone of the statue.

Bhaal must be very near, Hobarth thought, for it seemed to the cleric that the god leered over his shoulder. Hobarth acted as if by instinct, performing a ritual he had never seen, yet one that he knew without question or doubt. He sensed that Bhaal was pleased, and his god's pleasure was a thrill unlike any the cleric had ever known.

The black surface of the heart touched the white stone of Genna's breast. Yellow smoke hissed at contact, and trickles of clear liquid ran down the statue's stony robe. Where the stone was wet, it became a bright red, like freshly spilled blood.

Hobarth stared into the statue's eyes, and he saw the defiance that had been etched there begin to fade. He pressed his hand against her and was gratified to feel the Heart of Kazgoroth sink into the stone. More smoke spewed, nearly blinding him, but he kept his gaze fastened upon the statue's eyes.

His own eyes watered. The statue grew soft, and Hobarth's hand, together with the black stone, passed directly into the cold body. Quickly he drew forth his hand, empty, and the surface of the statue closed behind it. He looked again into those stone eyes.

Only it was no longer a statue, and the eyes burned with a far from stonelike fire.

\* \* \* \* \*

The low green mass of Corwell loomed to starboard. To port, invisible in the gray haze of sea-miles, lay the island of Moray. And below the keel of the sleek longship rolled the gray swells of the Strait of the Leviathan.

But Grunnarch the Red knew that the Leviathan was dead. Had not the Red King played a role in its demise only a short year earlier? He found the memory vaguely disquieting.

Now the ruler of the northmen stood boldly on the deck of his ship, the *Northwind*, and stared into the distance. Not north, toward Norland and home, but east, toward Corwell.

Why did that land hold such fascination for him? The Red King himself did not know, though certainly the roots of the answer lay in the disastrous invasion and his army's subsequent defeat. Grunnarch had been fortunate to escape with half of his ships and men, while many of his allies had suffered worse. The men of Oman's Isle, of the kingdom of Ironhand, had been virtually annihilated.

Now the *Northwind*, accompanied by the slightly smaller longship *Redfin*, sailed past that land after a long summer of raiding shores far from the Moonshaes. In less than a week, they would be home, but even the prospective homecoming could not lighten the Red King's brooding sense of foreboding.

True, the raiding had been highly successful. They had sailed south along the Sword Coast, plundering the towns of Amn, and even northern Calimshan. The *Northwind* rode low in the water from the weight of silver stowed along her keel, together with golden chalices, mirrors, fine tapestries and silks, and all manner of things treasured in the Moonshaes.

And there was the scroll. Grunnarch wondered why that lone treasure, scribed in a symbology he could not read, should figure so prominently in his thoughts about the trove.

*The lord mayor of Lodi stood before him, outlined by the blazing framework of his blockhouse. The man met his gaze without fear, but Grunnarch could see defeat in his eyes. The Red King, his bloody axe in his hands, watched the mayor with interest.*

*"I offer you our greatest treasure. In return, I ask only that you spare the children."*

*Grunnarch took the ivory tube, surprised at its lightness. He had expected the container to hold platinum, or at least gold, in quantity. Curious, he pulled the cap off and saw that it held but four small sheets of parchment.*

*"Treasure?" he said menacingly. "This is worthless!"*

*But the mayor did not flinch. "You are wrong. You have probably never held such worth in your hands!"*

*Grunnarch paused. The man's plea meant little—northmen did not slay children, so the town's youth had never been in danger. Truly the Red King had no use for a scroll. Yet, as he held it, he began to sense that it was indeed an object of rare worth.*

*A strange feeling came over him as he examined the exterior of the scroll case. He saw a picture of a beautiful young woman, sensual and rounded, and yet his reaction was a wish to protect her. Other pictures—a vast field of grain, a smooth lake, and a cozy fire in a hearth of stone—all beckoned him with sensations of warmth and comfort.*

*Disquieted, he took the scrolls gruffly. He turned on his heel and ordered his surprised crews back to their vessels, leaving Lodi almost unscathed. They took no other plunder but instead put straight to sea under the harsh urging of the Red King.*

And so came the scrolls with him to the Moonshaes.

This season of plunder had dragged on for Grunnarch,

for he lacked the fiery battle lust that had once made him relish the strike of steel against steel, the striving of man against man. Now battle was merely another tiresome task that faced him all too often.

After the raid on Lodi, the Red King had lost heart for battle altogether. Rationalizing that the season was late, he had ordered the two ships homeward, ignoring the surprised reactions of his crew. After two weeks upon the Trackless Sea, they had returned once again to the Moonshaes. Now they slipped between two kingdoms of the Ffolk, headed toward his own lands to the north.

And still that feeling of foreboding remained with him, perched upon his broad shoulders like some unnatural apparition.

\* \* \* \* \*

A great brown bear shuffled across the dead land, pausing to turn over a log with his broad forepaw or to snuffle under a stump with his nose. Once again, the spoor of even a tiny maggot or grub eluded him. Grunt huffed in frustration, too weak to take even a halfhearted swing at the offending stump.

There was no food here.

Grunt stumbled on, sensing that to stop was to die. Long gashes covered his shaggy flanks, now crusted with dried blood. One of the cuts lay freshly opened, a victim of some scrape against a looming trunk.

Even in the depths of his fatigue, Grunt moved with pride and purpose. His head held high, his posture was a challenge to any lesser creature that might cross his path. But his footsteps were unsteady, and the great brown eyes grew dull. There were no creatures to cross his path and behold his prideful agony.

This was land Grunt had known all of his life, yet he did not know it now. The grove of his mistress, Genna Moonsinger, the Great Druid of the isle, now festered and decayed. Many were the animals that had lived here, amid a lush blanket of greenery. Now there was no creature. Now there was nothing green.

Grunt growled, the sound rumbling low in his chest. He blinked, peering around as if trying to clear the nightmare vision from his eyes. Then he lumbered on, resolutely plodding across the wasteland in search of food or water.

Suddenly the bear lifted his great head and froze. His only motion was the twitching of his broad nostrils as they searched the air. Whatever it was, a scent excited the bear like nothing else in many days.

Grunt started forward faster now, breaking into a clumsy trot. He uttered one coughlike grunt, then another. Before him lay the former heart of the grove. Recently the bear had somehow sensed that this was the center of its corruption and had thus avoided it. But even the suspicion of the exciting spoor in the wind was enough to compel him there.

Genna? Hope swelled within the bear's breast. Was that not his mistress, standing there in the distance, staring at him? He sniffed at the air, lumbering closer. The scent was that of the Great Druid, he thought, but somehow different.

Blinking in confusion, Grunt struggled to focus his dim eyesight. He saw the short, rounded body, recognized the gray hair pulled tightly back from the face. He saw no smile upon that face, and the human's posture seemed stiff and unnatural.

Yet his eyes could not be wrong. He slowed as he reached the woman and grunted happily, leaning into her expectantly. The bear was surprised when she did not scratch his ears. What was wrong? Grunt looked at the round, wrinkled face curiously.

And in an instant, he recoiled in fear. Cringing low, the bear looked up at her like a whipped puppy, puzzled and pained by the look in her eyes.

She raised her arm, pointing, and Grunt obeyed. His huge body moved toward the black water, where once the crystalline Moonwell had reflected the blessing of the goddess. Quivering, he approached the water.

The bear turned once to look back at his mistress, his eyes pleading. She pointed again, and he dropped his head obediently. His muzzle touched the surface of the Darkwell. And then his life was gone as he gave it, unwittingly, to Bhaal.

\* \* \* \* \*

*Chauntea, as a goddess, was close in spirit to the Earthmother, though far removed in aspect. While the great mother's life lay in the earth itself, in the hallowed ground of the Moonshaes, Chauntea's being dwelled upon the joyous plane of Elysium, far removed from the world of mortals.*

*The Earthmother's followers were the Ffolk of the Moonshae Isles, led by their druids. Chauntea's believers came from across the planes, and even in the Forgotten Realms were spread among the many nations of the world. The tenets of the Earthmother's faith held that nature was sacred, and maintaining the balance of all things became the druidical creed. Followers of Chauntea held that the land should be farmed, that the growth provided by nature should be harnessed for the greater good of man.*

*Yet even despite their differences, the goddesses both were beings of health and growth, cherishing the plants and animals, working to protect the humans who held to their faith.*

*Now Chauntea sensed the power of the Earthmother waning. She also felt the looming presence of Bhaal. As that dark god moved into the power vacuum being created, Chauntea also began to move. Though she lacked Bhaal's awesome might and implacable evil, she was a being of great resource in her own right.*

*Now those resources would be tested.*

# ❦ 2 ❦

# LONG LIVE THE KING

For the first time, the wind seemed to be against them. It blustered from this direction and that in capricious gusts. To all sides stretched the sea, a gray mass of rolling swells, broken only by the foaming crests of the waves. The sky matched the water, a gray blanket of cold pressing heavily from horizon to horizon.

Overhead, the sail filled with air, spurring the ship across whitecaps and through deep troughs. Then the wind shifted, and the sail fell limp. The vessel slid crazily to the side, dropping between two rolling swells. A line drew taut as the boom swung across the stern. Two sailors dropped prone, while others hauled on a heavy rope until the sail once again billowed. The bow of the boat swung to port, angling across the waves on a slightly altered course.

Tristan Kendrick, heir to the throne of Corwell, stood in the bow of the *Defiant* and relished the cool spray against his face. It ran through his beard and soaked his heavy wool cloak. His feet were planted in a wide stance, and he swayed evenly with the rolling deck beneath his feet.

The ship lunged eagerly through the next swell, and the one after that. Each wave brought him and his companions closer to Corwell Firth and the castle on the little knoll, Caer Corwell.

Home.

Just a few short weeks ago, Tristan reflected, his first ocean voyage had carried him across this same water. Then, he had embarked on a mission of politics, to seek his coronation from the High King. Now he carried the crown of that same king—the Crown of the Isles—and he returned in triumph to his home. He knew he should be feeling joy and anticipation, but he could not.

He felt, rather than saw, a warm presence beside him and turned to see Robyn. Though she had slept little and eaten less during the past week, she had never looked so vibrant and alive. Her black hair, long and falling loosely around her shoulders and back, glowed with an ebony sheen, and her green eyes flashed with vitality. Her beauty increased every day, or so thought the king.

The druid joined him in the bow but avoided his eyes. He wanted to reach out, to put his arm around her, but he feared her rebuff.

"We'll be there soon—no more than two days, three at the most." He tried to offer encouragement, sensing her despair.

"But what will we find when we get there? What if we're too late?"

"We won't be! And whatever we find, we can best it! Together, with my sword and your faith, we can rid Gwynneth of any shade of evil!"

"I hope so." Robyn leaned against him and he held her, sensing the deep and spiritual fear that haunted her. He felt a vague sense of guilt for the time they had remained on the island of Callidyrr. He had known that she wanted to leave immediately following the defeat of the High King. Robyn feared deeply for the fate of her fellow druids, imprisoned as stone statues around the scene of their final battle.

Yet he could not have left then. And she had chosen to remain with him, rather than embark for home alone or with Lord Pontswain, who had taken the first available ship back to Corwell.

"I'm glad you stayed with me," he said. "I can't imagine facing the kingship without you beside me."

He thought of the many problems he had solved during his week in Callidyrr. He had settled an old dispute on fishing rights between the cantrevs of Llewellyn and Kythyss. He had pardoned the bandits of Dernall Forest, good men and women who had been forced to become outlaws because of the injustices of the former king. He had disbanded the few remaining mercenaries of the king's private army, the Scarlet Guard. The battles of the Ffolk, he had declared, would from now on be fought by the Ffolk.

With his ascension to the throne had come the discovery of the vast surplus in the High King's treasury, piles of silver coins, and some gold, which he had been able to return to the overtaxed lords of the land. This act alone would have done much to assure his popularity with the lords, but his wisdom and good judgment in settling the other disputes had insured their loyalty to his name.

"I'm glad I stayed, too," she sighed. "I know it was important to you, and to all the isles. You will make a splendid king.

"But all the while, I could not help wondering about the druids. Are they suffering? Are they dead? I wish I could have been both places at once. I know I cannot rest easily until I have seen evil excised from Myrloch Vale!"

Suddenly Tristan stiffened, lifting himself to the balls of his feet to peer in the distance. He squinted against the spray, and saw it again: a flash of crimson against the all-encompassing gray of sea and sky.

Robyn sensed his change in mood, and she followed his gaze, staring a few degrees to starboard of the bow. A foot shorter than the young king, she could not see what had alarmed him.

"Northmen," he grunted, pointing. She saw the flicker of color now. It could only be the square sail of a raiding long-ship, and it was facing them.

"Keep an eye on it. I'll inform the captain." Turning and sprinting like a seasoned sailor down the pitching deck, the new High King of the Moonshaes barked a warning to the laboring crewmen.

Robyn turned back to the south as the longship drew closer. She could now make out a second sail beside the first, veering to the side. The sleek vessels spread apart to block the *Defiant*'s path at either side. Some voice inside her said that she should be afraid, that these were dangerous and bloodthirsty foes. But instead she felt only a quiet anger as she faced another obstacle on the road to rescue Genna

Moonsinger, the Great Druid of all the Moonshaes.

But this was an obstacle she could counter.

By the time Tristan returned to the bow, she had unlashed her staff from its mount on the gunwale. Captain Dansforth, the taciturn master of the *Defiant*, regarded the approaching vessels through his long spying tube. The crew, two dozen steadfast Ffolk of Callidyrr, turned as a man to regard the raiders but maintained the course and sail of the *Defiant* without a hitch.

She was called the stoutest vessel, with the ablest crew, among the four kingdoms of the Ffolk. The proof had come when they sailed into the late stages of an autumn gale that would have kept any other vessel of the Ffolk in port. Racing through the Sea of Moonshae around the northern tip of Gwynneth, the *Defiant* had coursed through the Strait of Oman. Now they sailed south toward Corwell itself.

These northmen were obviously returning home—it was already later than the usual raiding season—but they would doubtless welcome one last prize before making port for the winter.

"The standard of Norland," grunted Dansforth. "That one, to starboard, would be the king's own vessel."

"Grunnarch the Red. I have fought him before," mused Tristan.

"So the stories say. And bested him." The captain looked at the king with just a hint of amusement in his gray eyes. Dansforth was not yet middle-aged, though his hair and beard had silvered until they matched his eyes. Yet he had an enigmatic manner of speaking that reminded Tristan of an old, but very smug, man.

"Can we alter course?" asked Robyn quickly. "To there?" She pointed straight toward one of the advancing longships.

"Why?" Dansforth was mildly incredulous. "They're cutting too wide. They underestimate our speed, I think. With a little luck, we can dash between them."

"We won't need luck if you can get close to one of those ships." Robyn spoke quietly, but there was a hint of great power in her voice.

"Do as she says," said Tristan.

"Very well," Dansforth said with a shrug. He stepped to the steersman, standing at the huge wheel amidships, and ordered the change in course. Then he hurried back to the bow as the *Defiant* heeled over with the turn.

The trio was joined by another pair. One was Tristan's friend Daryth, the swarthy, handsome Calishite who had become the king's chief adviser. Now he carried his gleaming scimitar lightly in his hand, awaiting battle with a half-smile across his dark brown face. The other was the halfling, Pawldo of Lowhill, a middle-aged adventurer whose wrinkled face and graying hair belied his vitality.

"What are you trying to do?" demanded Pawldo incredulously. "Let's make a run for it!" The diminutive con man had been a friend of the Prince of Corwell's for even longer than Daryth, and he now took it upon himself to protect the young king from the influences of others of a similar moral caliber.

"I hope you know what you're doing," grumbled Dansforth. "My men will stand by to repel boarders, but the crew of that one ship alone outnumbers us two to one!"

Robyn did not turn to look at the captain. "They'll not get near enough to throw a line."

Still skeptical, the captain turned to his crew while Daryth, Tristan, and Pawldo stood protectively around the druid. She closed her eyes in concentration and calmly caressed the smooth wood of her staff. The others held their swords ready. Tristan's own blade gleamed in his hand. The legendary Sword of Cymrych Hugh was a symbol of the ancient glory of the Ffolk. The fact that Tristan had discovered the potent blade after it had been missing for centuries explained to a great extent why the lords of Callidyrr had been so willing to extend to him the kingship.

The longships raced toward them with startling rapidity. One came head-on, closing rapidly. The other tried to veer in from downwind, battling the gusts to close with her intended victim. Soon they could make out ranks of axe-wielding northmen standing along the hulls, ready to leap into the *Defiant*. Others stood ready with lines and grapples, though the closing speed of the two vessels would make a grappling attempt risky at best.

The nearest longship veered slightly from their path, a hundred yards away, seventy, forty, closing fast. Robyn held her staff over her head, spreading her hands as far apart as she could. She clenched her hands and strained, as if trying to bend the stout shaft, silently mouthing a prayer to her deity, the goddess Earthmother.

An inhuman creaking assailed their ears as the longship suddenly lurched and twisted in the water. Nails flew through the air as the sleek hull bent tortuously. Boards snapped, the mast crumpled, and then came a harsh snap, like the breaking of a bone.

Suddenly the longship buckled, her keel torn in two. Bow and stern rose into the air while the center of the hull filled with foaming brine. The sail billowed gently into the water, belying the violence of the ship's demise, and forty men tumbled into the cold gray sea.

Tristan understood what had happened, though the reality of it stunned him. Robyn's power, the power of the earth, was keyed to all things wild, all creatures of nature. The oak trees that had formed the keel of the raider were such creatures of nature, and the druid had called upon those trees to change their shape, warping them into something different, something that would not support the frame of the longship.

He heard a thump on the deck beside him and turned to see Robyn, pallid and motionless, lying on the deck. "What happened?" he cried, kneeling and cradling her head in his arms. Her eyes fluttered open, and a look of panic washed across her features.

"I . . . I fainted! The casting made me weak! Why—how could it do that?" She groaned, but struggled to a sitting position. "I think I'm all right now."

The king sprang to his feet as the *Defiant* cut through the wreck, and Tristan could see the faces of the northmen who had been dumped so suddenly into the sea. He saw anger and hatred, but not fear. Even the display of ship-killing magic was not enough to quail the hearts of these fierce warriors.

Suddenly he saw a northman's eyes widen in terror. The man's mouth opened to scream, but he disappeared under the water before a sound could emerge. Another, and another of the raiders vanished with a desperate thrashing. Now the remaining men began to scream loudly, in mind-numbing panic. The gray sea turned green with the thrashing of scaly bodies, and red froth exploded from the torn shapes of sailors.

Tristan saw the other longship heel toward them and then suddenly lurch off course. Her sides became a seething mass of green scales as reptilian creatures climbed from the water over the smooth planks, to fall upon the crew with sharp teeth and wicked, slashing claws.

"Sahuagin!" gasped the king, recognizing the savage fish-men they had battled upon Callidyrr.

And then it was the *Defiant*'s turn to slow in the water as the attackers grabbed her hull as well. Tristan saw a fishlike head, bristling with spines above a snarling nightmare of a face, and he stabbed instinctively. The creature fell back into the water, but two more took its place. Their humanlike hands, tipped with sharp claws and webbed between the fingers, grasped the hull as they pulled themselves upward. Tristan stared into their blank, emotionless eyes. He saw the bracelets of silver and gold, the cruel tridents, spears, and daggers tucked into metal belts. The monsters tumbled onto the deck all around him as Dansforth's crew put up their weapons against this new assault.

The humans took sword and axe and crossbow and faced attack from the Claws of the Deep. These creatures, the sahuagin, they knew to be cruel and implacable foes. Still the fish-men rose from the sea, striking at the two ships while their brethren dealt a bloody end to the northmen still bobbing among the wreckage of the third.

\* \* \* \* \*

The Darkwell grew even blacker with each killing. Hobarth sat and studied the pool, praying and meditating. He had seen a panther and an owl obliterated in the last day, joining the bear, eagle, and stag in giving their lifespark to

Bhaal. Somehow, the god summoned these wretched creatures from the surrounding wasteland. Hobarth did not know why.

The fat cleric studied well the word of his god, and slowly he began to sense Bhaal's plan. At least, he began to understand his own substantial role in that plan.

He looked to Genna Moonsinger, sitting upon one of the crosspieces that had fallen from the ruined druidic arches around the Moonwell. She stared listlessly off into space, as if awaiting a command. The fat cleric wondered at the druid's docility.

She looked like the same implacable enemy he had faced a short month ago. The statue had become a being of flesh and blood when he pressed the Heart of Kazgoroth into it. She looked, sounded, and moved like the Great Druid of Gwynneth. Even the bear, Grunt, had been taken in.

But now she was unquestioningly obedient to the commands of Bhaal, and thus Hobarth. For several days, this had been but a pleasant diversion for Hobarth. He had not been with a woman in months, and so he had taken advantage of her willingness to follow his orders. Though she displayed no revulsion, neither did she exhibit any other emotion. Hobarth had eventually realized that her lack of passion turned the whole experience into rather a bore.

Then he commanded her to use her magic, wondering if that potent weapon had been lost upon her perversion to the will of Bhaal. The cleric was delighted when she called forth an inferno of fire from the ground itself, surrounding them with greedy flames. However, he noted a difference from her previous castings of the firewall. Now, as the flames licked across the ground, they left the earth tortured, blackened, and barren in their wake, whereas before the spell had made no mark whatsoever upon the land. This spell fascinated Hobarth particularly, for it was one that no cleric could perform. She had used it to telling effect when he had sent his army of undead against her, and now it was his to command!

Yet, if her body and mind remained that of the Great Druid, her soul was unquestionably altered. The heart beating within her breast was no longer her own. It was the foul organ of a black beast of chaos, and this was the thing that held her now in its thrall.

The difference was visible mainly in her eyes. Where once they had sparkled with vitality and wisdom, they now glowered darkly. At times, Hobarth imagined he saw a flash of red fire within them, not unlike the gaze of Kazgoroth itself. And her lack of emotion reminded him more of the zombies he had once commanded than of any human being he had known.

Now, knowing the will of Bhaal, he approached her.

"Druid!" he barked, and she looked dully at him. He realized that he had forgotten to order her to clothe herself after his latest indulgence. "Don your garments."

He waited as she pulled her tattered cloak about her, watching with interest. Though she was well along in years, her body had not succumbed to the flab of middle age. She was stout, but her flesh had a firmness that he found strangely attractive. Shrugging, he told himself that it was merely the lack of any younger woman that caused him to desire her.

"Bhaal has spoken. You are to go to Caer Corwell. There you will perform a certain task he has planned for you. Upon its completion, you will return here."

As he told her the plan, as Bhaal had told it to him, he watched her for some sign of reaction. After all, he was asking her to betray the land and the people she had striven all her life to protect. Hers was not a mission of attack, but something far more insidious. Bhaal faced two powerful human enemies on the island of Gwynneth. These humans were closely allied to each other. The mission of Genna Moonsinger, simply, was to drive these two allies apart.

"I understand."

"And you will obey?"

"I shall obey."

\* \* \* \* \*

Claws raked Robyn's calf as she slipped on the blood-slick deck. She whirled toward the sahuagin that had seized her, cracking her staff sharply against its spiny head. The creature dropped like a stone, its skull crushed. Forked tongues flicking from between rows of razor-sharp teeth, others scrambled across the deck as the *Defiant* heeled sideways. Robyn lurched against the rail, still dizzy and unbalanced, but the faintness seemed to be fading.

Tristan slashed at a fish-man. The Sword of Cymrych Hugh sliced through the air, and as easily through the flesh of its victim. The sahuagin leaped backward, clutching the stump of its arm. It opened its mouth wide, showing hundreds of teeth in the gaping maw, and then hissed its hatred.

The king leaped forward, and the monster dove cleanly into the sea. Tristan stopped at the rail and stabbed another creature just as it tried to scramble over the gunwale into the boat. It fell back into the water, dead, and he looked about the deck. He saw Daryth behead one of the monsters as it lunged toward Robyn's back, and Pawldo's keen dagger disemboweled another as the nimble halfling ducked beneath the monster's grasping claws.

And then, as suddenly as it had begun, the killing ended. The bodies of a score of sahuagin, and several sailors, lay in chaotic disorder across the deck. Red human blood, and the pinkish froth from sahuagin veins, mingled on the planks.

But there was not a moving sahuagin to be seen. Captain Dansforth stood with a knot of his sailors amidships, while Daryth, Pawldo, and Robyn were near Tristan on the foredeck. Tristan's great moorhound, Canthus, stood beside the druid. The dog's back was higher than her waist, and its shaggy brown muzzle was stained with sahuagin blood. More than once this day, he had saved the lives of his master and mistress.

"They still fight," said Robyn, pointing at the longship, where the battle still raged.

Tristan smiled grimly at the sight. He could see the northman chief, Grunnarch the Red, poised before the mast of his graceful ship. His men stood with him in a circle, facing outward, while twice their number of sahuagin slashed toward the kill.

"Make sail!" cried Captain Dansforth, sending his men to line and beam. He nodded at the king. "We can make a break for it before they finish 'em off!"

The *Defiant* had placed her port side to the wind as she drifted during the melee. In another second, the sail came taut, and the *Defiant* heeled sharply into the wind. As her nose passed the drifting longship, Tristan saw another northmen dragged into the mass of sahuagin.

"Come alongside!" he called, noting the shock in Dansforth's eyes. "To the rescue!"

"You're—"

The captain was about to call him mad, Tristan realized. The thought startled him, and he realized that his order must seem mad by most logical arguments. Why should they help the raiders who had, minutes earlier, been bent on their own destruction?

"Hurry! And send your bowmen forward, man!"

Dansforth only hesitated for a fraction of a second. Then he curtly gestured to four of his men who held heavy crossbows. "You heard the king! Move!"

The *Defiant* crashed against the waves again, slicing a path that would take her just past the longship. The distance closed rapidly while the bowmen knelt at the rail and took aim.

"Oh, good!" Tristan was startled by the shrill voice behind him. "C'mon, Yaz—we didn't miss the *whole* battle!"

"I'm scared—scared! W-W-We better get below!" answered another, equally shrill voice.

The bright orange shape of a tiny dragon, its butterfly wings fluttering excitedly, suddenly appeared beside the king, popping from invisibility as faerie dragons are fond of doing. The little serpent darted past the king to perch on the rail. "Oh, boy! Northmen! C'mon, let's get 'em!"

"N-Newt, don't! Stay back here with me—with me!" Without turning around, Tristan pictured the tiny sprite, Yazilliclick, cautiously peering from the hatch to the hold, his antennae no doubt quivering anxiously. The two faerie creatures had spent most of the voyage belowdecks, but now the chaos of the battle had aroused them.

"Newt, why don't you keep watch on the waters off the stern?" suggested the king. "See that they don't sneak up on us from behind!" And incidentally, he added silently, stay out of the way.

"Well, okay," the faerie dragon agreed, with a suspicious look at Tristan.

Quickly Newt buzzed away, and Yaz popped out of the hatch to follow him. The sprite was a small, humanlike creature, about two feet tall and distinguished by a small pair of gossamer wings and two antennae that sprouted from his forehead.

The young king turned his attention back to the battle, to see that the longship was very close now. He could clearly make out several northmen in desperate combat with the monsters, while other sahuagin held back from the fight.

"Shoot those farthest from the humans," said Tristan. "Now!"

The four bolts flew through the air, each finding a target in the mass of scaly bodies. The red-haired northman in the center of the deck cried out a challenge, and his crewmen pressed the attack. The crossbowmen reloaded quickly, and loosed a second volley as the *Defiant* started to turn, barely a hundred feet from the raider now.

These bolts, too, found home in the slick bodies of the fish-men. The spined heads of the sahuagin bristled as they turned to face the *Defiant*, hissing their rage and clashing their weapons.

Daryth and Robyn joined Tristan at the gunwale. The king climbed up on the rail, bracing himself with a hanging rope. The Sword of Cymrych Hugh was like a feather in his hand—a thirsty, violent feather. He saw perhaps two dozen northmen still standing, though the numbers of the sahuagin had thinned as well. And the red-bearded captain still led his men boldly, striking to both sides with his broad-bladed axe.

The two ships drifted closer as Dansforth smoothly maneuvered his vessel through a sharp turn. Then the *Defiant* paused, parallel to the longship and barely twenty feet away.

The rolling of the swell dropped the longship into a trough. Tristan looked down into the hull and saw a pile of bodies, white skin and green scales intermingled in death. At the same instant, he pushed away from the gunwale, swinging on the rope until he lost momentum. He hung poised over the longship for a moment, and then let go to land lightly among the bodies. He heard Daryth land easily behind him.

On the deck of the *Defiant*, Robyn chanted a prayer to her goddess, then waved her staff in the direction of the sahuagin. Suddenly the outline of fish-men bodies glowed white, outlined in cool, magical fire. The reptiles hissed their rage, though several cowered back in fear. They slapped and struck at the flames without success, though the fire did not appear to cause them harm.

The red-bearded northman bellowed a challenge of brute violence, cleaving a sahuagin to the waist with his axe. His comrades let loose a shout and attacked.

A great, green sahuagin lunged at the High King. Its toothy jaws gaped, and the spiny ridge along its backbone stood erect as sharp claws clutched at Tristan's throat. The white fire flickered and flared around the creature's ghastly shape, making a clear target. The vicious claws swept toward the king, but the silver sword found the throat of the monster first. Pink blood sprayed Tristan as the reptilian attacker clutched the lethal wound, still staggering toward him as it died.

The High King whirled toward the other sahuagin, the Sword of Cymrych Hugh marking a gleaming arc through the air before him. The northman leader crushed a green skull with his massive axe, and suddenly the fish-men lost their heart for battle. In one motion, still outlined in eerie flame, the remaining attackers slipped over the side of the longship and disappeared beneath the waves.

Tristan and Daryth stood poised for combat, watching the northmen. They saw tall, proud seafarers. The one called Grunnarch stepped forward. His red hair and beard flowed freely across his chest and shoulders, and his pale blue eyes stared warily back at the pair. His chest was broad, and strapping muscles rippled beneath the skin of his arms. The northman wore only a short wool tunic, of plain gray, and high-laced leather sandals. He looked every inch the sailor, taking no note of the rolling deck beneath his feet as he advanced, studying his rescuers.

Grunnarch the Red saw two men facing him, one fair and one swarthy. The fair one stood easily before him, holding that dazzling sword. He held himself proudly, like a ruler of men. His brown beard and hair were shorter than the northman's, but still long and full, as a man's should be. Though leaner of muscle, the swordsman had a wiry, solid frame that appeared to conceal hidden reserves of strength.

The other man, the swarthier of the pair, was clean-shaven. His skin was a rich brown, his hair as black as night. He carried a silver scimitar and stood balanced, catlike, upon the balls of his feet. Grunnarch noticed that, while the swordsman stared him full in the face, the man with the scimitar looked everywhere else, as if watching for a threat to his liege.

Then Grunnarch's eyes went to the ship, where a black-haired woman stood at the rail. She met his gaze boldly, with none of the shyness that would have characterized a woman of the North. For several moments, he stared, distracted by her beauty, until he remembered his surroundings.

The northman lowered his axe. He spoke in heavily accented Commonspeech.

"Greetings. I am Grunnarch the Red, King of Norland. I thank you for my life."

"I am Tristan Kendrick, High King of the Ffolk."

The longship lurched slightly as Dansforth's crew brought the two ships together, lashing the hulls side by side. Robyn sprang into the longship to stand beside the two men. Grunnarch turned and spoke a command in his own tongue, and the surviving members of his crew began to tend to their wounded and hurl sahuagin bodies overboard.

Grunnarch's eyes turned unconsciously to the woman again. He saw the supple curves of her body, poorly concealed by her loose cloak. She stood easily in the rocking hull, moving like a fighter, with balance and grace. He saw that the muscles of her arms and neck were tight, but her strength could not conceal the womanliness of her appearance.

And then he recognized her. He recalled a figure, high atop a tower of Caer Corwell, black hair streaming in the wind. He saw her with her staff held over her head, and he remembered the lightning that had crashed and crackled into the ranks of his men. With the memory came the stench of burned, blackened flesh, and even the feeling of hopeless panic that had arisen within him. It was at that moment, Grunnarch remembered, that he had realized that the northmen's campaign was doomed.

He shook his head suddenly, turning back to the young king who stood looking at him curiously, and he wondered at the oddity that brought the two of them, sworn enemies a year ago, standing face to face over the dead sahuagin.

"Why did you do this?" asked the Red King.

Tristan thought before answering. Why, indeed? At last he spoke. "I'm not quite certain. Our first instinct was to sail away, once we had secured our own ship.

"Your people and mine have fought for centuries, and, in truth, it seemed we should fight for centuries to come. But must it be this way?"

"You are Kendrick of Corwell? And of Freeman's Down?"

"The same."

"We have fought, ourselves, scarce more than a year since. You have great skill—and fortune."

"And you, lady?" asked the Red King, turning to Robyn. "You, too, fought well. Your sorcery helped break the spell of evil that bound us."

"Mine is the magic of faith, not sorcery. There is a great difference." She smiled at him faintly, her eyes inscrutable.

He nodded, not understanding the distinction. Suddenly he remembered the scrolls and the promise they seemed to offer. He bent and retrieved the long tube from beneath the deck, offering it mutely to her. He was not sure why, but it seemed right that she should have it. Perhaps it was a way of repaying the debt he owed these Ffolk for saving his life, though it was more than his sense of obligation that caused him to give the scroll to the beautiful druid.

"It was claimed as a thing of great value," he explained awkwardly. "Is it of use to you?"

Robyn took the ivory tube, barely stifling a gasp. She stroked the elaborate carvings reverently before looking at the northman. His face was taut with tension, she saw, as if he desperately hoped that she would value the gift.

She looked again at the runes. They were strange, not druidic in nature, but at the same time almost identical to a series of carvings her teacher had made along a short piece of wood, a runestick, that Genna had given Robyn as a gift. This was obviously a talisman of great power, sacred to some god not very different from her own.

"It's very precious . . . a thing of power. Where did you get it?"

From the look of sudden anguish on the fierce raider's face, she knew she had hurt him with her question. She guessed that the tube was the plunder of some raid, though why Grunnarch should be troubled by that fact she couldn't begin to guess.

"Never mind," she added quickly. "It is a thing of tremendous value. I thank you for giving it to me."

"It is a small reward for the gift of my life and my ship," replied Grunnarch solemnly. The Red King turned back to Tristan. "Your actions are more puzzling, as you must know I was with the army that would have put your home to the torch. How can you forgive one who has done you such evil?"

"For one thing, you're no longer accompanied by your powerful ally," remarked Tristan. The vision of the Beast, Kazgoroth, growing from the body of a man into a monster towering over a castle wall, came quickly into Tristan's mind. He remembered the terror and awe of that moment as if it had occurred yesterday.

Grunnarch's face flushed. "Ally?" he spat. "It was a thing of great evil! It slew one of our greatest kings and took his body for its own foul purposes! We were little more than mindless weapons in its hands!"

"Perhaps that can explain why we aided you. Evil such as that still haunts the Moonshaes. As long as we strive to destroy each other, we make the task of that evil so much easier. I ask you, Grunnarch, King of Norland, would we not do better to join forces to combat this evil?"

The Red King looked Tristan full in the face, then nodded slowly. "You speak with the wisdom of a much older king. But what of this evil you speak of? It still threatens our lands? Where, and how, shall we fight it?"

"Come with me to Corwell," said the High King. "We will talk of it there."

The histories of lands, peoples, and nations are made of many tiny events. Most are insignificant, their impact gone with the moment of their passing. But some of these events have an impact extending far beyond their occurrence. These events are things that can shape and change history for countless years into the future.

Grunnarch the Red extended his broad hand, and Tristan Kendrick took it in his firm clasp. Their eyes met, bold and frank.

An event of the latter type had just occurred.

\* \* \* \* \*

*The corruption of Genna Moonsinger struck the goddess like a physical blow. It fell all the more heavily since the great druid had not even been granted the dignified defeat of death but had instead become a tool of the very evil she had striven to defeat.*

*The Earthmother felt the presence of her servant's body but could not reach out to her soul. Genna had been freed from her prison of stone, only to be entrapped in a spiritual corruption more vile than any form of death.*

*For a time, it seemed as if the land itself would wither and die in sympathy with the mother's grief. Indeed, winter hastened its approach, reaching frosty fingers across the Moonshaes, eagerly striking the last leaves from those trees still carrying vestiges of foliage.*

*And then, briefly, the goddess looked up from her misery, away from the dark depths of the earth to the world of sky* and air and sun. She felt a small tingle of vitality, and with it came renewed hope. The Earthmother knew that her lone druid, Robyn of Gwynneth, still lived. Now she sensed that Robyn had come into contact with a talisman of great power and faith, a vessel of wisdom that could invigorate and vitalize her.

The Scrolls of Arcanus were not of the mother's own essence, but they were clerical scrolls of great antiquity, born of a faith not so different from her own. The clerics, like her druids, held that the balance of all things made the fulcrum of life. Too, the scrolls contained teachings of that balance and its fundamental principles that held keys to great power. They offered Robyn some semblance of knowledge and might, even though the Earthmother herself could no longer offer the same.

Perhaps it was not much, but she could fasten her hopes to nothing else.

# 🌸 3 🌸

# SEDUCTION

With a shrill cry, the vulture sensed the nearness of the sea. The bird hastened its flight, and soon the blue waters of Corwell Firth came into view to the west. The bulk of Caer Corwell stood dominating the foreground, and soon the bird was flying over the castle. It circled above the stone keep, following the line of the wooden palisade that protected the compound.

Caer Corwell stood perched upon its rocky knoll, commanding the ground around the compact fishing town and its sheltered harbor. The surrounding moor had browned with the approach of winter, but the bright afternoon sun of this day gave the place a warm, springlike look, especially as it reflected the brilliant azure hue of the firth.

The vulture, a dirty black bird with streaks of brown and gray across its wings, finally settled upon the parapet of the highest tower of the castle. It was an oddly formed bird, with great, misshapen claws and a twisted, crooked neck, as if it were an imperfect rendering of the real thing. Now the bird perched there, staring intently at the activity on the waterfront. With humanlike attention, it watched the progress of two vessels that approached the dock.

To a human, the sight would have indeed seemed odd. Here was a sturdy, deep-drafted vessel of the Ffolk, its sails mostly furled as the gentle breeze pushed it toward the wharf. Beyond, just passing through the breakwater, came a sleek, low-hulled longship of the type sailed by the raiders of the North. Any human who understood the ways of the Moonshaes could not have helped but wonder why ships of two such bitter enemies would sail together into a peaceful harbor.

Genna Moonsinger, in the body of the vulture, felt no such curiosity about the unusual flotilla. She was on a mission from Bhaal, concerned only with the location of her target. And he, she suspected, would be found upon one of those ships.

She had made the flight from Myrloch to Corwell in two days. Her druidic ability to shift her body into the shape of an animal remained, despite her corruption by the Heart of Kazgoroth, but the animal body she inhabited was distorted and malformed. Her motivation now had a single focus: to serve the will of Bhaal.

She soared from the parapet and glided into the courtyard, landing in a shadowed passage between several stables. Then the body of the vulture shifted, growing and bending into the shape of a young woman. Genna, aided by the Beast, adjusted the body to achieve the effect she desired. A brilliant tumble of red hair flowed loosely across her narrow shoulders, framing a perfect oval face. Her breasts grew large and firm, thrusting boldly forward so that only a man of wood or stone could have avoided taking notice of them.

The woman who stepped from the passage into the afternoon light of the courtyard bore little resemblance to the Great Druid of Gwynneth. Tall, smooth-skinned, and young, she moved with the supple grace of a cat.

Gliding across the courtyard of Caer Corwell, she slipped among the Ffolk who had begun to gather at the castle in anticipation of the king's homecoming. She had naught to do now but wait for her victim to fall into her trap.

*　*　*　*　*

"The children of the goddess were her most potent allies in the struggle against Kazgoroth. The Leviathan of the deep shattered our ships and scattered our fleet, but the power of the Beast slayed the great fish in the end. The Pack pursued the army of the northmen over the land, howling madly with their wolfen voices and tearing flesh with their great fangs when they brought the army to bay."

Hobarth paused in his narration, sensing Bhaal's keen interest in the tale. In truth, the cleric was surprised at how little the god knew about their adversaries.

"But the Pack, too, is gone, scattered to the far corners of the isle. The druid told me her goddess lacks the will, or the might, to summon it again." Genna had indeed provided the cleric with a wealth of information. She apparently retained all the memories of her former life, with none of the spiritual values that would have prevented her from disclosing them to one such as Hobarth.

"Now," he continued, "only the unicorn, Kamerynn, remains of the children. He is strong—I have faced him myself—-but his might is nothing in the face of your own."

Of course, the cleric did not speak out loud. Instead, he formulated the information in his mind, where his god claimed it for his own. This, too, is how Bhaal spoke with his servant.

*These children you speak of . . . the children of a god. The thought of them brings me pleasure.*

Hobarth waited, confused.

*I, too, shall create children—the Children of Bhaal. They will stalk the land beside you and bring death to all the corners of the world!*

"What form shall they take?" asked the cleric nervously.

His answer came in the form of a bubbling maelstrom forming in the center of the Darkwell. The black water foamed upward, releasing a stench of foul gas into the air. Then the froth moved across the surface as rings of ripples spread outward from the turbulence.

The surface of the water parted in a soft eruption, and a figure emerged. Oily water trickled off a broad, flat head, streaked across a feathered face, dripped from a short, blunt beak. Then the great brown body emerged, lumbering onto the shore and hulking over the cleric. Patches of shaggy hair, in places torn to reveal bare and scabrous skin, covered the creature's lower body. Hobarth looked up at a ghastly apparition, a nightmare thing that did not belong on this world.

He recognized the shaggy body of Grunt, the bear. The thing stood on its hind legs, twice as tall as a man, in the hunching pose of a great brown bear. But the face dispelled any notions of normalcy. It was flat and covered with feathers, with a short, downward pointing beak—a beak! It was the head of an owl, grown hugely out of proportion and placed upon the body of the bear.

The words of Bhaal came into the cleric's mind. *My owlbear. You shall call him Thorax.*

Scarcely did Hobarth have a chance to register his shock, remembering a large owl that had died from the poisonous touch of the waters shortly after the bear's demise, than he saw the water foaming and swirling a second time. This time, a pair of bizarre creatures splashed forth, pulling themselves into the air on the broad wings of eagles. They were followed by several more, and they all flew with the grace and power of that most regal of birds.

But the heads of these hideous things were all like the head of a proud stag. A broad rack of antlers spread above each of them. Only the mouths were unlike deer, as they parted in flight to reveal rows of sharp, wolflike fangs.

*The perytons. Witness the birth of my flock.*

Again the waters of the Darkwell churned upward and away, and the cleric stared dumbfounded as the next creature came slinking from the muck and the slime. It rose from the water with a heart-numbing growl, its yellow eyes flashing hatred. Its black coat glistened, and its wicked eyes held Hobarth enthralled as the monster crept toward him.

*Shantu, king of my children.*

The beast resembled a huge black panther, nearly the size of a horse. Its coat, dripping with the oily liquid, glistened with a hellish sheen. The gaping mouth displayed fangs as long as daggers, and it crouched menacingly, as if it would leap upon Hobarth himself.

But this was no ordinary panther, even allowing for its size. From each of the black shoulders sprouted a long tentacle, covered all over with moist cups, like the limbs of an octopus. At the end of each tentacle curved a sharp, bony hook, ready to rip into flesh like a giant claw.

Shantu growled again, and Hobarth felt the bile rise in his throat. Then the creature slinked past him, and he noticed something curious—though the animal dripped steadily from the waters of the well, the ground beneath it did not grow wet. Indeed, the astounded cleric noticed, the ground was wet several paces to the side of the beast!

As the creature moved away from the well, it made no tracks in the muddy ground—at least not beneath it. Instead, Hobarth saw tracks appear off to one side, though the creature looked and sounded as if it was directly before him. With awe, he witnessed the power of his god's creation. Here was a creature that seemed to be in one place, yet was actually somewhere else nearby.

*Thus is the displacer beast born, to take his place before you.*

"Glory to Bhaal and His magnificent children," murmured the cleric.

*They, together with my legions from the sea and you, my servant, shall spread death across this isle. When you are finished, when my will has been done, there will be not a single living creature upon this land that is not beholden to me. This island shall become a monument to death!*

The flock of perytons swirled overhead, strangely silent. The owlbear, Thorax, lumbered away from the well, clacking its huge beak awkwardly in the air. And the great, cat-like displacer beast prowled the shore of the pond, as if waiting for a command that was not long in coming.

*And now, my children, go forth and hunt. Journey far, and slay the enemies of Bhaal!*

\* \* \* \* \*

The homecoming was all the young king could have desired. Pontswain had indeed carried word of his coronation to the Ffolk of Corwell, and they turned out to meet the *Defiant* in huge numbers. Hours earlier, lookouts had spotted the vessels heading toward the harbor. Despite confusion and suspicion raised by the appearance of the longship, it was an eager crowd that moved toward the waterfront.

The throng grew steadily until, by the time they docked,

most of the town awaited them. As the *Defiant* pulled alongside the pier, the Ffolk erupted in a spontaneous cheer. The king felt a warm glow of gratitude and a rush of pleasure to again see his home.

Among the well-wishers greeting them at the dock, Tristan recognized Tavish of Llewellyn, the bard of the harp who had plucked him from the sea after his boat sank on the journey to Callidyrr. He had not seen her since his arrest at the hands of the former High King's personal guards.

The rotund minstrel flashed him a beaming smile as he stepped ashore. She embraced him in a crushing hug, and he was surprised to see tears on her cheeks. "I came here to get help, to rescue you," she explained, wiping her eyes, "but it seems you've handled things pretty well on your own."

Tristan heard the rumbling of the crowd to his left, and saw many of the Ffolk surge toward the dock as the longship pulled alongside. "Raiders!" "Murderers!" "Thieves!" and other invectives emerged from the angry men, and the king forced his way through the crowd to stand before the longship. He looked straight into the faces of the angry farmers and sailors before him, and slowly they backed away.

"Hold, you men! And listen well! These men of the north are here as my guests. We have fought together and bested a monstrous foe! They will feast with us, and join our celebration—and no harm will come to them while they are in Corwell!"

A burly farmer grumbled his discontent, and Tristan fixed him with an icy gaze until the man looked uncomfortably at the ground. One by one, the members of the mob grew silent, their anger replaced by expressions of confusion or doubt.

"I am your king, the High King of the Ffolk." Tristan spoke softly, and as he had hoped, the mob grew silent to hear his words. "This day marks a new beginning for us, for the Ffolk of all the isles. Let this be the sign of a new reign, as the northmen come to our town and join us at our table!"

"Wise words! Hail to the king!" someone cried out.

Tristan looked around in surprise, and saw the beaming face of Friar Nolan, the cleric of the new gods who had worked long and hard trying to convert the Ffolk of Corwell. Though his success had been limited, he was widely regarded as a man of great wisdom, and his healing magic had benefited many a resident of Corwell.

"Hail to the king!" cried another man, and soon the crowd took up the chant. Several Ffolk even came forward to help lash the longship to the dock. The pudgy friar, his bald pate bobbing through the group, pushed his way to Tristan's side.

"Splendid words, sire! You embark upon a wise course. The gods will surely smile upon you!"

"Some of them, anyway," the young king replied with a grin. "And thank you for your own words—most timely remarks, good friar!"

"Welcome home, sire!" cried another young man, pushing to his side. Tristan recognized him as Randolph, the young but very capable captain of the guard, whom he had left in charge of the castle upon his departure.

Before the king could respond, however, he was swept away, lifted to the shoulders of his countrymen and carried on a triumphant march to Caer Corwell itself. They carried Robyn beside him, and his spirits brightened further as he saw her smiling above the tumult. Though she had been moody and depressed the last few days of the voyage, he hoped that their arrival at home—and the fact that they planned to strike out for Myrloch Vale in the morning—would improve her spirits.

But first there would be a feast. It would be a celebration of the new king, his homecoming, and his success in the campaign on Callidyrr.

Tristan regained his feet in the castle courtyard and led Robyn and Randolph into the Great Hall of the keep, where they finally left the crowd behind. "Where's Pontswain?" he asked. "We must talk before the feast."

"I'll send a guardsman to find him. Lord Pontswain's tending to the last business of the food and drink. We trust you will be pleased, sire."

"No doubt. Now tell me, how fares life in Corwell?"

"We have missed you, but fare well. The Ffolk have been fairly bursting with pride since news of your coronation, sire. Great effort has been expended preparing for your homecoming!"

"And what news?"

"The only excitement was the presence of a band of outlaws, raiding cantrevs Dynnatt and Koart. We caught and hanged them. They seemed to be northmen who did not flee with their brethren last year."

Randolph went on to describe the state of the kingdom, from the poor harvest and meager catches of fish to the great successes of the huntsmen in the highlands. "The food reserves for winter are adequate. It seems that a great deal of wildlife has fled south from Myrloch Vale. Hunting has never been better."

"And what news of the vale?" asked Robyn.

"Puzzling, that. Shepherds say their sheep will not venture near it. The huntsmen who have climbed along the high ridge to look into the vale report vast desolation. Trees have died, and even the lake itself has lost its gleam. It is disturbing news indeed, sire, but the blight does not seem to have reached Corwell."

"Welcome home, my king!" Lord Pontswain burst into the hall, bowing deeply. He was a handsome man, clean-shaven, with a broad mane of elegantly curled brown hair that was the envy of many a maid. "I trust your voyage was comfortable."

"Indeed. Please be seated." Pontswain had been Tristan's chief rival for the throne of Corwell before the High Kingship had made that rivalry moot. Now he seemed to devote all of his energies to the welfare of his king. The transition had been so sudden, and so dramatic, that Tristan still didn't quite trust him.

"I will have to leave the kingdom in the capable hands of you both for a little while longer," he explained. "Tomorrow morning Robyn and I journey to Myrloch Vale. This devastation is caused by an evil cleric of great power, and we shall confront and destroy him."

"As you wish, sire." Randolph asked several more questions about the governance of the realm, while Pontswain sat quietly, a distant look upon his features. Shortly the two men departed, and Robyn and Tristan were left alone in the Great Hall.

"The whole vale devastated!" she whispered, horrified. "What manner of man is this!"

"A man who can be killed, by my sword or your spells. And he will be, I promise you!" He put his arms around her and she leaned into him, comforted by his confidence.

"Will you join me in our celebration tonight?" he asked. "We can do nothing more until the morning. We should enjoy our homecoming."

She forced a smile. "You're right. I have thought of little else than the Moonwell and the druids since our victory on Callidyrr. You deserve greater rewards than I have given you, and I'm sorry for that. Tonight we shall celebrate!"

"And tomorrow, I promise, we'll start for the vale." He looked at her somberly.

"Yes!" Robyn's voice grew more animated. "The scrolls that Grunnarch gave me . . . I've been looking them over. I think one of them offers a real hope, a chance to return the druids to their mortal forms!"

"You mean the statues? Bring them back to flesh?"

"Exactly! And with the druids of the isles gathered around, mustering all of our combined power, this foul cleric must certainly be defeated. Besides, this time we'll have your sword on our side."

"But tonight," Tristan interrupted, "we feast!"

He kissed her and she met his lips with the full force of her own embrace. For a minute, they relished the touch, the holding of each other.

"Tonight, as we celebrate—" Tristan began slowly, hesitantly—"may I announce to our people the naming of their queen? Will you be my wife?"

She smiled softly and kissed him again. He realized in surprise that her cheeks were wet. Then she pulled away to look him full in the face, and the love shining from her eyes brought a fiery warmth to his heart.

"I do want to marry you. And I shall, I hope—but I cannot make this promise now."

"But why not?"

"I can't make that commitment until we have rid the vale of its scourge. You see, I believe I am the only druid left now. I hope that, with the help of the goddess, we can free Genna and the others from their stone prisons, and then I can marry you. I will tell Genna that I cannot take her place as Great Druid.

"But if we do not succeed, then I shall be the only hope of the continuance of my order. Tristan, I love you, but that would be a calling I could not refuse."

"But could we not still marry? I'm certain I could help you with—"

She silenced him with a finger to his lips. "The Great Druid, and such I must then become, must be chaste. She cannot marry."

Tristan was silent, understanding her calling. The knowledge only fueled his determination to succeed. "I shall love you either way."

"And I you, my king!" This time their kiss was longer, lingering until the maids entered the hall to begin preparing for the feast.

"Perhaps we should bathe," he said with a smile, "and prepare for the feast."

They returned to their separate quarters, relishing the familiarity of their surroundings, and each of them dressed in linens unstained by travel for the first time in many weeks.

Pontswain had acquitted himself well in preparing for the celebration. In anticipation of the king's arrival, the lord had ordered pigs and a cow slaughtered, kegs of ale iced—Tristan, in defiance of local custom, enjoyed his beer cold—and a multitude of cakes and pies baked.

Tristan quickly found himself seated at the head of a huge banquet table in the Great Hall of Caer Corwell. Also at the table sat Daryth, Robyn, Pawldo, Pontswain, Friar Nolan, Captain Dansforth, Tavish, and Randolph. Robyn sat to his right, and at his left hand sat Grunnarch the Red. A score of other tables filled the hall, each with benches and chairs for a dozen or more Ffolk.

This, the largest room in the castle, was warmed by four great fireplaces, one on each wall, and illuminated by innumerable torches set in sconces along the walls. It felt good, Tristan decided, to dress in a fine tunic and sit at the head of such a grand table. The aromas of pork and meat puddings mixed with the smoke of the fires, causing his stomach to rumble eagerly.

"When do we eat?" Newt demanded indignantly, suddenly popping into view on Tristan's plate. "I've been waiting for hours!"

The king laughed, even as the kitchen doors burst open and kitchen maids, carrying heaping platters of food and foaming pitchers of ale, emerged. Newt buzzed delightedly into the air and disappeared again. Yazilliclick, presumably, was resting somewhere. Sprites are notoriously nervous among crowds.

Tristan took no notice, at the time, of the young woman in peasant garb who took the last seat at the king's table. No one seemed to know who she was, but her appearance was stunning, and since most of the occupants of the table were male, no objection was raised. With a toss of her red hair, she sat among them. Soon Randolph laughed at some humorous remark she made, and shortly thereafter Tristan forgot about her.

Robyn looked up suddenly, disturbed by a vague disquiet. She looked around the table uneasily, though her gaze passed by the strange woman without noticing her, as if the woman were invisible.

Events were moving too quickly for the king to fully accept that his long voyage had finally ended. Everyone talked at once. His mug seemed to fill of its own accord whenever the level of foam dipped more than an inch below the brim. It felt wonderful to be home, and he basked in the admiration of his people as Daryth, Pawldo, and even Pontswain described their adventures.

The crowd fell gradually silent at Pawldo's account of the battle against the monstrous forces of High King Carrathal and the Black Wizard Cyndre. The halfling's voice fell to a dramatic hush as he described the rage of the Earthmother, telling in vivid detail of the roaring torrent of sea that washed onto shore, carrying away not only great chunks of the island of Callidyrr but also the army of the former High King as well. Ever the showman, Pawldo paused a beat.

"Don't leave us hanging, fellow! What happens next?" Tavish demanded.

"That's the good part," the king said, laughing. "A few hours later, a fisherman sailed from shore to our island. He wanted to know what had happened to his bay. All we could tell him was that it had gotten a lot bigger!"

"And he brought you home to Corwell?"

"Oh, it wasn't that simple," interjected Pawldo again. "First we had to go to Llewellyn. The lord there had a feast for us all and summoned all the lords of Callidyrr to attend the official coronation." He looked at Tristan with pride, as if he personally was responsible for his old friend's ascent to the throne.

"The celebration went on for a week! Of course, Pontswain took the first ship out to bring word to Corwell, but those Callidyrrians—Callidytes?—couldn't get enough of our hero!" Tristan stole a guilty look at Robyn as Pawldo continued, and she smiled back at him.

Newt swooped back onto Tristan's plate, lighting among clean-picked bones, and looked around for a snack. "Here," Tristan joked, tilting his mug toward the dragon. To his surprise, Newt stuck his muzzle into the foamy ale and slurped loudly, smacking his lips as Pawldo continued the tale.

"Finellen and the dwarves decided to walk home, though how you walk from one island to another, I'm sure I don't know. Then the storm hit, and we had to stay in Llewellyn even longer—not that we minded, of course. But finally Captain Dansforth and the *Defiant* were ready to sail. And here we are!"

"This black wizard," asked Grunnarch as the guests turned again to their own conversations. "Is he an aspect of the evil you spoke of?"

"I'm certain of it." Tristan frowned at the memory. "The

Beast that corrupted your own leader, and the foul sorcery at his command, both conspired to destroy the peoples of the isles."

"But did they serve the same master?"

"The wizard was but a pawn, like we are," stated Robyn bluntly. Tristan looked at her in surprise as she continued. "The true nature of the threat we face is a chaotic force of evil far greater than magic, and even greater than the Beast."

"How do you know?" asked the northman.

"I have seen the corruption strike at the very soul of the land. My teacher, and the druids who fought beside her, with all the faith of the balance and the land behind them, were not enough to stop it!" Neither Robyn, nor anyone else, noticed the bright gleam in the eyes of the redheaded woman as she leaned forward to catch every word of the young druid's explanation.

"The power behind this evil is greater than could be wielded by any man, even a sorcerer such as Cyndre. The power is served by a cleric of incalculable evil, but even that cleric is but a pawn. There is only one answer: Our islands are threatened by one of the Dark Gods."

Robyn spoke softly, but all of those at the table looked furtively toward her as she spoke. All except Newt, that is, who took the opportunity to steal another, and then a third sip from Tristan's mug. The red-haired woman licked her lips, while the others stared with expressions of apprehension or disbelief.

Grunnarch frowned. "Why should one of the Dark Gods desire the Moonshaes when there are rich empires— Calimshan, Thay, Waterdeep—all across the Realms? What do we have here?"

Robyn bit her tongue, holding back an angry reply. She realized that he really did not understand. "These islands have a life of their own! Perhaps that is one reason our people make war on each other with such regularity. The Ffolk have always felt that the men of the north do not treat our land with the reverence it deserves."

She suddenly leaned against the table, wincing in discomfort, and Tristan took hold of her arm. Unnoticed by them all, the red-haired woman smiled and stared intently at the druid.

"What is it?" Tristan asked. "Are you all right?"

Quickly she shook off his hand, sat upright, and continued. "The Moonwells are the proof. Genna told me that when her grandmother was a girl, there was a Moonwell in every village of the isles. Druids by the hundreds patrolled the wild places, working the will of the goddess."

"Indeed," agreed Friar Nolan. "These isles have a peculiarly sacred nature, obvious to those of us who worship the new gods, as well as to the druids. Remember, not all of these gods are of the same vein as the master of this evil. Many of these clerics, as you, regard the Moonwells as benign and sanctified places."

"But there are no Moonwells on Norland!" protested the Red King, and then he looked thoughtful.

"Precisely! And as the faith of the people wanes, as more of the lands are taken from the Ffolk, the power of the goddess grows weaker." Suddenly Robyn shook her head violently, and the color drained from her face.

"But the enchantment of the land remains?"

"Yes. And becomes more susceptible to corruption with each passing year, each new blow against . . . the Ffolk." Robyn was trying hard not to state her points accusingly, but she was only partially succeeding. She had trouble speaking the words clearly, and an acute nausea grew within her. All the while, the strange woman stared at her, piercing the druid's skin with those cold black eyes.

"But the land is here, like all other lands, for the using!" argued Grunnarch.

"The using, yes, but not the abuse or destruction! It is when humans destroy that which supports them that the goddess suffers most keenly."

"You, like your king, are wise beyond your years," mused the northman. "I do not like the thought that my people are responsible for bringing this evil to the land."

"Perhaps you can help us to remove it." Tristan spoke earnestly, staring his guest in the face.

"I owe you my life. Ask what you will. If it is in my power to give, you shall have it."

"For now, I'll be happy to have your friendship," Tristan said warmly. "Let's toast: To peace between us, and between our children!" Both kings raised their mugs and drank deeply, thumping them back to the tabletop at the same instant. Tristan realized, suppressing a belch, that he had had a lot to drink.

"Time for some dancing!" proclaimed Tavish suddenly. She rose and unstrapped her lute, checking the tuning of a few errant strings. Eager Ffolk pushed some of the tables aside, and Tristan turned to Robyn, ready to kick up his feet. She shook her head in‑confusion, and he leaned over toward her, again concerned.

"I'm sorry," she said weakly. "I'm not feeling well at all. I think I'd better go to bed."

He offered to walk her to her room, but she declined. "Well, wake me at first light," he offered. "We'll ride at dawn."

She looked at him skeptically. "I'll wake you then," she said with a laugh, "but you'll surprise me if we leave before mid-morning!" With a forced smile, she left the hall.

Tristan turned back to the table and bumped someone who had not been there a moment earlier. With surprise, he saw the red-haired woman wiping the contents of a spilled mug from her apron.

"Excuse me," he said. "Let me—"

"That's all right," she interrupted. She smiled at him, a rich, glowing look that caused his blood to race. He had not noticed earlier just how attractive she was.

"Sit here," he said, not knowing why he offered the seat Robyn had just vacated. "Move, Newt." He pushed the faerie dragon aside, and Newt, with an indignant "Hmph!" disappeared.

The woman handed him another mug as he sat heavily beside her. He stared at her mutely as Ffolk throughout the hall rose to dance to the strains of Tavish's lute. Something very appealing, and a little wicked, gleamed at him from her eyes.

"You are a very handsome king," she said quietly. Her voice was soft and husky.

His head swirled, and lust rose unbidden within him. Her hand fell softly on his leg, and the pressure of her fingers burned into his flesh.

"Who are you?" He realized as he asked the question that her answer would mean nothing to him. It didn't matter who she was. He did know that he wanted her with a physical yearning beyond anything he had ever felt.

Tristan was unaware, or chose to ignore, the uncomfortable looks of Pawldo and Randolph as his two friends cast sideways glances at their king. He took no note of Pontswain's sneer, nor even of the hot anger burning in Daryth's eyes. The Calishite glowered at the girl, but she squeezed the king's thigh more tightly.

Abruptly she stood and swirled away from the table, her loose gown flowing around the full contours of her body. Tristan stumbled to his feet as she slipped away. A desperate fear rose within him—he mustn't let her get away.

"Sire?" came the call from behind him in Daryth's strained voice.

Friar Nolan stood and laid a restraining hand upon Tristan's arm, but the king angrily shook it off. The cleric shrank back into his chair under the intensity of Tristan's blazing stare.

But then the king had eyes only for the luscious creature that slid sinuously across the great room. She passed through the door, into a darkened hallway. He followed behind, eagerly hurrying to her side, but she twisted away and dashed up the stairs to the royal living quarters. Tripping on the first step, he regained his balance and followed her.

Somehow she found his bedchamber, and he followed her inside, pulling the door shut with a slam behind him. Her robe fell away, and the sight of her nakedness took his breath from him. He lunged toward her and they fell across the huge bed, his own tunic falling, unnoticed, around his ankles.

Desire took hold of his brain, giving him clear focus and

strong purpose. Nothing could be more important than this warm, wanton woman beneath him.

\* \* \* \* \*

Newt looked blearily at Tristan and Robyn from his invisible position next to a recently full pitcher of ale. Suppressing a belch, he squinted. What was wrong?

That wasn't Robyn! Sitting up in shock, the little dragon watched the woman—that floozy!—lead the unfortunate Tristan toward the door. This wasn't right, wasn't right at all! Where did Robyn go? What did that awful creature have in mind for his friend?

"I'll save him!" he vowed, blinking again. Already his mind whirled with illusions he could use, perhaps a nest of snakes in her hair, or a great, fat wart, right on her—

But he couldn't let them get away. Already the door was closing behind them. Newt sprang into the air, wings humming. But wait! His head was spinning uncontrollably from the effects of the ale. And what was wrong with his wings? Why were they flying him in *this* direction? And where had that great, looming pillar come from—the one right in front of his nose.

No one in the hall heard the tiny *thunk* as the dragon crashed, and Newt knew only blackness as he fell lightly to the floor.

\* \* \* \* \*

Once behind the solid oaken door to her room, Robyn began to feel better almost immediately. The sudden queasiness passed, and she decided it must have been a combination of excitement and too much food and wine. She lay on her familiar down mattress and dwelled for a moment on her glowing pride in Tristan.

He made a splendid figure of a king! She had always sensed a great destiny before him, but now she began to see it take form. Would that he could end the centuries of strife between northmen and Ffolk! And after that accomplishment, where would he go next?

She hoped, very deeply, that she would be able to share

that pride and progress with him, that they could have children and grandchildren who would see that legacy live on after them. And with him at her side, she felt confident that they could conquer the evil cleric and his legions in Myrloch Vale.

Suddenly she sat up, thinking of the celebration in the hall below. Her illness had passed. There was no reason she shouldn't go back and enjoy herself. And Tristan had been disappointed, she could tell, when she had left. She felt a twinge of guilt, knowing how important this homecoming was to him. There was no reason why they shouldn't have a night of enjoyment before embarking upon their quest. And she really did enjoy dancing.

She went downstairs and saw with surprise that Tristan was not there. Daryth left the party, too, as soon as he saw her come through the door. She thought he looked angry. Pawldo and Randolph didn't seem to know where the king had gone, though their answers when she questioned them seemed forced.

Perhaps he had been taken ill also. Could they have shared a piece of spoiled food? Concerned, she started back up the stairs. The first thing to do, she decided, was check his room.

\* \* \* \* \*

Tristan didn't notice the door swing open behind him, but the sudden wash of torchlight broke his concentration. Robyn's voice, as if from a great distance away, reached him.

"Tristan? What's wrong? What—"

And then he was cold sober as he turned to stare into the druid's shocked face. Robyn slowly lowered the torch, her mouth hanging slack in astonishment. The yellow flames reflected vast depths of pain in her green eyes. He tried to sit, but the tunic betrayed him and he sprawled across the woman, who laughed in delight.

And then the door to the room slammed shut with a force that shook the stones of the castle and sent its echoes reverberating through the long, empty passages of his heart.

* * * * *

Shapes slipped past overhead, dark green against the purple of the sea. The stream of bodies continued for many minutes, sinuous forms swimming easily through the depths, dark and scaly and silent, always silent. Ysalla stared upward all the while, watching the army gather above her. Her mouth gaped slightly and her forked tongue darted, unnoticed by her, back and forth from her maw.

The force gathered like a cloud in the sea, blocking the scant sunlight that penetrated this far down and surrounding Ysalla with a welcome darkness. The throbbing power of the Deepsong filled the sea around her and brought a fierce joy to her soul.

Below her, along the floor of the vast undersea canyon, another army gathered. This was a plodding, methodical force, lacking the speed and grace of the swimming sahuagin, but it offered its own terrors to any foe.

For the second army was a force made up entirely of death. The shambling corpses, animated by the dark power of her faith, dumbly awaited a command.

Her command.

Ysalla was a cleric of Bhaal, in her own way as powerful as Hobarth. However, while the human Hobarth presided over a domain of air and land and light, Ysalla practiced her craft in the dark, chill regions below the surface of the sea.

As Keeper of the Eggs, she ruled her scaly congregation together with Sythissal, the king. Her priestesses—yellow, sleek creatures, as opposed to the sturdy green warriors that made up most of her kind—enforced the will of Bhaal as that will was made known to their mistress.

Now Ysalla and Sythissal had assembled an army more vast than any in the memory of the Deepdwellers. Beside the legions of fierce sahuagin warriors at their command fought the dead of the sea—sailors who had drowned in the oceans of the Moonshae and had been animated by the power of Bhaal to serve as mindless servants of evil. And now, too, they had the remnants of the army of the Black Wizard. These troops, humans mostly, but also the dead remnants of the Ogre Brigade, marched beside the dead of the sea in answer to Ysalla's command.

And over them all swam the sleek legions of sahuagin, ready to burst forth from the surf to lay waste to the lands of northmen and Ffolk alike. They awaited but the command to march.

Summoned by the thrumming cadence of the Deepsong, the army massed in the city of Kressilacc, deep beneath the narrow realm of men. They huddled among the towers and domes of the vast city on the bottom of the sea, gathering force and ferocity from the song.

To the east, they had suffered rebuff and loss against the skill of the new king and the might of the Earthmother. Ysalla sensed that the goddess was not the threat she had been, and the new king was now a hated enemy. The king gave focus to Bhaal's hatred, in a new direction, and so he directed his priestess toward the west.

Toward Corwell.

Ysalla keened sharply from her temple, high on the canyon wall of Kressilacc, summoning her priestesses to the sword. Sythissal called his legions together, and they started on the march to the west. Propelled by the command of Bhaal, they would march to land and lay waste to all the settlements of man they found there. Northmen or Ffolk, it mattered not—the Claws of the Deep would slay regardless.

The god of murder dangled a tempting prize before them. Should they slay the humans along the shore and destroy the ports of Gwynneth, Bhaal would reward them in a way Ysalla could only dream about.

For if they emerged victorious, Bhaal had promised to sink the island. Gwynneth, and the kingdom of Corwell itself, would fall beneath the waves, to become the permanent realm of the sahuagin.

\* \* \* \* \*

*The Earthmother had reigned over the Moonshae Islands far longer than any of the men who had made their homes there. Even the graceful Llewyrr, the elves who had once claimed the islands as their own, had come to a land where the goddess already ruled unchallenged.*

*In those decades and centuries, she had witnessed the birth of creatures misformed by genetic accident. She had beheld the cruel ravages of disease, often deforming and crippling the animals that roamed her lands. All too often, she had been forced to bear the scars of war, the cruelest of such crimes for it was the most avoidable. Her forests had burned; whole villages had fallen to the sword, or the axe, or the fiery magic of evil sorcery.*

*But never had she witnessed a greater blasphemy than the Children of Bhaal. Their very existence was a challenge to the balance, and their birth, wrought by the magic of the Darkwell, was a challenge to her soul.*

*She looked upon all the creatures of the isles as her off-spring, and this compounded the outrage. Perhaps her heart bled most bitterly for the fate of the great brown bear. Grunt had been a faithful servant and protector of Genna Moonsinger for a very long time, measured in human terms, and the destruction of the bear and his subsequent perversion into a thing of evil were the cruelest cuts of all.*

*But all her knowledge, awareness, and outrage slowly faded as her weakness grew. A blackness, the expanding void of death, surrounded her.*

*And then she knew no more.*

# ❧ 4 ❧

# ON WINGS OF WIND

Recoiling in shock and grief—anger would not come until later—Robyn stumbled back to her room. There she took refuge in the Scrolls of Arcanus. Burying herself in these talismans of faith, she sought an answer that did not exist.

A tiny voice cried within her. Why? Why would he betray me thus? And then the plaintive voice vanished beneath the din of cold anger. Her rage swelled inside of her like an unnatural poison, hurting her but also directing a fiery scorn toward the young king who, hours earlier, had claimed her love.

Robyn's door thumped beneath a persistent pounding, and she vaguely realized that Tristan stood without, calling her name. She made no reply, and after a while he went away, allowing her to return to the scrolls.

Each was a sheet of frail parchment, inscribed at the top with a stylized rune depicting a blossoming rose within the circle of a blazing sun. The parchment curled of its own will, shaped by long storage within the tube. Each was covered with strange runes, symbols Robyn had never seen before.

All of the scrolls bore a similar border, inscribed in green ink faded to a dull brown. Delicate tracings outlined the thorny stems of roses, framing each page. The stems encircled a vivid image of the sun in each corner, then came together in an involved depiction of the rose blossom itself at the top center of the parchment.

The druid dropped her eyes to the writing on the page. The runes seemed to dance and waver before her gaze. Her vision blurred, and a dull ache throbbed in her forehead, but she held to her scrutiny. The pounding in her head grew to a roar, and the runes seemed to twist all over the page, as if attempting to evade her.

Gradually, by the force of her will, she began to bend the text to her understanding. The shivering of the runes ceased, and each lay flat and motionless on the page like a normal inscription. The pounding in her head diminished, and as it did, the runes became visible as symbols, and then the meaning of those symbols became clear.

As she read, she learned secrets deeper than any she had imagined. The scrolls were exquisitely preserved, but incredibly ancient. She was certain they predated even the age of Cymrych Hugh, before the very earliest era of the Ffolk.

*I believed that you, Tristan Kendrick, would be a leader as great as Cymrych Hugh. You would unite the Ffolk, I thought. You would be the light that would drive evil from our lands. How could you fail me so?*

The first of the scrolls told her of the gods of the planes and the delicate harmony of power that ebbed and waned between good and evil, law and chaos. She saw her own druidic doctrine of the balance reflected in this struggle and sensed that the message of the new gods was not so very different from her own faith in the goddess Earthmother. Where she had long known of the four elements, water, earth, fire, and air, the scrolls promised secrets of wind and stone, ocean and flame.

The writing on the scrolls was clerical in nature, strange to her eyes. Some of the symbols—those in which she sensed the greatest power—still hurt her eyes as she beheld them. Some mighty enchantment lurked within these runes. But she forced herself to overcome the pain and discomfort. If she had been weaker, the symbols might have blinded her or driven her mad, but her discipline was such that she bent the power of the scrolls to her will and mastered them. Instead of a threat, the scrolls became a source of spiritual nourishment and growth.

*How I wanted to bear your child . . . our child. He would*

have been so strong! He would have been so wise! We could have done so much together, you and I. How could you betray me?

The next of the scrolls held the tale of the elements and told how the gods had used them in the creation of the Realms. Prime among them rolled the great mass of the sea. Eternal, imperturbable, unchanging, the sea had marked the boundaries of the world since the dawn of time. Holding fast to the slender page of the scroll, Robyn came to know the gods as beings of and from the sea, forces whose original essence was the vastness of the oceans.

You, too, could have been a force of primordial power, Tristan. Your mark could have been as vast as the ocean! Your power, with me at your side, would have run as deep, your legacy have been as eternal, as the sea itself!

Then she took up the parchment that told of the secrets of stone. She read of the land's rising, bleak and lifeless yet solid and firm, from the bosom of the sea. Thus were the Realms born, and their earth made the foundation for all that would follow. Stone was the flesh of the world, and in this secret—and the mastery of stone promised by the scroll—she began to sense a hope for her fellow druids.

You were my foundation, my rock! You were the firmament upon which I rested my hopes, not just for us and ours, but for the land and peoples of the isles! You could have been the unshakable base for generations of growth and peace and progress!

The following scroll told the story of fire. Fire, hot to the touch, killing and cleansing in its heat. Fire was the forge of the world, the spark from which emerged all the multitude of life that came to live upon the isles.

And the heat of passion that burns within that life. How could that fire consume you so easily? How could you be so weak?

And last she read the tale of wind, the breath that gave life to the world. Vitality came to all things through the wind, she learned. Even the plants breathed, and air was the vessel that brought health to life and carried waste and corruption away. Wind, so tenuous and untouchable yet so pervasive and strong. Without the air that was its medium, nothing could live.

Was our love so tenuous, so weak? Could you be so frail that the touch of a strange woman's hand was enough to draw you from me? Is holding you like holding the air: You are here when I breathe, but gone as the breath leaves my body?

As dawn colored the eastern sky, her grief dimmed, only to be replaced by the cold fire of anger. She confronted the reality of Tristan's betrayal, and she found she could not forgive him.

She did not see the aura that shimmered around her as she stood. Her body thrummed with power. The enchantment of the scrolls possessed her soul. Her flesh became the earth, her blood the water.

The fire of anger burned brightly in her soul as she stood before the window, looking eastward toward distant Myrloch Vale. There, awaiting their rescue, stood her druids. She no longer needed the help of a sword at her side, especially one held by so fickle a hand as that of her king. The power burned within her, and she stepped through the window, high above the courtyard, to go to the rescue of her clan.

With a puff of air, she was gone, her body disappearing even before it began to fall. A gust burst from Caer Corwell, racing eastward toward the vale as Robyn, druid of Gwynneth, became the wind.

\* \* \* \* \*

Once again the vulture rose above Caer Corwell, this time soaring away from the sea. The bird's bright eyes searched eastward, for the darkness upon the land that was its destination. For two days the bird flew, never tiring, until it passed above the reaches of desolation and blackness that marked its goal.

Genna, the druid—but also Kazgoroth, the minion of Bhaal—arrived at her master's lair in the Darkwell. Her body shifted easily back to that of the druid, and she quietly informed her master that her task was done.

* * * * *

Tristan stormed back to his room. Robyn had not acknowledged his knock, and now all his shame, all his frustration, became anger directed at the woman who, he felt, had brought this upon him. He crashed through his door, ready to strike her or kick her. He would drive her from his castle!

But she was already gone.

He sat numbly upon his bed. The haze of drink had fallen from his brain, and now he thought about the woman. It didn't strike him as odd that he had never seen her before. Even as prince, he had never traveled across all of Corwell. Yet she had seemed to know him. And the effect of her eyes, and her body, upon him had been like a powerful drug.

Slowly he convinced himself of a lie: that she had bewitched him somehow into betraying his beloved. His mind would not accept the reality, that the betrayal occurred because his own will was weak.

He thought of the celebration, still proceeding in the hall. As midnight approached, the revelry would be reaching its height. The bitter knowledge of his shame held him to his seat. He could not bear the looks that would fall upon him from his friends, his subjects. Daryth's burning look of accusation as he had left the hall came unbidden into his mind's eye.

The longer he sat and brooded, the blacker his mood became. He leaped to his feet and paced the length of the large bedroom, raging silently. He would make it up to Robyn, he vowed! He would go to Myrloch Vale and confront the evil there with the Sword of Cymrych Hugh! Then she would know the depths of his love for her.

Somehow this made his shame bearable. He walked from the room, passing slowly by Robyn's door. Tempted to knock, instead he listened softly for a moment but heard nothing.

Then he went down the wide stairway and reentered the Great Hall. Tavish still played her lute, and most of those present sat quietly, enthralled by a ballad of young lovers.

Carefully the king returned to the head table.

The others turned as he sat. Pawldo quickly avoided his gaze, and he saw the look of disappointment, even anger, on Daryth's face. More annoying to him was the leer of amusement with which Pontswain regarded him. Grunnarch the Red smiled pleasantly, apparently unaware of anything untoward.

The king looked boldly at his companions, but he felt the red blush of his shame rise into his face. Never mind. His friends would forgive him when he explained his plan of action. And Tristan cared very little what Pontswain thought.

Tavish returned to the table as Tristan leaned forward to speak to his friends gathered at the table. The Ffolk at the other tables paid no attention as they joined again in their own conversations. He saw no sign of the redheaded woman, and for this he felt great relief.

"In the morning, Robyn and I embark for Myrloch Vale. There we will confront this foul cleric and destroy him—and when we return, the celebration can truly begin!"

Daryth's eyebrows rose in surprise, but his face remained masked by a scowl. Pawldo nodded, and Tavish, who arrived at the table as he made his announcement, beamed.

"This time I'll be there with you!" declared the bard. "There'll be a song in this that'll last for the ages, to be sure!"

"I, too, shall place my axe at your side!" declared Grunnarch solemnly, surprising the young king.

"Thank you, Grunnarch. But I cannot—will not—ask you to accompany us on this mission. We will fight a battle for Corwell's heart, but it is a battle that must be waged by the Ffolk." The Red King scowled, and Tristan wondered if he had offended his guest.

"There is a greater task you can perform, Grunnarch, if I can ask it of you," he hastened to continue. "Can you go to your people and tell them of our peace? Tell them that the time of war between Ffolk and northman is over?"

"That is no task for a fighting king!"

"Perhaps not. But I ask you, can you do it? The enemies of our islands lie not just in the heartland of Gwynneth. The sahuagin who attacked our ships are ample proof of that. Carry the word of our alliance to your people, and we can unite in a common strength that will defeat all of our foes!"

Grunnarch looked skeptical but held his peace.

"I will need to leave the castle's administration in your hands a little longer," Tristan went on, turning to Randolph.

"I will come with you," announced Daryth, though the black look remained on his face.

"Someone'll have to keep you two alive," grumbled Pawldo. "As usual, it might as well be me!"

Tristan felt a burst of relief as his two old comrades declared their intentions. He had not previously realized how much their support meant to him. The memory of his shame fell to the rear of his thoughts, now, as planning for the expedition accelerated. But then he noticed the Crown of the Isles, gleaming in its place at the center of the table, where he had placed it at the start of the banquet. Its purity seemed to mock him, its brightness causing a physical pain to his eyes. Impulsively he stood up.

"As long as the scourge of evil marks our island, my kingship shall not truly begin!" he announced to the guests at large, noticing the sudden hush that fell across the room. "I shall leave the crown, the symbol of my past victories, here at Corwell, awaiting my triumphant return! Then, and only then, it shall be placed upon my brow in my own castle—and here, before you all, I shall take my place as High King of the Ffolk!"

A thunderous volley of applause exploded from the people, warming the king and seeming to wash his guilt away. That would truly be a grand event, he imagined, with Robyn at his side and evil vanquished from the land!

In the excitement, he failed to notice Tavish's look of alarm following his announcement. She studied the crown with concern, then looked back to the king. She admired, and even loved him, but now she feared he was embarking on an act of folly.

Tristan sat again, and planning for the excursion continued. Tavish, he learned, had returned to Corwell upon the king's powerful stallion, Avalon, from the stable at Kingsbay, where Tristan had left him months earlier. His spirits rose still further at the knowledge that this sturdy steed would carry him into the vale.

Finally the details had all been addressed. The revelers had left the hall. Virtually forgotten was his momentary dalliance with the redheaded woman. Perhaps it had all been a dream. Certainly it seemed logical that Robyn would have forgotten about it as well.

He had managed to convince himself of this as, at dawn, he climbed the stairs to the living quarters. Before retiring, he would tell Robyn of their plans. She would be delighted, he knew.

But again there was no answer, and a sick feeling of worry gripped him. In panic, he smashed the door with his shoulder and then kicked it aside with his boot. He stumbled into her room, looking frantically around. He saw her window standing open, with its airy view high above the courtyard, but the druid, together with her staff and scrolls, was gone.

\* \* \* \* \*

The druid, in fact, currently relished a form of freedom she had never before imagined. As the wind, she gusted and eddied, sailed and then slowed. She felt a great expansiveness, freed from the cloak of flesh. Her senses probed everywhere, pulling in the touch and sight and smell of the world.

For a long day and through the following night she blew, caring little for the passing of time. Fatigue was a thing unimaginable. The moors rolled past, and she dallied and swirled in the foothills below the highlands. She paused at a tiny cantrev, and even the woodsmoke of breakfast fires tickled her nostrils with a delightful odor.

The white ribbon of Corwell Road meandered below her as she swirled toward the center of Gwynneth Island. Finally she judged the time had come to turn northward, toward Myrloch Vale.

The power of the scroll possessed her completely. The words—runes, actually—had been vibrant with power. Now that magic, sanctified by the gods in a time long past, became Robyn's tool. She used it with skill and vigor, becoming a new element in pursuit of her goal.

She hurled herself at the highlands, storming up a vale, roaring through a narrow defile. Now Robyn was a wind of storm, gathering strength as she rose into the chill, barren reaches.

The forested hills of Corwell still glowed green, as the fir trees cloaking them retained their foliage even against the approach of winter. She sensed little wildlife, as the deer and badger and rabbit had all migrated to the lower reaches for the cold season.

As she rose higher, the trees gave way to rocky, barren slopes. Great patches of snow lay in drifts along many of the ridges. Deep ravines fell into chasms, and then valleys that trailed to the warm, green country behind. She did not sense the waning of her enchantment, but the spell had begun to lose its potency. Though mighty, it could last for but a limited time.

Snowflakes pranced around her as she crested the great ridge, the summit that separated the human realms of Corwell from the wilderness of Myrloch Vale.

And here the storm broke into chaos.

Robyn crashed into a barrier of evil so potent, so pervasive, that her soaring momentum vanished into nothingness. Where the land behind her had been clean and healthful, full of nature's vitality, she recoiled now, faced with a vision of death, decay, and corruption. The devastation began at the crest and trailed into the vastness of Myrloch Vale.

Even Myrloch itself, a great lake of crystalline azure in Robyn's mind, had succumbed to the rot. Visible in the distance to the north, it was now dark and dull, the water seeming more a stretch of brackish swamp than a vast loch. The forests around it now sprawled lifeless, barren skeletons of trees rising forlornly from blackened ground.

The magic that had carried her thus far vanished in the face of a far stronger and more immediate power. In the flash of that instant, Robyn's body became flesh. She crashed among the rocks at the crest of the highest peak and lay there stunned, shivering, and bleeding.

But the worst injury had been inflicted upon her soul. The desecration of so vast an area, and the totality of the destruction, tore at every fiber of her faith. How could she cope with power such as this?

Dimly she realized that her arm lay behind her, twisted at an unnatural angle by jagged rocks. She shifted slightly, and pain knifed through her shoulder.

The immediacy of her suffering brought her attention back to her own predicament. She sat up, wincing in pain, and knew that her arm was broken, probably in several places. Her lips and mouth were swollen and bleeding. She spat, and several chips of teeth fell onto the rocks.

As she looked up, the expanse of the vale again came before her vision, and she moaned with despair. The cold wind, an inanimate thing now, pulled at her torn robe, sucking the heat from her exposed skin. Now flakes of snow swirled around her, stinging the scraped skin along her face and cheeks.

Mother, I have failed you, she thought in despair. She did not know if she spoke to her spiritual mother—the goddess, mother of all the isles—or to her true mother, the druid she had never known. It didn't matter, really.

I shall die on this rock. My anger has sent me on a fool's quest, but must the punishment be so harsh?

Slowly the pain disappeared from most of her body, though her arm and shoulder continued to throb. Was the chill numbing her senses, or had the pain indeed eased?

She twisted again among the rocks, trying to avoid a root she felt jabbing into her back, and then her mind began to work. There could be no root where there were no plants. The plainly wooden surface annoying her must be something else.

Biting her lip to keep from crying out, she turned to see her staff pinned between two rocks. Awkwardly, with her good hand, she pulled it out and laid it across her lap. She had no strength to call for its magic, but its mere presence comforted her nonetheless.

Another unnatural thing caught her eye, and she gasped

with relief as she saw the ivory tube containing the Scrolls of Arcanus. The container lay below her feet, in a shadowy crack beneath an overhanging boulder. With relief, she confirmed that she had carried her talismans with her.

The accoutrements of faith brought hope back once again. Perhaps she would not die here. It would take more than a few bruises to break the will of a druid of the vale!

She closed her eyes and slowly, carefully, rehearsed the words to a simple spell. She was weak, and her mouth was wounded. She could not take a chance on misstating the incantation.

*"Matro, karelius doniti . . . arum!"*

She whispered the words to her spell, and the healing magic spread through her shoulder, into the length of her arm. She felt the torn muscles mend, and even sensed the bonding as the shattered ends of bone fused again into one. For precious seconds, the curing spell tingled within her.

But then the magic faded, dying away in a last flutter of healing. She grew weak and dizzy, finally slumping against her rocky seat. For a moment, her world went black, and then she awakened with a start. She moved her arm experimentally, and pain again lanced through her shoulder, but it was more bearable now, and the arm answered the commands of her brain in its movement, however begrudgingly.

The healing spell of a druid was not potent, but it did help. And after a brief period of prayer, she could use it again. Closing her eyes and forcing herself to ignore her pain, Robyn relaxed. The familiar sensation of peace came over her, and she called upon the mother to restore her spell to her.

She awaited the smooth flow of power that would be the answer to her prayer, but there was nothing. Again, and a third time, she prayed for her spell, but she could get no response from her goddess. A chill sensation of fright and loneliness closed about her, and she found it impossible to concentrate any longer on prayer. Grim and afraid, she tried to move.

She found that she could stand up and did so. Carefully lifting the scrolls, she looked for a pouch or pocket in which to place them. Settling for her apron, Robyn carefully wrapped the tube in cloth, binding it against her back. She found that she had on the garments she wore at the time of her casting—robe, apron, belt and boots—along with her staff and scrolls.

But nothing else. She had neither flint to spark a fire nor dagger to strike it on. Her clothing was woefully inadequate to face a chill night, even one not spent atop a craggy, snowswept peak.

She turned, once, to look at the rolling foothills to the south, falling away to the green moors of central Corwell. The sun still beamed there, dancing among white clouds to illuminate a low hill or small copse of brilliant oak, blazing with the colors of late autumn.

But overhead roiled heavier, more ominous clouds. The snow became thicker by the minute and soon began to gather in the cracks among the broken rocks. The clouds lay like a leaden quilt across the breadth of the vale, casting the huge valley in a pall of shadow. Though the snow seemed to be falling only among the highest mountains, Robyn could see no sign of encouragement or comfort in the entire brooding vista.

Struck by a thought, she looked in the scroll tube for the parchment of wind mastery, but it was not there. She was not surprised, for she knew that a druidic spell written upon a scroll would vanish as soon as it was cast. She suspected that the clerical spells worked the same.

But there were other ways to travel, and many of them did not require her to walk down the side of this mountain. Once she had flown from Gwynneth to Callidyrr in the body of a hawk, and she could certainly cross a narrow band of foothills in the same form.

She closed her eyes, calling the birdlike image into her mind, preparing for the familiar shifting of her form. And then a blinding pain flashed behind her eyes and she sat heavily upon the jagged rocks. Reaching to either side, she balanced herself upon her hands—not wings, as she had expected—and opened her eyes. The same weakness that had caused her to faint after casting the healing spell drained her muscles of strength and caused her head to spin.

For an awful moment, she felt a horrible surge of panic rising in her stomach. What had happened to her powers? She shook her head, banishing the fear, and sought a logical explanation. It must be fatigue, she told herself—the weakness caused by her wounds and her lack of sleep. Certainly it would pass.

Resolutely she started toward the north on foot. Holding her staff in her right hand as an aid to balance among the treacherous rocks, she started down the long shoulder of the mountain.

For an hour or more, she made steady progress. The walking warmed her body, and all her attention was focused on the placement of the next step. She had no time to brood about her surroundings or her plight.

The steep ridge led to a broad shoulder. The air felt noticeably warmer here, and the snow had nearly stopped. She looked into the gray clouds surrounding her and imagined that she saw all manner of hideous, deformed figures there.

Suddenly she stopped in shock. Something had moved within those looming clouds. She saw it again, a vague shape that soared through a thinning of the mist, only to disappear again within the folds of the cloud. It could have been a great bird, or something else. Whatever its nature, it looked to be nearly the size of a man.

Nervously she tightened her grip on her staff. By instinct, she probed with her feet, finding a broad, flat slab to provide a secure foothold. All the while, her eyes searched the clouds on all sides and above her. For many minutes, she stood alert, unmoving except to roll her head to look everywhere.

But she saw nothing, nothing except the vastness of suddenly threatening nature. Her feet began to ache from the chill of inaction, and she started to descend again. Robyn moved more carefully now, cautiously planting each foot on the broken ground and then searching the skies for the hidden threat.

The length of the broad shoulder behind her, she once

again confronted a steeply descending ridge. She slid along a knife's edge of stone, ignoring the dizzying drop on either side. She saw two tiny lakes below her. One, to the south, lay beneath a white sheet of ice, covered by a thin layer of snow. A dusting covered the lake's small basin, only the larger jumbles of rocks poking through as proof of solid firmament below.

The other lake lay to the north, just beyond the narrow gap in the crest that marked the border between Corwell and the vale. Here no ice had formed, and no snow remained on the ground. The rocks of the valley floor were rounded and worn, a dark gray shade. The water itself festered in choking weeds. Patches of scum floated on the surface, among the brownish green tendrils of algae.

Robyn reached a sharp drop. She looked at a wide ledge, twenty feet below, and considered jumping. The alternative was to turn and face the rock, working her way carefully down one of the wide cracks in the stone face. At the same time, she would leave herself terribly exposed to any menace from the sky. She looked again at the drop and realized that a slight miscalculation in her jump would plummet her to certain death, off one side of the ridge or the other.

The clouds still oppressed her, but her descent had carried her far below the heavy gray mass. She stared intently for minutes but saw nothing moving among them. Tucking the staff across her belt and lashing it in place with the apron, she turned to face the rock and climbed over the edge.

A small fissure gave her a toehold, and she reached down to grab a spur of stone with her hand. She lowered her other foot and wedged it between two outcroppings of rock. And then she felt a presence behind her.

Instantly she let go of the rock, dropping free at the first prickling of alarm. Thumping to the ledge, she fell to the side to absorb the force of her fall and then whirled to stare upward.

Suddenly a creature crashed into the wall where her back had been. She heard a cracking of bone as the thing, eerily silent, fell beside her. She dared not look at it as she desperately tore her staff from her back and climbed to her feet, scanning the skies for any other attackers. Her timely drop had saved her life, for the thing would have smashed her body brutally if she had remained on the cliff.

But what was it? The limp body sprawled beside her, issuing a heavy stench of rot and corruption. She felt her eyes drawn toward the corpse, but then another flash of movement in the sky drew her full attention.

She saw another of the things—it looked like a great bird—diving from the clouds, with a third plummeting behind it. Now the staff was free, held in both hands before her as she stared in disbelief, and then revulsion, at the soaring creatures.

They came soundlessly, their mouths gaping. Their heads were skeletal but unmistakably the skulls of deer. And the broad, menacing antlers spreading above the head of each confirmed the monster's staglike origins.

But the body was feathered and gaunt, like some huge vulture. And each of them swooped like a hawk, still making no sound. Robyn could now see the sharp, wolfish fangs that filled each hungry maw.

The things came closer, straight at her face, and she swung the staff with all the force her weary body could gather. The stout shaft cracked against the first monster's head, knocking it aside, but the force of the blow nearly knocked Robyn off her feet. Instantly the second of the things struck her.

She brought the staff up and felt the shaft crunch into its feathered body as those awful antlers sliced her face and forced her back against the cliff face. The creature's teeth tore at her breast, and she forced the staff against the thing's throat as blood from a slash on her forehead dripped into her eyes. The creature snapped at her again, but she pushed it away.

The monster had black, soulless eyes, or maybe they were just empty sockets staring from that rotted skull. Robyn could not be sure. The teeth snapped again at her left breast. Suddenly she was acutely conscious of her pounding heart, thumping almost audibly from her exertions.

The beast lunged forward again, and this time she crushed its throat with the force of her resistance, and she understood its lust as it died. It hungered for her heart!

The body fell lifeless at her feet, and she stumbled back in horror as she saw the beast clearly for the first time. The stag-skull, framed by a proud rack of antlers, could have been taken from the body of a deer and transplanted onto the headless corpse of a great eagle, for all its gory looks. But the thing had lived!

And one other, at least, still did. The first monster, the one she had clubbed aside with her staff, suddenly swept upward from the valley. It had taken a long dive, but now it attacked with undiminished fury.

Robyn, through a bloody haze, saw it coming and staggered to the edge of the ledge. She could barely raise her staff, and the creature was soaring toward her with savage momentum. In that instant, she realized the futility of further combat. If she stayed to fight this thing, she would die, for she had no more strength.

In that same instant, she fell back upon her faith and her skill. If her magic failed her now, she would be dead. The monster raced toward her, its wicked antlers spread like a score of lances. But Robyn no longer stood before the attacker. Instead, she dropped to all four of her feet and scuttled toward a crack in the rock. Her tail whisked out of sight as the creature thumped into the rock wall.

Her tiny heart pounded, many times a second, as she turned to stare anxiously from her sheltered niche. She chittered and chirped nervously, unable to restrain her invective.

The monster landed outside and slashed at the crack with its crooked claws. But the furry marmot that was Robyn of Gwynneth drew farther back in the cave and chattered an angry challenge.

*　*　*　*　*

*The great unicorn trotted across the wasteland, his white head held high. His ivory horn rose in apparent challenge to any minion of horror that might arise before him.*

And indeed, Kamerynn would have relished the death of any of the servants of evil who now defiled his home. For weeks, he had lived among the desolation of the vale, slaying the living carrion that served the cleric of the Darkwell.

Once the unicorn had discovered and fought a hideous flying creature, a cross between hawk and stag. The thing was incredibly evil, but it had flown away before Kamerynn could slay it.

Through those weeks, he had wandered around the breadth of Myrloch, watching the great lake die. The desolation had spread quickly, and now he could only feel a hopeless sense of defeat. Kamerynn was only an animal, but an animal of such intelligence as to make normal human intellect dim in comparison.

To him, the fate of the world was now obvious, writ upon the face of Myrloch Vale. This blackness and death would claim all. Abruptly the unicorn halted in his tracks. He lifted his head even higher, flexing his pink nostrils in the fetid air. Though no odor nor sound reached him, he sensed a message, or was it a cry for help?

His broad heart quickened as he felt the gentle tug upon his spirit once again. The mother called him! He could not know that the goddess lay inert within the earth, paralyzed by the blackness, nor that the call came not from her but from a druid of great faith, in dire danger.

But he recognized the summons, and the command. With a mighty bound, he galloped off in a new direction, thundering across the dead ground. A streak of white across a landscape of unbroken black, he raced to answer the call to his soul.

# ❧ 5 ❧

# INTO THE DARKNESS

Tristan opened the chest, and immediately the musty smell washed over him with memories of his father. He inhaled slowly, cherishing those remembrances in a way he had never cherished his father while he lived. Then he shook off his reminiscence and reached into the large trunk.

The silver chain mail gleamed untarnished, as if he had put it there yesterday. In reality, the armor had lain here undisturbed since the end of the Darkwalker War more than a year earlier.

He lifted the shirt of mail, noticing again the lightness of the metal, the unblemished nature of the craftsmanship. Yet experience had shown him the strength of the armor. It had saved his life more than once.

And it would do so again, staying with him as trusted protection. Not like his companions, damn them! Not like Daryth! The Calishite had not spoken to him all morning as he went about his own preparations with surly concentration. Even Pawldo was subdued.

Of course, they all worried about Robyn, as did he. But they would find her, rescue her. Tristan knew that they would.

He raised the legacy of his father over his shoulders and felt its solid weight come to rest upon his frame. The armor felt good, a solid cloak protecting him from the deadly assaults of his enemies. Would that it offered the same protection from the pain emanating from his own heart!

Angrily he shook off the thought. Guilt was for weaklings!

He stalked through the castle, down the stairs, and out the doors, then across the courtyard to the stable. There he found Avalon. The great stallion whinnied a soft greeting.

The steed had been well cared for. As he threw the heavy saddle across the stallion's back, the king saw that Avalon's snowy white coat gleamed and his nostrils flared with eagerness, as if he sensed impending adventure. He pranced anxiously as Tristan cinched the saddle and loaded his few provisions into panniers.

He only vaguely noticed Tavish and Pawldo preparing their own mounts, a gelding and a small pony, elsewhere in the stable. Pawldo was well outfitted for travel and adventure, with sturdy leather garments and his trusty sword. Tavish had borrowed a shortsword from the castle weapons room. She had it strapped to her saddle so she could carry her lute. Her saddlebags bulged with a variety of foods and several skins of strong wine.

Newt and Yazilliclick buzzed around anxiously. Both the faerie creatures were eager to return to Myrloch Vale, but the sprite's natural shyness prevented him from talking when everyone else remained silent. Noticing the difficulties Tavish had with packing her ample provisions, however, the sprite offered his aid. The bard finally saddled him with a wineskin.

The normally loquacious Newt seemed unusually subdued. This morning his scales were a sickly greenish color. He waited on one of the rafters in the stable until the others were ready, then buzzed down to ride on the horn of Tristan's saddle.

Daryth already sat astride his chestnut mare, waiting for them in the courtyard with Canthus. His silver scimitar rested easily against his thigh. Daryth looked toward the gate, ignoring the rest of the party as they gathered in the courtyard.

Tristan glanced awkwardly at the others when they gathered before the gate. They were all acutely aware of Robyn's absence, he felt certain. His embarrassment caused his voice to grow harsh as they started out.

"Robyn's gone. I'm certain she's headed for Myrloch Vale,

to the grove of the great druid. We will follow and find her."
He nudged Avalon with his knees, and the great stallion
started into a brisk trot, passing through the gatehouse as
the other companions fell in behind.

Tristan unwillingly recalled in vivid detail the events of the
previous night. How could he have hurt Robyn like that?
What could have gone through his mind? A part of him still
wanted to claim that the woman had bewitched him somehow, used foul enchantment to beguile him with her charms.
But he suspected that this was not the truth.

Tristan remained constantly aware of Robyn's absence,
though he tried to ignore his role in her sudden departure.
His father's chain mail armor rested heavily on his shoulders, and he quickly grew saddle sore. Nevertheless, he
would find her. Of that he was certain. The others could
come with him or remain behind.

He didn't really care.

\* \* \* \* \*

Now the north wind howled with the threat of approaching winter, but the lone longship of Grunnarch the Red
sliced through each mountainous crest as if it could smell
the security of its home port. Manned by thirty brawny
northmen, several of whom Grunnarch had recruited in
Corwell's taverns and one whom he had liberated from the
town gaol, the sleek vessel raced northward.

"Hold steady!" the king ordered his helmsman as he made
his way into the bow. The gray water rolled on all sides as
far as he could see. Dusk settled over the Sea of Moonshae,
and the Red King's thoughts turned to the cookfires of
home, the great smoky council lodge near the shore, and
the welcoming embrace of his woman.

It would not be long before those things were his again,
and this knowledge brought him a keen pleasure. Truly,
homecoming was always sweet, but this one would be
sweeter than most.

Still, his eyes fell, unbidden, on the gray swells that slowly
turned to black with the vanishing light. He recalled the
sahuagin that had boiled upward from the mysterious

depths to claim the lives of so many of his countrymen.

The fish-men still lurked down there, he knew. He couldn't be certain, but he suspected that their depredations were not finished. Grunnarch did not even suspect that the horrors of the sahuagin had barely begun.

\* \* \* \* \*

The great dog led the way unerringly, selecting the easiest path up the rocky defile. Tristan followed, leading Avalon by the great stallion's bridle. The wind picked up, and he pulled his cloak tightly about him with his free hand.

As they climbed through the foothills into the highlands, progress slowed for the first time in the four days of the journey. From his previous venture into Myrloch Vale, Tristan knew that this was the roughest part of the trip.

"Let's hunt some firbolgs!"

The suggestion came from the back of Avalon's saddle, where Newt rested comfortably. Tristan ignored the faerie dragon, but the top popped from one of the saddlebags to reveal Yazilliclick.

"Are you c-crazy?" he stammered, his tiny antennae quivering in agitation. "W-We've got to find Robyn—Robyn!"

"Well, maybe she's been captured by a firbolg! I mean, that's as likely as anything, if you ask—"

"Shut up!" growled Tristan, whirling to face the dragon. Newt dropped his head and sulked as the king glared at him for a moment. Beyond the dragon, Tristan could see the figures of Tavish and Pawldo, each leading his mount up the trail behind him. Daryth's tiny figure, occasionally disappearing around some bend in the trail, brought up the rear to guard against surprise.

"Or perhaps to avoid my presence," mumbled Tristan. In truth, the Calishite had avoided his gaze and made no offer to converse with him. As they had made camp each of the last three nights, Daryth had found an excuse to wander away by himself, returning only after Tristan had retired.

The bright sunlight of their journey thus far, even with its pale, wintry glow, had seemed to mock the king. The noble purpose of the quest seemed an empty memory now. Daryth should be helping me, offering me friendship and comfort, damn him!

He tried to avoid thinking about his own actions, but his mind was inexorably drawn to the fateful night of their homecoming. Robyn's absence had surprised and mystified him, but he had suspected immediately that she had gone on to the vale alone. How she had left her room without drawing attention, he couldn't guess.

But now she must certainly be in great danger. And he was equally aware that his own lack of faith had sent her away. He cringed inwardly at this awareness, but there was no other way to look at it. He had betrayed her.

"She could be killed!" he hissed, shaking his head as if to ward away the fear. He pushed himself harder, looking ahead to Canthus.

The great dog stood now at a narrow niche in a ridge at the top of this high valley. His sharp nose pointed into the wind, the moorhound gazed majestically into the valley beyond. There, Tristan knew, lay Myrloch Vale. There, too, would be Robyn.

Or so he devoutly hoped.

\* \* \* \* \*

The marmot cowered within its niche while the great predator, with apparently infinite patience, crouched just outside the crack. For three days, it had remained motionless, like a statue of itself.

But it still was there, waiting only for the appearance of its prey. The strain of the shape-change had exhausted Robyn so much that she had slept for a day and a half. Now, as she slowly regained her strength, she listened carefully. Robyn's tiny ears, more keen than those of her human body, heard the steady thumping of the monstrous heart. The druid knew that she was trapped.

Her ears were not keen enough to hear the distant clopping of hooves upon the rocks below. The monster could hear, and see, however. Its vacant eyes stared at the muffled figures, four of them, below. The humans led their horses and were preceded by a great dog. The peryton watched them make their way through a high pass and descend into the broadening valley beyond.

The peryton twitched anxiously, shaking its broad antlers. The commands of its maker had been clear—guard the vale, attack strangers, report large groups of intruders.

But now it had a dual task, for was it not still engaged in the attacking of the stranger now trapped in the cave? Yet these were intruders below, as well, and didn't their numbers make them the greater threat? But the prey in the trap was an intruder close at hand, and as is the way of stupid beasts, to the peryton, the thing close at hand was the important thing.

So the monster kept its watch upon the tiny marmot, for sooner or later, the creature would need to emerge and eat. And all the while, the four intruders, with their horses and dog, grew smaller and smaller in the north.

Robyn's senses had a new aspect now. She was no longer crippled with fear. Her wounds, over the past three days of enforced rest, had healed. She was hungry, and eager to proceed with her mission. Now the fear of the monster that had driven her into the tiny cave was gone, replaced by an angry flame that slowly grew into a crackling rage.

She reached a decision easily. Once she had decided to escape, she was satisfied. All that she needed now was a plan.

She would attack the thing and drive it from her doorstep! First, though, she would need a new body. She considered the limitations of her cave, with an entrance less than a foot high and little wider. She would have to emerge with a small body but one that was powerful and tough, equipped with weapons that could slay the hideous creature that lay in wait.

She thought of the body of a great wolf, but she immediately discarded it as too large for the cave entrance. Then she considered that of a scaly serpent, but she realized that the cold weather would make her slow and lethargic.

And then she thought of the creature she would become, and as quickly as she thought, she shifted. Her body crouched in the rodent's posture but grew longer and broader. Her back widened, but did not rise much higher than the marmot's. Her tiny claws, however, stretched and grew hooked until they rested on the rocky floor several inches ahead of her four paws. Her muzzle grew until wicked fangs protruded from her curling lip.

Her heartbeat slowed as that muscle grew to accommodate the larger body, and her black eyes took on a reddish cast. The growl that rumbled unconsciously from her chest could never have been uttered by a marmot.

But the marmot had become a wolverine. Robyn flexed her powerful rear legs and slipped through the cave entrance with a single fluid motion. The monster leaped backward, flapping its great wings in surprise. Its ghastly mouth gaped in rage, and it hissed a challenge.

The wolverine's forepaws reached out and clutched the thing's body in a steely embrace. Robyn's teeth sought its throat, and only the monster's desperate twisting prevented her from administering a fatal bite. The creature tumbled backward as the wolverine clung tightly to its breast. Her rear legs flexed and kicked as Robyn used those sharp claws in an effort to disembowel her opponent, all the while ignoring the pounding of its wings against her head.

All of a sudden, the creature's twisting evasion took them over the ledge. Robyn felt them both falling, bouncing against the rocky cliff. But now her animal instincts—instincts among the most savage in the natural world—compelled her to cling to her victim tenaciously. This tenacity saved her life as they suddenly crashed into the ground, and she felt the creature's body break beneath her.

The frenzy of the wolverine's attack did not abate, however. Robyn slashed and bit and growled until the remains of the unnatural monster had been torn into shreds. Feathers covered a circle ten feet wide, and bits of cracked bone lay scattered over a similar distance. In the center of the circle, only the staglike head, lying flat on the ground with its antlers spreading treelike above, remained as mute evidence of the beast's nature.

Finally her rage faded, though Robyn, still cloaked in the body of the wolverine, paced restlessly around the remains of her foe for some time. Every so often, she paused and glared at the sky, as if challenging another of the creatures to attack.

Eventually she sat up on her haunches and tried to concentrate, to call up an image of her own human body. For several minutes, her mind whirled with a confused blur of pictures, none of them familiar. She found her attention wandering to thoughts of food.

Instinctively she growled, and the sound shocked her back to awareness. I must think! I must shift . . . now! A deep fear began to grow within her. Perhaps she had waited too long . . . perhaps her powers had waned too much for her to change back!

With a desperate strain, she pictured herself, and called upon all the spiritual power gathered in her tiny, muscular form. The world spun around her, and she gasped for air, feeling her windpipe contract. A sickening sense of nausea rose in her stomach, and then she lost consciousness.

Robyn awakened some time later. Dehydration swelled her tongue, and her lips cracked painfully as she struggled to open her mouth. But it was a human mouth, and a human tongue! Still, a great sense of lethargy lay upon her, as if the effort of the shape-changing had drained more of her strength than she had to give.

She sat weakly on the rocky ground as her world spun madly. "Mother, what is happening to me? Where are you?" But as before, when she had tried to pray, there was no answer to her question. It took her several minutes to regain her strength.

She noticed a gnawing ache in her stomach and realized with chagrin that she had neglected to bring any food with her. Nor had she brought a bedroll, or a waterskin, or any of the other equipment that was necessary to this mission in her human body. Somehow she had felt that she could reach the well and work her magic in the form of the wind, with no mortal accoutrements.

Softly she cursed her lack of foresight. Then she took up her staff and scrolls, which had made the shift with her, and looked around. She had tumbled nearly to the foot of the mountain during the course of the fight. The path before her, to the north, now curved gently along a sloping ridge. She started walking, and the movement swiftly drove the stiffness from her muscles.

In an hour, she had entered the low country, following the vestiges of a trail that had once been pastoral. Now it twisted toward the blackened trunks of dead, rotting trees. A fetid odor of decay arose from the land itself, and Robyn pulled her apron across her face. Even this could not dampen the pervasive stink.

She paused at the edge of the forest, but she knew that this was the path through Myrloch Vale, to the grove of the Great Druid. She took several deep breaths, as if sensing she breathed the cleanest air she would taste for many days.

Then, shouldering her staff, she spoke a quiet prayer to her goddess. Like the others, the prayer went unanswered. Nevertheless, she stepped forward resolutely and entered the dead forest.

\* \* \* \* \*

A padded foot, as broad as a bear's, fell softly on a pile of dried, dead moss, yet no sound emerged. Another paw, identical to the first, reached forward to pull the sleek body along. The rear feet, when they moved in turn, fell exactly in the soundless prints of the forefeet.

Above, all was blackness, except for the yellow slits in the creature's eyes. Should any moonlight have broken through the midnight clouds, an observer could have seen the long, curving teeth exposed by the widespread jaws. One could have marveled at the liquid muscle rippling below the sleek black hide, or shuddered at the ghastly tentacles protruding from the creature's shoulders.

Shantu, the displacer beast, moved to the hunt.

Shantu did not hunt from hunger—at least, not from the desire to fill its belly. Shantu's hunger was of another kind. It was the lust for fresh blood to cool its tongue, for the soothing death-cry of a victim to ring musically in its ears. It was spiritual, for Shantu longed for the feel of a warm body growing cold in its mouth, to drive the breath of life from a living creature.

Shantu was not hungry for food but for death. And now, patiently, with complete silence and stealth, the displacer beast moved through the deadness of Myrloch Vale. It sought anything alive, anything that held that spark that would give the beast sustenance in its extinguishing.

And so the displacer beast crept through the night, looking for something to kill.

\* \* \* \* \*

"We'll stop at the first good camping place," Tristan announced. The party had drawn together as darkness closed in, and now Tavish and Pawldo stood beside him as they rested. Daryth stood, almost invisible in the dusk, a few feet away, ostensibly observing the trail behind them.

"I wish you guys could see in the dark! I'm not tired yet!" Newt declared his disappointment loudly.

"Be quiet!" hissed the High King, looking into the dead woods around them. They had left the rocky highlands behind, but this forest of rotted trunks seemed even more barren. "Start looking for a place to camp. And another thing—there'll be no fire tonight!"

"This is still high country!" argued Pawldo. "We'll freeze without a fire!" The halfling huddled on his pony, a picture of discomfort and misery.

Tristan ignored him, turning back to the trail. He was riding Avalon now—they had all remounted beyond the high valleys—but he realized the futility of blundering on in the utter darkness that would soon descend.

"There's a grove of sorts," announced Tavish, pointing to a stand of dead pines as her gelding skittered nervously to the side. The towering skeletal trees offered better shelter, and softer bedding, than the rocky ground, so they entered the grove and prepared to make camp.

Unsaddling Avalon and watching the darkness close upon their camp, Tristan felt a sense of aloneness around him. The nearest community, he knew, lay beyond the rocky highlands, two days hence.

Where are you, Robyn? His mind voiced the question that

possessed him. His throat tightened and he shook his head angrily, but though he struggled to overlook his own role in the druid's flight, guilt soon rode roughshod over his feelings. And following the guilt came self-pity, and then the anger he directed at his companions.

"Damn!" he cursed at the darkness. He tried unsuccessfully to shake off his mood as he joined his companions over their cold bread and cheese.

"We'll have to stand watches. I'll take the midwatch." Tristan grabbed a large chunk of dark bread and chewed angrily.

"Have some wine," offered the bard, and the king gratefully took the wineskin.

"I'll take the first watch." Daryth said as he finally entered the camp.

"And the morning watch for me! We'll let the halfling sleep in," piped the bard, chuckling.

"I can stand watch, too! How come I never get a turn?" Newt was indignant. "I can see in the dark better than any of you!"

"Take the morning watch with me. I could use the extra pair of eyes!" Tavish tried to humor the dragon, and Newt, satisfied, curled up to sleep.

"I can't b-believe this is Myrloch Vale—Vale!" Yazilliclick looked around nervously. Dark clouds pressed ominously overhead, and the lifeless forest stretched to the horizon on all sides. "It—it's all so dead—so dead! Wait till Genna sees this—till Genna sees!"

Tristan took another swig from the wineskin, then turned to Daryth. "Let's check the horses before it's too dark to see."

The Calishite shrugged and followed him to the little clearing in which they had staked their mounts. The king tugged on the line that held Avalon, while Daryth checked the other horses. Tristan stared at his companion all the while, but Daryth would not meet his gaze.

"Look at me, Daryth! Why won't you look at me?"

Daryth turned to stare at the king, but the look was more painful than his avoidance. Tristan saw great depths of accusation in the Calishite's black eyes. Then, wordlessly,

Daryth went back to his task.

"Why this silent invective?"

"You drove Robyn away," whispered Daryth, in a voice that thundered in Tristan's mind. "She could be dead!"

"And she could be alive! We'll find her, I swear it—and it'll be easier if we work together! When we do find her, she will accept my apology and forgive me. She knows I made a mistake!" The king spat his answers, one after the other, before taking another pull of the wine. The liquid cooled the heat of his throat and seemed to calm his pounding heart. "By the gods, she will forgive me!"

"You ask too much of her," replied the Calishite in a voice of silken quiet.

"Too much? It's asking too much to forgive a simple mistake?"

"You have the love of the finest woman I have ever met. What cause do you have for throwing it away?"

"Stop it! I command you, as your king! You took the oath to serve me, as binding as upon any lord of the Ffolk!"

"And serve you I shall . . . sire. But you cannot command the feelings inside a man. Until now, I would not have thought you fool enough to try."

Tristan's hand went instinctively to his sword, but the bitter edge of truth in Daryth's words held him back. Instead of drawing his weapon, he stared in anger and pain at his friend.

"I chose to follow you, remember?" Daryth continued, his words spilling forth in heat. "You spared my life, true, when I would have stolen your purse. Since then, we have fought great enemies side by side, and I have watched your power grow. I have always felt that you were a man with a great destiny before him, and I was pleased to help you reach that destiny. But now to see you throw that away for a trivial encounter with a maid—"

"I did not throw anything away! I will make it up to Robyn! How does that mean I have renounced my destiny?"

"You have proven yourself unworthy of her love!"

Tristan stepped back as if he had been struck, but then he stopped and stared at his companion. He studied Daryth carefully and came to a startling realization.

"You love her, too, don't you?" Daryth flushed and turned away while the king took another drink. "I don't know whether to cry out in rage or in laughter!"

"Laughter? She could be dead right now, or in the gravest peril, and all because you drove her away! And now you talk of laughter!"

"Get out of here!" shouted the king. "Leave me alone! I don't want your help or your presence! If this is the loyalty you offer—" He stopped, jealous heat choking off any further words.

Daryth spun on his heel and stalked into the night, away from the camp. After two steps, he disappeared from sight, and Tristan realized that the twilight had passed.

"Wait!" The king cried out once, softly, though he knew Daryth would not stop. In truth, Tristan realized that he was relieved the confrontation was over. Daryth had awakened too much guilt within him, and each of the Calishite's words had seemed to drive another wicked dagger home.

The darkness grew thick, a blanket of night that fell in an almost physical cloak around them. The clouds above, and the gaunt trees around them had all vanished into the utter darkness. Tristan stumbled back to his companions, stifling an angry curse as he tripped over a root. He sat against a tree trunk, some distance away from Pawldo, Tavish, and the two faeries.

The king noticed that his hands shook. Tension boiled within him, and he wanted to lash out against something. But he forced himself to remain still, and eventually heard the deep breathing of his companions. Canthus came to him and, with a soft whine, curled up at his feet.

He lifted the half-empty wineskin, but suddenly the wine tasted bitter, nearly gagging him. Spitting it out, he leaned back in disgust. So Daryth loved Robyn. . . . How could his friend have kept a secret like that? How painful had it been for him to see Tristan and Robyn together?

As he reflected, he began to remember a look he had seen on the Calishite's face occasionally at unguarded moments. He thought of the attentive way Daryth listened to Robyn speak, the way he laughed when she laughed. I could have noticed it any time I wanted! I just never paid attention.

And then Canthus growled, very softly, and every fiber of Tristan's being was jolted back to the present. He stood quickly, soundlessly, and listened, trying to project his senses into the surrounding night.

Something was out there!

Tristan heard a soft scuffling sound, and he felt Canthus grow tense beside him. The noise came again, from the direction of the trail behind them. For a moment, he wondered if it was Daryth returning, but he remembered that the Calishite had gone to the north, in the opposite direction. Even Daryth could not have circled the camp that quickly and soundlessly.

Tristan let the Sword of Cymrych Hugh rest in its scabbard, safe at his side. The brilliant blade would illuminate their camp if he drew it, but that would only serve to help whatever was out there to spot them.

He felt Canthus drop into a fighting crouch and slink forward. Tristan stepped carefully beside the great moorhound, trying to move silently and cursing the rasping of each footstep against the dry ground. The feeling that something approached them grew stronger.

Once again he froze at full attention, desperately seeking any clue from the still, dark night. He thought of waking his companions, but for what? He still couldn't be certain there was anything out there. Only his keyed nerves, and the suspicious Canthus, led him to suspect a threat.

But then he heard a clear sound, a footfall, and he knew that something approached their camp. The sword, almost of its own will, leaped into his palm, and the clearing stood stark, washed in the magical light of the enchanted blade. With a low bark, Canthus sprang forward.

Pawldo sat up in his bedroll as Newt darted into the air, buzzing anxiously toward the prince. Even Yazilliclick popped his head out of the saddlebag he had chosen for a bed. "Wh-what is it—is it?"

Tristan saw the shape emerge from the darkness. He watched Canthus stop in shock, then bound ahead with a yelp of greeting. The great moorhound nearly knocked Robyn off her feet as the druid embraced the dog.

"Robyn!" The king coughed out the word, his voice choking. She was here, and she was safe! The clearing seemed suddenly a warm and cheery place, and in his relief and joy, he stumbled forward to greet her, forgetting the thing that had driven her away.

But there was no forgetting in the druid's eyes as she looked coolly at him, and then at his companions. She stepped past him into the camp, and the night again grew forbidding and chilled.

\* \* \* \* \*

More silent than the faint breeze passing through dead limbs, Shantu slipped through the darkness. His passing seemed to bring even more intense blackness, an increase in the night's oppressive cloak that was not imaginary.

Ever southward the beast hunted. Not once had it noticed the spoor of a quarry worth its efforts. Most of the animal life had been driven from the vale, and the few pathetic creatures Shantu detected could not attract the beast's interest, though scarcely a creature that breathed escaped the stalker's keen senses.

But the spoor of a rabbit, a squirrel, or even a deer did not interest the beast. It hungered for grander game, for prey whose killing would serve the dark purposes of Bhaal.

At last Shantu found such a worthy quarry. The scent came faintly from the distance, in the blackest part of the night. The beast did not pause to confirm the spoor as a normal hunter would. Instead, Shantu sprang to the south, toward the source of the signal that had triggered the displacer beast's hunt.

Now Shantu became a black streak, a tireless shape slipping through the dead forest at startling speed, yet making no more sound than the flight of a night owl. And as the monster ran, its mouth gaped more broadly than ever. The curved fangs seemed to grin in anticipation as Shantu raced toward the kill.

\* \* \* \* \*

*Mother, give me the patience and the strength to forgive him. Allow me to welcome his help, to use his strength to fight for your cause.*

*And give me the might that I may work your will and restore your body to you, that I may tend you as my destiny calls. Please, my mother the earth, answer me. Give me some sign that you live and recognize me.*

*But there was only the awful, lonely silence of the night.*

# ❧ 6 ❧

# SHANTU

Bhaal relished the concentrated evil of the Darkwell as he observed the actions of his minions. He sensed Ysalla marshaling the sahuagin and their mindless servants, the dead of the sea.

He knew that the cleric, Hobarth, now worked his way north through the wasteland of the vale on a mission for his master. In a few days, Hobarth would reach the sea, and there an important phase of Bhaal's plan would begin.

And Bhaal, too, was aware of his children. He heard the hissed reports of his perytons as they flew to and from the well. They swirled above in sweeping flocks, observing and protecting the periphery of his domain. Savage and dimwitted, the perytons would serve as admirable guards and warriors in the defense of their master's domain.

Thorax, the owlbear, lumbered aimlessly through the wilderness. Bhaal had no worries about this creature. Though stupid, it was equally ferocious. Soon it would find victims, and the legend of its horror would begin.

The god of murder sensed, most palpably, the bloodlust of the king of his children, Shantu. The displacer beast had found the spoor of a victim, and Bhaal waited eagerly for the battle and the kill that was sure to follow.

For Shantu was the greatest of hunters, made of blood and muscle and senses among the most deadly to be found on this world and augmented by a spirit and instinct for cruelty that came from planes far below the Forgotten Realms. Shantu was ultimate stealth, implacable cruelty. No creature of the Realms could match its keen instincts for surprise, its utter fearlessnesss, and its arcane, other-dimensional power.

And soon, Bhaal knew, Shantu would kill.

\* \* \* \* \*

Daryth moved softly into the night, anger tearing at his soul. But even the turmoil of his emotions could not still the native caution of his movements, and each step over the broken ground fell with care.

The forefront of his mind roiled with thoughts of Tristan. How he had admired his king! He would have served him for life! He would gladly have sacrificed his own life to save that of his king, or the king's lady.

But even as this knowledge tormented him, the back of his mind counseled caution and alertness. Though the Calishite walked rapidly over rough ground in inky darkness, most of his steps fell in utter silence. His ears remained alert to any sign of warning from the dark, and his scimitar rested loosely in its sheath at his side. In an instant, the blade could become an extension of his arm, offering sudden death to any threat.

His dark figure picked its way carefully along the faint trail, avoiding cracked boulders and rotted, festering trunks. He had no destination in mind, but simply a desire to distance himself from Tristan. Daryth didn't know how long he paced or how far he had come, but eventually he halted, trying to decide what to do next. Should he spend the night here? His pride balked at the idea of returning to camp. Tristan had sent him away. So be it. But should he stay here in the darkness? He immediately discarded that idea and turned his footsteps back toward their darkened camp. He would claim his horse, and leave.

Angrily he slipped back along the trail. The route led mostly upward, though he hadn't been particularly aware of walking downhill when he had left the camp.

But he was not lost. Even in the blackest night, with a complete lack of landmarks, the Calishite would have been capable of making a very accurate guess as to his location. Now, though the night was dark, he remembered many landmarks along the trail to confirm his direction.

He moved as quickly as he could while still maintaining silence. Inevitably his haste drew an occasional scuffing sound as his boot slipped along the side of a rock, or a dull crack as he stepped on a dried twig. These slight sounds concerned him little, however, since all he had seen thus far told him that Myrloch Vale was now completely lifeless.

Soon he detected a break in the consuming darkness before him, and in a few more steps, he recognized the silvery glow that could only emanate from the Sword of Cymrych Hugh. Tristan, you fool! His thoughts raged. It's not enough that we camp within a few paces of the trail. Now you have to announce our location with that confounded glow!

And then, as he came closer, he heard voices, though he saw Pawldo and Tavish curled in their bedrolls. Tristan was speaking, and someone else replied.

Robyn! She was safe! Somehow she had found their camp. Daryth stole closer, suddenly tentative. Where had she come from? How would she treat the king whose betrayal had sent her away in the first place.

The Calishite reached the bole of a thick tree and peered carefully around it. Tristan's sword leaned against a rock, casting its illumination on the little clearing. The king stood beside it, an expression of anguish on his face. Daryth could not see Robyn, but he could hear the ice in her voice.

"Don't speak of love to me now, or faith. I saw enough of that at Caer Corwell!"

"You condemn me for a single mistake! It was the woman. She bewitched me! Any man can—"

"Any man? You are the High King of the Ffolk, Tristan, the man who would have been my husband! Don't talk to me of what any man would do!"

"But I love you! She meant nothing to me! I don't even know who she was, or how she—"

"Don't know?" Robyn was incredulous. "You seemed very well acquainted to me!"

Tristan groaned and turned from Robyn. "By the goddess, I'd give anything to take back that night!" The king stalked away, but then stopped and spoke more softly. "Still, we must work together, don't you see? You had no chance out here by yourself!"

"Perhaps. But I had no desire to be out here with you. However, you're right. Our best chance of success is to cooperate." Robyn's voice contained no hint of forgiveness.

"What are you planning to do now that we've reached the vale?" Tristan asked.

"I will tell you when we reach the well. First we must negotiate the terrors of this defiled vale."

"But . . ." Tristan's attempted argument faded before it even began. "Very well," he sighed, defeat resounding in his tone.

Daryth whirled away, disgusted by Tristan's voice. He leaned against the tree, breathing heavily. How could you have fallen so? he wondered. He accused Tristan and then tried him in his mind, and in the verdict, found him wanting. Clenching his jaw in suppressed anger, Daryth stumbled blindly away from the camp, back down the trail to the north, his horse forgotten. He could not bear the thought of confronting Tristan or facing Robyn now. Perhaps, in the morning, he would feel differently. But in his heart, he suspected that something very fundamental to his life had changed.

Once again this night, Daryth of Calimshan became a thing of the darkness, slipping cautiously and quietly through the dead forest, pausing to listen for any sound. He searched the air with his nose, sniffing to see if he could discern any alarming scent among the overpowering odors of rot and decay.

Then he moved again, with no destination save distance. He desired only to leave the couple that he loved, to leave them and their pain far behind. Occasionally he moved more quickly than caution warranted, but he caught himself at such moments. Then he would stand motionless in an open area and for several minutes listen and smell the woods around him.

Once he climbed a rounded rock to stand solidly upon its smooth crown, watching and listening with the patience of a stalking predator. It was at this moment that he began to suspect he was not alone in the forest.

He stood for nearly five minutes like a frozen statue atop the boulder beside the trail. No scent came to his nostrils. No sound reached his ears. Yet the hair at the nape of his neck slowly prickled upward, and he found himself whirling around to stare into the impenetrable blackness.

Something *was* out there!

Daryth touched the haft of his scimitar, reassuring himself with its smooth feel. The keen blade carried its own enchantment, not as potent as the Sword of Cymrych Hugh but still sharp and deadly. He resisted the impulse to draw the weapon. He could have it in his hand the same moment he desired it, so quick were his reflexes, but it would serve him no purpose now as he tried to discern the nature of the threat.

Carefully, silently, the Calishite lowered himself to the ground and started again along the trail, moving farther into Myrloch Vale. Now he moved with utmost stealth, creeping slowly, not making the slightest whisper of sound. Yet he could not escape the disturbing suspicion—no, the knowledge, he corrected himself—that something was out there in the darkness.

After a hundred paces, Daryth froze again, but again no signal reached any of his senses to confirm the existence of a threat. Yet he needed no confirmation, so utterly convinced was he that some dire creature lurked in the darkness.

And that dire creature was almost certainly stalking him. As he moved farther, the prickling on the back of his neck remained. He hastened his steps, ignoring the faint sounds he made as he broke into a trot, and still the feeling stayed with him. He stopped suddenly and listened, but again he heard no sound from the blackness surrounding him.

Daryth made a full circle back on his trail, but he was able to detect no single direction the threat came from. Instead, it seemed to be everywhere at once, indefinable in its nature but awesome in its might. The Calishite told himself that he was imagining things, that in fact there was nothing here to menace him except his own frayed nerves.

Indeed, the sudden arrival at camp of Robyn, added to his confrontation with the High King, had certainly agitated him to the point of anxiety. Now he was in a strange, admittedly terrifying place, in darkest night! It only seemed natural that his nerves would play games.

Considerably relieved, he started again down the trail and soon came to a narrow gorge where high rock walls loomed close on either side of the trail. He could not see them in the blackness, but a sudden coolness in the still air around him told him of their presence as surely as if his eyes had confirmed it. In a few minutes, he had passed through the gorge and entered the dead forest again. He noted that the path was more level here, as though it had finally emerged from the foothills and entered the vale proper. The stench of rotten plant life assailed him even more intently, and he thought sadly of the pain Robyn would feel as she entered this bleak region.

Daryth's temper had calmed, and he began to think of returning to the camp. The others would be asleep, and in the morning he would be able to face them both and still retain his composure. Indeed, this was a plan that offered him some hope, and even promised the chance to get some rest.

And then a low growl emerged from the darkness. Instantly Daryth dropped into a catlike crouch as his blade sprang into his hand. He held the scimitar before him, horizontal to the ground so that the keen blade was ready to slice into an unseen attacker. The faint glow of the enchanted weapon barely penetrated the thick darkness.

Every sense of his body grew taut as he strained to see and hear. He tried to reconstruct the sound he had heard. It had been faint, but not because of distance. Fear thrummed through him—fear such as he had never known. It became a dread panic that rooted his feet to the ground and clouded the already hazy senses of his eyes and ears. The pounding of his heart echoed through his brain and seemed to reverberate into the forest itself.

Whatever was out there growled again, and Daryth could

sense it feeding upon his fear. The growl had been soft and deep, not like a bear—indeed not like anything he had ever heard! Swiveling, still catlike, on the balls of his feet, he tried to look around.

Suddenly he knew that the thing out there was some kind of cat. It had aspects of a great feline in its growl, and Daryth began to picture a massive cat-body crouched to spring. But it was more than this, he knew as well. This threat was not just a cat, but a cat-creature of great, all-encompassing evil that defied all laws of animal creation.

Slowly, forcefully, Daryth struggled to gain control of his frayed nerves. He recalled the basic lessons he had learned, many years ago, in the Academy of Stealth: *Fear is a state of mind. As such, it can be conquered by a stronger state of mind.*

The Calishite suspected that the teacher of this lesson had never felt fear such as he now felt. Nonetheless, he concentrated on the discipline of that lesson and others that had helped him to master his body's more primitive urges. Slowly he felt the pounding of his heart subside. His hands, mercifully, did not shake. And most important of all, his mind began to free itself from the paralysis of terror.

The thing would attack him, Daryth sensed, but it seemed to be in no hurry. Perhaps he could improve the odds by the time the assault came. The first order of business was to choose the ground for the fight.

Daryth felt the presence of open woods on all sides, naught but gaunt, barren trunks to protect his back. Slowly, carefully, he sheathed his weapon and reversed his direction, remembering the rocky walls that had loomed on either side of the trail. The narrow gorge lay close behind him.

For several minutes, he glided through the night as quickly as caution would allow, until he felt the cool reflection that told him he had entered the narrow gorge. He stopped for a second, and although he heard no sound of pursuit—he had not expected to—the presence of the unseen menace still lurked out there in the blackness.

Daryth backed against the wall, taking care to move in

complete silence. He forced his breathing into a slow, rhythmic pattern and tried to relax when he at last leaned weakly against the cold granite.

Something stroked across his shoulder and he gasped out loud, whirling instantly and drawing his weapon in the same motion. The blade cast a faint glow across the rocky wall, and he saw that it was a trailing tendril of dead moss that had startled him. Cursing silently, he again turned his back to the wall and stared at the small circle of light around him.

Though he knew that the light made him more visible to anything lurking in the darkness, he did not sheath the blade. It would take too long to regain his night vision, he assured himself. In reality, the dim circle was the only comfort he had in the terrifying night, and he could not bring himself to relinquish it.

Calmer now, he tried to take stock of his assets. Besides his blade, he had a coil of sturdy rope around his waist and a small pouch containing various picks, wires, and probes. He wore the smooth gloves he had discovered in Caer Allisynn, which contained wire picks of their own. He knew that lockpicks would be of little use to him now.

And he had his belt, a pouch of drinking water, a small box of tinder, a flint, and a short, sharp dagger. Most of these items rested in a compact pack in the small of his back, though the dagger was concealed in the back of his right boot.

Of them all, only the scimitar seemed to offer immediate help. He still held the weapon before him, the blade across the height of his body. The magical light of its enchantment gave him a sense, inflated perhaps, of power. The weapon had been crafted of hardened steel, ensorcelled by some forgotten weaponsmith so that its edge remained keen, its point sharp, and its strength unfailing.

He had always intended to name it, Daryth recalled now—something grand and heroic. The proper name had never really occurred to him, and he had decided to wait until it did. Now he saw the weapon gleam and curve before him, and he saw it as a larger version of an animal's claw or fang—a weapon he found himself facing, or suspecting that he faced, now.

"Cat's-Claw," he whispered. The blade seemed to glow with a warmer light, as if the cold steel had been warmed by the naming. Daryth sliced the air in a back-and-forth motion, and Cat's-Claw floated like a feather in his hand.

Then he saw the eyes.

Two great yellow orbs stared at him from the darkness, beyond the protective glow of Cat's-Claw. Each seemed as large as a melon, slitted with a long, evil pupil. They remained upon Daryth, unblinking, as the Calishite leaned back against the wall. He imagined the fetid breath of the creature on his face, and it seemed to suck his very spirit away.

For a second, Daryth felt his knees grow weak and he began to sink to the ground, but as quickly as it began, the impulse passed and he stood firm again. He would not kneel before this vision from hell!

The eyes continued to bore into him, and he felt the cold bile of terror rising in his throat. Again the growl came from the darkness, pushing him against the cliff with an almost physical force. Still holding Cat's-Claw before him, Daryth groped at the cracked face of granite with his left hand, discovering several wide ledges. He studied each of these with his fingers, not daring to turn away from the staring eyes until he had completed his exploration.

Then he spun sideways and leaped onto the stone wall. By memory, each of his feet and his free hand found purchase in a narrow irregularity in the rock face. The force of his spring lifted him several feet above the ground and allowed him to brandish the scimitar outward with his free hand.

Carefully he raised one leg, then the other, until he could lift himself another foot. Still he held the blade at the ready, while his left hand stretched upward to grab another firm hold. Then, pulling himself up, he repeated the process.

The yellow eyes still stared from the darkness, but the creature moved no closer. Once Daryth saw the eyes disappear, and he gasped in panic, but they instantly returned, and he realized that the thing had merely blinked. Again and again, he pulled himself higher on the wall. Finally he reached a ledge he guessed to be about fifteen feet from the ground, and here he paused to rest.

He stood with his back to the cliff, staring outward and down. The predator had disappeared again, whether because it had moved or because he had carried the light source farther away, Daryth couldn't tell. He derived little comfort from the fact that he couldn't see it anymore.

After his heart ceased its pounding, once again Daryth turned to climb. He began to wonder if he might not avoid the creature by scaling this granite face to the top, where the four-footed predator would be unable to pursue. He felt with his fingers to find a handhold above his head while he stood on the wide ledge. At last he found a grip, and he quickly pulled himself upward. Once again he held the scimitar away from the rock, ready to strike in the event of any surprise attack.

Now came another growl from the darkness, this time deep and heavy. It rumbled off the rock and echoed through the silence with a sinister resonance. Daryth could see nothing below, but he sensed the thing slinking toward the bottom of the cliff. With a detached sense of wonder, he thought it uncanny that the creature always seemed to move in perfect stealth, never giving even a whisper of sound at its passage.

Turning back to his task, Daryth pulled himself up the rock wall with practiced skill. He concentrated less on silence than on speed, for he sensed safety in the unseen heights above him. Pulling on tiny cracks in the rock, forcing his boots into impossibly narrow wedges, he made steady progress up the wall.

And then the awful approach came from behind him, and his heart failed for a moment. With a soft moan of terror, he clung to the rock as he felt the presence, immediately below him, of death. The creature sprang to the ledge the Calishite had just left, landing soundlessly on the narrow shelf of rock. Daryth couldn't hear or see the leap, but he knew that the thing once again crouched very near.

He forced himself free from the paralysis of his terror and

stared below, holding Cat's-Claw out from the rock so that the blade shed as much light as possible. Those great yellow eyes, slanted up at the corners in oriental fashion, gazed hungrily at him from just a few feet below the level of his boot.

The light from the scimitar spilled over the ledge where the creature perched, but though the Calishite could see the rock and patches of fungus and the huge eyes of the thing, he could see nothing else. A black shadow blocked his view of some of the rock, and from this he discerned a long, feline shape. He had to guess the creature's shape more from what he couldn't see than what he could.

Heavy lids drooped over those terrible eyes in a slow blink, and immediately Daryth hurtled himself up the face. Perhaps, with luck, the ledge below would prove too narrow for the monster to gain footing to spring.

His left hand forced into a wedge, while his right still held the blade. Daryth kicked and scraped at the rock with his boots, looking for a foothold. One boot caught on a rough spur, and he hoisted himself up with growing desperation. In a frenzy, he probed with his other foot, seeking any support that would hold his weight.

A hot wound slashed through the leather heel of his boot, into the sole of his right foot. He cried out in pain as he felt a tug. Instinctively Daryth slashed downward with Cat's-Claw into the black space below his foot. His other hand began to slip from its hold, but then the keen blade bit into something that twisted angrily beneath the impact and the tugging ceased.

Gasping, he pulled himself up another few feet and wedged himself into a narrow, chimneylike crack that stretched vertically above him. Turning his back to the cliff, he held the blade across his lap and stared, wide-eyed, into the blackness.

Even as he struck the thing, he realized, the creature had made no sound. Where was it now? Had it fallen back to the ground or to the ledge below? Or was it even now creeping up the cliff toward his tiny shelter? Was this where he was destined to die?

Cursing silently, Daryth attempted to cast off these morbid thoughts. He realized that his hands—his whole body, really—were shaking from the close call. Oddly, the first biting pain in his foot had given way to numbness. He twisted his leg awkwardly to try to get a look at the wound. Resting Cat's-Claw on his lap, he used both hands to pull his foot around, ignoring the pain that again flared with the movement.

His eyes widened in shock, and the world began to spin around him. With a moan, he leaned back into the crack, afraid he would faint. Mercifully, after several seconds of dizziness, his senses calmed somewhat. He felt terribly weak, but he forced himself again to look at the wound.

His foot was gone—or at least half of it. Numb with disbelief, he saw that some horribly sharp thing had ripped through the bottom of his boot and torn off the forepart of his foot. Nausea rose in his throat at the sight of the white bone, its red mass of flesh glistening, and the blood that dripped freely from the gaping wound.

He leaned forward and vomited over the side of the rock, heaving until his stomach was empty. Weakly he leaned again into the crack, not sparing a hand even to wipe his mouth. Then he forced himself again to look at the wound.

Though the heel and ankle remained intact, Daryth sensed that the wound had crippled him for life—however long that life might be. The Calishite decided he would gladly settle for one more sunrise at this point. He would make it to the dawn!

With that determination, his thoughts once again focused on his enemy. Where was the creature? The camp seemed very near now. . . . Wasn't that Robyn stroking his forehead? How gentle . . .

Startled, he snapped to wakefulness. The cold rock poked into his back, and his cramped muscles tormented him. He had lost consciousness. For how long? he wondered. Curiously, the knowledge terrified him more than had any of the events of the night. Death did not cause him great fear, as long as he could die fighting. But to grow weak, to lose consciousness so that death could creep up silently and claim him while he remained unknowing . . . this he could not allow!

He looked down again, and again he saw nothing but vast blackness. Whether he had dozed for seconds or an hour, he couldn't know. How long could it be before dawn? He felt with sickening certainty that night's cloak would last for many more hours.

Grunting in pain, he wrapped the wound crudely, using cloth torn from his tunic. The binding quickly soaked through with blood, but it would serve as minimal protection. Next he tried to lift himself from his awkward seat. Only with great exertion did he finally pull himself free from the crack. His muscles shrieked in protest. Once his wounded foot thudded into the rock, and the resulting explosion of agony threatened to drive him mad. Gasping and choking, he clung desperately to the rock until the pain subsided.

Slowly, inch after pain-wracked inch, Daryth reached upward with his left hand. Scraping his blistered fingertips across the rock, he found another of the tiny cracks that had helped him climb this far.

Then he discovered another problem. Allowing his injured foot to dangle loosely, he tried to hold the scimitar in his right hand while lifting his other foot higher on the rock. But the tiny handhold, gripped only with his fingertips, didn't afford him enough purchase for the move.

Grimacing, he slid Cat's-Claw back into the scimitar's sheath, reluctantly realizing that he now needed both hands for climbing. Gaining a hold with his right hand, he pulled himself up until he could wedge his left boot into another crack. Once again he repeated the process.

This time his right foot crashed into a jagged spur of rock, and he cried out from the pain. Instantly biting his tongue, he clung to the sheer rock face while the world closed in around him. Fiery gouts of pain erupted along his leg, and tears flowed freely from his eyes.

Daryth's fingers began to slip from their precarious holds, and he sensed the certainty of death below him. "If I let go, I die." He whispered the words aloud, over and over, and from somewhere he found the strength to hold on. But even as his grip strengthed, a great well of blackness opened up in his mind as his pain threatened to swell up and swallow him.

"Don't faint . . . don't . . . faint!" He chanted the words desperately to himself, struggling to retain consciousness, and finally the haze in his mind began to dissipate. Nevertheless, he held tightly to the rock for several minutes until he finally felt ready to proceed.

In this way, he worked himself up the cliff, moving with great deliberation, taking care not to strike his wound on anything. Occasionally he wouldn't be able to find purchase for his good foot, and at such times Daryth lifted himself solely by the strength of his arms and shoulders, holding his position with one hand until he reached through the darkness to find another hold.

As he climbed, he felt the horror that had cloaked him dissipate. The prickling of his scalp lessened, and finally he was left with a sense of being alone in the night. Not a friendly night, to be sure, but only the night.

Did he spend minutes, or hours, finishing his climb on the wall? The Calishite had no idea, though the time seemed to drag on for a half a lifetime. He could have climbed fifty feet or five hundred. The whole nightmarish ascent blurred together in a collage of pain, endurance, despair, and determination.

But at last he reached the top. He sensed immediately, as he crawled onto the flat surface above a sheer face of granite, that no more cliff lay before him. He felt the wind on his face, and it carried the strong odor of forest rot. Gasping in relief, he pulled himself away from the brink and found the stump of an old tree to lean against.

He sat facing outward, toward the cliff. It took him several minutes to convince himself that even a monster of supernatural ability would not be able to scramble up that face. Only something equipped with hands, or wings, could make such a climb.

He looked toward the sky and saw nothing but vast and inky blackness. How much longer could this night last? Wea-

rily he pulled Cat's-Claw from its sheath, using the faint illumination of the blade to look around.

Isolated trunks of the dead forest stood arrayed around
him, as if the wood had crept toward the precipice to look
over the edge. Large broken pieces of rock lay upon the
ground, and these were covered with a phosphoresence
that caught the light of his weapon and amplified it. The
patches of reflective fungus gave the tiny clearing a friendly, welcoming aura.

And then, between two of the tree trunks, at the limits of
his vision but unquestionably atop the precipice with him,
he saw the two yellow eyes, still unblinking, and coming
closer.

\* \* \* \* \*

"Where's Daryth?"

Tristan, standing lonely guard duty over the little camp,
spun in surprise as Robyn emerged from the darkness. He
had assumed she slept.

The Sword of Cymrych Hugh still leaned against the rock,
casting its light around their small camp. Tristan worried
about the possibility of the dim light giving their position
away, but somehow this night had seemed too dark, too
black to face without some form of illumination. He wondered if it was cowardice that caused him to leave the
sword out as a light.

"He . . . went off into the night." Tristan didn't want to con-
fess that he had sent his companion away. "We had an argument. He got angry."

Robyn didn't look surprised, just concerned. Tristan felt a
need to talk to her, but he didn't know what to say. How
could he make her understand?

"We fought about you," he blurted suddenly.

"Oh?"

"He can't forgive the way I hurt you. I understand that—
believe me, I can't forgive myself!" Tristan groped for words
to continue, to keep her looking at him, talking to him.
"Daryth . . ." But he couldn't bring himself to tell her of the
Calishite's love.

"You fought, and then you sent him away?" The words were cool and accusing.

"No!" The denial was instinctive, and he immediately regretted it. "Yes . . . I did."

"What's become of the man I loved?" Robyn seemed honestly puzzled. "Why do you do such things? You have friends, followers, people who love you and wish to help you! And one by one you drive us away!"

"I didn't wish that! I was bewitched by something, some force I don't understand. I only know that I feared for you when you were gone. If harm had come to you, I could not have lived with myself!"

"Rest assured, sire, that if harm comes to me it will not be your responsibility to bear! I have control of my own destiny; I have chosen this mission for myself. If I suffer because of that, so be it. The responsibility is mine."

"Very well," said the king quietly. "But will you let me help you?"

"Yes," replied the druid, equally softly. She turned and looked into the night surrounding their camp. "I wonder where Daryth is. . . ."

\* \* \* \* \*

*Taggar, shaman of Norland, threw down his ash-streaked deerskin and paced angrily around the smoky lodge. The signs, he was forced to admit to himself, were all bad.*

*First, the king should have returned by now. Grunnarch the Red, of course, always pressed his raids late into the season, but winter was about to begin and there were still no signs of the Red King's longships.*

*Second, the storms had roared into Norland from the Trackless Sea every other day for a fortnight. Every shaman knew that seven storms in fourteen days bespoke great ill.*

*And thirdly, most awful of all, was the news brought by the abject farmer who even now stood outside the leather-bound shaman's lodge. The wretch had lost nine sheep in one night!*

*Each of these omens, in its own right, would have forced Taggar to call a prophecy of ill will for the coming winter.*

*But all three together . . . it was too much to conceive!*

Indeed, Tempus was mightily displeased. And Taggar thought that he knew why. Tempus, brawny god of war and the deity worshiped by most of the northmen, relished the clash of battle, the shedding of blood, and the triumph of routing the enemy from the field. In normal circumstances, the northmen were the perfect tools for furthering the aims of Tempus. They had chosen him as their god, and he favored them with his blessing.

But during the last war, the northmen had crusaded under the auspices of a different god, though the warriors themselves had been ignorant of that fact. Tempus must have been angered by the slight, and the men of the north had done nothing since to gain his favor.

Taggar was now convinced, in the absence of his king and of any plunder of battle, that Tempus would call down his anger upon his people when they were most vulnerable, during the cruel months of winter.

For the god of war was not a patient deity.

# ❦ 7 ❦

# TIGER'S-TOOTH AND
# CAT'S-CLAW

For a long time, Daryth did nothing except meet the cold gaze of the predator with his own unblinking stare. Neither the monster nor the man moved a muscle, though the Calishite strained to keep his eyes open. He felt it would be disastrous to blink.

He wondered how the creature had climbed to the top of the cliff. It had appeared off to one side, not directly behind him, so he deduced that it had gone up or down the gorge for a distance until it found a place where the sides were not so steep. Then it must have climbed the slope and come along the crest to find him.

Suddenly the creature moved. Daryth saw the eyes disappear behind the bole of a tree, then appear again, still boring into him. The thing slipped sideways through the woods, marking a semicircle around him but not moving any closer.

"Why don't you attack, beast?" hissed Daryth, feeling a bit giddy from the strain. "Are you afraid? Yes, you know my cat's-tooth has a sharp bite!"

The creature did slink a little closer at his words, and Daryth found himself wishing it would leap at him or do anything but this patient stalk. The beast was, he sensed, playing games with him, the way a cat plays with a wounded mouse. The analogy struck him as decidedly unpleasant, if accurate.

Gradually the man became aware of a dull grayness diffusing through the air. It could not yet be called light. It seemed more a slight lifting of the total darkness that had blinded him for so long. A smoky haze drifted among the gaunt tree trunks, reminding him of the scene after a devastating fire.

As the light gradually increased, Daryth witnessed the advent of a heavily overcast, foggy day. Even the minimal illumination was far preferable to the inky darkness. And he decided something else, changing a decision he had made in the depths of the night: It was no longer enough to simply live until the dawn.

He saw the creature take form against the forest, a nightmare thing of purest black. He saw the great shoulders and massive, soundless paws. The gleaming teeth, clearly visible in a widely gaping maw, seemed to hunger for his flesh. And he saw the long, sickening tentacles that coiled and twisted from the thing's shoulders, clearly dispelling any suspicions he might have had that this was simply a great panther.

And now, with the coming of daylight, he formed a new goal for himself: He would slay this nightmare creature. He didn't know exactly how, for the monster's physical tools far superseded his own. But that left him a battle of wits, and the Calishite had always been proud of his wits. Indeed, he resolved to outsmart the creature and bring it to its well-deserved death!

But how? Obviously, he told himself, with a trap. The designing of a trap was a thing well taught at the Academy of Stealth, and a tactic at which Daryth excelled. Of course, he had never tried to trap anything like this before, but that was no deterrent. A basic rule of trap design states that no good trap is identical in purpose or execution to any other trap. The very concept of repetition, in a trap, becomes a weakness.

He looked again at the monster. The yellow eyes stared back into his own, but the beast had not moved. It crouched between a tree and a rock, poised as if to spring. The tentacles, which he could see more clearly as dawn progressed, writhed and twitched like disfigured snakes along the cat's back or over its head.

His first decision to make was, should it be a killing trap

or a capturing trap? Killing, obviously. Or if the trap could not be ultimately fatal, it must at least smash the creature hard enough to allow Daryth to administer the *coup de grace*.

Next he must take stock of the tools at hand. He had Cat's-Claw, of course, and the dagger, and rope . . . fire-starting tools, and trees, lots of trees. And there was the precipice, he reminded himself.

He thought about his selection for a moment and realized that the precipice seemed to offer the greatest chance of doing the cat harm, though, of course, if he could lure it under a large, leaning tree trunk, he could also hope to give it a sound thump.

The third consideration, the approach to the trap, did not offer ready inspiration. The woods here were open, and the little existing underbrush had withered and rotted away. The cat-creature could go between the trees wherever it pleased.

Neither did the cliff seem to offer an auspicious location for his trap. Though the rocky lip was sharp, nowhere did the ground slope down toward the precipice. Instead, it marched straight and level, right up to the very edge, which meant it would be difficult to get the monster to slide toward the drop.

He looked again at the creature, which still held that unblinking gaze. The monster watched the Calishite almost curiously now and seemed to be in no hurry to attack. Slowly Daryth climbed to his feet. He had to determine how mobile he could be.

A terrible aching throb exploded from his right foot when he tried to rest even a fraction of his weight on it. Wearily he leaned against the tree and slumped back to the ground. He would need a crutch for any movement at all.

He stretched to his right and reached the end of a stout stick that had fallen from a tree. Pulling it across his lap, he began hacking at it with his dagger, all the while watching the creature as it watched him. Soon he had cut off a short piece of branch, which he lashed across the end of the longer piece for an armrest.

Switching Cat's-Claw to his left hand, he climbed slowly to his feet, leaning his weight on the crutch. With an awkward hobble, he started moving away from the creature, determined to find a location that would provide him with his trap.

His foot continued to throb, but the pain had become a fact of life, and he no longer took special note of it. He hopped for several steps, then leaned against a tree as he suddenly grew dizzy.

And then the monster made its first audible footfall, directly behind the Calishite. Daryth whirled in shock, dropping his crutch and transferring Cat's-Claw into his right hand. The creature had bounded a hundred feet or more in mere seconds! Now it snarled savagely, only a few paces away.

Daryth firmly anchored his back against the tree, feeling the rotten bark peel away under his weight. He hefted the scimitar in both of his hands and stared the creature full in the face. He felt no fear of the thing, just a cold anger that, like his pain, seemed more a fact of life than a raging emotion.

The cat-beast came closer, creeping a pace at a time. The shiny black body crouched as if it prepared to spring after each slithering step. With repugnance, Daryth saw the suction cups lining the leathery tentacles. The moist lips of each flexed and pursed as if seeking contact with the flesh of their victim.

The Calishite took no notice of the sun, which at last broke through the morning haze as it crested the ridge across the valley. Though the woods remained shrouded in fog, the small area on top of the cliff stood outlined clearly in yellow sunshine.

A deep, heart-stopping growl rumbled from the creature's cavernous chest, but even this awful sound could no longer bring a tremor to Daryth's hand. He carefully studied the approach of the monster, marshaling his strength, planning his blow.

Staring at the center of the monster's forehead, he concentrated on the placement of his weapon. He doubted that he would have a second chance, but if his first blow could somehow puncture the bone there, driving into that wicked brain . . .

Smoothly he raised the scimitar, but not so high that the creature could slash in under his guard. The cat came on with no apparent fear, creeping almost to within his range without springing. Each breath the beast took now was a prolonged and rumbling growl.

Suddenly Daryth struck. The silver blade sliced downward faster than a mortal eye could follow, straight and true toward its target. All the muscle in the Calishite's shoulders and arms, and all of the skill in his heart and mind, poured into that one blow.

The blade fell true, striking exactly at the point of aim, but it passed straight through the point, and the air beneath it, to crash harmlessly into the ground. His already precarious balance gone, Daryth pitched forward and fell on top of the blade.

There was nothing there! He whirled into a sitting position and reached out to touch the image of the monster, squatting beside him and glaring balefully. His hand passed right through the sleek black side, and he knew the creature there was nothing but air!

Then the monster snarled again, and the sound brought a chill of horror to Daryth's spine. The snarl came from behind him! In an instant, Daryth understood the nature of the beast. This was a creature that appeared to be in one place but was actually somewhere else! Daryth's blow had been strong and true, at the image of the beast, while the beast itself crouched behind his unprotected back!

An electric surge of alarm propelled Daryth into a crablike scramble to the side. Even as he moved, he felt the thump of a great body landing beside him, smelled the pungent scent suggestive of a great panther, somehow corrupted.

The Calishite whirled on the ground, ignoring the pain from his wound. His hand came up, Cat's-Claw gleaming, and then the blade bit into something fleshy and muscular. The monster shrieked, an exaggerated feline cry of pain and rage. Its image, now beside Daryth, recoiled several feet at the same time as the man heard the beast retreat before him.

The jolt of energy gave him strength to stand, and once more Cat's-Claw darted forward. The blade whistled through the air, striking nothing, but on its lightning back-stroke, Daryth again found blood.

His frenzy continued unabated as he pressed the battle against the ungodly beast, shrewdly estimating its true location before each silver slash. The monster recoiled, stunned by the savage attacks, but it quickly recovered.

A lashing tentacle wrapped both Daryth's legs in a snake-like embrace, pulling him to the side as it twirled around him again and again. He raised Cat's-Claw, taking aim at the thing from feel since he could not see the tentacle that imprisoned him.

But then the other tentacle wrapped tightly around his neck and his mouth. It jerked his head backward, and he gasped loudly as the air exploded from his lungs. The moist, sucking cups fastened themselves to his face, and he couldn't draw a breath. Suffocating, he squirmed fruitlessly in the grasp of the beast.

Then his heart was gone, torn from his ribs in a single crushing bite. And with it went his life.

\* \* \* \* \*

"The North Cape! Home!"

The cry of the lookout brought Grunnarch the Red racing to the bow. He stood behind the proud figurehead and let his eyes bathe in the view. The fir forests of coastal Norland gave the strip of land a green and lively cast, especially when compared to the unrelieved gray across the Sea of Moonshae.

Always the autumn homecoming was a time of reverence and thanks for the Red King, but this year the feeling struck him as especially profound. There would be great wailing in the lodges tonight as the cost of this mission—a ship and a full crew—became known.

This weight did not bear as heavily on his shoulders as it

would have in years past, however, for this year he brought back a thing he had never found on a raid before. Always he returned with plunder, sometimes with slaves, and ever leaving new enemies behind.

But now, for the first time, Grunnarch the Red returned from a raid with an alliance. The news would be greeted with mixed emotions by his people, he knew, but he was enough of a leader to make them understand the properness and usefulness of the move.

He watched his steersman take the sleek vessel around the rocky prominence of North Cape and into the Bay of Norland. His own town lay on the shore, dead ahead, and he could already see the signal fires sending the message of their approach from the cape to the town. His people, and his woman, would quickly gather and be waiting for him on the docks.

Ingra would understand. The Ffolk didn't have to be the enemy! And with her help, he could make the rest of his people understand and accept.

The longship pulled alongside the stone quay just before dark. As he had suspected, a silent throng had gathered there. Eighty men and two ships had embarked from this same quay seven months earlier. Now only half of those men returned, and many voices from the crowd were raised in grief. The Red King ignored the wailing of the women as he stepped proudly down the plank.

Ingra stepped forward to greet him, and he swept her into his arms, relishing again the feel of her softness. She did not weep, for it did not befit the wife of a king to display her emotions in public, but he could sense her relief as he held her.

And then he set her down and turned to look at the faces of his countrymen and -women. They looked back with a mixture of hope and apprehension as he spread his arms to the sides and allowed his voice to boom across the waterfront.

"Summon the fathers of the tribes! I will meet the chieftains of Norland in my lodge five nights hence! I am calling a Council of Winternight! We return laden with treasure, and

those families that have lost their men shall be cared for.
The remainder shall be divided at the council!"

And with this news, he dispersed his people, planting
seeds of hope and curiosity. A Council of Winternight was a
rare meeting, for travel over Norland this late in the season
was a hazardous affair. The northmen understood that a
matter of great import would be discussed, and they sensed
correctly that their king was not about to tell them what it
was.

But word went out to the hill villages and to the towns
along the coast. The fathers of the tribes packed for the
journey, and by longship or by horse, they began to make
their way to Norland, to the lodge of their king.

\*   \*   \*   \*   \*

Four figures moved cautiously forward, leaving the scant
shelter of the dead forest. They crept across a field of
brown mud, toward a black circle of water. Each of them
was shrouded beneath a thick fur cloak, though their arms
swung easily outside the garments. Two of them carried
slender swords, while the others were not visibly armed.

One of the figures gestured to another, the smallest of the
band, and the latter paused. A strand of blond hair fell from
the fur hood as the slender form gestured angrily. Wide
brown eyes glared from the depths of the garment. At last,
with obvious reluctance, it turned back to the woods and
took shelter among the bleak trunks.

The trio approached the dark water, stepping between
two white statues. One of them studied the stone image, the
likeness of a young woman dressed in sturdy fighting garb.
Then it turned back to join the two as they came to the very
shore of the water.

*Come closer . . . a little closer.* Bhaal willed the strangers to
advance, to touch the water. The god longed to reach forth
and strike them down, but he lack the physical means to
push himself beyond the surface of the water, so he must
wait for the victims to come to him.

Bhaal sensed that these were ancient beings of enchantment and peace. Vibrant and very humanlike, they were

nonetheless not human. Their souls were more lyrical than the rough spirituality of humanity, and the dark god sensed that they would taste very sweet.

Finally one of the figures knelt and reached forward, extending slender fingers to the water's surface.

Immediately the blue light exploded upward, hissing and crackling as it outlined the suddenly rigid body. The light sizzled through the air to strike the second, then the third figure. The silver swords blackened, and the fur burned from the hoods and cloaks of the victims.

Then the fire faded, and the three figures stood scarred and misshapen, killed but not truly dead. The shells of their bodies shuffled slowly around the rim of the well, taking up stations as Bhaal's sentries. He did not hear the fourth figure scream, nor did he see it turn and flee from the well.

The god was satisfied for now, but the frustration of waiting for the victims' approach still irritated him. The physical location of the Darkwell began to seem a closed door rather than an opened window. And as Bhaal drained more of the Earthmother's might, turning that power to his own purposes, he longed to take more of a role in his machinations.

He would have to find some way to project himself beyond this watery veil.

\*　\*　\*　\*　\*

Tristan awakened with a jolt of alarm. He sprang from his bedroll, the Sword of Cymrych Hugh gleaming in his hand, and dropped into a fighting crouch as he looked around for the source of his fear. Before he came fully awake, he would have disemboweled any intruder.

But all he saw was the dim gray light of an overcast dawn and the sleepy figures of his companions, stirring in their own bedrolls. Tavish, on guard duty, leaned against a tree and regarded him with raised eyebrows.

"Jumpy this morning, sire? Indeed, you slept poorly. I've seen dancers that moved less and singers more quiet than you were in your sleep."

"Yes . . . jumpy," he agreed ruefully, looking at the ghastly woods and its supernatural cloak of fog. "But with good cause, it would seem. Did Daryth ever return?"

"No, sire," said the bard, growing suddenly somber. "I'm worried."

"So am I," muttered the king. A gnawing dread tugged at his subconscious. "I'll put Canthus on his trail. We'll find him. That forest is no place for a man to be alone."

"The sight of it's enough to send a shiver down my spine," agreed the bard. "Though the lonesomeness is relieved some by your rising. The last hour before dawn, now there was a time I kept a nervous eye over my shoulder!"

"It's not the hour," interjected Robyn, stepping into the clearing. She had slept several paces off. "It's the place."

"Myrloch Vale?" asked Tristan.

"Myrloch Vale now, as it has changed. The valley has been taken over by some evil of vast power—more awful than that lone cleric, certainly. Perhaps he is in direct contact with his god.

"The dark force must be centered in the grove of the Great Druid, for that is the matrix through which flows control of the entire vale."

"And that, also, is where the druids remain entrapped in stone?" asked the bard.

"Yes. I intend to go there and break the power of this god!"

Tristan immediately wondered how Robyn planned to do this, but he dared not ask her. Tavish, too, seemed curious for more details, but she settled for a shrug of her broad shoulders. "Well, I'm in till the end this time. I've a hunch I missed some great ballad material when I left you on Callidyrr!"

"I'm famished!" Pawldo's voice emerged from the depths of his bedroll. "I'll have three goose eggs, turned oh-so-very easy."

"Eggs? There must be bacon, too . . . and cakes. Let's eat!" Newt lifted his head from beneath the saddle that had served as his tent.

"Cold bread," said the king, suddenly irritated by his companions' good humor. "And we'll hit the trail in ten minutes." Tristan stretched his stiff muscles as he slid the chain mail over his shoulders. Even the heavy wool padding did not prevent the chill of the iron links from penetrating to his skin.

He saddled Avalon, then lifted Daryth's saddle to the back of the Calishite's frisky chestnut mare. There he met Robyn as she brought their friend's bedroll to be lashed onto the horse.

"Daryth went down the trail last night, farther into the vale," he explained. "I want to put Canthus on his trail. If he's strayed from our path, I'll try to find him. I'll catch up with you later."

"By all means," she agreed. "But we shall all go." She looked at him without anger. "Our first priority must be to find him."

By the time they had packed their meager camp, Tristan had located the Calishite's trail and shown it to Canthus. The moorhound immediately grasped his master's meaning and started along the path at an easy lope, his nose held inches off the ground.

Tristan, atop Avalon, rode behind the moorhound. Robyn, on Daryth's mare, came next. Newt also rode the mare, perched possessively on the saddlehorn before the druid, while Yazilliclick rode in front of the king on Avalon. Pawldo and Tavish brought up the rear.

The horses broke into a slow trot, unimpeded by any underbrush in the dead forest. The trees here had once been lofty pines, but now each was a bleak spire, prickly with the brittle array of its dead branches and surrounded by a small heap of rotting needles. Their path, a former game trail, meandered among these trunks, then gradually left the hill country and entered the bottomland of Myrloch Vale itself.

Tristan put a hand on Yazilliclick's tiny shoulder to steady the sprite as the horse took them over a rough part of the trail. He took care to avoid crushing his companion's frail butterfly wings, but nevertheless he noticed the faerie's body trembling under his touch.

"What is it, Yaz?" he asked, leaning forward and speaking softly.

"It—it's *this!*" squeaked the faerie, gesturing around them in despair. "Of all the places in the world—the world, this one here, the v-vale, was the closest to F-Faerie! And now it's all dead—all dead!"

"Faerie? I've heard it's a magical place, unlike any other realm. Is that so?"

"Oh, y-yes!" Yazilliclick brightened perceptibly. "It has b-beauty and magic—and a w-wonderful peacefulness!"

"Where is it?"

"I d-don't know for sure. You go through a g-gate and you're in Faerie; it's that easy—easy. There are so many gates, especially to here, to the v-vale."

"Did you come through one of them?" Tristan tried to divert the sprite's attention from his misery.

"Oh, yes! L-Long ago, I came here to the vale—the vale. It was so beautiful here, just like F-Faerie. Wh-why did they have to kill it all?"

"It is not gone forever. Whatever is causing this must have a weakness. We'll find it."

"It's all d-dead," wept the faerie, unconsoled.

Tristan looked at the wasteland through new eyes and wondered at the evil before him. This vale had never been more than a vast wilderness to him. It was well stocked with game, to be sure, but he knew that, to Robyn, it was very much more. It was the center of her faith and the heart of her goddess's power. He began to picture, very vaguely perhaps, what its desecration meant to her.

Canthus never hesitated for a moment as he trotted through the twists and turns of the path. Somehow Daryth had followed the trail through the thick of the night, and the king marveled at this evidence of his friend's nocturnal skills.

The trail suddenly dropped into a rocky gorge, and here Tristan called Canthus to slow as the horses made their way carefully down the steep and gravelly path. The moorhound sprinted ahead and then waited impatiently. He pranced in a circle in agitation, then dashed forward as soon as Avalon drew near.

Tristan lost sight of the hound as Canthus leaped around a bend in the gorge wall. As always, the moorhound hunted silently, so the king heard no barking to help locate his dog.

Spurring Avalon into an easy trot, the fastest gait he dared on this rough ground, he came around the same bend. The stallion reared back in surprise, his nostrils flaring, and Tristan's hand darted instinctively to his blade.

But the shock before them was in its tale, not in its terror. Canthus had stopped at the bottom of the sheer granite wall of the gorge. The hound stood up on his hind legs, his forelegs reaching up the wall higher than the height of a man's head.

Following the gaze of his dog, the king looked up to see a garish streak of blood across the face of the rock. The stuff had dried to a reddish brown color, but its nature was unmistakable. Tristan raised his eyes and saw bloodstains running down the entire side of the gorge.

Robyn came around the bend then, and he saw her face grow pale. She looked first to the right, and then to the left. "Back up the trail! We can get out of the gorge and come around on top!" No sooner had she spoken than she whirled the mare around and sent it racing up the trail.

Canthus dashed between Avalon's legs and raced up the gorge past Robyn. Daryth had been the dog's trainer and beloved teacher, and Tristan sensed dire urgency in the dog's manner. The gnawing dread he himself had experienced all morning broke into cold terror. Pawldo and Tavish, bringing up the rear, turned quickly and led the column out of the gorge. They raced along the rim, dreading what they would find.

\*　\*　\*　\*　\*

Hobarth walked among villages of leather-covered huts huddled in glens among the great fir forests of northern Gwynneth. This land contrasted sharply to Corwell, which lay upon the southern shore of this same island. While Corwell was pastoral and open, a place of farmers and fields, this was a place of hunters and warriors. While the Ffolk of Corwell looked to the land for their sustenance, the northmen looked to the sea. But they would die just the same, mused the cleric. And their dying would give as much pleasure to his god as would the passing of the more peaceful Ffolk to the south.

Finally the cleric reached the shore and saw the work of Bhaal in all its glory. The northern shore of Gwynneth was separated from Oman's Isle by the Strait of Oman. Upon Oman's Isle was the great fortress known as the Iron Keep, former palace of the northman king Thelgaar Ironhand. Oman, and especially Iron Keep and its sheltered bay, were the focal points of northmen power in the Moonshaes.

But this focus, already dimmed by the catastrophic Darkwalker War, was about to be diffused.

Already the waters of the strait lay heavy and dark in the channel. The cleric could see the rocky bulk of Oman's Isle, but his attention was drawn instead to the sea itself.

Great patches of brown scum and thick foam floated across the water. Hobarth, invisible to man, observed the distress in the northmen villages as sleek hulls began to show signs of early rot and a putrid odor rose from the waves and wafted ashore.

He witnessed the consternation of fishermen as they pulled bloated, rotting fish from the strait. He watched with delight as a swollen, drowned body washed into a quiet cove and frightened a group of women.

Soon the northern folk would ignore these trifling inconveniences, as Hobarth's god put his plan into action. When that happened, the existence of pollution or poor fishing or foul scent would mean naught to these humans. By then, they would be confronted by the ravaging menace of the sahuagin.

And worse.

*　*　*　*　*

Kamerynn galloped through a stretch of marshy fen, his broad hooves sucking effortlessly from the muck with each supple bound. Brown water splashed and foamed all around him, streaking his flanks with grime. His thick fetlocks clung to his legs, soaked in a mass of putrid ooze that spattered to his belly.

But he held his head high, and his mane floated, unblemished, behind him. His ivory horn remained proudly upright, a challenge to the desolation all around.

Soon he charged up a smooth slope and stopped on dry ground once again. Normally he would have paused to nibble a patch of clover or very young grass, but now there was no food to be found.

Every day the unicorn progressed farther in his exploration of the devastated vale. And each day, the scene around him grew more miserable, more hopeless. Kamerynn's ribs now showed clearly through his dirty hide, but his stance remained ever proud and unbowed.

And then he was off again, moving with the easy canter he could maintain all day. He loped through a chaotic jumble of hills, where all the dead trees had lost their roots in the sandy soil and lay like matchsticks, a nearly impenetrable tangle. The unicorn forged ahead, forcing his way among the trunks and nearly getting stuck before he emerged from the other side.

He came into a shallow draw and followed a pebbly stream bed, now dry, down the center. This was free of trees, so he was able to canter again.

Finally the unicorn stopped in his tracks, his nostrils flaring. His great head swiveled as he looked this way, then that, before turning his attention to the ground. A spoor lay there, crossing the path that Kamerynn followed. As a trail, the spoor was completely invisible, for the thing that had passed had neither disturbed even one tiny stone nor broken the most insignificant of twigs.

Nevertheless, its passing was written boldly on the land for the eyes of the unicorn. Kamerynn saw the mark of four huge paws, carrying a heavy body of supple grace. But the thing that made the unicorn's ears perk upward and widened his large eyes was the fact that the spoor on the ground was written not in trail sign, but in sheer, palpable evil.

\* \* \* \* \*

*The god of murder sucked hungrily at the warm life of the Moonshaes, like a vampire claiming the blood of its vic-*

tim. And like the vampire's prey, the goddess Earthmother's strength faded toward eternal nothingness.

The history of Bhaal is a tale of treachery and betrayal, murder and death, on a scope undreamed of by most creatures. Creatures of the lower planes, creatures of the mortal world—all had tasted death at the hands of Bhaal and his minions.

But his killing had never before claimed a god.

# ❧ 8 ❧

# OATH OF BLOOD
# AND DESPAIR

Canthus, leading the others along the trail, discovered the body first. The moorhound probed Daryth's corpse mournfully as Tristan dismounted and walked slowly to the remains of his friend. He heard Robyn behind him, but he did not turn.

He had no doubt that the Calishite was dead. A ghastly wound had torn away half his chest. The scene lay under a blanket of blood, more blood than Tristan could imagine. Numbly he watched as Robyn knelt beside the body and closed Daryth's eyes. She bowed her head, and he followed her example, too stunned to compose a prayer of his own. The others stood back silently, sharing in their grief.

*I did this to him!* a voice screeched in Tristan's mind. He watched Robyn's back, saw her shoulders shake as she wept. At that moment, he dreaded, more than anything he had ever feared, that she would turn to him and accuse him of the very thing he was blaming himself for. If she did that, he knew that his grief, and his guilt, would surely drive him mad.

In a moment, she rose and looked at him with tear-filled eyes. Her gaze held no accusation, only a deep, aching sorrow. "I shall find a place to bury him," she said and walked into the woods.

Tristan nodded dumbly and watched her go. As Robyn disappeared between the trees, his eyes were drawn unwillingly back to the corpse. Angrily he tore his cloak from his shoulders and knelt beside Daryth, covering him with the garment. And then he wept.

"By all the gods, my friend, I know I failed you!" He spoke softly, to himself only, and to Daryth. He hoped devoutly that the Calishite could know his sorrow. "I did not deserve the loyalty of one such as you, and yet you gave it to me."

Tristan raised his eyes to the gray sky, staring upward through the blur of his tears. "By those same gods, I vow to avenge your death. I know I cannot bring you back, but I can only pray that your memory will grant me forgiveness!"

He wept for the loss of his friend, and for his own terrible guilt in that loss. He seemed, everywhere, to be confronted by evidence of his own failure. He felt as if his life was degenerating into chaos. All of his failures seemed to culminate in the lifeless body of his friend, growing cold in this dead forest.

"No more!" he hissed, almost inaudibly. Pressing his fists to his eyes, he willed his tears to stop. He started at the touch of a hand upon his shoulder and looked up to see Tavish beside him.

"He was a brave man, and true," she said, her own eyes moist.

"And I was the one—" Tristan began angrily.

"Don't say it!" warned the bard, an iron edge in her voice. "You are the High King of the Ffolk, king of us all. Our destiny is wrapped within yours, and some of us will die before you reach that destiny!"

The king listened. He wanted to argue, but the tone of her voice compelled him to remain silent.

"It grieves you to witness the death of those who serve you, and that is good, for you must share our pain. But you cannot carry the blame for those deaths. You must have a goal, and that is the goal for all of our people. That goal is the important thing!"

Tristan wanted to shout at her, to tell her that this was different. This was a death for which he bore special responsibility, for it was brought on by his own selfishness and arrogance.

But he said nothing. Instead, he thought about her words. It seemed a long time that he stood there, while Tavish sat beside a tree and began to strum a slow anthem on her lute.

The music floated around him, sweet and heartbreaking at the same time. It was full of minor chords, yet it resounded with a triumphant pattern that urged a listener to look up, not down.

"I always knew he needed me to look after him," said Pawldo miserably. The halfling's face was red with grief. Tristan had always suspected that the diminutive adventurer cared for the Calishite more than he had admitted.

Newt and Yazilliclick curled up dejectedly on the ground. The faerie dragon's scales had darkened to a deep purple, a hue the others had never seen him take on. Yazilliclick peered into the woods nervously, his antennae twitching in agitation. Robyn returned, having found a suitable grave site, and Tristan carried the body behind her. The others offered to help, but he would have no assistance for this task.

They prepared Daryth for burial as best they could, covering his body and its horrible wound with his favorite red cloak. Robyn tenderly brushed his hair, and finally Daryth had the look, almost, of one who rested peacefully.

Tristan gently removed the Calishite's ensorcelled gloves and laid Daryth's hands across his chest. Turning to Pawldo, he held the soft leather objects toward the halfling. "These came from a place of long ago," he said haltingly. "I think he . . . he would have wanted you to have them."

The despondent Pawldo said nothing, but he took the gloves reverently and slid them onto his hands. Though they had been too large for the halfling while Tristan held them, they quickly shrunk to a skintight fit.

They laid Daryth to rest in a small clearing, high above the winding gorge. Robyn said a quiet prayer over his body, asking the goddess Earthmother to help his spirit in its search for fulfillment. Tavish strummed another anthem, heartbreakingly beautiful, and they stood for a moment of silence.

Tristan stared at the rough ground, the dirt he had piled with his bare hands. He had never felt more forlorn. But all the time he had labored, a grim resolve had begun to crystallize in his mind, a determination that this drifting of his life into chaos must end.

\* \* \* \* \*

Hobarth decided that the community before him must be the largest on this forsaken shore. He stood on a high, bald hilltop less than a mile inland from the town. From the summit, he could see the wooden and animal-skin buildings scattered around the shore of a small cove. Rickety wooden piers jutted into the water, and a number of small boats bobbed at rest.

It wasn't much of a town, but the other human settlements he had discovered were even smaller, tiny fishing villages of a score or two buildings. The north coast of Gwynneth seemed a poor place for an attack, if plunder was the object. The plans of Bhaal were not obvious to his humble cleric, however. Here Bhaal had ordered the attack, and so here it would be.

The waters of the strait were devoid of boats, as the filth of pollution now spread thick across the surface. In the far distance, he could vaguely make out the bulk of Oman's Isle, faintly outlined through the haze. The sun had passed into afternoon, but many hours of daylight remained.

The cleric spent several minutes exploring the hilltop, finding a jumble of rocks that marked its highest point. He walked in a tight circle around this summit, chanting a careful litany and dropping a powder made from finely crushed diamonds. As he cast, a glowing pattern of lines formed across the rocks, until he had inscribed a circle of magic around the crest. The lines seemed to have been carved into the rock itself, and they shimmered with a silvery cast, enclosing the cleric in a circle of enchantment.

His glyph of warding cast, Hobarth could now prepare his major spell in security. He knew anything trying to interrupt him would be stopped by the glyph, or surprised very rudely if it tried to penetrate the magical barrier.

Finally Hobarth sat upon the summit and closed his eyes. He called upon all the faith in his black heart and all of the knowledge in his twisted mind, then began the spell of summoning. For long minutes, he sat as motionless as a statue, his face wrinkled in concentration, his eyes tightly closed. Only the flaring of his wide nostrils gave visual proof that he still lived.

But if an observer could have looked beneath the veneer of optical senses, he could have seen the real proof of Hobarth's vitality. Concentrated in the invisible employment of magic, the cleric's spirit sent out a call deafening in strength to those who could hear it, and compelling in nature to those same listeners.

Beneath the brackish waters of the Strait of Oman swam one listener who heard and immediately moved to obey the summons. Ysalla, high priestess of the sahuagin and devoted cleric of Bhaal, had long awaited the call from her human counterpart.

Ysalla hovered in the upper reaches of the sea, where the sun's illumination penetrated dimly. The water here was shallow, and the smooth bottom was heavily layered with silt, but the priestess took no notice of this. She drifted slowly between the surface and the bottom, waiting.

All around her waited the legions of the sea. Standing abreast upon the bottom stood the rank of ogre corpses that had perished in battle, only to be reanimated by her priestesses and the power of Bhaal. The fat bodies resembled monstrous maggots, swollen from their immersion. The blue-black water swirled around them, but the stolid corpses remained immobile, awaiting the command of the priestess and the black power of her god.

Behind the ogres came the dead of the sea, the thousands of drowned sailors, fishermen, and soldiers who had also been animated from death to serve Bhaal and his minions. Only after these vast ranks of undead came the sahuagin themselves, the Claws of the Deep. They would swarm ashore in the wake of the dead army and complete the annihilation of the foe. Glory to Bhaal and his legions!

And to his legions across the strait, where King Sythissal and more of the sahuagin warriors massed in similar might. As Ysalla sent her charges onto the shores of Gwynneth, Sythissal would send his own fighters, lusting for blood, into the human settlements on Oman's Isle. When the coastal communities had been ravaged, the two armies would combine to enter Iron Bay and bring the great keep there to ruin.

Now the summons came, and Ysalla sensed its source. The great yellow fins along her spine bristled, and the priestesses of her order saw the signal. Their own spines bristled in silent acknowledgment, and the legions surged forward.

The dead marched stolidly across the silt, climbing the sloping shelves toward the beach. The sahuagin swam slowly behind them, the entire mass gliding through the water like great, sinister fish.

Then the broad ogre heads broke through the listless surf, and eyeless sockets fastened upon the shore. The bloated bodies lumbered from the shallows, their clubs, axes, and great hammers held high. The skin of the lifeless monsters had bleached to milky white during the long immersion, and the waterlogged bodies moved slowly, heavily forward.

They were indeed slow—but they could not be stopped.

\* \* \* \* \*

Koll's heart pounded as he left the tiny inn and walked the few steps to the pier. The *Starling* bobbed prettily at dockside, even amid the scum that had coated the water lately. Though small, the little sailboat was the perfect setting for his purpose.

And here came his purpose. Gwen walked to the boat with just enough eagerness to excite his hopes and just enough restraint to calm his nerves. For weeks, he had been trying to get her to go off alone together with him.

Now she smiled at him, her brown eyes sparkling with a secret promise that inflamed his passion. She was not overly pretty, was Gwen, but she had a lively manner that had caught Koll's attention when he had first purchased a shield and jerkin from her father, the leatherworker of Codscove.

Short and slightly plump, Gwen greeted him with a shy smile. Her red-brown hair was cut short, and Koll liked the way it framed her round, smiling face. Indeed, as he was unusually tall even for a man of the north, they made an oddly matched couple. His soft beard had finally covered his chin the past spring, and now he stroked it self-consciously as she made her way to the dock.

He helped her into the boat, enjoying the unsteady moment when she lost her balance and leaned on him.

"Sit here," he offered, lowering her to the bowseat. The line came easily free from the dock, and he pushed the *Starling* away, as if worried that someone would come along and stop him. The breeze was sluggish at best, but the little craft caught what little wind blew, and they pulled steadily away from shore.

For some time they didn't speak. Koll tried to ignore the lifeless brown of the sea, without complete success. Indeed, fish were dying in whole schools; catches were nonexistent or diseased. Even these placid northmen of Gwynneth were once again talking of raiding as a means of survival.

Koll tried to banish such thoughts, knowing that Gwen was of a family of native Ffolk, while his ancestors were the plundering northmen who had claimed these lands as their own a century before. Instead, he concentrated on his passenger's eyes as she demurely looked away. Such pretty eyes they were! Shy, but not afraid. Gwen had always fascinated him with this air of demure courage, so unlike the women of the northlands.

He finally pulled in the sail and drifted calmly. Codsbay was a distant mark on the shoreline, though Koll could still distinguish individual buildings. With the easy grace of the sailor, he moved to the bowseat and took Gwen's hand.

She giggled briefly, but she did not turn away as he bent to kiss her. She was warm and soft, her slight plumpness filling his arms as he embraced her. Suddenly he felt her grow rigid, and he saw her eyes open in shock, staring at something over his shoulder.

Gwen screamed as Koll spun around, his own eyes widening. The most horrible creature he had ever seen slithered over the transom, flicking a forked tongue toward him. Its pale eyes bulged, and rows of sharp wicked teeth gleamed in its widespread mouth. Its vaguely humanlike body was completely covered with green scales, and it used clawed hands, with webbed fingers, to pull itself into the bottom of the boat.

In the instant of his turning, the northman froze in panic. What could he do? He gaped in terror as the manlike form slithered forward. Suddenly his fear galvanized into action, and he reached for one of the long oars. He lifted the oar from its lock and brought it crashing down onto the creature's head as the monster tried to stand. It slumped to its knees, and he crashed the oar down upon it again, snapping the wooden shaft in two but dropping the creature senseless into the hull.

"What—what *is* it?" gasped the maid as Koll slumped weakly to the bench.

For a moment, he could not speak. Bile rose in his throat, and he feared he would lose his breakfast, but finally his tongue freed itself from his terror. "I—I've heard tales of the fish-men, dwellers of the deep. Sometimes they struck ships, but only far at sea." The northman spoke slowly as he regained his breath.

"Look . . . Codsbay!" cried Gwen, pointing to shore. They watched in horror as a wave of huge white bodies plodded menacingly from the surf and entered the town, striking down any humans who did not flee before them. And then another wave of invaders rose from the sea, and still more hastened in their wake.

Koll pulled the sail taut as they watched, and soon the wind pushed them slowly toward the strait.

"Where are you going?" cried the distraught young woman as she saw his course. "My family's there. We've got to go back!"

Koll nodded at the town. Flames had already begun to flicker upward from the buildings. "They've either fled, and are safe, or they did not flee. . . . In either case, we will not be able to help them."

She turned with a sob to watch the shore, seething in chaos behind them.

"We'll go to Oman's Isle," he promised. "There we can get help and sail home as soon as possible!"

Of course, he couldn't know that Sythissal and the

sahuagin already swarmed across the length and breadth of Oman's Isle, and that the survivors were already fleeing toward the cramped security of the Iron Keep.

\* \* \* \* \*

They rode steadily toward the Darkwell, each immersed in private thoughts, but they all shared the common purpose now. Nothing else mattered until they could confront the root of the evils that plagued the land and had slain their friend.

Tristan wondered what Robyn would do when they reached the well. Some secret with the scrolls, she had indicated. Why had she refused to give him more details? This, he realized, was just another evidence of the depth of the change between them. She no longer confided in him or sought his advice. He realized with sharp clarity just how much he missed her. For the thousandth time, he cursed himself, cursed the red-haired woman, cursed all the circumstances of that fateful night.

All he could do now was strive for atonement, and so he would. To start, he would see that the companions all reached the grove of the Great Druid, and the goal of their quest, alive.

For a while, they rode in silence, all of them sharing their grim purpose. Even Newt seemed to sense their resolve. He sat forlornly ahead of Robyn in the saddle, curled against her stomach, silent for once. Behind her, lashed to the saddle, rested Daryth's silver scimitar. Tristan had offered it to her as they buried their friend and, reluctantly, she had accepted the gift.

All the riders looked nervously this way and that, sharing a grim apprehension yet seeing no visible threat. Tristan took a measure of comfort from the fact that the sharp-eyed halfling rode at the rear of the party. Then a blackness gripped him, and he thought of how much more secure they would have felt with Daryth's keen senses protecting their flank.

He shook off the thought and looked again toward Canthus. The moorhound led the party as they advanced carefully into the heart of Myrloch Vale. Yazilliclick sat before the king on Avalon's broad back. The little sprite held his tiny shortbow ready, with one of his silvery, dartlike arrows nocked in the weapon. His antennae quivered, and the king wondered if they helped him to search the woods for enemies. He hoped that they did.

Though the season was autumn, the chill in the air and the low, leaden sky bespoke more of winter. No snow had fallen here yet, but the bleak wind blew off the highlands with an icy bite that penetrated their cloaks and clothes and flesh, cutting right to their bones. Shivering, Tristan pulled his woolen cape more tightly around himself, but even that offered little comfort.

They followed a faintly visible trail through the black trunks. Though fallen leaves, now rotting, covered parts of the path, Canthus seemed to have no doubts as to the trail's location. Their route took them on a gradual decline into the flat basin of the vale.

Soon they came to the shore of a bleak and stagnant fen. The vast marsh reeked with an air of death and disease, and Tristan nearly gagged as the trail moved along the fringe of the swamp. This must, very recently, have been a thriving wetland, teeming with ducks and otters and other creatures. Now it lay brown and still, a lifeless smear upon the land. A few barren tree trunks jutted from a vast swamp of brown, stagnant water. In other places, patches of thick scum covered the surface.

He felt relief as the trail again returned to the woods, climbing gradually away from the fen. The return to the forest was only a slight improvement, for still there was no sign of greenery or animal life, but at least the abhorrent stink of the swamp grew more faint in the air. Still, the whole vale, forest and fen alike, gave him a chilling sense, as if they were all cloaked in a blanket of death.

The king watched as Canthus stopped and sniffed nervously at the ground. He saw the hackles rise on the great dog's neck, and he quickly dismounted.

"W-Wait for the others! B-Be careful—careful!" squeaked Yazilliclick.

Tristan looked back, surprised to see how far the rest of the party had fallen behind. "Watch my back," he ordered. "I want to see what's bothering Canthus." He saw Robyn spur her mare into a fast trot as he turned back to his dog.

Canthus stood at a bare spot in the trail, turning his huge head this way and that. Abruptly he growled and began to back toward the king. The hound's body, stiff with tension, poised like a coiled spring as he bared his great teeth at a threat that remained, to Tristan, unseen.

Suddenly the ground began to convulse under Tristan's feet, and he crashed to his back, the wind knocked from his lungs. Gasping, he saw Canthus leap backward with a prodigious bound that took the dog clear over his master's body. Then came an awful ripping sound, as of a body being torn asunder, and he felt the ground quiver beneath him again.

Suddenly the firmament beneath him fell away! For a sickening split second, he felt himself hang in the air. In that same instant, a stinging wave of gas exploded from the yawning space below him, sending fiery fingers into his chest as he gasped for air. Great roots dangled from the broken ground, hanging into the hole, and Tristan felt poised, for a moment, at the brink of doom. And then he started to fall.

A great fissure had opened in the ground along the trail, and now the stunned king lay at its lip, sliding into bottomless darkness. Noxious fumes rushed upward from the chasm, again biting into his lungs, and then blackness claimed him.

The moorhound rebounded instantly from his leap and sprang forward to seize his master's arm in his jaws. As Tristan's body dropped into the pit, the dog tightened his grip and held the king back from certain death. Canthus's paws began to slip along the ground, and he growled savagely as he felt himself pulled toward the chasm. Suddenly he tumbled forward, unable to hold the king's weight, but even then he would not let go. The dog still clawed desperately for footing as both of them dropped over the edge.

\* \* \* \* \*

Randolph stepped wearily down the long staircase at the

heart of Caer Corwell. Once again, another day drew to a close as he left unfinished the great majority of the tasks he had set for himself that day.

True, his duties as captain of the guard occupied him for many hours each day. But more significant was the burden of governing the kingdom in the absence of King Kendrick. He would not have believed the petty bickering causing strife among the populace were he not forced to hear the complaints himself!

Pontswain, of course, was no help whatever. The lord enjoyed the bounty of Tristan's cellar and pantry and the hospitality of his keep, but he did little to aid Randolph with the daily chores of office. Instead, Pontswain was more likely to sit brooding in the Great Hall, alone or with one of his favorite kitchen maids. The lord would glower at the Crown of the Isles, gleaming where Tristan had left it upon the great mantle, and declare to all and sundry that the real honors belonged to him.

Randolph passed beneath the wooden arch into the Great Hall and saw Pontswain sitting in his usual position. The lord sprang to his feet as the captain entered.

"What's the meaning of spying on me like this?" demanded Pontswain.

"Don't be ridiculous, my lord. I'm simply going to the kitchen on my way to check the stables—and by what right do you challenge me?" Randolph had grown tired of Pontswain's constant suspicions and accusations.

"By the words of our liege, who left responsibility for his kingdom entrusted to both you and me!"

Angrily the captain stomped through the hall, his appetite gone. He disliked Lord Pontswain heartily, and the man's every word seemed designed to irritate him further. He hated to place personal prejudice above his professional caution, but a conclusion was inescapable.

Lord Pontswain would bear watching.

\* \* \* \* \*

Robyn absently stroked the back of the faerie dragon. Her mind dwelled on thoughts of Daryth, despite her attempts to remain alert to the possibility of danger around them. The devastation of the forest weighed heavily on her spirit, and she found it difficult to look at the bleak terrain. Thus, she strayed easily into reminiscence.

She thought of her first meeting with Daryth, when he had just stolen her prince's coin purse and Tristan had caught the thief after a long chase. She remembered the flashing humor in his black eyes, and the even match between the Calishite's skills and Tristan's, though even then, as the two men had formed their friendship, the prince had stood out clearly as the leader.

Tristan! How her anger flared whenever she thought of him. She did not blame him for Daryth's death, though it occurred to her that she could. But whenever the picture of Tristan's infidelity came again into her mind, the bitter ache of anger flared brightly within her. Coupled with the rage, and there was no other word for it, came a bleak sense of utter confusion. It seemed that all the things upon which the foundations of her life rested had begun to fall apart around her.

Desperately she sought an explanation for the absence of the goddess, for her deity's silence when the druid prayed. All the possible answers loomed as too frightful for contemplation. Had the goddess perished forever from the earth? Had Robyn unknowingly enraged her spiritual mother and thus cut herself off from her comfort and power?

And Tristan. Had the woman in Caer Corwell bewitched him? Or was his love so frail that he could be drawn from Robyn by a simple flirtation? She desperately hoped that the former explanation represented the truth, but even if it did, she wondered if she would ever be able to forgive him.

She whispered a soft prayer, but the words seemed to echo hollowly through the dead woods. Never had she felt so alone, so separated from her goddess. It was as if a great void had opened up, and neither her faith nor the mother's might was great enough to bridge it.

With a start, she came back to her surroundings, surprised as Newt jumped to his feet before her. The faerie dragon arched his back like an angry cat and stared around the mare's neck, straight at Tristan.

"Something woke me up!" he complained. "Hey, what's the matter with Canthus?"

Robyn saw the dog leap, felt the ground shake as the fissure exploded below the king, and instantly kicked her mare into a gallop. She saw Tristan fall to the ground. Yellow and red clouds of gas burst from the hole, seething through the woods. Her heart rose into her throat as she saw the king, apparently unconscious, slip into the crevasse.

Newt buzzed into the air, his gossamer wings invisible with the speed of their flapping. Like an arrow, he darted toward the fissure.

A fear like none she had known gripped her as she saw Tristan disappear from sight. The struggling Canthus slipped closer to the edge, and then his forefeet dropped away. She was too far away to reach them, and she could see that even Newt would not get there until they had plummeted to whatever fate awaited them.

*"Glorus, vih-tali essatha!"*

Robyn cried the words to a desperate spell, an enchantment that offered minimal hope of arresting their fall, but it was the only action she could think of that might help. She cast her spell of plant growth.

The casting of a druid spell summons the power of the Earthmother directly, using that might for the working of the magic, but the power for this spell came from Robyn's heart, and for a moment, she felt dizzy and weakened.

Even as her vision blurred and she swayed in the saddle, she saw the roots and brush at the fringe of the fissure begin to spurt upward. Canthus disappeared from her view as the growing tangle of vegetation sprouted around him. The thicket continuing to grow, writhing constantly, along the edge of the fissure. She could not see whether its tendrils extended down the inside of the pit.

In another moment, she had reached the gap. Quickly she leaped to the ground, though she staggered unsteadily and had to grip the reins of the mare for support. The awful terror she felt held her back, and she could not bring herself to look into the fissure.

Newt, appearing and disappearing rapidly in his agitation, buzzed around the fissure. "They're here! You saved 'em! Come on, you guys. Get out of there! Hey, Tristan, wake up!"

Weakly she stumbled to the lip of the gaping pit, gagging on the stench of the gas that rose from the wound in the earth. Though the tangle created a weblike mass of branches, she slipped among them with the druid's natural ease. Then she saw the king, clutched firmly in the grip of the young branches, held motionless against the dirt wall. Canthus was caught in the bushes as well, but the moorhound squirmed his way upward as Robyn reached down for the king.

Newt continued to buzz overhead until a whiff of gas swirled around him. The dragon turned instantly from green to orange, sneezing loudly. With a sudden bolt, he darted to the side of the pit and landed, coughing and gasping.

Tristan's face was blue. Though the gas had thinned out somewhat, Robyn suspected that he had breathed it heavily. Had it already killed him? She banished the thought, somewhere finding the energy to heave upward on his limp body. It wouldn't budge.

"I've got you, honey. Let's pull!" She heard Tavish's voice as she felt the bard grab her waist, but even pulling together, the two could not free the king. Horrified, Robyn watched Tristan's lips grow black.

"*Glorus, desitor ehahy!*" cried the druid, once again summoning a spell. She felt herself grow dizzy, but she forced herself to retain her grip on the king. All around her, she could feel the plant growth recoiling, twisting free and pulling away from her.

And from Tristan. The king fell free from the plants, with Robyn barely managing to keep a grip on his arms. Then Tavish heaved mightily and they pulled Tristan's limp form onto the lip of the fissure. Weakly she pressed her mouth to his, forcing air from her lungs into the king's. She pressed downward against his chest to force out the bad air, then blew inward again. Over and over she repeated the process, with Tavish taking over when the druid collapsed from exhaustion.

Desperately she watched the king's face, begging for a sign of life, but his color remained that awful blue.

"It—it's the p-poison!" stammered Yazilliclick, slumping mournfully beside the druid. "He gets the air—the air, but the poison takes his l-life."

Robyn sat up weakly. Of course . . . the poison of the gas! Why hadn't she realized that? She leaned over the limp form and pushed Tavish aside.

"*Banlie, venali!*" she gasped frantically, pressing her hands firmly to his lips. Once more she felt the magic flow from her body as she called upon a potent spell of druidic healing. It would work only to relieve the effects of venom. Devoutly she prayed that the poison was the real menace to Tristan's life.

And then the dizziness rose within her again, as once more the power of her spell was drawn directly from her soul. The void between herself and her goddess remained vast, so she could only draw upon her own, suddenly depleted, reserves of magic. Her vision blurred, but she saw Tristan's eyes flicker open and heard his lungs gasp great, sweet breaths of air before she lost consciousness and slumped motionless across him.

Tavish lifted the druid gently and laid her beside the king, checking to see that her heart still beat and her breathing remained regular. Pawldo had galloped to the fissure and dismounted. Now he knelt beside Tristan, taking the king's large hand in both of his own. Tristan coughed and gagged, drawing deep and raspy breaths. The halfling's eyes, however, never ceased darting about the woods as he watched for an attack from that quarter at any moment.

But the scene remained, for the moment, quiet. A great oval had been ripped in the earth beside them. The bottom lurked in the invisible depths, where seethed a riotous mixture of yellow, green, and orange gases. A powerful odor, sulphurous in nature, with a stinging bite of even more sinister and unnatural substances, rose from the pit and filled the air around them.

Tristan sat up, still groggy, and his eyes widened with

alarm at the sight of Robyn's motionless body.

"She'll be all right," said the bard softly. "She used her magic to save you. It seemed to take a lot out of her."

"I'm getting lightheaded," said Pawldo suddenly. "Let's get away from this hole."

"Good idea," said Tavish, lifting Robyn easily in her broad arms. Tristan climbed awkwardly to his feet, while Newt and Yazilliclick darted into the air, ready to look for a suitable resting place. Pawldo, aided by Canthus, gathered the mounts that had drifted away from the noxious site.

"The cloud drifted toward the fen in the lowlands," observed the bard. "Let's make our way upslope."

By the time they reached the crest of a low hill beside the trail, Robyn had regained enough strength to walk slowly, aided by Tavish. They collapsed on the first level patch of ground they could find, and Robyn looked at them all with a tentative, fearful gaze.

"What is it?" asked Tristan, reaching for the druid's hand. She let him take it, but she looked past him as she replied.

"They're *gone!*" she whispered, frightened. "The spells I cast . . . they come to me through prayer. And when I cast, the power of the enchantment is the power of the goddess herself.

"But the goddess gave me no power for the spells I cast today. It's as if each was torn from my memory, whole. There's nothing left!"

"But can't you pray to the goddess to get them back again?" asked Tristan.

"I can no longer hear her. I don't know if she speaks or even lives. It's as if we've entered another place or a different plane—one where my goddess has no presence."

"You must conserve your strength," said Tavish. "Use your magic only if it's absolutely necessary." They were all aware, but none mentioned it, of how necessary her magic had already proven that day.

"I'm ready to go now," the druid announced. "We must keep moving!"

"I'll take the lead this time," offered the bard.

"And me!" piped Newt.

"Yaz and I will bring up the rear," added Pawldo.

This left Tristan and Robyn riding in the center of the group. For a time, the king followed the druid, riding in silence, but when they reached a place where the woods opened into broad clearings, he pushed Avalon gently forward to her side.

"Tavish told me what you did," he started out awkwardly. "I owe you my life. . . ." He trailed off, unable to express his gratitude and his love.

She turned, and for a moment she smiled at him like the maiden he had fallen in love with. Only her eyes, dark and somber, betrayed her maturity and purposefulness. "The land of Corwell needs you," she said simply.

"And what of the druid Robyn?" asked Tristan, his heart pounding. "Does she need me?"

"I . . . need to serve my goddess, to the whole of my being." Robyn's voice carried firm resolve. "That is the most important thing in all the Realms to me." A door slammed shut before the king, and he was left shivering in the cold.

"Hey, you guys, get up here!" Newt darted from the trees to hover before them, his tiny mouth split in a toothy grin. "You've never seen anything like it before, I'll bet! C'mon . . . hurry!" The faerie dragon dashed away, dodging like a hummingbird among the tree trunks.

The pair called to Pawldo and urged their horses into a run. In moments, they broke from the woods to gaze upon the bleak shore of something the like of which, to be sure, neither of them had ever seen before. It was the size of a small lake, with a smooth surface of glistening black.

"Tavish says it's a tar pit, though how she knows that, I'm sure I can't tell you!" The dragon darted across the flat surface before them, pausing in midair to sniff at a bubble. He flew back to them and lighted upon the stuff.

"No!" cried Tavish, too late. The dragon's four feet touched the sticky surface, and though he tried to spring back into the air, he found himself stuck fast.

Tristan laughed, in spite of himself, and drew the Sword of Cymrych Hugh with a flourish. "To the rescue, wyrm!" he announced, leaning forward to slip the blade, flat side up, under Newt's belly. He lifted with a smooth motion, and the dragon popped free of the tar. Newt flew off in a huff to rest upon a tree limb and try to clean his sticky paws.

"There was never anything like this in Myrloch Vale before," observed Robyn solemnly. Tristan sensed that this was yet another example of the blasphemy that had fallen upon this sacred ground.

Suddenly he heard Canthus bark from the shore of the pit, and he saw the halfling, still mounted, galloping toward the dog. Just then, Yazilliclick popped into sight. "Over th-there! It's a firbolg—a firbolg!"

"A firbolg!" cried Tavish. "Now, that's more like it. At least there's a monster I can understand!"

Tristan and Robyn ran along the shore of the tar pit, with Tavish close behind. The king still held his sword and Robyn her staff. The bard brandished her lute, keeping the borrowed shortsword in its scabbard at her waist. In moments, they reached Pawldo's side. The halfling stood with an arrow nocked in his shortbow, but he didn't shoot. Canthus stood before him, growling at something lying on the very shore of the tar pit.

The creature was indeed of the race of misshapen, hunchbacked giants known as firbolgs. His black, beady eyes glittered at them over a great bulbous nose, and his face split into a gap-toothed snarl that revealed only a few yellowed, crooked teeth. He lunged suddenly at them but fell short, and Tristan saw why the creature's attack had been frustrated.

"Why, he's stuck in the tar!" said the bard in amazement. "I've always wanted to see one of these things up close. What an opportunity!"

"Be careful," warned the king. Suddenly he grabbed Tavish and pulled the bard backward as the firbolg lunged a second time, a bit farther than he had at first. "He's shrewd enough to fake us into coming closer."

They saw that the firbolg had somehow embedded both feet, to midcalf, in the edge of the tar pit. He had managed to fall backward onto solid ground, but his feet were firmly anchored and he could not break free. Instead, he snarled and snapped at them, then jabbered something in his crude, brutish tongue.

"I feel sorry for the poor thing," said Robyn. Tristan, to his great surprise, found himself in full agreement—perhaps only because the firbolg represented a familiar thing. Though an enemy, the firbolg was a natural element of the vale, the first such they had encountered in this bleak place.

He leaned forward to get a closer look at the firbolg's plight, and was rewarded with a swinging club of a fist that would have crushed his skull had he not skipped out of the way. "I'd be inclined to help him," he declared ruefully, "but I don't think he'll let us."

"Maybe I can help." In a swift motion, the bard lifted her lute from her shoulder and strummed a pleasant chord. She followed it with a trill of light notes, then several more rich and gentle chords. Tristan saw the firbolg look at her in amazement, and the belligerent look on his face faded to an almost trancelike glaze.

The king moved closer, and the creature started to turn toward him, but Tavish strummed vigorously and the firbolg turned back to the music. "We'll have to use one of the horses to get him out," whispered Tristan.

He whistled to Avalon. The firbolg turned suddenly at the note of dissonance, but the thing had been pacified again by the time the stallion trotted over. Tristan unwound coils of his long rope and approached the giant, while Robyn lashed the other end to his saddle.

Keep playing! Tristan thought, concentrating on the music as he reached around the waist of the monster and looped the rope as far up on his chest as he could. The firbolg remained entranced by the music, a look of utter placidness on his face, as the king backed away and fastened the other end of the rope to the stallion.

"We're taking an awful chance," whispered the concerned halfling, a nervous observer of the preparations. "What if he gets free and suddenly changes his taste in music!"

Smiling with more confidence than he felt, Tristan turned to the stallion. "Go!" he cried, slapping the steed on the rump. In an instant, Avalon sprang forward, the rope came taut around the firbolg, and the monster gave a thunderous bellow of surprise. Scarcely pausing, the stallion lunged farther, and the giant toppled to the ground. With an additional grunt, Avalon pulled him free of the clutching tar.

The monster leaped to his feet with an even louder bellow and turned toward Tavish, the nearest of the companions. The bard smiled broadly and stroked the lute, a softer, slower rhythm than she had played before.

The rage fell from the creature's face as the music again held him in thrall. The firbolg cocked his head to the side, as if to hear better. When Tavish stepped away from the tar pit, the firbolg followed mutely. "What do I do now?" asked the bard, slowly growing concerned.

And then the horror exploded from the woods.

\* \* \* \* \*

Kamerynn loped tirelessly along the spoor of evil that lay like a broad stripe across the land. He followed it for a day and a night, never resting.

A sense of urgency gripped him, as if he knew that here, among all the evil and corruption around him, was the focus for his vengeance. Here was an enemy he could fight.

The unicorn came upon a scene of battle, where the beast had attacked a man. Kamerynn paused in surprise, for the spoor of the man was unusual in the dead vale. He saw that the man had been driven to a cliff by the approach of the monster, and that he had suffered a bloody wound as he had climbed away from the danger.

Then the unicorn followed the spoor once more, to where the creature had raced along the base of the cliff to a gap where the slope was more gradual. Here it had bounded easily to the top, though the climb was still precipitous. It was only with great difficulty that Kamerynn struggled up the same slope.

And then he came upon the scene of blood and death. The man had died, and other humans had come. . . .

Kamerynn froze, his nostrils widely dilated, as he sniffed at the footsteps of these other humans. His heart quivered with hope, but the scent was so faint! He found the place where they had buried the man, and here his hopes were confirmed, where the one he hoped for had knelt beside the grave and left a strong scent for his nose.

The druid had returned! She was in the vale! Eagerly he explored the area, finding with a chill that the great beast had lurked in the woods close by while the humans had buried their dead companion.

The unicorn's chill turned to black terror as he saw that the creature had come out of hiding to follow the path of his beloved friend, stalking her and her companions as surely as the cat stalks the mouse.

\*　　\*　　\*　　\*　　\*

*A great sigh arose from the land as the Earthmother's spirit fled the drained corpse. Bhaal leered hungrily over her flesh, and all of Nature paused a moment to sense the historic passing.*

*Across the land, raging storms died. Windy skies became still, and the rolling swells of the seas flattened into utter calm. The lands themselves did not look so very different. Crops still thrived, animals bred, and the Ffolk and the northmen went about their business with scant notice of the change.*

*But to those of keen eye and sensitive soul, the change was apparent. The land had lost a certain luster, a quality of aliveness that was unique to these insignificant isles.*

*Thus ended the long reign of the goddess Earthmother.*

# ❧ 9 ❧

# THE TRAP

Hobarth watched the attack on Codscove with rapt fascination, once his own part of the mission had been accomplished. He had felt the priestess's response to Bhaal's command, and he knew that the legions were ready. Now the fat cleric had naught to do but enjoy the carnage.

Of carnage there was plenty. The ogre corpses lumbered through the town, smashing doors, attacking the few humans who tried to oppose them. Hobarth chortled at the sight of a brawny northman who lurched from an inn, wielding a massive axe. The warrior bellowed in berserker frenzy, striking the arm from one of the ogre corpses, but another undead stepped in and crushed the man's skull with a blow from a heavy club. The armless one stepped over the body and smashed in the door of the inn, lumbering inside. From his hilltop, the cleric observed other patrons leap from windows or bolt from the back door.

He saw the dead of the sea shuffling in the wake of the ogres, seizing fiery brands and flinging them atop the thatched buildings. These dead moved slowly, but occasionally a victim fell into their clutches—such as one woman who hurried back to retrieve her toddling child. The cleric saw the zombies fall upon the pair, seizing the babe and tearing it from the screaming mother's arms. More and more of the monsters joined the slaughter, forming a lurching, frenzied mob that completely buried the doomed humans.

The final wave of the attack struck with the most savagery, for though the undead killed unhesitatingly upon command, they did so without emotion. The sahuagin, coming on the heels of the animated corpses, slayed with relish. Hobarth saw the fish-men search through the rubble for survivors. Dragging these unfortunates from concealment, the monsters dispatched them with carefully placed stabs of their tridents or cruel, deliberate slashes with sahuagin claws. Always the death was lingering and painful.

Finally the pace of battle slackened, and the huge cleric rose from his rocky vantage to lumber down the hill. The undead had shambled inland, in pursuit of the fleeing populace, and the sahuagin were left in control of the town. Before he entered the ruined settlement, Hobarth mumbled a quick spell, one that enabled him to speak to these monsters and be understood. He had no doubt that his message would guarantee him free passage.

A trio of sahuagin spotted him as he stepped between the ruins of two buildings. Hissing, they turned their tridents toward him and advanced.

"Take me to your mistress, the high priestess Ysalla!" commanded the cleric, his voice a booming human command. But the words registered clearly in their dim brains. They paused in surprise, hissing among themselves, clearly taken aback by the appearance of this human who could speak their tongue.

"We will do as you say," announced one, finally stepping forward. His sibilant speech was clearly understandable by Hobarth.

"You are wise." The thing led Hobarth to a gory scene at the shore, where torn human bodies formed a massive pile. Hundreds of the sahuagin were gathered around, reveling in a feeding frenzy. Many of them turned and hissed or started toward the cleric, only to be turned away by a command from Hobarth's escort.

A huge sahuagin suddenly reared before him. It bristled with a headdress of sharp spines, its color bright yellow, in contrast to the green of most of its companions. Hobarth sensed immediately that this was Ysalla.

"Greetings in the name of Bhaal. You have won a mighty victory," he began.

"You are the human cleric." The creature looked at him with pale eyes, devoid of emotion. Suppressing a shudder, he sensed that the high priestess would as soon eat him as speak with him. Only their obeisance to a shared master restrained her. "What are the commands of our lord?"

"We are to await his order here. He will send us either against the Iron Keep or Caer Corwell. When he does, the might of Bhaal will be revealed to the humans in all their folly."

Ysalla's sibilant voice did nothing to quell Hobarth's unease. He felt as though he spoke with a snake. The sahuagin cleric loomed over him, her sleek body displaying lines of tough, wiry sinew. Her yellow scales glistened, streaked as they were with red human blood.

"Why are there two targets?"

"The Iron Keep is close by and sits astride your route from Kressilacc to Gwynneth. Corwell is more significant, as it rests upon Gwynneth itself."

"I know this Iron Keep. Many of the longships rest there or return there after they cross the sea. It is a good target. The humans there have displeased our god?"

"They are . . . in the way." Hobarth found the concept of the attack difficult to explain. He himself had doubts about assaulting a target not directly useful to the defense of Gwynneth, but his god had commanded the attack. He explained to Ysalla the words of Bhaal: "The humans will then have no place to flee to when we complete the destruction of this island, Gwynneth. Bhaal will claim as his domain the lands in the heart of the isle. You and your king are free to claim the coast."

Ysalla hissed, which Hobarth understood was an expression of eagerness or perhaps bloodlust. "And you will swim with us to Iron Keep?"

"I shall walk my own paths," said the cleric, looking at the water with a shudder. How he hated the sea! "But fear not, I shall be there when you arrive."

"What is fear?" asked the high priestess, puzzled. And then she turned back to her bloody feast, and the cleric slipped quietly away.

\* \* \* \* \*

Thorax the owlbear grew more and more angry with the passing of each day. Though it stalked the vale tirelessly, pressing ever outward, away from the Darkwell, it could find no trace of prey. Like Shantu, Thorax desired blood for the joy of the kill, not for any need for sustenance. But the owlbear lacked the displacer beast's cold cunning and shrewd sense of stealth. Thorax was a creature of stupid nature and brute strength.

And so the malformed brute lumbered along. It turned its feathered head around on its broad shoulders, looking behind itself like an owl. The owlbear walked sometimes on all four of its massive paws, and other times it walked upright, but it remained always hungry, always seeking prey.

Finally its search was rewarded.

\* \* \* \* \*

A cracking in the dried brush provided the first alarm, though Tristan didn't hear it. He stood still, warily watching the firbolg as the creature gazed blissfully at Tavish and her lute.

Canthus, however, whirled with a sharp bark, the first to notice the attacker bursting from the woods. Tristan turned at this sound of alarm, shouting a warning to his companions. Then he raced forward, sword at the ready, prepared to face . . .

"What in all the Realms is *that?*"

He heard Robyn's gasp behind him, and Pawldo shouted in surprise. But his attention remained riveted on the thing that bore down upon him with frightening speed. The horses shrieked and whinnied in terror, turning to bolt along the shore of the tar pit.

At first, he thought it to be a huge bear. Indeed, the broad shape, shaggy coat, and lumbering gait all came from an unmistakably ursine body. But that head! The thing uttered a screeching shriek, like some monstrous bird, and lunged for him with a widespread beak. Its eyes glittered amid a face covered with brown feathers, like the beady orbs of a bloodthirsty hawk.

Canthus lunged past him and bit the creature, whirling away before the owlish bear could land a return blow. The moorhound dove and ducked, barking and snarling, but the creature continued to advance on the companions with deadly purpose.

The king's astonishment slowed his hand a bit, or perhaps he underestimated the tremendous speed of the monster. He slashed his blade at the last minute and felt the steel bite into the thing's shoulder. His sword tingled in his hand, joyously cutting into the obscene flesh. But then a massive paw struck him full on the chest. The silver chain mail absorbed the force of the blow, but he still flew twenty feet through the air before landing in a stunned heap. The Sword of Cymrych Hugh fell, still gleaming, some distance away.

The monster spun with another screech and leaped toward the king. Suddenly it turned to the side as Tavish darted forward. She brandished her shortsword awkwardly, as if she wielded a giant fork. Tristan groaned and tried to sit up, fearing desperately for Tavish, but the monster again moved too quickly. It reared onto its hind feet, towering over the bard, and lunged toward her.

The firbolg, growling and grunting in his crude tongue, sprinted with amazing agility to the bard's side. The giant bashed one hamlike fist into the monster's snout, momentarily knocking it backward, and Tavish dodged out of the way. The bear returned the blow and the firbolg fell, kicking a huge foot into the monster's belly even as he crashed to the ground. The creature dropped to all fours and prepared to spring upon the prone giant.

Once again Canthus closed, sinking his fangs into the owlbear's haunch. The dog sprang away in the split second before the blow that would have crushed his body struck.

Shaking his head, his vision still blurred, Tristan sprang to his feet and scrambled to retrieve his sword. "Hey! Over here!" he cried, and the monster turned to regard him with those wickedly gleaming eyes. At the same time, the owlbear swiveled quickly, swiping at something in the air behind him. For a moment, Newt popped into sight, darting at the monster's rear end. But in the next instant, the faerie dragon again disappeared, and the monster turned back toward Tristan.

This time the king was ready. He dropped into a fighting crouch and approached the beast, relieved to see it turn its attention back to him. He noticed several tiny arrows bristling from its shoulders. Obviously Pawldo and Yazilliclick had found the range, though the tiny weapons could do little to slow the monster.

He feinted a thrust, and the owlbear reared back. Good . . . it had learned to fear the blade. Then it lunged forward. Tristan stabbed desperately, feeling the sword sink into the creature's massive chest, and then another powerful blow from a paw sent him reeling. The king did not fall, but he felt hot streaks of blood flowing down his left arm.

Robyn watched helplessly. Her staff offered little hope of harming the beast, and Daryth's scimitar remained lashed to her saddle on the fleeing mare. Unlike a sorcerer, the druid knew no spell that would smite the thing with a ball of fire or singeing magical arrow. Suddenly, however, she had an idea.

"Newt, come here! Quickly!" she called, and the faerie dragon instantly popped into sight before her.

"What is it? I was having a great time chewing on his tail! Can't I do it some more? Please?"

"This is more important. Remember those wonderful illusions you showed us when we fought the firbolgs in the fens? Can you show us some more?"

"Now?" Newt, disappointed, looked back at the fight. The king was giving ground steadily to the rushes of the beast. "I suppose . . . but the battle looks like a lot more fun to me!"

"Not just any illusion. This must be a very special one," she said conspiratorially.

"Oh, good! That's more like it!" The dragon hovered beside Robyn as she explained her plan, then giggled in delight as he darted away, ready to work his magic.

"Tristan! Over here!" Robyn called to the king, whose dance against death grew increasingly desperate. He backed away from the owlbear, dodging another lightning blow, and dashed toward Robyn.

"Now, Newt!" she cried, and to Tristan added, "Follow me!"

The druid sprinted along the shore of the tar pit. Tristan followed, trusting that she had some kind of plan, while Canthus remained behind, snapping and barking at the monster.

"Canthus, come!" he called, and the dog sprang obediently after him.

Tristan stopped, amazed at the sudden appearance of two brawny swordsmen. The fighters seemed to spring from the ground in front of the monster, both heavily armored and carrying great spears. Each wore a headdress of ridiculous yellow feathers. They fell back slowly, an illusion so real that the king could not distinguish them from truth.

Neither could the owlbear. One of the fighters appeared to stumble, while the other seemed to turn and run directly away from the monster. The beast crouched, screeched, and sprang, landing on the illusion that had stumbled.

The magic dissipated with the monster's touch, revealing only an expanse of black, sticky tar. All four of the owlbear's feet landed in the stuff as its leap carried it well beyond the pit's edge. Twisting and turning in a desperate effort to break free, it only succeeded in wrapping itself entirely in tar. Squawking in rage, it turned hate-filled eyes upon the companions until finally its screeches drowned in a gag of sticky, deadly goo.

\* \* \* \* \*

The waters of the Darkwell seethed in a black tumult of rage. Bhaal greeted the death of Thorax not with sorrow, but with an explosion of boiling hatred. The god thrashed within his oily medium, cursing his lack of physical form. Bhaal desired to smash objects, to strike solid blows, but his watery form denied him that power.

As he raged, his will crystallized into actions. The perytons, gliding in eerie silence, flew from throughout the vale to gather at the Darkwell. His clerics, Hobarth and Ysalla, paused briefly in their own plotting as the stuff of their faith shook from the deep disturbance. Each recoiled before the rage of his deity, and each likewise felt immense relief that the rage was directed elsewhere.

Instead, Bhaal's rage brought them a command, imperious and irresistible. *Level the Iron Keep!* Bhaal's intense anger needed slaying before it would cool, and at that fortress there would certainly be many humans gathered, seeking the imagined safety of its high walls. But those within were not reckoning on the mighty power of the god of murder and his minions. His clerics instantly set to work upon the plan.

And then Bhaal gave another command, this to his flock of perytons. The monsters had gathered at the well and circled, a great cloud of corruption, above the center of their master's power. And they heard his command.

Bhaal sent them soaring across the vale, silently gliding above the wasteland of death. He ordered them to find those who had slain Thorax and kill them.

Their wings scarcely flapped as the hawklike bodies sliced gracefully through the air. Their ghastly antlered heads stood proudly upright, their eyeless sockets scouring the land. Like the clerics, the perytons hastened to obey the command of Bhaal.

\* \* \* \* \*

The *Starling* sailed on into the long, dark night. Gwen cried herself to sleep on the bowseat as Koll stayed at the tiller, torn by an agony of doubt.

Had he done the right thing? His action in fleeing the massacre at Codsbay had been too instinctive to question at the time, but now uncertainty writhed within him. The vilest of afflictions that could strike a man of the north was cowardice, and he feared that it was cowardice that had spurred his flight.

Rationally he knew that his presence in the doomed village would have made no difference to the outcome of the fight. The monsters that had swarmed from the sea would have, in all likelihood, dragged the *Starling* under the waves before he even reached shore. But should that have been his only concern?

He looked at the maid before him, her tear-streaked face finally peaceful in sleep. Koll had no family in Codscove, but the village had been Gwen's lifelong home. She couldn't know if her parents even lived. Yet they could not have saved them even if they had made it to the village! The thought was only slight consolation.

He looked at the wicked dagger he had tucked into his belt, the prize from the fish-man that had climbed into their boat. The creature must have been some kind of scout for the army, Koll had decided, since they had seen no more of the monsters near them. He had dumped the body overboard but kept its weapon.

They had no food and very little water in the boat, but this did not concern him greatly. The crossing of the Strait of Oman was a voyage he had made many times and required but a single day—or night, as the case may be. By dawn, they would be in sight of Ramshorn, the village on Oman's Isle closest to Codscove. There they would recruit help and spread the alarm. Certainly the hot-tempered northmen would flock to the rescue of their kin on Gwynneth.

His certainty died as the dawn's light showed more than that he had been true to his course. The village of Ramshorn lay directly before him, visible from far out at sea. That visibility killed his hopes, for the village was marked by a tall, oily column of black smoke.

"What's that?" asked Gwen sleepily, staring before them. Koll hadn't realized that she had awakened.

"Ramshorn. It's been razed as well. The attack is far more broad than I feared."

"What can we do?" she asked anxiously, turning to him.

The pleading look in her eyes banished all thoughts of cowardice. Koll had a responsibility, he realized, to keep this woman alive and safe—as safe as they could be on the surface of an ocean teeming with enemies.

"We can sail to Iron Keep. There will be a gathering of warriors there, I'm certain, and there we'll be safe from this scourge."

\* \* \* \* \*

"Daryth always told me that a trap could often be more effective than a weapon," explained Robyn, "and since I didn't have a weapon that would be of any use against that abomination, I tried to think of a way we could trap it."

She stopped speaking suddenly as a shadow fell across her face. Closing her eyes, she turned away from the others. Tristan took her hand gently, understanding her pain. The mention of Daryth had brought his grief to the forefront as well.

"As a trap, it was well done—very well done!" exclaimed Tavish, hastily strumming another chord as the firbolg stirred restlessly. "I don't mind telling you that the beast had me a little worried!"

"Worried?" Newt scoffed. "It was a great fight! I haven't had so much fun since we burned down the firbolg lair!"

"B-But Tristan, Tavish—they could have been killed— killed!" Yazilliclick glared at the faerie dragon. "Our arrows were helpless against it!"

"But not my magic! That was the best illusion I ever thought of, I'm sure!"

"*Who* thought of it?" The bard grinned mischievously at the dragon.

"Well, maybe it was Robyn's idea, but I added the yellow feathers! That was my idea!"

They sat at rest finally, watching the descent of another inky night. The gray clouds had dropped even lower as the day progressed and would certainly block out any trace of moonlight or starlight. Robyn had discovered a small grotto, surrounded with high limestone walls, where they could take shelter from the wind. The companions had climbed across a stretch of low, barren hills to reach the hollow. The walls towered close to them on all sides except for the wide, sloping entrance. A narrow crack split the walls behind them, where a steep, winding gully dropped toward a bleak stretch of swampland.

Once again they dared light no fire to drive back the darkness. They all felt the presence of some sinister, nameless aura in the vale, and they did not want to call attention to themselves.

Tristan looked uneasily at the firbolg, wondering if it had been a mistake to bring him along. During the Darkwalker War, the firbolgs had been among their most implacable and hated foes. For all his life, he had known them as the natural enemies of humans, dwarves, and Llewyrr.

But now there seemed an unspoken bond that had developed between this monster and themselves. Perhaps it was because they all belonged here on the isles. They were a natural part of this world. As such, they made natural allies in the fight against a supernatural foe. The creature had shuffled along with them for the entire afternoon, occasionally calmed by a trill of the lute. After its courage in the fight against the owlbear, none of them wanted to send it away.

"You know, speaking of the firbolg lair, this isn't far from where we first met Newt," remarked the king. Tristan and Pawldo had made a brief reconnaissance of the area before dark. "The gulch out in back of our shelter drops directly into a swamp, and I think it's the Fens of the Fallon."

The firbolg looked up, blinking his oddly small eyes. "Fall-lon?" he grunted.

"And where you found the Sword of Cymrych Hugh? That's what it says in the Song of Keren." Tavish strummed a few chords of the ballad, as if to remind them.

Tristan nodded. "Yes, in the stronghold of the firbolgs."

"I wonder what's left of that place?" mused Pawldo. "It was quite a fortress. But then, we burned most of it down before we left!" The halfling's eyes suddenly glinted at a secret memory, and he turned his face away from the others to hide his sly smile.

"I'm sure there's quite a mass of ruins remaining," mused the king. "After all, most of the place was made out of stone."

"Fall-lon," grunted the firbolg again, pointing at himself.

"Firbolg." The bard pointed at the giant.

"Fall-lon. Firr-bowlgg." The creature was obviously pleased with himself.

"Human," offered the bard, pointing to herself, then Tristan and Robyn.

"Hu-mann! Firr-bowlgg!"

"He's smarter than I thought!" Tavish began to enjoy the lesson. She taught him more words, and he absorbed lute, sword, hand, head, and fist in rapid succession. "Tavish," she offered, pointing to herself.

"Hu-mann?"

"No . . . I mean, yes, but humans, that's all of us. Me, I'm *Tavish!*"

"Taff-ish?" The giant blinked, and then his face brightened. "Taff-ish," he said, pointing at her and then at himself. "Yak!"

"You're Yak? That's wonderful!" She proceeded to teach him the names of the others, and soon "Triss-tun," "Robb-inn," "Pawll-doo," and "Noot" had been formally introduced to their new companion. The firbolg stumbled on "Yaz-lick . . . Yoos-oo-luk, Yizz-ill," and finally settled on "Yuz," much to Newt's amusement and the sprite's discomfiture.

They chatted idly for a time, trying to avoid the pain lurking very near the surface of their awareness. All of them keenly felt the loss of Daryth. Tristan's own guilt tore ruthlessly at him though he tried, quite unsuccessfully, to bury it. The Calishite was dead, in large part because of Tristan's own stupidity in sending him out of their camp. It was an act performed in anger, resulting in tragedy.

All he could offer, and it was very little solace, was a prayer for Daryth's soul and a silent plea for his forgiveness. And he had his own determination to succeed and, by doing so, atone for his mistake.

Tavish once again pulled one of her wineskins from her pack, though the king declined the proffered drink. The others took small sips, but the sack remained mostly full.

The bard offered to take the first watch and continue the language lesson, so the others retired, each taking a shift in turn. The night, like the previous eve, was pitch black. At least the high walls of the grotto kept the worst of the wind from their camp, but even so, the temperature fell below freezing.

None of them slept well. Tristan and Robyn spent the night in lonely grief, each mourning the loss of their close friend. For the others, too, the combination of death among them and the universal death around them made for miserable rest.

Even so, dawn found them ready to move on again, if only to alleviate the stiffness and chills of a night spent sleeping on a bed of stones. They wasted little energy in conversation as they wrapped their meager bedrolls and started to load the horses. Tristan, looking nervously around the chill grotto, wondered what new horrors the day could offer.

Once again it was Canthus who saw the first sign of attack. With a sharp bark, the hound called their attention to the sky.

"Look out!" cried the king. "Look to the sky!" His sword came instantly to his hand, as if moved by a will of its own, and he raised it to meet the diving winged creatures above them.

A flock of birdlike forms swirled downward from the clouds, numbering two score or more. Many veered away from the narrow hollow, but several continued to dive right toward the party. They made no sound as they swooped in to the attack.

"What *are* those things?" wondered Pawldo aloud, swiftly nocking and drawing an arrow.

One of the creatures swished over Tristan's head, and he thrust at its belly but missed. He stared, amazed, at the staglike head of the creature and its black, cold eye sockets. Its pointed, misshapen antlers appeared deadly, as did the sharp claws on the monster's feet.

Pawldo loosed an arrow that darted through the wing of one of the creatures. The thing made no sound but settled awkwardly to earth, where Canthus set upon it with a growl and a flash of white fangs. The two creatures rolled across the ground in a blur of feathers, fur, antlers, claws, and teeth, until finally the moorhound stood with the monster's neck in its mouth. With one final shake, the dog cast the corpse aside.

Many of the winged creatures landed at the lip of the little grotto, perching like vultures waiting for the kill. Others swooped in aggressively to the attack. Yazilliclick and

Pawldo sent arrows after these intruders, but the missiles whizzed harmlessly past their intended victims. Finally, in order to conserve arrows, they held their fire.

Tristan ducked as one monstrous bird flew over his head. Then he slashed savagely upward and sliced off its wing, killing the beast with one quick thrust as it flopped to the ground. Once again the Sword of Cymrych Hugh sang joyously in his hand.

"Rock!" Yak grunted from somewhere nearby.

"Yes, rock," Tristan panted, too distracted by the fight to pay attention to the firbolg.

"Rock . . . kill!"

Suddenly the giant pitched a stone the size of a man's head at one of the monsters perched on the rim of the grotto. The missile struck the creature in the chest, and it disappeared in a cloud of feathers.

Newt buzzed into the air and sank his teeth into the tail-feathers of one of the creatures, but the monster twisted and raked at him with its claws. Several more of the bird-things swarmed around the little dragon, and Newt disappeared with a shriek. He did not become visible again until he was safely on the ground, watching the battle from a vantage point between Robyn's ankles.

A shrill whinny of terror jerked Tristan's attention to the horses. Horrified, he saw Pawldo's pony pitching and rearing while three of the bird-things clung to its back. Their talons tore through the pony's skin, and then another of the monsters landed and drove its ghastly antlers into the poor steed's chest. With a squeal, the little horse fell heavily to the ground, where the beasts attacked with their sharp teeth.

The king raced toward the scene, with an inarticulate cry of rage. Before he reached the dying pony, he saw one of the creatures tear through the animal's breast with its razorlike teeth. It pulled forth a pulsing, bloody chunk of flesh, the pony's heart.

Immediately the other horses whinnied in terror, rearing and kicking frantically. Avalon sprang high, and a sharp kick of his forelegs knocked one of the monsters from the air. The stallion leaped upon the thing and pounded it to a pulp with his hooves. At the same time, half a dozen of the beasts swarmed around the chestnut mare. In seconds, she joined the pony on the ground, screaming as cruel teeth, claws, and antlers tore into her body.

Tristan reached the steeds and drove the monsters away with sharp swipes of his sword, but the mare kicked weakly and could not rise. All four of her legs were ripped badly, and one of her eyes had been poked out. Crying in pain, she lay upon the rocks, breathing quickly and heavily. With a sob, Robyn stepped forward and cut the mortally wounded horse's throat with a swift strike of her scimitar.

They looked around and saw that the entire flock had finally settled to the ground around the rim of their little shelter. Perched in sinister silence, the creatures chose vantage points beyond the range of Yak's rocks or the arrows of the halfling and the sprite. Now they resembled vultures more than hawks, with the hunched and patient appearance of carrion eaters. Their skeletal heads and sharp antlers added a surreal touch to the scene.

"Why don't they make some noise?" groused Pawldo. "At least they could screech or something!"

"And why did they stop attacking? Not that I'm complaining, of course!" The bard looked up in puzzlement.

"I suspect because they can't maneuver well in here," suggested the king. "The hollow is too small for them to attack from all directions."

"Wh-what *are* they—are they?"

"Corruption!" Robyn's voice was bitter but certain. "They are a living, breathing desecration of life itself, like that bear with the head of an owl. The god that is killing the vale is not content with the mere destruction of life. He must twist and pervert it to his own ends." And then her voice rose to a scream.

"He must be destroyed!"

The flock shifted nervously, several monsters flapping their wings or stepping awkwardly to a new perch. But they quickly settled back to their vigil.

"So they can't maneuver in here. That makes me wonder how we're going to get out," Pawldo reflected.

"That gully you mentioned last night," Robyn said to Tristan. "Could we get down it? And is it narrow and deep enough to keep these deathbirds from following us?"

"It's possible, but the horses could never make it. Even Canthus might have a hard time."

"What about waiting right here until they go away?" asked Tavish.

"That won't work," Robyn answered quickly, then told them about her experience with the deathbird that had waited three days for her to emerge.

"Can we cross the open ground out the front and fight our way to the woods?" the king wondered aloud. The answer was obvious to all of them. Although the confines of the grotto provided them temporary shelter, they would be torn to bits if they gave the flock ample room to attack. The gully began to look like the only solution.

"Mayhaps we can try the descent and get the things to follow us. One of us can wait behind and spook the horses. The steeds might have a chance to get away, at least." Tavish offered the only real possibility.

"Let's try it," agreed the king, trying to ignore the ache in his heart. "I'll stay back with the horses."

"No! Let me do that. You lead the way down the gully!" Pawldo argued hastily, albeit reluctantly. They all knew that the last one down would be in grave danger.

"Thanks, old friend. But, no, I will do this myself. Now get ready to go!" Tristan felt some small measure of pride in his role. Perhaps this was a way for him to begin his atonement.

The white stallion stood silently, watching them, and Tristan had the eerie feeling that Avalon had understood. He went to his steadfast mount and wrapped his arms around the horse's solid neck, leaning sadly into his broad flank. "Run for me, boy. Run like you've never run before! You can make it!"

They unsaddled the mounts and loaded food, water, tinderboxes, and an assortment of supplies into their own packs. Tristan and Tavish each took a length of sturdy rope, after they tried and failed to convince Yak to coil the strands around himself. The giant snarled and backed away, and only the soothing strains of Tavish's lute kept the firbolg from bolting from the camp. After he saw the companions lifting their backpacks, he tried to mimic them, however, and eventually they succeeded in loading a heavy saddlebag onto the firbolg.

"The gully is back here. It's more of a narrow chute, actually." Tristan led them through a crack in the rock walls to the head of the gully. They saw a narrow, rock-filled slide dropping steeply for several hundred feet. Far below them, the black waters and gaunt trees of the Fens of the Fallon stretched into the distance. To the far north, they could barely see Myrloch, covered with a thin haze and lying flat and lifeless in the valley.

The one consolation of the route was the steep, high sides of the chute. Its twisting floor would make attack by the flying predators very difficult.

"I'll lead," Pawldo offered. "My king, stay back until all of us have gotten a good start. Then scatter the horses and come after us. Good luck, sire!"

"And to you."

Tristan stood as Pawldo started down the chute, followed by Tavish. The hefty bard immediately lost her footing and started to slide toward Pawldo, but Yak reached down with one brawny paw and grabbed her by the collar. Thus steadied, the bard worked her way carefully over the loose rubble with the surefooted firbolg beside her. Newt and Yazilliclick used their wings, flying slowly down the chute and staying near the ground. Finally Robyn came to the edge of the gully.

She looked back at the horses. "Do you think they have a chance?"

"Yes . . . a chance. No more than that."

She reached forward as if to embrace him but hesitated and then placed a hand on his shoulder. "Now, go, and good luck to you!" she whispered, then started down the chute.

Already he could hear Pawldo and Tavish shouting, trying to attract the deathbirds. Several of the creatures soared like vultures overhead, observing the party's progress, as Tristan stole back to the horses. He waited while several more of the creatures took to the air. Finally the whole flock, still silent, took off and circled toward the chute. If the horses had a chance to escape, this was it, now while the deathbirds couldn't see them!

"Go!" he hissed, slapping the gelding on the rump. The black horse bolted toward the wide entrance to the grotto. "You, too! Off with you!" He stared at Avalon but did not strike him. The stallion looked at him quizzically, then suddenly turned. With a kick of his hooves, the great white steed blazed after the gelding.

The king raced through the cut and started down the chute, slipping and sliding on the stones in his haste. He ignored the cuts on his hands, desperate to join his companions and lead the deathbirds away from the horses.

Then he looked up and jerked to a horrified stop. The creatures, as a flock, soared over his head back toward the hollow! In moments, they drifted out of sight behind the rocky shoulder of the hill, back toward the camp and the courageous steeds.

The screaming of the horses followed the companions all the way to the bottom.

\* \* \* \* \*

*The fabric of the myriad planes of existence is a material of many parts. When a single panel grows weak, the whole grows weak as well. When a portion tears away, a void is created and chaos reigns.*

*The stuff of the fabric is the stuff of the gods. And now a tear in the fabric began to open in the Forgotten Realms, where the Moonshae Islands served as a tiny portion of the whole.*

*The death of the goddess sent a soft ripple through the ether that connects the myriad planes. The gods of chaos greeted the news with delight, the gods of law with concern. The former would try to rip the fabric asunder, the latter to patch it. The gods of neutrality cared little about the opening of the void. They would seek to prevent it from growing but would not strive to close it.*

*But Bhaal, dark god of chaos and evil, the most base of*

aspects, had claimed a place in this void before the other gods could act. Now Bhaal tore the fabric wider.

Other deities sought to stem the disaster, led by Chauntea, benign goddess of health and nature, but the force of Bhaal's black evil drove them away. Other gods, led by Tempus, stormy god of war and favorite of the northmen of the Moonshaes, strove to contain the hurt, so that it would not spread to the rest of the Realms or the planes beyond. They built and strained, creating barriers of strong magic to cast in the murderous god's path. But even they were daunted by the force of Bhaal's evil and the power of his base in the Darkwell. By moving the center of his essence into the well, Bhaal could project more of his energy into this struggle than the gods who fought him from other planes.

If the fabric was to be saved, the gods knew the acts that saved it would not be godlike in origin. Bhaal had insulated himself from them, and they could not stop him.

It remained for someone of the isles themselves, a hero of mortal nature, to stem the tide.

# ❧ 10 ❧

# FALLEN FORTRESSES

It is given to some mortals, to those of great faith and loyalty, to know some of the secrets of the gods. To those of such faith, and even greater loyalty, a deity might reveal secrets of awesome portent and supernatural might. And to mortals of the greatest obeisance, and the greatest skill, the greatest of mortal knowledge is imparted.

Hobarth, devotee of Bhaal, was one such: a cleric who had given all his life to the service of his dark god and who had attained the greatest levels of knowledge and skill. Among the knowledge that had been revealed to him was an understanding of the nature of the planar fabric, and an ability to use that fabric to suit his own ends. Now Hobarth did just that.

He abhorred the sea and despised the thought of crossing it upon mortal conveyances such as boats, so he employed his knowledge to step through the very fabric of worlds, into other, darker realms. Here he walked among beasts of unfathomable evil. These monstrous beings paid him no mind, for they recognized him as one who was cut from the same timber.

A thing these nether planes lacked made them very desirable to the cleric: They lacked oceans and seas. Hobarth gladly picked his way among seething mountains of lava and great islands of oblivion, all the while rejoicing in the absence of water.

Finally he stepped again through the fabric of the planes, into the world we call the Forgotten Realms. He had arrived at his destination in good time, and dry, for he found himself standing in the valley upon Oman's Isle below the Iron Keep. He looked toward the vastness of Iron Bay and knew that Ysalla and her legions had not yet arrived. Yet the fortress stirred with activity, as refugees crowded within and ranks of soldiers marched out. Ships of every variety crowded the bay, all filled with northmen seeking the sanctuary of the keep.

Little did they know how much they needed that sanctuary, or how illusory it would prove. For of them all, only the cleric knew that the sahuagin swarmed in a deadly mass toward the fortress, and that the dead of the sea came rapidly in their wake.

\* \* \* \* \*

Black water soaked their leggings, and each step became a struggle against the clutching mud. Now Tristan led the way, hacking the tendrils of ropelike vines out of their path, trying to pick a route connecting the few dry patches of ground.

Inevitably their path through the Fens of the Fallon took them across more water than land. Making the situation even more uncomfortable was the fact that the air temperature had been dropping steadily, and the inescapable water was icy cold.

"They're still there," whispered Tavish, looking toward the sky from her position behind the king.

The news came as no surprise to Tristan. The shrill, panicked cries of the horses still echoed in his mind. He pictured, all too vividly, Avalon's white flanks streaked with the stallion's own red blood. He shuddered at the thought of monstrous teeth slashing through the stallion's breast to tear out that proud heart. But then the flock of bird-creatures had returned to their original quarry, and now they circled above the party as they marched through the dismal wetland.

Angrily Tristan hacked at another of the dead branches that entwined them. In the fens, as in the rest of the vale, the trees had died, shedding their leaves and leaving a putrid stench of rot. A heavy scum coated the brackish water, and each footstep brought noxious gases bubbling from the muck on the bottom.

At least the predatory creatures in the air did not dive. The interlocking branches overhead apparently prevented them from flying to the attack.

Tristan stopped to catch his breath, worn by the exertion of slogging through the mud and water. His boots, long since soaked through, numbed his feet more with each step. The spindly branches offered little protection from a biting north wind, and as the king paused, the air knifed through his garments and brought an involuntary shiver.

Canthus, beside him, stepped in front of his master and then stopped, his ears raised and his nose carefully sniffing the air. He, of all of them, seemed best able to cope with the cold and damp.

Tristan looked to the rear and saw Tavish leaning weakly against a tree. The bard unsuccessfully attempted a smile, and the king noticed her mud-spattered leggings and cape. Her lute, slung over her shoulder, had somehow managed to stay clean. She, too, shivered as a sudden gust of wind iced across them.

Pawldo slogged slowly up to Tavish, grasping branches and tree trunks to pull himself along. The water, knee-deep on the humans, sloshed to the halfling's waist. Pawldo looked at the king, and Tristan saw that his lips were blue and his teeth were chattering uncontrollably.

Yak lumbered slowly behind Pawldo, apparently having more difficulty ducking under the low-hanging branches than he did with the mud and water. Robyn came last in line.

"I'm worried about Pawldo," murmured Tristan, speaking to Tavish.

"I'm f-fine!" The halfling had overheard.

"You're starting to sound just like Yazilliclick!" The king spoke sternly before turning back to Tavish. "Do you think Yak could carry him for a while, at least until his legs are dry?"

"Yak!" Tavish turned to the firbolg. "Yak carry Pawldo?"

"Yak carry Pawll-do!" The giant grinned and plucked the

halfling from the water, cradling him like a babe in one of his brawny arms.

"Hey! Let me go!" Pawldo twisted fruitlessly, then finally noticed the comfort and security of his perch. He settled back against the firbolg's shoulder. "Well, if you insist . . . but only for a little while."

"Say, where are Yazilliclick and Newt?" the bard wondered aloud.

Tristan looked around but saw no sign of the faeries. "Probably exploring somewhere. I'm sure they'll catch up."

Robyn wearily came up to her companions. Her face was pale, and she drew each breath with a ragged gasp. "I . . . can't take much more . . . of this. We'll have to rest soon."

"We will," promised the king, "though we'll have to keep a sharp watch on those deathbirds overhead."

"I think we'll be safe in the woods," declared Pawldo.

"I hope you're right. We'll stop as soon as we reach dry ground again," the king declared, shivering again. "We can't stop here in the water. We'd get too cold."

Robyn nodded dumbly, and he waited for a minute or two while they all caught their breath. Grimly Tristan took his place at the front, following Canthus across an open stretch of shallow water. Here, at least, he didn't have to hack the ubiquitous vines out of the way. Since the path was narrow and winding, the deathbirds were not tempted to attack.

The wind became more savage, raging from the north, full into their faces. The companions trudged silently forward, Tristan trying to keep their heading as close to true north as possible. The thick clouds prevented him from plotting their course by the sun, but many of the larger trees had streaks of dried moss upon their permanently sunless north sides, and he used these as a guide.

Canthus stopped with a sudden growl, up to his belly in water. His hackles bristled, and he turned his proud head to the left.

Tristan saw a bubbling eruption of water and mud through the trees, and he felt the ground quiver beneath his feet. Instinctively he backed away from the disturbance, watching as clouds of greenish gas drifted upward from the ground. Waves rolled outward from the site, and then water began to pour into the newly formed hole with a thunderous roar.

"It's another one of those fissures, like the one that almost finished me!" He stood, awestruck, watching the land's torment from a safe distance. Then, as the gas began to spread away from the pit, he led his companions away as fast as they could march.

"The whole vale is being destroyed," said Tavish, horrified. "That tar pit, these fissures—everything points to destruction far beyond anything the isles have ever known!"

She was right, Tristan sensed. Robyn had known this for many days, but the reality of the menace had taken longer to crystallize in his own mind. Now there could be no doubt: The very survival of the vale, perhaps of all Gwynneth and the Moonshaes, was at stake!

Desperately he forced his way through the swamp, now hacking at the branches that seemed to reach out to drag him back, now forging along a brief, open stretch of marsh. Finally he noticed the water growing more shallow, and then he stumbled onto a low hillock of soggy ground. Barely the size of a small farmyard, the land jutted no more than a foot or so out of the water, but at least it was dry!

He collapsed on the bank, exhausted, as one by one the others joined him. After a moment's rest, he pulled his boots off, shocked at the pallid lifelessness of his legs. His toes had begun to turn blue, and all feeling had long since gone from his feet. Desperately he massaged the chilled flesh, trying to restore circulation before it was too late.

The others, too, worked desperately to prevent frostbite or worse as the chilling wind moaned through the trees. They all shivered uncontrollably, but it looked as though none of them would lose any toes—at least for the time being.

"Newt and Yazilliclick still haven't returned," said Robyn suddenly. Tristan realized with a start that he had forgotten about their diminutive companions.

"Those two will bring all kinds of trouble back with 'em, I'm sure," grumbled Pawldo. "They probably found some horrible monster, woke it up, and made it mad, and now they're on their way back with it!"

"I'm worried," admitted the king. "It isn't like them to go off on their own for this long. Just the same, they've both spent all their lives in the vale until recently, and if any of us can find our way around in here, it's Newt and Yaz!"

He felt a sudden, stinging touch at the back of his neck and slapped the spot instinctively. Then he felt another on his hand, and one on his face—not so much stinging as cold. A quick look around confirmed his suspicions, even as Robyn made the observation.

"It's snowing." White, icy crystals of snow, driven by the wind, had begun to sift down through the gaunt branches. As they watched, the snow thickened and swirled, becoming a white shower of cold. The wind increased in force, and the snow quickly grew thicker, so that they could see no more than ten or twelve paces into the woods.

Slumping against the ground, the king felt an overwhelming sense of hopelessness, as if Nature herself conspired with the evil that opposed them, striving to bring their quest to an ignominious end.

"That's all we need!" groaned the halfling.

"I don't know . . ." mused the bard. "It might make the woods a little prettier. I was getting tired of looking at black and brown all the time. I'd like a little white!"

Robyn laughed suddenly. "We can build snowmen!" she exclaimed, and Tristan sat up in surprise. He looked at her as if she had lost her mind.

"Or build a sled!" This came from Pawldo. "I'll bet Yak could pull us all in comfort!"

Tristan couldn't help but laugh himself. "If you're all going to be so damned cheerful about this, maybe now is the time to get moving again!"

"Right you are," agreed the bard, heaving herself to her feet.

"Boy, this place sure has changed! I can't find anyone around here to tease anymore!" The shrill voice, with its familiar whine, came as a welcome surprise to them all. In another second, Newt became visible, hovering before Tristan with an indignant look on his now orange face.

"Where have you been?" demanded the king.

"Why, in the vale, of course! I should think that would be quite obvious even to—"

"Don't do that again! It's important that we stick together." Tristan didn't try to conceal his anger.

"We were all worried about you." Robyn took a softer tone, casting a harsh look at the king.

"Worried? About me?" The faerie dragon looked pleased. "And well you should be! I have been *so* bored! I used to find deer and squirrels to scare with my illusions, and even bears and boars. But none of them are left! You don't suppose I frightened them away, do you?"

"No, I should think not. But you and Yazilliclick should stick closer to us from now on." Robyn tried to sound stern. "We can't afford to get separated."

"Where is Yazilliclick?" asked Tavish, suddenly concerned.

"Why, with you, of course! At least, that's what I thought. He didn't want to go exploring. He's really kind of a party pooper, sometimes. Hey, Yaz, where are you?"

But the only answer was the moaning of the wind, and all they could see was the cloak of blinding snow closing in more tightly around them. They shouted for the sprite several times, but there was no response.

"We can't risk calling too much attention to ourselves," cautioned the king. "I hope he catches up with us, but we'll have to press on without him."

"Do you think the deathbirds have gone to ground?" asked the bard, noticing that none of the soaring creatures were visible in the swirling snow.

"Could be, but we can't count on it. Still, the snow might give us a chance to cover our tracks. Let's go."

Robyn turned to the faerie dragon. "You didn't happen to see anything we could use for shelter, did you? Near here?"

Newt shook his head. "You mean like a house? Or a castle? Nah . . . there's nothing around here but the ruins of that big firbolg lair we burned down."

"Ruins?" Pawldo's eyes lighted. "Where? How far?"

"Oh, not far," Newt replied, shrugging. "In fact, they're just over the next patch of water. But why do—"

"Is there enough left of them that we could take shelter there?" asked Tristan.

"I should say not!" Newt sniffed at the very thought. "Why, it's damp and drafty, and there's soot all over the tunnels, and it's *still* huge. I can't imagine why you'd even *think* of such a thing!"

"It's better than these naked trees! Can you lead us there?" Tristan tried to direct the dragon's attention.

"What? Oh, sure. But, hey, aren't we going to have something to eat first? I'm starved! I suppose you guys sat around here all afternoon and took it easy, but I've been—"

"The ruins! Take us there *now!* Then you can eat!"

"Humph! No need to get angry about it. I guess too much rest can do that to a person. All right, all right. I'll take you there!"

The snowstorm continued to grow in fury as the party once again plodded into the fens. Tristan hoped that the dragon was right and that there was enough left of the firbolg stronghold to provide them some shelter. Though the deathbirds remained invisible somewhere in the storm, the king knew that they were doomed unless they gained protection from the snow and wind beside the warmth of a fire.

\* \* \* \* \*

Thick snow swirled in an eddy, gathering against a sheer rock wall. The drift grew quickly, covering the narrow shelf to a depth of several feet. Above, a craggy face of granite soared upward and disappeared into the night. Below yawned a vast chasm.

The only movement here was the endless shifting and blustering of the snow. But then came a more solid motion, and a figure appeared, climbing slowly along the steep shelf. It walked upright, like a human, yet it was heavily muffled in a cape of thick fur. It left manlike footprints with its high, thick boots, but these footprints quickly vanished under the persistent onslaught of fresh snow.

Darkness was almost complete, yet this figure walked

with precise steps along the very edge of the precipice. When it reached the high drift, two mitten-covered hands emerged from the cape. The figure took a blunt, hoelike object from its back and quickly cut a footpath through the drift. It followed the path as it was cut, and even as the snow drifted across the path behind it, the figure emerged on the other side of the drift and continued up the ledge.

Finally it stood at the crest of a sheer ridge, where the full force of the north wind carried the snow up the far side. Ducking against the increased force of the gale, the figure began to descend. Moving steadily through the night, as the snow grew deeper, it pushed its way down the high mountain ridge and into the still snowy but less windy reaches below.

The snow lay heavy on the low country, drifting into deeper and deeper piles. Here the figure paused and awkwardly reached beneath its cape to pull forth a pair of snowshoes. Attaching these to its feet, it shuffled onward, still making slow, steady progress against the storm.

The body was entirely cloaked in fur—the fur of winter garments. Only a pair of wide eyes, with large brown pupils, were visible beneath the furs, and even those eyes peered from the depths of a fur-lined hood and woolen scarf.

All night, and into the white dawn, the figure never once stopped to rest or eat or drink. It followed an unmarked trail, somehow finding its course through a snowy wasteland of leafless trees and barren hills.

Then it climbed across a broad, snow-swept hillside and found a wide path entering a hilltop grotto, concealed by high limestone walls and somewhat sheltered from the violence of the storm. Here, in this small vale in the hills, the traveler finally paused.

Here it stood still for some minutes, looking around the grotto. Finally the figure pushed through a drift of snow higher than its head to reach a niche in one of the limestone walls. And there it found what it sought.

The traveler knelt beside another creature, this one a great white horse, now blood-spattered and torn. The stallion's flanks were still and its eyes were closed, but a wisp of steam emerged faintly from its bloody nostrils.

The traveler removed the mittens, revealing humanlike hands that were very slender, with long, narrow fingers. Gingerly those fingers reached for the stallion's head.

\*     \*     \*     \*     \*

The *Starling* rounded the head of Oman's Isle and at last raced with the wind. She leaped foaming crests of gray sea in her eagerness to make the shelter of Iron Bay. There, in the most powerful bastion of the northmen inhabitants of the Moonshaes, Koll and Gwen would certainly find shelter from the ravenous hordes that had fallen upon their home.

At least, that was the plan. Koll guided the little vessel through rough seas that he knew heralded the first storms of winter. The pair had eaten no food in two days and had drunk the last of their water twelve hours ago. Not until the Iron Keep hove into view did he allow himself a measure of optimism, but finally it looked as though they would make safe landfall.

The fortress loomed high above the bay. The dark stone of its walls gave it the reddish-black hue that had provided its name. Though not truly made of metal, the Iron Keep's walls were hard and its position unassailable. It had stood for a hundred years as a symbol of northern might, and no doubt would stand a hundred more.

Koll and Gwen, far from shore in the bay, could not see the cleric Hobarth poised beneath the walls of the fortress. Nor could they see the masses of undead swarming from all across Oman's Isle to finally converge upon the fortress. They were not aware of the Claws of the Deep emerging from the shore of Iron Bay to march upon the fortress from seaward.

And they could not hear the words of Hobarth's powerful chanting as he called upon the might of his god to lend power to the cleric's most awesome spell: the earthquake.

But they saw the effects.

Dumbstruck, the pair watched the high wall of the Iron Keep crack, crumble, and fall before their eyes. A breach a hundred feet across fell open, and Koll and Gwen could see the massive army crawling into that breach to meet the thin line of northmen who recovered from the disaster in time to take up arms.

The result of the battle was perhaps not preordained, but it may as well have been. Thousands of attackers poured into the breach, to be met by hundreds of defenders. The defenders could not stand, nor did they.

The *Starling* bobbed to a halt in the choppy waters of the bay as her two passengers fell silent, stunned observers of the end. Nor did they turn about until flames had erupted from every part of the castle, ample proof of evil's triumph.

"And where can we go now? What is left to us?" demanded Gwen.

"We can't return to Gwynneth. We've seen what awaits on that shore." Koll did not consider the possibility of landing in southern Gwynneth. The Ffolk of Corwell were every bit as much the enemy to him as were the Claws of the Deep. "Likewise we have seen the fate of Oman's Isle—our fate, to be sure, if we make landfall here.

"I see but one choice. We shall sail on to Norland. There, if that land has been spared the fates of these, we shall find help. King Grunnarch the Red rules there, and his vengeance will be terrible when he hears of these outrages."

He did not mention that, to get to Norland, they must sail without provisions into the teeth of the first winter storm across the breadth of the Sea of Moonshae.

Oh, yes, all this in a boat not meant to sail beyond the sight of land.

\* \* \* \* \*

Wide yellow eyes watched the circling of the flock, but Shantu did not move toward the grotto. The beast, with an unnatural patience, waited for the chance to slay a lone member of the party. One by one, they would die, but there was plenty of time.

Shantu saw the flock depart and then return. It heard the screams of the horses, and the beast sensed that its prey had departed. With stealth and speed, it loped around the hill and found the chute into the Fens of the Fallon.

Here, though the companions had traveled through water, in many places leaving no physical trail, the displacer beast again took up the trail. Slipping silently through the chill mire, now a thing of the swamp, Shantu moved quickly in order to close with its prey.

Then came the wind and the snow and the storm. This, of all things, was hateful to the beast, for it was a creature of blackness and fire. Shantu growled into the face of the wind, but the weather blustered even harder. Finally the storm did what neither fatigue nor hunger had been able to do: It forced the displacer beast to seek shelter and delay its hunt.

Shantu found the root cluster of a massive tree, recently fallen, and it curled up in this slight protection, still snarling its rage against the storm. The killing, for now, would have to wait. . . .

\* \* \* \* \*

"Throw another stick on the fire," suggested Pawldo lazily, leaning back against a slab of rock and wiggling his hairy toes at the very fringes of the fire. "Oh, yeah!" He watched tendrils of steam curl upward from his feet.

"It hurts to thaw them out again, but I love it!" the bard agreed as her own feet absorbed the welcome warmth of the blaze.

They had found a large chamber, partially underground and completely insulated against the wind and snow, in the ruins of the firbolg lair. Though the inferno they had created—more than a year earlier, upon their escape from this place—had damaged it heavily, destroying the wooden beams that had supported the stones, much of the original structure remained intact. Stone ceiling tiles rested upon solid stone or earthen walls, creating long passages without obstruction. The larger rooms had all collapsed, and in places the corridors were blocked with piles of rubble, but much of the stronghold remained habitable.

An interconnecting network of passages remained, sheltered by the huge stones of the fortress that had fallen in upon themselves. Some of the fortress had been underground, and those tunnels remained virtually intact. After a little exploring, they had come upon a large room connected to the outside by a winding corridor, with several other passages apparently leading to the depths of the building. The deathbirds remained outside the narrow entrance, perched in the branches of nearby trees.

This roomy chamber had been the best of many they had discovered. It had a slow but steady draft that carried the smoke from the room, and yet it was far enough from the outside that the light of the fire would be invisible to anyone beyond the walls of the lair. And now the fire had generated enough coals to warm the chamber appreciably.

Robyn and Tristan, too, massaged their numbed feet beside the fire. The moorhound lay sound asleep, curled between them and unmindful of the steam sizzling from his drenched coat. Yak snored loudly in a corner of the chamber, and Newt had gone off somewhere to explore the ruins.

"I suppose we'd better wake him when his fur starts to singe," Robyn said with a smile, gesturing at the dog.

Tristan nodded. Weariness flowed through his body as he relaxed for the first time in days. "I never thought I'd be glad to see this place again!"

"Nor I. We were glad enough to get away the first time! I only wish Yazilliclick had turned up. I fear for him."

"Yes." Tristan felt a wave of melancholy. He thought of the good friends he had had, and lost, in the time since they had first discovered this lair and he had gained the Sword of Cymrych Hugh. Keren, the master bard, who had died in the fight against Kazgoroth the Beast. Hugh O'Roarke, bandit lord of Callidyrr, fallen in the battle against the High King. And of course, Daryth.

"Hey, you guys! Get up! Let's go exploring!" Newt darted into their chamber from one of the side passages. "There's *all kinds* of tunnels, and a deep well— Oh, and there's a bunch of dead firbolgs that got squished when the place—" He stopped suddenly, with a guilty look at Yak, but the giant snored on.

"I don't think we're going anywhere for a while," groaned

Robyn. "My feet are finally getting warm and dry again, and I'm keeping them that way for as long as I can!"

"Awww! You guys are no fun at all! Say, what's for supper? Didn't you say we could eat after we found shelter?"

Newt eagerly dove at a piece of hardtack, seizing the dried biscuit and chewing contentedly. Despite his bluster and humor, his color had faded to a bluish green, and Tristan saw him glance frequently toward the entrance. Even the faerie dragon was worried about Yazilliclick.

"How far is it to the grove of the Great Druid? That's where the druids are now, right?" Tavish asked Robyn.

"It used to be two days march or so to Myrloch and along the eastern shore, about halfway up the vale. Now, what with blizzards and gas fissures and tar pits, I don't know how long it will take."

"And what will we do when we get there?"

Tristan had wondered about the same thing for some time.

"I assume that things have gotten worse since last I saw the Moonwell. At that time, the surviving druids of the vale, a score or so of them, had been frozen into stone statues by the power of the goddess. It was either that or face death at the hands of zombies and walking skeletons under the command of the evil cleric.

"Now, with the extent of the corruption through the vale, I can only guess that the Moonwell itself has been desecrated. It is the spiritual heart of the islands, and only through it could enough power be channeled to cause destruction on the scope we're seeing."

"But how do we face something that powerful?" Tristan didn't like the odds.

"I have a single hope, found in the scrolls the northman gave me. Those parchments, the Scrolls of Arcanus, contain secrets of ancient clerical lore. They were scribed by a cleric of another goddess, called Chauntea. But many of the tenets of her faith are very close to those of the Earthmother. Included among them are the mastery of the four elements!"

"Air, water, fire, and earth," interjected Tavish.

"Yes, earth . . . or stone." She told them how she had journeyed to the vale by using the mastery of air and becoming part of the wind itself. "The other three scrolls allow similar control—either to summon, shape, use, or actually become the element, once per scroll.

"I shall save the scroll of stone. When we reach the well, I shall use my mastery of stone to free the druids from their statues. Together we might have enough force to purify the well."

"Keep the scrolls safe," suggested Pawldo. "It's not much of a plan, but it seems to be the best we have."

"Let's take advantage of the shelter we have for tonight. This may be the last warmth we feel until this is over." Tristan remained well aware of the snow falling outside and the impact that the weather might have upon the rest of their mission.

"I have no problem with that," agreed Tavish. "I'll take the first watch. I want to dry out my pants."

"I'll get up for the last watch," blurted Pawldo, very hastily. The others took no note of his urgency as they divided up the rest of the night. All of them except Tavish quickly settled down to sleep.

The bard awakened Robyn after several hours. She in turn called Tristan to the watch for the third quarter, then returned to sleep. The king finally awakened the halfling as night approached dawn.

Pawldo stood a nervous guard duty until he saw that the king had fallen asleep. Then he silently checked over his gear—shortbow, sword, rope, and lockpick. With a last look at his sleeping companions, he turned into one of the dark passages and started to make his way deeper into the firbolg lair.

*　*　*　*　*

*Taggar, shaman of Norland, sat back from his ashes with a frown. The pattern was clear, unmistakable to such a devout follower of Tempus. He knew that Grunnarch had called the Council of Winternight for the following evening. All day the warlords of Norland had been arriving, taking* up quarters in the best lodges in Norland town.

The prophecy so plainly indicated by his ashes surely must refer to one of these worthies . . . but which one? With a shrug, the shaman climbed to his feet. If Tempus did not want to reveal any more, so be it. The cleric would tell his king all he knew of the prophecy. It would be up to Grunnarch to figure out what it meant.

He found his liege feasting in his lodge with Eric Graybeard and Urk Bearstooth, two of his favored lieutenants. Grunnarch bade him speak in the presence of them all, so Taggar told of the casting of ashes and of the message Tempus had given him therein.

"Sire, the message is this: One will travel to see you, bearing a message of great import and a plea for help. You must heed his call."

"Hmph!" The king scoffed at the message. "When is the day someone does *not* come to see me with an important message and a plea for my aid?"

"But, sire, consider the rest of the prophecy: This one will not walk nor swim to Norland. Nor will he ride cart or steed or ship! But he will arrive, just the same."

And then the cleric went back into the night, wondering at the ways of gods and kings and men.

# ❧ 11 ❧

# SUN-SIGN OF CHAUNTEA

The *Starling* bobbed and dipped in the choppy sea. Each crushing wave poured more water over the little boat's bow, and the hull was soon awash to knee-depth. Koll held the tiller against the strain of fatigue and cold, shivering uncontrollably. He tried to avoid looking at Gwen but could not tear his eyes from her miserable form.

She huddled in the bow, wrapped in the tattered shawl that was their only protective garment. She had bailed until her strength failed, and then she had collapsed. It had been hours since she had moved, and Koll wondered if she was dying.

The wind roared out of the north like a vengeful dragon, lashing first one side of the boat, then the other, as Koll tacked his way into the teeth of the wind.

By dawn of their second day at sea, he forced himself to face the truth: They would never make it to Norland. He had been a fool for even trying the voyage, and his foolishness would cost them both their lives. Why hadn't he taken her to Corwell? She, at least, with the blood of the Ffolk in her veins, would have been safe there.

He felt a sudden jolt against the hull and feared for a moment that he had struck a rock, but that was impossible. They were in the middle of the Sea of Moonshae, with no shoals for a hundred miles. Again the little boat lurched, and he heard the unmistakable scraping of stone against wood.

Suddenly the *Starling* heeled violently to the side, and he saw her frail timbers cave in under the force of a violent collision. Instinctively he lunged forward, grabbing Gwen as she rolled to the side, and then they both tumbled into the frothing sea.

His shoulder crashed against something hard and unforgiving, unmistakably stone, and then he found himself sprawled on a flat surface, holding the unconscious maiden to his chest. The water drained away around them, and he looked up in astonishment and awe to see four towering spires rising above him, looming on each of the points of the compass.

The wreck of the *Starling* was carried away by the rushing waves, but he remained in place, sitting upon a surface of flagstones. Too stunned to speak, he stared at the four high walls of a great castle that had somehow appeared around him.

It had risen from the sea! His boat, he realized, had smashed itself into the crenellated parapet of the castle wall, dumping them into the courtyard as it foundered. Now he sat upon the floor of the courtyard, looking at a few dozen fish that flopped helplessly as the rest of the water drained away.

Gwen opened her eyes and looked around in a daze. "Where are we?" she asked weakly. "Is this a dream? Are we dead?"

"We're not dead, and this is no dream. I don't know what this is or where we are, but this place has saved us!"

She sighed and leaned against him with a frail smile. "That's nice," she whispered and closed her eyes again. He noticed with grief that her lips were blue and her breathing shallow. Once again he looked up and saw a wide stairway leading to a massive pair of doors in the castle wall.

He wrapped the shawl more tightly around Gwen and lifted her in his arms, surprised at how little she weighed. Still not sure he believed this whole thing, he started up the stairs. Perhaps there was something in the castle that could help them. In any event, he was determined to take every advantage of this unexpected chance to remain alive.

\* \* \* \* \*

Pawldo slipped silently down the darkened passage. He paused every few steps to listen but heard no sound from any of the labyrinthine passages. His eyes, far more keen than their human counterparts, penetrated the blackness enough to show him where a side corridor joined the one he was in or to warn him, as now, of a gaping pit that suddenly yawned at his feet.

He stepped around the pit, which had apparently been created when the stronghold had collapsed, and continued deeper into the maze.

His destination was a chamber etched firmly in his memory, but its location had become more problematical. The halfling chose his route partially from memory, partially from an intuitive sense, and often because pieces of the collapsed structure blocked corridors he would have chosen to follow.

Often he scrambled over piles of broken granite or spilled earth. Once he was forced to squirm underneath a broken, charred beam.

But he pressed on with singleminded determination, motivated by the one great love of his life: treasure. He remembered the room they had discovered upon first entering this stronghold, the gold and silver coins piled in great heaps, the gems scattered among them, gleaming with all the colors of the rainbow.

He felt certain that the treasure room lay very close now. A sharp jog in the corridor looked very familiar, and then his pulse pounded as he saw a dead-end passage leading to a heavy oaken door. This was it!

Nothing disturbed the stillness of the labyrinth. Musty beams, jagged pieces of rock, and a heavy coat of dust filled the passage. Pawldo saw that the heavy door stood firm, unaffected by the force of the cave-in. Carefully he wormed his way under another beam and around a boulder until he reached the door and examined it. He had no doubts as to what chamber it protected. The spot had burned itself indelibly into his mind, and even the chaos wrought by the cave-in and fire could not erase the image.

He examined the heavy lock, remembering that Daryth

had picked this same lock with no difficulty during the Darkwalker War. Pawldo removed his trusty lockpick from his belt and carefully slipped it into the narrow hole. Let's see, a little probe this way, a pull that way, and . . .

*Snap!* "Hey! What's going on?" Pawldo leaped, or rather tried to leap, backward, but the sudden clasp of a pair of metal handcuffs held him securely to the door. "Damn!" he whispered. "A trap!"

Indeed, two firm iron bracelets had sprung from the door when his probe had pulled on the lock. Now they pinched his wrists in a most uncomfortable, and permanent-looking, fashion.

Pawldo suppressed a momentary surge of panic. What would Daryth do at a time like this? For the first time, the halfling grudgingly admitted to himself that the Calishite had been a master at such tasks as opening locks and finding traps.

He remembered Daryth's gloves, which Tristan had given to Pawldo after the Calishite's death. They had shrunk to fit the halfling's hands perfectly, so much so that Pawldo had forgotten that he still wore them. Now he looked at them on his fingers, barely visible in the dim light. At the same time, he tugged very gently at the handcuffs imprisoning him.

His hands came free! They slid right through the manacles, as if the gloves could not be held in such confinement. Murmuring a quick prayer of thanks to Daryth, wherever he was, Pawldo drew one of the wire lockpicks from its pouch in the glove. Once again he probed the lock, and this time it popped open quickly.

Pawldo's eyes flashed, and the pounding of his heart threatened to shake more rocks from the ceiling as he seized the door and pushed it open. The halfling darted through the portal, his darkness-attuned eyes flashing as he stared eagerly around the room.

And then his eagerness turned to shock, then disbelief, then anger. This was indeed the firbolg treasure room, but it was virtually empty!

"What happened to the treasure?" he groaned. "Thieves! It's been stolen! Why, those scum! If I get my hands . . ."

He slumped to the floor, stunned. A single coin gleamed mockingly from beneath the layer of dust. Pawldo picked it up and brushed it off to reveal a virtually worthless copper piece. The dust covered everything in the room nearly a half inch thick, so he knew that the plundering had occurred long ago.

Perhaps the few surviving firbolgs had carried their treasure away when they abandoned the ruins of the stronghold. Or maybe a band of dwarves—avaricious fellows, dwarves!—had come upon the place. For several minutes, the halfling stewed, his rage building as he groped for someone to blame.

Finally he realized there was little point in trying to pinpoint the blame. The bulk of the treasure had been removed, and that was that. He saw several other dust-covered coins and checked each one, but all of them proved to be copper.

"Not just thieves, but discriminating thieves!" he grumbled.

He saw an irregularity in the dusty surface beside a fallen beam and brushed it away to reveal a glint of gold in the form of a thin chain. He tugged on it and pulled forth a round medallion as big as his hand. Here was something worthwhile! The medallion was pure gold, in the circular shape of the sun, and it surrounded a large rose made from several rubies. Eagerly he tucked it into his pocket, reaching below the beam with his tiny hands. Perhaps the plunderers had missed a spot!

His efforts were rewarded as he pulled out a few gold and silver coins. Pawldo then encountered an odd shape, and tugged at it a few times to bring forth an unusual object. It was a pair of spectacles. One lens was cracked, and one of the temples had fallen off. The halfling started to toss the thing aside, but something stayed his hand. With a shrug, he stuffed them into his pouch with the rest of his loot and went back to the search.

Near the end of the beam, he found something that caused his heart to quicken again. At first, his touch told him it was merely a pebble, firmly wedged beneath the wood. But his delicate fingers felt the pebble carefully and detected numerous facets on a very smooth surface.

"Stones don't have facets," he murmured. "But gems do!"

As a pebble, the stone was rather small, but if it indeed was a gem, it was one of quite respectable size. Eagerly he got out his dagger and pried at the bottom of the beam. In moments, he was rewarded as the object popped free and rolled onto the open floor.

"That's it!" he gasped, picking it up. Even in the darkness his keen eyes could make out the crystalline outline, fatter than his finger. The hard surface felt cool to his touch, and he suspected that he held a gem of surpassing wealth, though he could not discern its nature. From its great size, he judged that it would be an amethyst or bloodstone, since it was too large to be a ruby, emerald, or diamond. Still, the thieves had missed something valuable after all!

Then the beam he had moved shifted again with a dull thump. He heard a scraping sound from the ceiling and scampered out of the way just as a great rock broke free and tumbled onto the chamber floor. Another rumbled free, and Pawldo quickly dove through the door. A thunderous crash emerged from the room as the entire ceiling collapsed, sending a cloud of dust into his face and shaking the foundation of the stronghold.

The walls around him rumbled, and then the whole place started to collapse.

*　*　*　*　*

"What if he doesn't come back?"

"What?" Randolph looked up, irritated, from his mug. Pontswain's question, after an hour of total silence, jarred him unpleasantly.

"The king. What if he doesn't come back from his quest?" Pontswain leaned forward, his eyes alight.

The two men sat alone in the Great Hall of Corwell. A low fire smoldered in the hearth, and the hour was late. Each of them held a large tankard, now nearly emptied of ale.

"What kind of a question is that?" Randolph did not try to hide his annoyance.

"A good question . . . quite practical. I should think, to you and me, it would be a question of great pertinence." Pontswain smiled, his lips creased in an oily grin.

The lord's eyes flickered, just for a moment, to the heavy oak mantle. The silvery glow of the Crown of the Isles caught his pupils, illuminating them unnaturally.

"I will consider what do when the king fails to return *only* if he fails to return. Are you suggesting that a week's absence is sufficient cause for usurping the throne?"

"Of course not," Pontswain soothed. "I was just wondering, that's all."

"Good night, sir," snapped Randolph. "And I'll thank you to wonder about something else." The captain stalked out of the hall, but he could not shake a vague sense of disquiet.

"What if he doesn't return, indeed?"

*　*　*　*　*

Yazilliclick shivered in the growing storm and settled to the ground in the shelter of a gaunt and skeletal tree. Where had everybody gone? Why didn't they come back and find him? The sprite had tried to fly after the others, but the wind had blown so forcefully that he had little control over his course. So now he sat and watched the snow settle on his wings and cover his legs.

The sprite shook more from the effects of loneliness and fear than from cold. Though dressed only in the leafy green tunic and leggings that were his permanent and sole garment, he—like most creatures of Faerie—did not suffer extremely from the ravages of weather.

But flight was another thing. Yazilliclick was a strong and steady flier, but he weighed very little. Flying against the wind was always a challenge, and he had no chance at all of making progress into the teeth of this northern gale. Plus he still carried the wineskin that Tavish had given him before they started out, when he had asked to help. That dragged him down still more, and now his friends had all forgotten him!

Certainly Newt should have noticed his absence, shouldn't he? The two creatures, both with roots in Faerie, had developed a deep friendship that was as close as two such flighty creatures could come to love. But even the faerie dragon had elected to continue on with his more mundane companions.

The sprite's shoulders hunched and shook as he wept. His antennae wobbled, and great, round tears rolled to the tip of his pointed nose. There they gathered, one on top of the next, until a small icicle had formed, growing until Yazilliclick sneezed it away.

Well, he had to do something. The sprite got to his feet and started trudging through the snow toward the north. He dreamed wistfully of happier times, times spent in Myrloch Vale when this was a living and pastoral place, and even more distant times spent in the realm of Faerie itself.

Ah, Faerie! Now, there was a land for the likes of a sprite, or a faerie dragon, or a pixie—or indeed any of the myriad creatures who originated in that place of magic and beauty. Yazilliclick, plodding through snow piled higher than his knees, lost himself in reverie.

Faerie was a distant land, far from the Realms, but in some respects it was very near. He remembered making the journey from his homeland to the Moonshaes. It had simply been a matter of stepping into a narrow crack in a mossy tree trunk and popping out the other side in Myrloch Vale.

He, like many of his brethren, had stayed in this world. Perhaps he had not been able to find his way back, or perhaps he had not wanted to return. Certainly he had never spent much time looking for a gate back to Faerie, for there had always been so much to do here. Then, of course, he had played with the other sprites of the vale, and taunted the pixies, and followed the dryads. In those days, Myrloch Vale had been a place so much like Faerie that it seemed as if he and his kind belonged here.

Now, of course, things had changed. In fact, for the first time, he wondered what had become of the pixies and sprites and other faerie creatures of the vale. Had they returned home, leaving him here alone? Or had they all been killed by the monsters and the evil cleric?

That thought was too horrible to contemplate, and so he

didn't. Instead, his mind returned to the awful, miserable present, to the snow that now reached his waist, and the biting wind that stretched his wings behind him, and this depressing vista of death and decay that even the white snow could not conceal completely. There, like that looming dead tree stump before him, with the ugly crack down the side. He could see the places where moss had fallen away from the stump, leaving only ghastly barren patches of rotting wood.

And then the crack widened and a great, clawed hand reached out to grab the sprite by the tunic. It pulled, Yazilliclick squealed once, and then he was gone.

\* \* \* \* \*

"What was that?" Tristan sat bolt upright, wide awake and already drawing his sword. Again he heard the rumbling, and he felt the unmistakable shaking of the ground beneath him.

"Cave-in!" Robyn jumped to her feet and looked around. For a moment, all was still, and then another distant rumble shook the earth.

"Yipes! Who did that?" Newt demanded.

"Everyone outside!" shouted the king. "Hurry!"

"Where's Pawldo?" Tavish gathered her possessions and noticed the halfling's empty bedroll.

"He took over the watch when I went to bed. He's got to be around here somewhere!" Tristan lifted a glowing brand from the fire and swirled it in the air until it blazed into flame. Then he looked around the chamber as the others gathered their things. "Pawldo? Where are you?" For several moments, they froze and listened, but the stronghold mocked their ears with complete silence. At least the rumbling had stopped again.

"Let's have a look around," suggested the king. "He might be hurt."

A quick search of their chamber and the adjacent passages revealed no sign of the halfling. Though the rumbling did not resume, Tristan had grave doubts as to the security of their shelter.

"Everyone go outside. I'll take Canthus and see if he can follow Pawldo's trail. We'll join you as soon as we can, but it's not safe for all of us to remain in here."

"You'd better take Yak with you," argued Tavish. "He'll be able to move rocks and stuff out of your way. And that means you'll have to take me, 'cause I'm the only one he listens to!"

"I'm coming, too," said Robyn quickly. "There's no sense in breaking up the group still further. Besides, things seem to have settled down."

"For now." Tristan was tempted to argue with them, but he knew that would be fruitless. "All right." He turned to the great moorhound. "Canthus, find Pawldo. Where's Pawldo?"

The moorhound looked at him quizzically for a moment, and then his ears pricked up excitedly. He bounded around the chamber, his nose to the floor, and then he started down the tunnel that led toward the heart of the firbolg stronghold.

Robyn and Tavish each grabbed a torch and followed the king in a flickering procession through the darkness. Canthus leaped ahead, then waited until the humans caught him before bounding ahead once again. Newt hovered over the dog.

It seemed like a long time as they pushed deeper into the ruined lair. Fortunately no new rumbles disturbed the silence, but neither was there any sign of the halfling. They had only their faith in the moorhound's keen nose to convince them they were on the right path.

"What could he be up to?" wondered Tristan as Robyn came up behind him.

"I think I know. Remember the gold and jewels, all that wealth that we left in here when we fled? I suspect he's gone back after it."

Tristan groaned. "Of course! I should have known he'd do that! Why didn't I think of it?"

"You can't think of everything." Robyn touched his arm and, as always, the pressure of her hand upon him calmed his nerves and cooled his judgment.

Suddenly Canthus stopped before a huge pile of rubble. With a soft whine, he started pawing loose rocks and broken pieces of timber out of the way. The king dropped to his knees beside him and started pulling more wreckage aside.

"Pawldo? Are you there?"

The voice that responded was faint but was unmistakably the halfling's. "Help! I'm stuck!"

Tristan's heart leaped at the sound. Pawldo was alive! "Wait'll we get you out! I'll strangle you! What kind of a prank is this?"

"I'll *let* you strangle me! Just get me out of here!"

The king heard the strumming of the lute behind him and looked up to see the firbolg leaning curiously over him. "Yak dig?"

"Yes!" gasped Tristan, already exhausted. He sat against the tunnel wall. "Yak dig!"

The giant pulled a heavy beam out of the way, then roughly shouldered several boulders aside. He reached a brawny paw into the rubble and pulled roughly.

"Ouch! My neck! Hey, that hurts! Urf!" Yak ignored Pawldo's protests as his shoulders tensed. Tristan imagined he heard a popping sound as Pawldo suddenly burst from the pile of rubble.

Yak held Pawldo by the scruff of his neck, lifting him up so that the others could see. The giant's face was split by a wide grin. "Look! Yak find Pawll-do! Hi, Pawll-do!"

"Put me down, you behemoth! . . . There, that's better." The halfling cleared his throat a few times and dusted himself off before glancing sheepishly at his friends.

"Uh, thanks, everybody. I'm, uh, sorry about all this, but I didn't know the place was going to collapse just because I moved a stupid board! Besides, I, uh, I wanted to explore the ruins a little—"

"Explore my eye!" exclaimed Robyn with a scowl. "You went looking for the treasure room, didn't you?"

"And I found it, too! Except someone else had been there first—they cleaned out everything!"

"Everything?" The druid eyed him shrewdly.

"Well, just about everything. I did sort of find a few things

. . . nothing too great. There's this—" Pawldo reached into his pouch and pulled out the medallion, its ruby heart scintillating in the torchlight.

Robyn gasped and seized the golden talisman, though Pawldo kept a tight grip on the chain. "This is the same symbol that marked the Scrolls of Arcanus! It's the sign of the goddess, the one called Chauntea."

Pawldo grimaced but relaxed his hold on the chain. "Well, if you know what it is and all, and you came to rescue me, I suppose you should have it. Is it magical?"

Robyn took the talisman and held it up, examining it in the flickering light. "I don't know. But it's certainly sacred to followers of Chauntea. Thank you. I shall keep it with the scrolls."

"Why don't you wear it?" suggested Tavish.

Robyn looked startled. "No! I couldn't! It wouldn't be right, or proper. . . ."

"I know of this Chauntea," persisted the bard. "She is a great and powerful goddess, worshiped throughout the Realms. She is a goddess of growth and life, plants and animals, and nature. Is that so different from the great mother?"

Robyn shook her head reluctantly, and the bard continued. "Now, a matter of faith is a thing you must decide in your heart, but you have told us that the goddess has grown so weak that you cannot hear her answer your prayers. Nor can she restore your spells. Surely she would welcome the help of another goddess, one of great power and similar beliefs, if it will aid us on our quest!

"And a clerical talisman of such great value must indeed be a thing of power. Perhaps the symbol of Chauntea could work to our benefit. She is certain to despise and resist the presence of evil around us!"

"Perhaps," wavered the druid. "But—"

"And didn't you cast a spell of Chauntea, from the scroll, to travel here?" asked the king. "Might not wearing the medallion aid in the use of the other scrolls—perhaps even to free the druids?"

"Very well. I shall wear it." Robyn lifted the golden chain

over her head, lifting her long hair out of the way so that it settled around her neck. The medallion itself, the shining crimson rose centered in the golden image of the sun, came to rest between her breasts, glowing warmly.

"I also found these. I don't know what good they are—they're kind of busted up—but I took them anyway." Now the halfling produced the battered spectacles, dust-covered and cracked. "I figured that since they were in the treasure room, they must be something valuable."

"Let me see those," said the bard. She took the glasses and held them up to her face, perching them on her nose. They tilted at an awkward angle, since the left temple was missing. The lens over her right eye was marred by a spiderweb pattern of cracks, but Tavish squinted comically and looked around.

"They don't do much for me . . . kind of hurt my eyes," she admitted. "I don't know why they would have been stored with the other valuables. Maybe that's why they were left behind." She removed the glasses and offered them to Tristan, but the king had turned back to the halfling.

Pawldo squirmed awkwardly as the others examined the glasses. Finally he spoke again. "There was—that is, there is—uh, one more thing. It was under a beam."

Hesitantly he reached into his pouch and pulled forth the fat gem. In the torchlight, they could all see the unmistakable glimmering of its many facets.

"A diamond!" gasped the halfling, surprising himself.

"It's huge!" murmured Tavish, leaning close to examine it, though she did not attempt to remove the stone from Pawldo's fingers.

"I guess, since you all went to the trouble of getting me out of there, this really belongs to all of us," admitted the halfling. "I'll hang on to it for safekeeping, but when I can sell it, we'll each get a share."

Tristan hid his surprise, but he looked at his old companion through new eyes. The avaricious halfling had accumulated quite a hoard over the years, but this was the first time the king had ever heard him offer to share any of it.

"Well, at least we've discovered a way out of here by

which we might be able to avoid a confrontation with the deathbirds," said Tavish.

The others looked at her in amazement.

"What are you talking about?" asked Tristan.

"Why, over there . . . where the light is coming from. Hey, where did it go?" Tavish looked in amazement up a side tunnel. "I swear I saw daylight in that tunnel, just a minute ago. . . . "Wait a minute!" The bard, excited, put the spectacles back on her face and looked up the passage. "Yes, I can see it! We just have to go around a corner or two, and there's a shaft of light coming through the roof! We can get out there!"

"You're looking *around* the corners?" asked the king, incredulous. Nevertheless, they followed the bard as she quickly led them up the passage and through a winding corridor that connected to it until they reached a hole in the ceiling. They stood in a circle, looking up at a glowering patch of gray cloud, unmistakably outside the lair.

\* \* \* \* \*

*Kamerynn held to the trail of his quarry through the growing might of the winter storm. Even when the ground upon which the hateful thing had walked became buried beneath a thick blanket of snow, the spoor of evil lay like an obscene snake across the earth.*

*The unicorn never hesitated nor wavered from his mission. He sensed that the killing of the thing he followed would not bring back the world he had known, would not free his beloved druids from their stony prisons. But he sensed that killing this creature was something he could do, and that had become all-important.*

*The trail entered the Fens of the Fallon, a region Kamerynn had rarely trod before. But now he charged forward, wading through the freezing water and boldly forcing his way through the entwining foliage. The proud spire of his horn remained upthrust before him.*

*Finally Kamerynn sensed the presence of the thing itself, and for the first time, he hesitated. His nostrils dilated as he searched the air, seeking confirmation of the awareness that seemed to penetrate directly to the depths of his soul. A great darkness lurked nearby, and all the unicorn's senses urged attack.*

*His mind, however, counseled caution, and so he slowed to a deliberate walk, facing the blustering wind, still holding his head high. He approached a great dead tree, its huge root cluster rising before him like the gaping maw of a hungry dragon, and he knew he had found his enemy.*

*The beast exploded from its shelter in a snarling attack of yellow eyes and long, drooling teeth. Sharp claws raked the unicorn's flanks as Kamerynn's hooves lashed out, driving the monster backward. The creature crouched on the ground before him and then sprang again.*

*Wiry tentacles lashed out toward the unicorn's flanks, but he skipped aside. Kamerynn reared and kicked again, but he missed the lightning-quick body of his foe. Driving his horn downward, the proud animal thrust. Kamerynn struck only air, but at the same time he heard the clamping of mighty jaws behind him. His sudden attack had thrown off the cat-beast's aim.*

*Once more the horn missed the black pelt, and the unicorn's blood streaked his snowy flanks. Kamerynn reared backward, crying out a shrill challenge as he fought on.*

*It was a fight that could only end in the death of one of the combatants.*

# ❧ 12 ❧

# THE SECOND SCROLL

"And now we shall turn to Corwell."

"Such is the will of Bhaal." Ysalla nodded her head, the yellow skull-spines bobbing in agreement. "But first my people shall have their feast and their celebration."

"But we must make haste!" Hobarth, hissing in the language of the sahuagin, argued. He himself had already gathered a hefty sack of gold coins, not so much for his own use—Hobarth had little need of material wealth—but because he thought it might prove useful in furthering the plan of Bhaal.

"You make haste, human. We have won a great victory, a battle we have fought for the spoils. You shall not cheat us of those spoils."

The cleric looked at the high priestess, surrounded by a rank of her own sahuagin clerics, and knew that further argument was pointless. "Very well. I shall await you at the mouth of the bay."

Hobarth was not a gentle man, nor was he burdened with a surplus of kindness, but the 'celebration' of the victorious sahuagin was a thing he had little stomach for. The sheer scale of the massacre could not help but raise glimmers of doubt and fear in his almost inhuman psyche.

Not, of course, that he would mourn the deaths of the many men, women, and children of the north who fell beneath the Claws of the Deep. Their deaths had been willed by Bhaal, and as such, Hobarth's role in bringing them about could not be questioned. These people were not necessarily enemies of Bhaal, but their existence was an inconvenience to his lord. Therefore their extermination should bring him joy.

But instead it raised the growing specter of fear in his soul. Bhaal's aim, of course, was to make of Gwynneth an island of death, a monument to his inhuman evil. The fact that this massacre occurred on the much smaller neighboring island of Oman could be dismissed as a diversion, or a rehearsal for the annihilation of Corwell. That kingdom, of course, would be their next target.

Yet for the first time, Hobarth wondered about his own role in his master's plan. He had been a true and devoted cleric for all of his adult life, giving all of himself for the greater glory of his god. But soon Bhaal's will would be done, and then what of Hobarth? If the god of death wanted no human life to mar his island, what would become of his unmistakably human cleric?

Grimly Hobarth shook off these doubts. He had cast his die, and he would live—or perhaps perish—with the roll. Certainly he would hasten his own destruction if his master should suspect anything less than total obedience.

Thus far, Bhaal should have no complaints. Hobarth's earthquake spell, the most powerful of all his enchantments, had torn the wall from the Iron Keep. Exploiting the breach, hundreds of sahuagin had poured into the suddenly exposed castle. The dead of the sea had followed, lumbering up the steep slope and through the wide gap until the entire keep had been overrun.

Now the animated corpses lolled senselessly about the battlefield, for they depended upon the commands of Ysalla's clerics for movement or any other action. And those clerics were now, with the rest of the sahuagin, embarked upon a frenzy of killing, eating, and looting.

This left Hobarth to worry about the next phase of the plan. Of course, it was irrational that he worry. The might of Bhaal had proven unstoppable thus far, and if the fishmen wished to revel in their victory for a night before embarking for Corwell, so be it.

Still, Corwell was an ancient kingdom, protected not just by doughty warriors but by some kind of benign and supernatural force. Or so it seemed. The Beast, Kazgoroth, had not been able to break the might of the kingdom. Of course, Kazgoroth could not cast the earthquake spell, and his minions had been living, breathing warriors, capable of failures of morale.

Nevertheless, Hobarth felt a strong sense of urgency, an urgency that was not shared by his allies. He took up a position at the mouth of Iron Bay, sitting upon a rocky promontory overlooking the scene of fire, chaos, and death below. He closed his eyes and prayed to Bhaal for a restoration of the spell he had cast during the battle. The recovery of the earthquake power would take most of the night, anyway, so he might as well put the time to good use.

And as always, his god Bhaal heard him and answered his prayer.

\* \* \* \* \*

Snow spilled down the narrow hole, but the broken rock of the fallen ceiling had created a natural stairway. Tristan led the way, holding his sword in his right hand as he used his left to pull himself upward, out of the firbolg lair and onto the snow-covered ground.

"It's clear," he whispered. "Come on!"

He reached down to hoist Robyn to the ground beside him, and then the pair of them flanked the hole as Yak helped Tavish, Pawldo, and Canthus up. Newt popped out under his own power, and the firbolg had no difficulty lifting himself from the underground labyrinth.

They emerged into a landscape of black and white—black where the trunks of the dead trees towered from the snow, stark against the gray sky, and white everywhere else. The snow had stopped falling, but the wintery blanket covered the ground to a depth of a foot or more.

"The deathbirds are gone, or else they're still watching the entrance. Let's make some time!" Tristan started to move away from the ruins and suddenly stopped short. He looked up toward the gray sky, but the overcast gave no hint of the sun's location. "Which way is north?" he wondered aloud.

Robyn, directly behind him, looked around at the bleak forest. Tavish, meanwhile, pulled out the broken spectacles, perched them on her nose, and looked at the sky. "Just as I thought! These glasses let me see things as they really are! It's really quite remarkable. For example, I can tell you that the sun is over there. That must be east, so north is that way!"

"Seems as good a guess as any," grunted the king. "To the north, then."

For several hours, they pushed across the snowy ground. Tristan led for a while before turning the lead over to Robyn. It proved much easier, in the snow, to follow in the exact steps of the leader, so after this they changed the order of march frequently and took turns breaking the deep snow.

The warmth of their evening camp had revitalized all of them. Though they talked little, they made steady progress, and the firbolg lair fell quickly behind them. They saw no sign of the ghastly birds and began to hope that the predators had also been left behind.

For Tristan, Daryth's death still burned like a deep wound. His own part in it seemed an act of tremendous evil. But he was now convinced that the challenge before them offered him a way to absolve himself of that guilt.

In most places, they walked among the gaunt trunks and tangled branches of the forested fen. The patches of land they encountered now seemed larger than those of the previous day.

An unlikely benefit of the cold temperature became apparent the first time their path took them from one of the hummocks of land back into the wetlands of the fens. The cold temperatures had frozen the water, in most places creating a layer of ice thick enough to walk on. In these cases, they put Yak in the rear of the party, since the firbolg's weight always caused the ice to give way. The rest of them made it across several such icy patches with little worse than an occasional wet foot.

Tristan took over the lead after one such stretch, looking behind at the plainly visible path they left in the snow. "I hope those birds are too stupid to follow a trail," he said to Robyn as she stood aside to let him pass.

"I'm afraid not." She pointed to the sky, and his heart sank as he saw a soaring shape wheeling just below the level of the low clouds. It was soon joined by another, then several more.

"They're pretty far away," he said hopefully.

"But I think they're coming this way."

The king started breaking trail with a vengeance, as if he hoped they could outdistance the awful creatures, but more and more of the flock appeared in the sky. Though they did not chase the companions with any apparent urgency, it was clear to the companions that the deathbirds were getting closer.

"What will we do once we're past the fens?" asked Robyn, bringing up a question Tristan had avoided thinking about. "Can we stick to the forests and keep them off our heads there?"

"I doubt it. The woods are too open to provide much of an obstacle. "We might be forced to fight them," said the king, without much hope. They all knew the odds of such a fight were grim.

Right now he faced a more immediate problem, as he hacked a network of dead vines out of the way and pushed himself through a tangle of trees, only to stop short.

"What do we do now?" he groaned, gesturing to the obstacle he had discovered.

Before them, neatly bisecting their path, stretched a steep-sided gorge that had once been a riverbed. The bottom was only about twenty feet below them, but the smooth, rocky sides offered few promising handholds. Snow lined the bed of the gorge, revealing the tops of huge boulders. On the far side, they could see well beyond the fens, for the ground rolled away uninterrupted by trees or any other cover, descending gradually to the north. In the distance, unfrozen and dark, sprawled the polluted expanse of Myrloch.

*　*　*　*　*

Yazilliclick squeezed his eyes shut. He felt the grip of massive claws on his shoulder and waited to be killed. And waited some more. Still nothing happened.

He began, without peeking, to take stock of his surroundings. He could hear the deep, raspy breathing of some creature beside him. A warm, smoky smell filled the air, and he thought he detected the scent of meat roasting on a fire. Indeed, he could hear it sizzling.

Against all his attempts to stifle it, his belly rumbled from hunger. Of course, he reminded himself, that wouldn't matter after this horrible beast had killed him. And still he waited, and still he wasn't killed.

Daringly he decided to sneak one eye open a tiny crack. He peeped from beneath the trembling lid and caught sight of a huge warty nose, flanked by a pair of beady eyes. A troll! Immediately he squeezed his eyes shut, and he once again waited to be killed.

"Well? Why'd ya nock?" The gruff voice, propelled by a burst of unimaginably bad breath, rumbled in his ears. He didn't dare move, or speak, or look, or anything.

"Woke me up, ya did! Banging on the gate, you wuz—I heard ya!"

"G-Gate?" The sprite dared another look at the thing. "Gate to what?"

"Why, to Faerie! You is a stoopid one, ain'tcha?"

"Y-Yes, I mean, n-no! I m-mean, I didn't knock—didn't knock. I am stupid, though. You're right—right!"

Yazilliclick looked up hesitantly at the troll again. The creature's green skin was covered with warts, and it towered over the faerie, even as it squatted before him. In size, it nearly equaled a firbolg.

It was much skinnier, however, with spindly arms and legs that looked awkward and frail. The sprite knew they were lined with supple sinews far stronger than any human's, however. The great, hooked nose wagged menacingly at him, and those gleaming, incongruously tiny eyes fixed him with a baleful glare.

"Did ya wants in or out? I kin pitch ya back out if ya wants!"

"N-No! Y-Yes! N-Yes! I did wants—want—-in! And you heard m-me! You're a guardian troll, aren't you? And this is a gate to Faerie—to Faerie!" Now the sprite opened his eyes wide. He wanted to leap up and hug the troll, but common sense suggested this might be a bad idea.

"Bright fella, ain'tcha now? 'Course this is Faerie! An' I'm a troll, ain't I? An' I'm guardin' the gate, ain't I? Whaddya think?"

Bolder now, Yazilliclick looked around at the 'gate.' It wasn't much, really. It passed right through this troll's earthen lair, but the sprite couldn't even locate the exact spot he had entered. Of course, his eyes had been squeezed tightly shut, but it seemed he had been pulled through a tangle of roots growing from the dirt wall on the far side of the lair. Elsewhere, he saw a crude stone fireplace where a succulent piece of meat sizzled on a stick. A few clean-picked bones lay in a heap in one corner, and a heavy oaken door stood in the wall opposite the tangle of roots. He noticed a collection of jugs and kettles, all covered with filth and dirt, scattered around the room. Then he remembered the troll's question.

"What do I th-think? I think I'm h-home! I—I just wanted to come home so bad—so bad! And you must have h-heard me think about it. That's it—that's it! I didn't even know there was a g-gate here!"

"Didn't know! Is you blind?"

"B-Blind? I am not blind!" Yazilliclick became indignant. "It's j-just that everything has changed so much out there that none of the gates even l-look like gates anymore! You should t-take a look at what you're g-guarding sometime, then you'd s-see!" He gasped for air, unaccustomed to such long speeches.

The troll chuckled. "You been gone a long time, not to see gate!"

"Oh, I have—I have! And I'm never going away again—again! N-Now that I'm home, I'm going to stay r-right here!" And then Yazilliclick paused. For the first time since he had sensed his impending death, he thought of his friends. How were they faring in the desolate wasteland of the vale? The sprite knew that he couldn't abandon them.

"Kwitcher yakkin'," groused the troll. "I is thirsty. Give me rotgut." He pointed to a filthy jug of unknown origin and equally unknown contents.

Now Yazilliclick's terror had passed, and he knew he had to do something to help his friends. He began to develop an idea for doing so.

"How'd you like some real g-good wine?"

"You gots wine?" The troll was all ears.

The sprite nodded solemnly. "A whole bottle, and I'll g-give it to you—to you, for a small f-favor!"

"What favor?" The troll's eyes squinted even smaller. "Maybe I just take wine!"

The sprite felt a flash of panic. "Y-You can't! You're a guardian troll—you told me—told me! And you're sworn to help and p-protect those who come through your g-gate!" He hoped the troll had some sort of respect for the laws of Faerie.

"Hmph!" But the troll made no move toward him. "What favor?"

"W-Well, you must know where the gates are here in Faerie. Lot's of 'em go to the vale—the vale! Can you take me to the others and help me find my f-friends?"

The troll considered the offer, and soon his black tongue extended, licking his lips. "Okay. First wine, then gates!"

The sprite's elation caused his hands to tremble as he reached into his pouch and pulled forth the bottle. He felt very proud of himself.

"First w-wine, then g-gates!" Yazilliclick repeated. "I don't m-mind if I have a little drink m-myself—myself!"

* * * * *

Koll pushed on the great bronze door, half afraid he would find it locked. The other half of him feared what he would find inside. He still carried Gwen, who lay motionless in his arms, her eyes closed.

But the massive portal swung silently open, revealing a huge hall lined with gleaming granite columns. Every surface was wet and gleaming. An array of windows circled the hall near the ceiling, their colorful panes of glass filtering the gray light of the outside world into a rainbow assortment of cheery hues.

"By all the gods!" he whispered. "It's a miracle!" He didn't try to hide the sense of awe and wonder that held him rooted to the spot.

"Hmmm?" Gwen's eyelids fluttered open. "What is this place?" She twisted to see, and he set her down, supporting her with one of his arms as she stood weakly and looked around.

"It could be that we've died," Koll said.

She shook her head with sudden vehemence. "No. We're alive. And like you told me before, this place is real!"

"Look . . . through that hall. You see the glow?"

She followed his pointing finger and saw a rosy light flickering down one of the hallways leading from this vast chamber. "Let's see what it is!"

"No! Wait, there might be danger!" Koll's heart pounded and sweat soaked his palms. He loathed the fear within him, but he could not banish it.

"Nonsense! It seems perfectly cheery to me!" Gwen smiled, nodding at the warm light. "Let's see what it is—please?"

The woman led the way now, taking Koll's hand and starting down the corridor. The passage was short and opened into a small room. They saw several bearskin rugs on the floor and assorted furniture—a couch, several wooden chairs, and a gleaming table—none of which appeared to have been disturbed by the presence of seawater in the room.

But the most amazing feature of the chamber was the cheery blaze that greeted them from a huge fireplace. Several massive logs, carefully arranged, burned smoothly and evenly, showing no trace of the steam that should have hissed from wet wood.

They sat on one of the rugs, soaking in the welcome warmth of the blaze. Already their clothes had begun to dry, and lifegiving heat once again seeped into their flesh and bones.

"I give up trying to explain it," muttered Koll. "Maybe this whole place will vanish in two minutes and plop us back into the ocean."

"No," said Gwen firmly.

"I hope you're right. Even if you aren't, I want you to know that, well, I'm sorry I've gotten you into this."

"You saved my life. You have nothing to be sorry about."

"If we are about to die, at least I have the comfort of spending my last moments with you."

Gwen smiled and leaned over to kiss him affectionately. Then the young woman shook her head. "I'm sure we have been saved for a reason—and not just to dunk us back into the sea! I don't know who saved us or why, but I suspect we'll find out soon."

And then they both froze in shock. The feeling beneath them was unmistakable, and yet it seemed to defy explanation even more than the appearance of this citadel before them.

For now the castle had begun to move!

\* \* \* \* \*

"The flock's on our trail. I don't think they've seen us yet, but it's only a matter of time." Robyn balanced upon a limb of a desolate oak tree, looking back along their trail.

"That's all we need!" Tristan turned to look at the gorge, but he was fresh out of ideas. They could leap or climb down into the rocky gulch, of course, but they would be easily trapped when the deathbirds reached them. The terrain on the far side of the barrier offered no hope of concealment, either. They seemed to be trapped no matter what they did.

"This was once a river not so very long ago," said the druid, climbing down to stand beside him.

"Too bad it isn't anymore. Then all we'd need is a boat. We could float down the gorge a lot faster than we can walk through this stuff."

"I've got a boat!" Tavish offered. "Remember?"

Tristan looked at her in surprise, then in remembrance as she pulled a narrow wooden box from her pack. "All I've got to do is say the word, and it'll fold into as pretty a craft as you could wish."

"I do remember. I owe my life to you, and that boat, when you fished Daryth and me out of the Strait of Alaron." Pawldo and Robyn nodded as well, for they had both heard the tale of Tavish's marvelous folding boat. It was good-sized and a most seaworthy vessel that, upon the speaking of her word of command, folded into the compact box she now showed them.

"It still doesn't offer much help, with no water to put it in," remarked Pawldo sourly.

"I wonder . . ." Robyn paused, looking at the riverbed curiously. Impulsively she reached for the ivory scroll tube and removed the top. She pulled out a sheet of parchment, looked at it, and then pulled out another. Satisfied, she returned the first one to the tube and resealed it.

"The Scroll of Arcanus that offers mastery of water," she said quietly. "It might be the solution to our problem."

"Well, let's find out in a hurry. Those birdies are getting closer," announced Pawldo. They could all see a score or more of the soaring creatures, wheeling gracefully over the fens several miles away. But the size of the flock was growing, and their meandering course undeniably brought them ever nearer to the companions.

Robyn stepped to the edge of the gorge, unrolling the sheet of parchment and holding it open before her with both hands. Slowly, deliberately, she began to read.

The words were strange to Tristan and the others, and it seemed they were strange to Robyn as well. More than once she paused, pronouncing a long word very slowly and carefully, but she never misspoke nor repeated a phrase.

The king stood protectively beside her and noticed a strange phenomenon as she read. One by one, the runes upon the scroll disappeared from the parchment, apparently in time with her reading. As she finished and lowered the page, he saw that the entire surface was blank!

He forgot the parchment as he heard a splashing sound. As one person, they looked down into the gorge and watched the snow melt along the bottom, carried away by a shallow streamlet of clear water. It originated, apparently, from the stones themselves, for there was more of it than could possibly have been created by the melting of the snow, but the trickle remained far too shallow to offer any hope of floating a boat.

As they watched, however, the water slowly grew deeper, and deeper still. Soon it babbled along like a mountain stream some three or four feet deep. And still it continued to rise.

"How deep will it get?" Tristan asked, disbelieving the evidence of his eyes and ears.

"Who knows?" whispered Robyn, staring intently at the steadily increasing flow. Unconsciously she placed her hand around the rose-in-sun medallion she wore around her neck.

For a full minute, the water level rose, storming up the sides of the gorge, filling the narrow passage with its clean, frothing mass, and rushing ever downward toward Myrloch. Finally the current slowed to a forceful, steadily rolling pace, still racing down the riverbed but deep enough to bury most rocks and obstacles in the gorge. Like a smooth green carpet, it lay before them, a few feet below on the only possible route to safety.

"If I live to be a hundred, I'll never ask to see anything like this again," said Tavish, awestruck.

"I'm older than that, and I've never even *heard* of anything like this before!" whispered Pawldo. Even Newt sat quietly for once, gazing at the miraculous flow.

"No time to lose now!" Tavish shook off her reverie and placed the folding boat on the rim of the gorge. "Everybody get ready to jump in. Once it unfolds, its own weight will topple it into the water, and we won't get a second chance. You, too, Yak!" She gestured at the box and the water, though the firbolg managed to look more confused than ever.

"*Garanday!*" she cried. The box immediately flipped open, doubling its size. But it didn't stop there. The sides flopped down, unfolding again and again until the rough outline of a boat took shape. Then the keel stretched forth from the bottom of the box, and the whole craft tilted crazily, barely balanced on the rim of the gorge.

"Get in!" shouted the bard, diving toward the tiller and seizing the shaft in her hands. The other companions leaped in a similar chaotic fashion, and even Yak and Canthus tumbled into the boat as it slipped off the rocks and splashed into the water. A cascade of icy spray soaked them, but then the bard steadied the helm.

The current swept them along, rolling down the gorge with startling speed. Tavish hauled on the tiller with all her strength, narrowly missing a huge outcrop of rock, and then they slid wildly around a corner. Their launching place, and the end of their visible trail, quickly disappeared behind them.

\* \* \* \* \*

With a sharp cry, Kamerynn reared. He sighted on the creature's flat skull and brought his front hooves down to crush it. Then he lurched to the ground in surprise as his attack met no resistance, for the thing was not where it appeared to be!

The unicorn felt raking claws dig into his flank, and he whirled in desperation, flailing at the air with his sharp horn. He felt the horn meet resistance and drove it forcefully against the invisible form there. Kamerynn was rewarded by a shrill cry of pain and rage.

Then one of the monster's horny tentacles wrapped around the unicorn's throat, and he felt once more the raking claws across his breast. Kamerynn reared and kicked with his powerful forehooves. For a moment, the monster twisted, impaled on the horn. Kamerynn looked at the snarling, hateful face below him and tried to guess at the monster's actual position.

He ducked his head and kicked forward into the air to the left of the creature's apparent location. But he was terribly, fatefully wrong.

Once again his attack met no resistance, and this time, he felt an awful weight land upon his back, twisting his heck backward as the creature remained impaled. Claws sank *deep into Kamerynn's flanks, and the creature's tentacles lashed his neck again and again. The unicorn reared backward, but he could not dislodge the supernatural predator.*

*He bucked and kicked, tossing the beast around and trying to drive his horn ever deeper into the twisting body. But then, with a sharp snap, the horn of the unicorn cracked and broke off. It remained stuck in the monster, but it no longer held it away from the unicorn.*

*Then Kamerynn felt the long fangs at his throat, felt the powerful jaws close and drive the teeth through his skin, his muscle, his windpipe. With a strangled gasp, the unicorn fell to the ground.*

*Then the jaws completed their deadly work, snapping the bones of the proud neck, and Kamerynn—the last of the children of the goddess—kicked his last and died.*

# ☙ 13 ☙

# A DEEPER DARKNESS

"Hold on!" Tavish grinned with delight as the boat ducked and bobbed through the water. She handled the tiller with skill, avoiding the numerous obstacles that reared suddenly in their path.

Tristan looked behind them and saw no sign of the deathbirds. Could it be that they had seen the last of the things? A curtain of icy spray suddenly drenched him, and he forgot about their pursuers as he clung tightly to the gunwale.

He and Robyn sat in the bow of the little craft, while Pawldo rode beside Tavish in the stern and Yak sat amidships. Canthus bounded nervously from one place to another, while Newt perched on the prow as a living figurehead.

"Yippee! Here comes another one!" The faerie dragon's exhilaration was not shared by the other passengers as the boat darted down a narrow, foaming chute to burst into more placid waters.

"Ride water!" shouted Yak, his face split by a gap-toothed grin. "Look!" The giant pointed at a craggy rock formation and stood up to get a better view.

"Sit down!" shouted Tavish and Tristan together as the boat heeled dangerously to the side. Puzzled, Yak sat and the craft righted itself.

"That was a close call!" groaned the king, wiping spray from his face.

"What was so great about that rock, anyway?" demanded Pawldo.

"It probably reminded him of his mother." Tavish seemed to be enjoying their ride down the rapids.

For a short time, the vessel bobbed peacefully as the water meandered through a wide, deep stretch. Then the walls narrowed, looming above them, and again the river became a raging torrent. The boat raced between the rocky sides of the gorge, but Tavish's steady hand on the tiller kept them in the center of the channel.

"The water's deep enough to cover the big rocks," said the bard. "That helps a lot!"

"How long do you think it'll last?" Tristan looked at Robyn, still amazed by the power she had displayed in bringing the river to life.

"I don't know. The wind spell lasted for a long time, but faded as soon as I reached the vale. I suspect it's harder for the magic to work here, so I assume we only have an hour or so."

"We're making great time, anyway." Tristan had been surprised and delighted by the speed of their boat. "We've already made half a day's progress!"

The gray sky still glowered its threat of snow, but for the time being, no flakes fell. Nearly a foot of snow lined the banks of the river, however. The temperature remained below freezing, and in places where the water splashed up on the rock walls, it left an icy sheen. Only the forceful current prevented the entire waterway from freezing.

Best of all, there was no sign of the deathbirds. The flock would have been hard put to keep up with the racing boat, and the depth of the gorge often screened the river from view from the sky.

Once more the river widened, and they relaxed their holds. Tristan noticed that his knuckles were white from the strain of gripping the gunwale, and he stretched his fingers in relief at the temporary respite.

The water rolled, a deep gray-green below them, washing against what was now a flat shore.

"We can beach the boat anywhere along here," offered Tavish. "It'll be a lot harder to do once we drop into the rapids again."

"Let's take advantage of the river while we've got it." Tristan spoke for all of them in preferring to stay with the boat, however hair-raising the rapids, to another long overland trek.

Soon the rumbling of the torrent grew in volume again, and they saw the walls of the gorge rising high above the water before them.

"Sounds like a pretty fast one," admitted the bard, looking a little worried for the first time. "Everybody get a handhold!"

Tristan looked ahead and saw the water drop away. He couldn't see what lay beyond, but the roaring grew to a thunderous crescendo, and then the boat flew into the chute.

The gorge became a blur of rock and snow as the craft heeled and lurched through the rapids. Spray flew from all sides, drenching and chilling them, but none of the companions dared let go of his precious handhold. The boat crunched into a rock, jerking to a sudden halt before breaking free to race along with the current again. Tristan, alarmed, saw water spurting through several of the planks in the hull, but he dared not let go to bail.

The river dipped into a hole and flew out the other side, carrying the boat with it. For a desperate moment, the craft seemed to drop away from beneath them. Tristan felt an odd sensation of flying before he slammed back onto his seat. A small shape, whirling through space, passed through the corner of his vision.

"Pawldo!" cried the bard as the halfling was torn from his seat. She dared not release the tiller to reach for him, and in the next instant, the boat lurched again and the halfling flew over the side.

Tristan whirled in his seat, reaching out his hand toward Pawldo, receiving only a faceful of chill water for his effort. The halfling bobbed under the water as the current swept him away from the boat.

Canthus sprang over the side of the boat in a single leap, splashing into the foaming rapids near the spot where Pawldo had disappeared. In another second, the moorhound vanished under the water.

Canthus popped to the surface some distance away, and Tristan saw his teeth firmly clamped around the halfling's shirt. "Come on, boy!" he whispered, willing the dog back to the boat.

Robyn leaned over the side next to him, and Tristan seized her around the waist to prevent her from being swept overboard. She extended her staff, and he saw Pawldo, his arms thrashing, grab desperately for it. For a split second, the dog and the halfling disappeared again, but then Pawldo surfaced with the tip of Robyn's staff in his hands.

"Pull!" she cried, leaning back into the boat. Tristan heaved as well, ignoring the sickening rocking of the craft and the icy spray that continued to fly into his eyes. Robyn, still clutching her staff, fell on top of him.

They scrambled back to the gunwale to see Pawldo hanging on to the hull like a drowned rat. Canthus bobbed in the water behind him, frantically trying to swim in the torrent. Tristan reached down and grabbed the halfling by the arms, quickly pulling him back into the perilous safety of the boat.

Immediately he leaned back toward the water, grasping for the fur of his dog. Canthus yelped once—a gasping, choking sound—and tried desperately to swim toward his hands, but just as he got close, an eddy of violent water swirled him away, and the moorhound disappeared below the surface.

"No! By the goddess, no!" The king leaned far out of the boat, aware of Robyn's hands now grasping him by the legs. He flailed at the water and would have hurled himself in but for her firm grip. "Canthus!" His voice was a wail, but the dog did not reappear.

Then another jarring crunch shook the boat as it twisted in the grip of the raging current. For a moment, the vessel hung between two giant boulders, and Tristan got a brief impression of the gorge walls towering overhead, appearing to lean in on them. The boat suddenly broke free, riding again with the current, but now water swirled about their ankles, pouring in through another gash in the hull.

"Shallows! We'll have to find a bank and land her, or we'll be torn to pieces!" The bard shouted over the thunder of the rapids, twisting the tiller in her hands. But no flat shoreline presented itself. If anything, the walls were steeper and higher here than at any point along the journey, and they continued racing downstream.

Tristan saw more and more rocks sticking their craggy heads above the surface of the water, and once again he felt the awful scraping of granite against wood. How much more punishment could the little boat take before it came apart?

The king looked anxiously across the whitecaps of the river, desperately seeking any sign of Canthus, but the dog had never surfaced again after their last glimpse of him. Still, Tristan could not bring himself to believe that the great hound was dead. Not Canthus, too! he thought. There is too much death, too much killing! We must stop it!

A savage swirl in the current suddenly twisted the boat around, and for a hair-raising second, they rode sideways, beam to the current. In that instant, they smashed into a huge rock jutting out of the middle of the stream, and the little vessel came to pieces around them.

Tristan flew from his seat in the bow, grabbing Robyn's hand as she, too, was hurled into the water. The current forced them up against the rock, and for a moment, they remained there, poised in the rapids, as the crumbling pieces of the boat floated away to either side. The weight of Tristan's chain mail dragged him down, and he flailed his arms, grasping a leather saddlebag, salvaging a few of their possessions. They saw Yak standing in the streambed, shaking his head angrily, and then Tavish and Pawldo floated up to them. Newt had disappeared, no doubt invisible in his agitation, but Tristan didn't doubt that the faerie dragon had flown to safety.

And then Tavish stood before him, and he realized that the water was indeed quite shallow. He put his feet down, easily reaching the rocky bottom, and as he stood, the water level fell even farther. In seconds, it washed around his waist, then his knees, and then his ankles.

"The spell!" Robyn gasped. "It must have run its course."

Soon the stream was no more than a memory, reflected in the rapidly freezing sheets of ice that coated the wet rocks. The companions, bedraggled and wet, huddled in the bottom of the gorge with the wreckage of Tavish's boat around them. An icy wind raced down the riverbed, driving a deadly chill into their soaking bodies as it grew to a mournful, howling gale.

There was still no sign of the moorhound.

\* \* \* \* \*

"I sell a catch along the north coast now and then," explained the grizzled fisherman. He looked down, avoiding Randolph's eyes. "They pay good, and we got enough down here, anyway. It's not like I'm disloyal!"

"Go ahead, man. Get to this news you say is so urgent!" The captain of the guard waved impatiently to get the man to continue.

"Well, you see, I was takin' a batch of salmon—nice catch, for this season—up to Codsbay, only I sailed into the cove, and the town was gone! I tell you, it was burned, or trampled, or somethin' even worse!"

Randolph leaned back in his large chair and stared at the man. He could think of no reason why the fisherman would make up such a story, especially since he confessed in the telling to selling food to the enemies of the Ffolk.

"What exactly did you see?"

"Well, there was some ashes. And other buildings, with the walls just caved in, it looked like. I don't mind telling you that I didn't land when I saw that. I took off outta there faster than you can say 'firbolg'!" The fisherman looked around anxiously, as if searching for evidence to corroborate his story.

The pair sat in the Great Hall of Corwell, before the grand fireplace that had burned so brightly on the night of Tristan's homecoming feast. Above the blaze, on the broad oaken mantle, rested the Crown of the Isles, right where the king had left it. The symbolic icon of his authority was well guarded by Randolph, and now the young captain looked at it, as if hoping for guidance. He didn't know what to make of this strange news.

"Could the damage possibly have been done by firbolgs?" he asked.

"I don't think so. They don't like fire much, from what I hear. It'd not be like them to burn the place."

"Well, what then? You can't suspect that the northmen have raided a village of their own people!"

"No, I don't, nor do I know what did it. If you want my guess, it was something that come from the sea, it was! Something more terrible than firbolgs or northmen, though the goddess knows what that could be! I just come to tell you what I seen."

"Thank you. You have done well." Randolph dismissed the man with a wave, then stood up, thoroughly alarmed. If it were true that some ravaging scourge had attacked the north coast of the island from the sea, was it not possible that Corwell was also on the enemy's agenda?

He heard a footstep and looked up to see a familiarly handsome face, surrounded by a frame of brown curls. Pontswain collapsed easily into the chair the captain had just vacated, looking at him curiously.

"What did the beggar want?"

Briefly Randolph recapitulated the fisherman's story. "I'm worried," he admitted after he finished. "I think we should take steps to prepare for a possible attack!"

"Bah!" Pontswain waved away the suggestion with irritating casualness. "No doubt the drunken ravings of a man who has been at sea too long! And even if something did happen to the town, there's no saying it didn't happen over a year ago, during the Darkwalker War!"

Randolph shook his head firmly. "There's more to it than that. For one thing, the northmen did not attack their own towns during the war. And second, I saw that this man was genuinely afraid—worried enough to give us the warning!"

"Probably hoped for some kind of reward."

"I think we should raise the militia and start a watch on the coasts. I intend to send out the summons this very afternoon!"

"Wait a moment!" Pontswain stood and glared at the captain. "We share the rulership of the kingdom, remember? And I will not sanction a muster with winter approaching. Think of the cost, man!"

Randolph clenched his teeth, biting back an angry reply. He knew that without the support of this influential lord, he could not expect the other cantrev lords to respond to his call for a muster. "We must do something! What if some unknown menace descends upon us now, gathering force while we do nothing?"

"Well, then, you do something!" said Lord Pontswain. "Take a band of your guardsmen and investigate the report. See if we really have anything to worry about. I can tend to the needs of the kingdom while you're gone."

The suggestion jangled a hundred alarm bells in Randolph's brain. He could not trust the kingdom to the care of this ambitious lord even for a few days. But he still had to do something.

"I will send scouts," he decided. "If they bring proof of a threat, then will you agree to call the muster?"

Pontswain shrugged. "Perhaps. Certainly if the proof is conclusive." He tried unsuccessfully to hide his disappointment in Randolph's decision to remain in Corwell.

"Very well." The captain turned on his heel and left the hall, frustrated by the lord's lack of concern.

Pontswain remained in the Great Hall for a few more minutes, sitting in the great chair and watching the fire. Then he got up and went to the mantle. As he had done a thousand times before, he examined the Crown of the Isles, relishing the sight of its golden frame, its elegant shape, and the small but perfect diamonds that gleamed from each of its eight points.

What a shame, he thought, that it had been won by the wrong man.

\* \* \* \* \*

The muffled figure remained beside the wounded stallion for several days. The slender hands cleaned and then bandaged the grievous cuts, offering the horse handfuls of tender grains and then building a small fire to melt enough snow to offer Avalon a drink.

It was fortunate indeed that the great horse had found this niche in the grotto wall. In any other position, the stallion would have been torn to pieces, but as it was, he had reached this shelter barely in time. Dragging himself, slashed and bleeding, into the narrow cut, he had saved himself from the attacks of the horrid predators. This, alone, was why he had survived the attack.

But now it was the ministrations of the fur-cloaked stranger that kept the horse from perishing. Avalon ate a little food and drank a little water, and slowly the awful wounds began to heal.

After a time, Avalon was ready to stand again, albeit unsteadily. The stallion dwarfed the slender figure as he gained his feet, stumbling from the niche into the open grotto. Slowly the horse regained his balance and learned to stand firmly on his bandaged legs.

The stranger acted in the manner of one who knew horses, leading the stallion with a gentle hand on his neck or his muzzle, never pulling or startling the mighty steed. And after Avalon had regained his feet, the figure bade him walk and led him from the grotto, across the barren hilltop, into the dead forests of the vale.

It led the stallion eastward, toward the fringe of Myrloch Vale, and Avalon followed it willingly, perhaps perceiving their destination. Or perhaps he understood the words of the stranger, when it finally spoke softly into the stallion's ear. The voice was soft, speaking in light, musical tones.

"Come, Avalon, this way. Let us go home."

\*　\*　\*　\*　\*

Koll leaped to his feet as soon as he felt movement in the castle floor below him. "Come on! Let's get out of here!" he cried.

Gwen leaned back on the rug, the look of contentment on her face quite at odds with her companion's agitation. "I think we're perfectly safe," she said with a sigh, "and I'm going to stay right here!"

For a moment, the northman considered reaching down and sweeping the woman into his arms. Damn her blind naivete! He wanted to carry her to safety, but he admitted to himself that he didn't know where safety lay. Koll's heart pounded, thumping in his ears. Somehow he spoke without screaming.

"Stay here, then, if you want to! I have to see if we're sinking!" He sprinted through the corridor, back into the Great Hall with its shimmering stained glass, and out the great bronze doors into the courtyard.

For a moment, he felt relieved. Water was not, as he had feared, pouring into the castle. It did not appear to be sinking back beneath the waves. Then he looked to the sky and saw the clouds sailing past the castle walls, appearing to move from the north to the south.

Koll dashed across the courtyard and found a stairway leading to the parapet high above the wall. Scrambling up the steps three and four at a time, he stumbled onto the rampart and looked in disbelief at the water below.

The castle wall, like the prow of some impossibly massive ship, plowed through the gray swells of the Sea of Moonshae, tossing up solid curtains of spray from each mountainous wave. The citadel moved across the surface of the water on a steady northerly course! He looked behind them and saw a broad, foaming wake in their path.

"Am I mad?" he asked himself. After a moment's reflection, he decided that the movement of the castle across the ocean did not seem any more improbable than its rising from the depths at the precise moment his boat had sailed above it. It *all* seemed impossible and unbelievable!

He stood there for a long time, like the captain on the bridge of a massive warship, watching the gray swell rolling to the far horizons. Eventually he felt a presence beside him and turned to see that Gwen had joined him on the rampart. She took his hand and leaned against him.

"It *is* a miracle," she said. "The fire told me."

"What?" Koll turned to look full into her face, but he could see no trace of madness. In fact, she looked more confident and self-assured than he had ever seen her.

"I know it sounds crazy," she continued, laughing, "but the fire—I heard it talking to me while you were gone. It spoke with a woman's voice. This is her castle, and she is—was—a queen of the Ffolk who died long ago. Queen Allisynn, bride of Cymrych Hugh."

"You know of her?"

"Her husband was the great hero of my people, the first of our High Kings."

Koll was prepared to believe almost anything now, so the news that the fire had spoken to Gwen did not shake him. Some distant part of himself watched in amazement as he calmly discussed the issue. "And what did she say?"

"She is taking us someplace where there is a task we must perform. I don't know what it is, but it is important, and we are suited for it because I am a daughter of the Ffolk and you are a son of the North."

He turned back to the water, watching the gray waves roll past the castle walls. His seaman's sense told him they sailed north, or perhaps just a little west of true north. He made a guess, based upon their course and his knowledge of the Moonshaes.

"I believe she is taking us to Norland," Koll pronounced.

\* \* \* \* \*

Tristan led the way, blindly driving himself along the bottom of the icy gorge, pulling his companions by the force of his rage. Savage images cavorted through his mind. He saw Canthus, drowned and dead, Daryth mauled beyond recognition. He pictured Yazilliclick frozen in the snow somewhere, Avalon torn and bleeding. He stared unwillingly at the image of the red-haired vixen sprawled naked on his bed and Robyn's wounded face as she opened the door.

I'm going to fail!

The knowledge burned within him, steadily growing into an inferno of fury and threatening to consume him with its fire.

I deserve to fail!

He groaned aloud in his pain, unmindful of Robyn's presence as she followed closely behind him. The others had fallen farther back, unable to maintain his punishing pace. Once he slipped on an icy patch of rock, falling heavily onto his side. The pain was a welcome thing, like a deserved punishment for his multitude of failures.

He attacked the trail even more savagely then, leaping down treacherous, slippery expanses of rock, wedging his way between two boulders as if he would hurl them out of the way. Newt buzzed to his side, looking at him curiously, and the king swatted a hand at the faerie dragon with no more thought than he would have given to striking a bug. Hurt and confused, Newt retreated to accompany Tavish, Pawldo, and Yak.

It was nearly dark by the time they reached a sloping portion of the gorge wall, a place where they could at last climb out of the riverbed that threatened to become a trap. Tristan scrambled up the steep slope, slipping and losing his balance several times as Robyn struggled to stay close. She feared for him, but she dared not interfere.

At the top of the gorge, Tristan started immediately to the north, ignoring the plight of his companions. Yak stayed to help Tavish and Pawldo, both of whom were shivering and exhausted, while Robyn struggled to keep up with the possessed king.

The land above the gorge was barren of trees and gently rolling. It descended toward Myrloch through a series of broad ridges, each of which was bare and snow-covered. At one time, these would have been meadows replete with flowers and bees, but now their very smoothness added to the aura of death.

"Tristan! Stop!" Robyn cried finally, as her own strength began to fail. She stumbled after him, afraid she would fall and that he would continue on, vanishing into the dead vale forever.

But he paused, shaking his head as if trying to awaken from a deep and troubled sleep. As she caught up to him, she saw that he wept like a baby.

For a time, she held him in her arms, willing him to exhaust his grief. She said nothing, hoping that the reassuring embrace would calm him. An ironic image of the maid in his bed came to her, and she stifled an urge to push him away angrily. Suddenly she wanted to hurl his treachery in his face, to remind him of his betrayal.

But instead she held him, wishing him comfort, even wishing that she could forgive him and forget her pain. This she could not do.

He shook his head again and leaned back, looking at her with red, bloodshot eyes. "I'm sorry," he moaned. "By the goddess, I wish you knew how sorry I am!"

"Be quiet," she whispered, pulling him close again. "We need you now! Don't do this to yourself!" She reminded herself of the mission, of their need for Tristan's leadership and his sword. Those things were every bit as important as her own power, and she told herself that it was for their sake that she consoled the king. Her king.

"What can I do? Everything comes to failure and death! How many more of you will I kill today?"

"You haven't killed any of us! Your strength, your mind, and your sword have done nothing but help to keep us alive! Don't let us down now. We need your help more than ever!"

He looked up, as if a thick fog had parted before him, and saw Tavish stumbling toward them, followed by Yak. The giant carried the shivering halfling in his arms, and Newt was perched on his broad shoulder.

"We've got to camp before dark," Tristan said quietly. "Let's see if we can find some shelter."

The barren ridges offered little in the way of protection. The king tried to wrap his arm around Robyn's shoulders, feeling her shivering as he drew her close, but she pushed away and walked alone. The chattering of Pawldo's teeth was plainly audible. Their wet garments sucked the heat from their bodies, and once again the icy wind had become the primary foe.

Tristan set a more deliberate pace, conscious of the growing darkness around them. Finally he saw an irregularity in the snowy ground and led the party to a small cluster of boulders. The flat earth among them was relatively free of snow.

"It's not much, but I think it's all we're likely to find," he said. He threw his ice-crusted cloak on the ground and gestured Yak to place Pawldo down on it. Robyn and Tavish knelt beside them, grateful for even the minimal shelter offered by the rocks.

"It keeps the worst of the wind off of us at least," said the bard with a forced attempt at cheer.

Tristan leaned back against the frozen rock. "That's not enough, though. If we don't have a fire, we'll never make it to morning."

The truth of the statement was apparent to all of them, just as was the complete lack of firewood within the limits of their view. Pawldo shivered violently, and the chattering of his teeth sounded like a company of horses charging across smooth paving stones.

"I'll try to find some wood. The rest of you stay here and keep as warm as possible." Tristan rose to leave, wondering which direction was the most likely source of fuel.

"Wait," said Robyn. "There's another solution."

Without another word, she reached into her pouch and pulled forth the third scroll, carefully checking to see that the fourth and last one remained safely stored. As she opened the scroll tube, none of them noticed the tiny ruby in her medallion glow and glimmer faintly in its golden sun circlet.

"The mastery of fire," whispered Tavish. "But don't you still need fuel?"

"I have fuel."

Robyn read the scroll quietly, with the same diligent care she had used when casting the mastery of water. As she read, the words disappeared from the parchment, and then the frail skin itself burst into soft, blue flames.

Tristan gasped and reached forward when the flames spread to Robyn's hands, but Tavish held him back. He watched in awe as the flames spread across her arms, and her torso, at last appearing to flicker across her entire body. The fire kept its blue tint, shedding little light, and Robyn gradually faded from view as the flames grew warm, then hot.

Soon a silky blaze wavered before them, reaching six feet

or more from the ground. It flashed and shimmered, a narrow column of fire that radiated warmth like a mound of hot coals. Heat washed over the little party like a soft blanket of hope, and such it was.

The druid became both flame and fuel for the fire that saved their lives. Their wet garments drying, the chill slowly driven from their bones, the little band of companions huddled around the blazing image that no longer bore any resemblance to a human being. The blue fire flickered throughout the long night, and though none of them slept for more than a few minutes at a time, it renewed and revitalized them, bringing hope and heat and life to them all.

Dawn had already begun to lighten the eastern clouds when it began, once again, to snow.

\* \* \* \* \*

*The Darkwell grew mightier, and ever blacker, as the other gods recoiled from the power of Bhaal. The god of murder held forth in the inky pool and felt the greater portion of his presence now lay claim to this place in the Forgotten Realms. Of course, he retained his link to his home plane of Gehenna via a long thread of blackness, invisible to all but those attuned to the will of Bhaal. The thread crossed the myriad planes, through the ether as well, assuring the god of ready contact with his place of origin.*

*Now Bhaal began to view the Darkwell differently than he had in the beginning. Now he saw it as a temporary prison, not as the gate that had allowed him to leave Gehenna and project his self into the prime plane.*

*But, he reasoned, if the thread could be extended not just from Gehenna to the well, but from Gehenna through the well, could he not project himself beyond the limits of the Darkwell? In short, could he not free himself to walk unrestrained upon the Moonshaes, and indeed all of the Realms, not just enjoying the evil of his minions vicariously, but actually participating in that evil, commanding the minions at the point of battle?*

*In his black heart, Bhaal knew that he could. And so he set his energies toward strengthening the thread, giving him* the physical form and the means that would allow him to move beyond the Darkwell. His power grew, aided by the retreat of the other gods and the corresponding enhancement of his own status.

Soon the Moonshaes would tremble, not only under the assault of Bhaal's legions, but also under the footsteps of Bhaal himself.

# ❧ 14 ❧

# FAERIEWALKERS

Tristan awakened slowly, feeling the chill of his rocky backrest penetrating into his flesh. The heavy overcast remained overhead, eternal as ever. Dawn now lightened it from its impenetrable black to a smoky gray. Large, wet flakes of snow drifted slowly downward, melting as they touched his skin but gathering in an ever-thickening blanket on the ground.

Still sleepy, the king reached forth a hand to scratch Canthus's broad head, knowing that the dog would, as always, be curled beside him. Then the memory of the previous day doused him like icewater. He sat up in sudden grief, realizing that the moorhound would never again be there.

He saw Robyn lying motionless on the ground and gasped at the sheer whiteness of her skin. She looked drained of blood, and he wondered if the expenditure of magic that warmed them throughout the night had killed her.

Trying to restrain his alarm, he leaned over the druid and saw that she still breathed, though her breath came in short, shallow gasps. He took her up in his arms and held her close, frightened by the chill within her that seemed to drain the heat from his own body. But gradually, as he leaned back and wrapped her within his cape, her body warmed and her breathing grew deep and steady.

The king heard a stirring beside him and turned to see Tavish sitting up, blinking sleepily and stretching. Pawldo, too, arose, and even Yak's snoring began to sputter. A flurry of snow exploded from what had appeared to be a small

❧ 233 ❧

rock, and Newt's head popped free from his powdery blanket. This morning the dragon's scales were a deep blue, almost purple.

"What's for breakfast?" he asked.

"The usual," groaned the bard, pointing to the only food satchel they had salvaged from the wreck of the boat. "Soggy bread, waterlogged cheese, or wet dried meat—all frozen, of course."

The dragon turned his nose up at the fare, but nevertheless he shook himself free of the snow and buzzed over to the pack to select a few morsels.

Robyn moaned softly, and her eyelids fluttered open as Tristan pulled her closer. She curled against his side, and his heart lifted in momentary elation. Finally she, too, sat up and stretched.

"Will you come with me to the top of the ridge?" Tristan asked. "We need to discuss our route."

She nodded and took the hand he offered as she climbed to her feet. The snow, more than a foot deep now across the barren landscape, crunched beneath their feet as they walked the short distance to the top of the gentle incline that had sheltered them from the worst of the wind.

They saw Myrloch, huge and close now, no more than a mile away to the north. The lake was unfrozen. The dull expanse of its gray surface seemed to absorb what little light filtered through the clouds. It stretched far to the west, and to the full limits of their vision to the north. Only to the right, the east, could they see the shoreline meandering away from them. The snow did not fall thickly enough to obscure their vision much but rather seemed to render the whole scene an image viewed through a foggy window.

"Where do we go from here?" Tristan asked.

Robyn pointed to the eastern shoreline. "Once we reach the lake, we follow as close to the water's edge as we can as we head north. You see those dead trees, there? That's the forest south of Genna's grove. Once we get through those trees, we'll reach a stream—probably dry now, if the other streams and rivers are any indication—that marks the border of her grove itself. We should be there in less than two days' time."

They stood in silence, sharing the vista that had once been so pastoral, so clean. Now the evidence of pollution had become so pervasive that even the snow couldn't cover it. Indeed, the land seemed to dirty the snow, so that the wintery blanket looked gray and muddy in the distance.

"It used to be so beautiful. When I first came to study with Genna, these hills were bursting with every kind of wildflower, and the lake gleamed with such a light that it hurt your eyes to look at it."

"Perhaps it will again, when we are through."

"I don't know. . . ." Robyn turned to look at Tristan, her eyes somber. "I can't help but think that something very profound is happening, something that will change the nature of these isles forever. I doubt that they will ever be the same again."

"We have to try!"

"I know that, and we will try—we *are* trying! And if we triumph, this will not be the place of evil that it is right now. I just feel that it will never again be the Myrloch Vale of the past."

Tristan didn't understand exactly what Robyn felt, but that fact did not surprise him. He had always been rather mystified by the intricacies of her faith.

"We should get started soon," he suggested, "before those damned birds catch up with us again."

"You're right, though we did lose them rather handily yesterday."

"*You* lost them, you mean." Tristan took Robyn's shoulders in his hands and looked full into her green eyes. She started to turn away, then met his gaze, though he could not read her expression. He continued. "You gave us the river that allowed us to escape. You kept us alive last night, when we would all have frozen. You have even given me a reason for living, when it seems as if everything around me is dying because of my own shortcomings!"

"You *cannot* blame yourself! We have all blundered our way through this quest, and we're lucky to still have some hope of reaching the well! But you can't feel sorry for yourself because of the cost." Robyn's tone softened.

"Tristan, you're a good leader. People *follow* you. You are High King of the Ffolk, and you are the finest fighter I have ever seen. This quest is yours as much as it is mine.

"It may be that things between us will never be the same. I don't know. I do know that the most important thing in the world to me is reaching the well and excising the power that holds the druids in stone. I need you to help me get there. Will you do that?"

He looked at her with a new clarity. Her words about the change in her feelings sent a cold knife into his belly, but he understood the task before them, and knew that he had to try. He nodded and answered.

"Let's get started."

\* \* \* \* \*

"Wh-where's the next gate?"

"I is tired! Rest now!"

"C-Come on, Honkah! Just one more gate, then we rest— we rest!" Yazilliclick's urging finally lifted the troll from the mossy log he had collapsed onto. The sprite buzzed into the air, hovering on his gossamer wings, as the troll lumbered along beside him.

"Yer friends gots wine?"

"Oh, yes! L-Lots of wine!" Yazilliclick exaggerated slightly, but hoped that his companion would overlook this slight indiscretion.

The creature, who had confessed to the name of Honkah-Fah-Snooei, reluctantly started across yet another flower-bestrewn meadow, amid clouds of hummingbirds and fat honeybees.

"Dis way."

The sprite flew joyfully above, beside, and around him, delighted to be back among the pastoral reaches of Faerie. Overhead beamed the never-setting, gently warm sun that gave this realm a constant springlike air. Faerie was a small realm, not even as large as a single of the Moonshae Islands. It was enclosed in a bubble of magic that held it safe from the intrusions of more violent and brutal planes.

Yazilliclick saw that it hadn't changed much, if at all, since he had departed through a gate to the Forgotten Realms. They came upon a band of satyrs—manlike creatures with tiny horns on their foreheads, and the hind legs and tails of goats—playing their pipes and dancing in the sunshine. A beautiful wood nymph appeared, her silken gown shimmering in the soft sunlight. She glanced coyly at Yazilliclick, and he blushed and looked away from her tiny, alluring eyes. Then the satyrs spied her and took up the chase, calling and crying to the nymph to stop and please them.

She giggled, her voice a trill like a tiny brook, and flew through the woods, leading the satyrs on a long and delightful chase. The sprite knew that they would never catch her. After all, they never had before, and things in Faerie never changed.

They saw other creatures of Faerie, kin to Yazilliclick's own folk, such as pixies, dryads, and leprechauns. These dwellers called and beckoned to the odd pair, but the sprite kept the troll directed on his mission.

"How did you g-get your name, anyway—anyway?" asked Yazilliclick. "D-Does it mean anything?"

"Honkah-Fah-Snooie good name. It mean 'He-whose-nose-casts-shadow-over-ten-thousand-blossoms.' " Honkah proudly gestured to his impressive proboscis. "My nose great nose, even for troll, eh?"

"Oh, yes, it is—it is! I—I have never seen such a wonderful n-nose!"

Pleased, Honkah picked up the pace a bit, stepping across a crystalline stream on a series of strategically located stones. Dozens of fat trout looked up at them from the water as they crossed.

Yazilliclick turned suddenly as the bushes beside him rustled. He saw a brown canine face, topped by perky upraised ears, looking at him. A pink tongue lolled from a wide mouth as the creature seemed to smile at him.

"A b-blink dog—dog! Hi there!" The sprite hovered lower to pat the dog on the head, but suddenly it disappeared from view. Yazilliclick looked around and saw it grinning at him from behind a tree several dozen feet away. He darted over to it, but it blinked again, this time teleporting itself to the far side of the stream they had just crossed, where it was joined by a half-dozen of its fellows.

"I give up," the sprite said with a laugh. "Y-You just can't catch those guys—guys!" But the chase delighted him as had little else in recent years.

He buzzed back to Honkah's side, for the troll had begun tapping his foot impatiently. A feeling of warm well-being grew within the sprite, making him want to remain in Faerie forever. This was such a delightful, pleasant place. He found it hard to remember why he had ever left in the first place.

But then he remembered his friends and his mission. In truth, his companions were becoming a blurry memory to him already. He even had a hard time picturing Newt in his mind, unless he concentrated very hard. But he felt certain that they needed his help, and were in terrible danger, and some driving force within him compelled him to go to their aid. Perhaps he had been changed by his years in the Realms, for such a compulsion could certainly never have affected a creature who had spent all his life in Faerie.

"Here gate," grunted Honkah, pointing to a bank of earth exposed at the bottom of the steep hillside.

The sprite saw that this gate, like the half-dozen they had already visited, was framed by a thick layer of green moss and lay in a shady part of a lightly forested area. There was nothing about it to tell the unaware explorer that this was anything other than a bare patch of ground.

He realized how fortunate they were that the gates in Faerie were much closer together than their connecting points in the other worlds. This had enabled them to investigate a variety of locations in a few hours, covering distances that would have taken several days to reach had they been traveling through Myrloch Vale.

"T-To Myrloch Vale?"

"Yup, to vale. Lotsa gates to Myrloch Vale."

"Well, I'll see if I can find some sign of my friends," said the sprite. He stepped up to the bank of dirt and put his hands out, feeling the moist earth until he discovered a place where he met no resistance. Boldly he stepped through.

He popped back out in a second, sputtering and soaking wet. "It's under w-water! I c-couldn't see anything—anything! Wh-what kind of a g-gate is this that goes to the b-bottom of a lake or a river or s-something?"

Honkah looked puzzled, scratching his flat head. "Not under water last time. Must be wrong place."

"I *told* you things have ch-changed! Oh, I g-give up! I—I don't th-think I'll ever find them—find them!"

"What that?" asked Honkah, cocking his head to the side and listening.

"Wh-what's what? I didn't hear—"

"Shhh!" The troll lifted a warty finger to his mouth, still listening. Yazilliclick, too, concentrated, and then he heard the sound from the gate.

"Something's howling! Wh-what can it be—it be?"

"Honkah look." The troll stood up and leaned through the gate. It looked to the sprite as if the top half of the troll was buried in a hole in the ground, and only his lower torso and legs remained visible. Then Honkah reappeared, clutching a squirming shape in his broad arms.

The newcomer sprang free and leaped to the ground. In the same instant that Yazilliclick recognized him, he shook his body from head to tail, spraying both of them with cold water.

"Canthus! How are you—are you? Wh-what were you d-doing in the water? Wh-where're Robyn and Tristan and N-Newt? Are they all right—all right?" He stopped suddenly, feeling a little foolish as he realized that the dog could not understand him.

The dog greeted him with a slurping lick across his face that knocked him down, then turned to regard Honkah suspiciously. Yazilliclick stood and patted the dog's head, meanwhile taking Honkah's large hand. This apparently convinced the moorhound that the troll was no threat, and he began to sniff the air and look around curiously.

"C-Canthus, welcome to Faerie!"

\* \* \* \* \*

Shantu raised its blood-spattered head as the distant call came to its upraised ears. The displacer beast spread its lips in a snarl of challenge, returning once again to tear at the bloody form of its victim. The sharp, driving fangs tore into the unicorn's flesh to rip away another chunk of meat.

The wound in Shantu's flank still caused the beast searing pain. The snapped horn of the unicorn remained wedged at the base of the monster's tentacle, and all of its efforts to knock it free had only succeeding in driving it deeper.

The deathbringer crouched possessively at the side of the kill. It growled at the surrounding woods, a rumbling challenge to any who dared dispute the beast's claim. Shantu was king of the vale! King of death! And the king would tear the life from any usurper.

But even the king has a master, and now the summons from that master came once again into Shantu's black head. The beast growled and backed away from the bloody corpse, raising its head once again to snarl its challenge at the heavens and the earth.

With a last lingering look at the torn, mangled carcass, Shantu the displacer beast turned back to the woods and disappeared. Its gait was slow and awkward, since the biting pain of its wound raged anew every time the beast's right forepaw touched the ground. The horn stuck out from the shoulder, wedged between two bones. Limping, Shantu started the long trek commanded by its master.

It ran to the north, for it had been ordered back to the Darkwell.

*　*　*　*　*

The massive lodge of Grunnarch the Red had been specially adorned for the Council of Winternight. The plunder of a lifetime of raiding was hauled from cellars and sheds, from storage and from use, to decorate the rough-hewn log walls of the great councilhouse.

Now the lords of Norland entered and took their seats at long tables, heavily laden with food and drink, amid splendor such as rarely seen by the men of the north. From the ceiling hung three crystal chandeliers from the master craftsmen of Amn. Tapestries and silkworm rugs of exquisite workmanship, the plunder of many raids along the coast of Calimshan, decorated the walls.

The tables themselves were covered with golden and silver finery—plates, platters, and goblets of precious metal from as far as Waterdeep and other ports along the Sword Coast. Candles perched gracefully in the chandeliers, and several massive fires set in huge fireplaces cast a golden light across the gathering that was only partially obscured by the growing haze of smoke in the air.

For a long time, the feasting proceeded with good humor and great appetite. Boars and sheep and heaping platters of fish were all consumed in turn, as were keg after keg of smooth, imported wine and whiskey. Finally, as the last of the meat was reduced to clean-picked bones, Grunnarch the Red pushed back his thronelike chair and stood.

The Red King, as was his right and custom, sat at one end of the rectangular lodge, at a table on a platform somewhat higher than the main floor of the room. As he stood, his red beard bristling and his equally scarlet mane flowing smoothly about his shoulders, he became plainly visible to all the men in the lodge. Slowly their conversations died as they waited to hear why their liege had summoned them for the unusual winter council.

"Lords of Norland and the north, warriors of my country, I greet you at a time of grave importance, a crossroads in the history of our people on these isles.

"Norland is the greatest nation of the north, the leading light among those of us who have come to the Moonshaes in the past centuries. Yet in the recent past, we have suffered gravely for the errors of our neighboring kings, for the wrongful war we were compelled to fight by a force beyond our understanding!"

The hush was complete now, as Grunnarch's surprising words sank into the ears of his listeners. Rarely would a man of the north admit a mistake, even in the confidential council of his closest friends, and here was their king stating that they had made an error before the assembled lords and fighters of Norland!

"I have just returned from a kings' council with an ally of great standing, a wise ruler who was once our enemy. He has guided his people with good judgment and rare compassion. I shall declare before you all that he is now a friend of the North.

"He is a man who came to my rescue, and the rescue of my crew, only minutes after we would have claimed his ship as a prize. Then he offered the hospitality of his keep, the comfort of his food and wine, and the repairs to see our ship safely home."

A quiet rumble began to spread through the hall, for those of Grunnarch's men who had returned with him from Corwell understood of whom he spoke. Disbelief spread through the room as they shared this knowledge, in whispers, with their neighbors.

"Our ally, a king who will be my friend unto death, is King Tristan Kendrick of Corwell, High King of the lands of the Ffolk!"

The whispering died in sudden shock, and then the growing murmurs of outrage became audible, growing quickly in force and articulation.

"What madness do you say?" demanded Eric Graybeard from his seat at the king's own table.

"My brother fell in battle at Corwell!" proclaimed Urk Bearstooth, also at the Red King's table. "You cannot ask me to forget a bloodquest!"

Grunnarch stood impassively before them, allowing their rage to run its course. He remembered Taggar's prophecy and hoped the old cleric was right, as he had been many times in the past. A messenger to the council such as the one Taggar had foretold—perhaps even one of the men seated before him—could offer valuable words at this time of emotional torment. But no one voice rose above the tumult, and it began to appear to Grunnarch that the rage of his followers was growing in fury, not dying away.

"Silence!" His command rang through the lodge and, within a few seconds, was obeyed by all.

"You speak of bloodquests, and madness, and a tradition of war! I ask—nay, demand—that you look where these traditions, where our warfare and raids and plunder have gotten us! You know that the fish are dying in our waters! You know that our own brother, Thelgaar Ironhand, was slain by a Beast which then used us—you and me—as tools to achieve its own foul ends! Can it be that . . ."

Grunnarch stopped, seeing the door at the opposite end of the lodge burst open. He immediately thought of the prophecy and the messenger Taggar had predicted. Could this be the messenger?

He saw a trusted warrior, a man who had served the Red King for twenty years, standing there with his face flushed and his jaw hanging slackly. The man, the king remembered, had been assigned as lookout over the bay for the duration of the council.

"Speak, man! Why have you interrupted us?"

"Your kingship," the man stammered, his voice barely a croak. The others in the room turned in astonishment, amazed at the impudence of the intruder. "S-Sailing into the bay, even now approaching the docks . . . It's . . ." His voice trailed away, and he looked pleadingly at his king.

"Tell us!" roared Grunnarch the Red. "What manner of ship do you see? What flag does it fly?"

"No flag, sire . . . no flag at all. And it is—I should say it isn't . . ." His voice died, and it was clearly a great effort to speak. "Sire, it isn't a ship at all, though it sails across the water with speed and purpose.

"It is a castle!"

*　*　*　*　*

The gradual descent to the shore of Myrloch passed easily for the companions. The snow crunched underfoot, packing into a solid path for the second and subsequent companions, and once again the group alternated the lead.

Once they passed another of the great, smoking fissures that commonly marred the ground of the vale. This one, a gaping slash more than a hundred feet long, issued gouts of colorful smoke and noxious gas, but not as constantly as did the freshly formed crevasses. They skirted the gap carefully, giving it a wide margin and noting that it must be a source of heat, for the snow had melted back from the edge on all sides.

Finally they stood upon the shore of the great lake, amid snow-covered boulders. The dark water lapped at the fringes of the stones, in stark contrast to the whiteness of the land all around them.

Dead fish floated, belly up, along the visible length of the shore. Long tendrils of sick-looking weeds snaked through the water, brown and putrid in visible evidence of the pollution. Robyn turned suddenly away from the lake, unable to look at it.

"Yuk!" Newt commented, hovering over the water and looking down.

"Let's go," urged Tristan. Even he was repulsed by the look of this lake that had, all of his life, symbolized pristine natural beauty. "This way."

He led them to the right, following the shoreline but remaining a short distance from the water to avoid the rocks that prevented easy passage near the lake. As it was, they were able to pick a relatively smooth and unobstructed path.

"Look. Sticky stuff!" It was Yak who called their attention to the water after they had walked along the shore for half a mile or so.

"What *is* that?" Tavish wondered aloud, seeing the patch of black slime atop the water that had caught the firbolg's attention.

"Looks like more tar." Tristan stepped to the water's edge, but he didn't need to touch the stuff to confirm his identification. "It seems to be seeping up from the bottom."

"Let's go!" Robyn's voice, nearly a shriek, startled them all. "Let's get away from here!" She started into the lead, desperate to escape the growing evidence of desecration.

Finally they made out the gaunt outlines of leafless trees, a dark line on the horizon before them. The scene was heartbreakingly bleak, but Tristan found it a relief to have some kind of physical goal before them—anything but the awful monotony of the snow-covered fields and blackened water that had surrounded them for so long.

And, too, he knew that somewhere within those woods awaited their destination.

They all quickened their pace unconsciously, and gradually the distant mass of the forest became individual trees. The wood was as bleak and desolate as any other in the vale. Even the snow covering the branches of the trees did not alleviate the bleakness of the scene. If anything, it served to highlight the death of the forest.

Tristan again took the lead, heading toward the wood on a path that veered slightly away from the shore, when he heard Robyn approach from behind.

"Do you feel anything strange?" she asked.

He stopped and looked around, wondering what she meant. His eyes were drawn to the forest, to the still trees and the barren, snowy ground. As he stared, he felt a prickling along the nape of his neck.

"Yes, I do. It's like something is staring back at us from the woods."

"I feel it, too. I don't know why, but the feeling is very strong. There's something there!"

"Should we change our course?" he asked, wondering where they could go instead.

"I don't think so. We're getting too close to the well now. We'll just have to go in with our eyes open."

And our swords loose in their scabbards, thought the king, though he said nothing out loud. The feeling of being observed, that an unknown presence lurked in the woods, grew stronger as he resumed the march. He felt terribly exposed here on the flat, open ground, but he could see no ready alternative to approaching the forest, so he led the companions on.

They moved still closer to the woods, until they had to crane their heads to look up to see the tops of the trees. Every tiny branch was now visible in sharp relief, and they could see the falling snow sifting down far back into the uncannily still forest.

"Look . . . behind us!" Robyn's cry of alarm whirled the king in his tracks, and his heart sank as he looked up into the sky.

"It's the deathbirds! The whole damned flock!" shouted Pawldo, breaking into a run.

Indeed, the ghastly predators soared eerily toward them, gliding silently below the layer of clouds. The companions' concentration on the woods had proven to be a tragic mistake.

"Run! To the trees!" Tristan shouted, drawing the Sword of Cymrych Hugh in the same instant. He urged Robyn, Tavish, and Pawldo past him. Newt hovered at his shoulder and Yak spun beside him, shaking a hamlike fist at the sky as the creatures dropped into a shallow dive.

"Hurry!" Tristan cried, stumbling after his companions. The trees did not offer perfect safety, but they would provide some protection against the swooping flight of the predators. He sprinted through the snow that now seemed to clutch his boots with pernicious intent, striving to drag him down. Desperately he raced on, casting a look back over his shoulder at the flying monsters.

In his heart, he knew that they wouldn't make it to the woods.

\* \* \* \* \*

Once again Hobarth walked the dark passages between this world and the next, following the contours of the planar fabric that allowed him to enter in one place and emerge in a different location when he returned to the Realms.

In this particular instance, he crossed from Oman's Isle to Gwynneth, into the kingdom of Corwell, and finally to the town itself. He returned to the prime plane on the outskirts of Corwell Town, near dusk on a chilly wintery eve.

Of course, the sahuagin and the legions of the dead would take longer to make the same journey, but not too terribly much longer. And when they arrived, he would be ready.

He found a town that was friendly and warm, with pleasant fires burning in the hearths of most of the wooden cottages of the Ffolk. Several larger buildings made of stone commanded the waterfront, and the whole community was surrounded by a pitiful little wall, no more than waist high.

Hobarth found a small tavern called the Inn of the Great Boar. The place was warmed by a pleasant fire, and he went inside to rent a room. He thought it would be pleasant to sleep in an actual bed for a change, and in truth, the weariness of his travels had begun to weigh heavily on him.

Hobarth enjoyed watching the Ffolk of Corwell going about their petty tasks of barter and purchase, consumption and labor. How they would regret their foolish complacency! In a few short days, their lives would change irrevocably—for those few that survived.

He enjoyed a glass of warm ale, and then another, strolling out onto the porch of the inn as the grayness began to fade to black. He could barely make out the outline of Caer Corwell, perched so proudly and so precariously on its little knoll. The cleric smiled a secret smile as he thought of the earthquake spell Bhaal had restored to him.

Soon that ancient fortress, the original stronghold of the Ffolk, would come crashing down about them. And even as it fell, the sahuagin and the dead would emerge from the sea.

*　*　*　*　*

*Chauntea, mistress of agriculture, had recoiled with the other gods from Bhaal's roiling presence in the Darkwell. She had grieved for the destruction of land and life as that murderous god had worked his will.*

*But now she sensed a glimmer of life, and of hope, from near the heart of his realm. It was not strong nor constant, but it seemed to be her only promise, however faint, of a tool to use against the god of murder and death.*

*Chauntea had suffered much, perhaps more than any other god, from the passing of the Earthmother. The two deities had shared more than immortal sisterhood, for they had both cherished notions of growth and health, nature and life. The balance, prime tenet of the Earthmother's faith, was a necessary conviction of those who would work the land and grow crops and raise livestock. Without winter, of course, there could be no spring.*

*Now the passing of the goddess and the claiming of her*

lands—her body, in truth—by Bhaal struck Chauntea as a grievous wrong, a blight upon the face of all the planes.

But there was a hope now, at least the glimmer of one, in the person of this flicker of life and strength near Bhaal's own foul stronghold. Chauntea studied the signs well and came to know this thing as a human follower of the goddess, a druid.

This human would no doubt paint Chauntea, with the broad brush used by such druids, as one of the new gods and hence an enemy of the land. However, she was a person of great strength and faith, plus a powerful aptitude. Her use of scrolls normally reserved for Chauntea's own clerics provided ample proof of this. And she carried a medallion of faith, for this was how Chauntea knew of her presence.

Perhaps, if this druid remained strong, Bhaal would not gain a complete triumph. Perhaps some vestige of the land would remain in its natural state.

Perhaps.

# ❦ 15 ❦

# DANCE OF THE DEATHBIRDS

The snow dragged against Tristan's feet, slowing him to an agonizing plod. He saw Pawldo fall, with the tree line a good twenty paces away. The halfling struggled to his feet, whirling and unslinging his bow in the same motion, and Tristan turned to fight beside him.

The Sword of Cymrych Hugh hummed with anticipation as he raised it toward the oncoming flock. The leading deathbird swooped toward him, its antlers spread like a phalanx of deadly spear tips.

Tristan saw a flash of motion out of the corner of his eye, and Pawldo's arrow darted into the sky, piercing the monster's wing and bringing it tumbling to the ground. Even in pain, it made no sound, though the thump of its body and the cracking of its neck were plainly audible as it crashed.

More of the monsters swerved toward the king, seeming to blacken the sky before him. Silently he vowed to slay as many as he could before he fell, and the sword in his hands thrummed with the shared conviction.

A volley of arrows arced through the air over his head, knocking six or eight of the beasts from the sky. Instinctively the king readjusted his defense to face the nearest surviving attackers, and then his mind reacted. A volley! From where? Pawldo was a rapid archer, to be sure, but no man could shoot several arrows simultaneously!

But he had no more time to contemplate the source of this unexpected succor as two more of the monsters slashed toward his face. The sword flicked upward like a lightning bolt as the deer-skull face of one attacker ducked to drive its antlers home. The point drove deep into the creature's breast, and the sword sang with grim satisfaction.

The second deathbird veered to avoid the falling body of its partner, and as it did, the point of an antler struck the king a glancing blow on his shoulder. The sturdy chain of his father's armor absorbed the blow and snapped the tip of the horn, and one blow from the gleaming sword struck the creature on the back of its neck and lopped its stag-skull from the bird's body.

More of the things were on him instantly, and it seemed as if his world had been reduced to a vision of frantically beating wings, sharp antlers, widespread mouths hungry for his blood, and hollow, empty eye sockets. Antlers scraped his face, and blood flowed freely into his eyes. He took repeated heavy blows to his chest and back, which only his armor prevented from driving deep into him.

He fought back desperately, a whirlwind of slicing, slashing death. He cut the deathbirds from the air, slaying one, driving another back with one leg hanging limp, flopping a third to the ground as he severed its wing.

Another volley of arrows, gleaming silvery bright even under the bleak overcast, whistled overhead and struck several more of the monsters from the sky. Suddenly the entire flock was swirling around the companions in a vicious melee, antler against sword and dagger and even fist, for Yak waded into the thickest of the flock, bashing tirelessly with his great, clubbed hands. A deathbird vanished in a cloud of feathers and bones, annihilated by a single powerful blow. Another twisted and squirmed as the firbolg seized it around the neck and squeezed the life from its obscene body.

Tristan caught a glimpse of Robyn, surrounded by a swirling cloud of feathers and antlers. Silver gleamed, and the scimitar she had inherited from Daryth of Calimshan claimed an unnatural victim. The druid wielded the weapon with skill and grace, using it like a sickle to harvest the foul creatures from the sky.

The king lunged and hacked his way to her side. Pawldo fought alongside him, sticking and thrusting with his dag-

ger and somehow managing to hold the deathbirds at bay.
Yak stood protectively over the bard as Tavish poked awkwardly with her shortsword at the swirling predators.

A fountain of colored lights exploded among the flock,
scattering them temporarily, and Newt popped into view in
the center of the display.

"Scatter, you stupid buzzards, or I'll turn you all into spar-
rows!" With a great display of teeth, the faerie dragon dove
at one of the deathbirds, sinking his fangs into the thing's
tail and sputtering away with a mouthful of feathers. The
monster swerved around and joined several others as they
dove at the faerie dragon.

Once more Newt disappeared, deciding invisibility was
the safest defense against the raging fowls. The predators
darted and swooped in the direction of their vanished quarry, and Tristan took advantage of the confusion to stab
another in the belly, dropping the creature like a stone.

The attackers turned once more toward the companions,
and the king heard Robyn, behind him, cry out in pain. A
rack of antlers struck him in the back, jolting him forward
and knocking the wind from his lungs, but he somehow
maintained his footing. Once again the chain mail had prevented a wound. Spinning, he cut the creature from the air
as it tried to climb away.

Then he saw a line of figures, perhaps half a dozen of
them, advancing through the snow. Dressed in white furs,
they emerged from the trees and moved toward the battle.
He saw longbows and quivers slung across their backs, but
now they attacked with silver swords extended. Again the
king whirled to protect his flank, slaying another deathbird,
but he turned back in the next instant to stare at the newcomers.

Who were they? Where did they come from? These and a
thousand more questions stormed through his brain, but he
saw several of the silver swords dart through the air and
slice into the obscene avians. Whoever they were, they
were friends.

Robyn stumbled, a bloody gash on her shoulder, and Tristan hurried to her side. One of the monsters flapped toward

his face, revealing wolfish fangs in its bony maw, but the king brought the sword of his ancestors crashing down onto the thing's skull and it tumbled into the trampled snow. With a quick thrust, he killed it.

Now the fur-cloaked figures were fighting all around them, and the odds were shifting in their favor. As the newcomers moved easily across the ground, Tristan saw that each wore a pair of light snowshoes. Perhaps half of the deathbirds had fallen, and the remaining creatures could no longer gang up on an opponent four or five at a time. Tristan could see little of the strangers beneath their winter garments, but he caught a glimpse of wide brown eyes beneath one hood. A long lock of blond hair spilled from another.

Yak lunged forward with a loud bellow, seizing a flying deathbird by its claws. The firbolg swung the creature around in a circle before smashing its skull against the frozen ground. Tristan, Pawldo, and Robyn joined in the charge, disrupting the flock with a sudden attack. Then the strangers followed their lead and rushed forward. The entire flight of monsters lurched into the air, beating their ungainly wings in an attempt to evade the deadly swords.

Tristan lunged at one that passed high overhead, and the Sword of Cymrych Hugh seemed to pull him upward, striking the creature's belly at the height of the king's prodigious leap. In moments, the horrid creatures had risen too high for their blades, flapping their great wings with unseemly urgency as they fled the scene of battle.

The newcomers threw back their hoods and unslung their bows. The king saw, with instant recognition, the shocks of golden hair, the slender and serious faces, the breathtaking beauty of each of the warriors. He stood, amazed and exhilarated, watching the silver arrows dart into the sky, bringing down more and more of the monsters until at last the survivors, no more than a dozen or so, had flown out of range to the north.

Tristan did not speak until the last of the bows had been lowered and the leader of the band of warriors turned to regard him with her wide brown eyes.

"Brigit, your arrival could not have been better timed! I feared that we faced the end of our quest right here on this snowy field."

The sister knight's face lightened with the barest suggestion of a smile. "Your quest is the hope and prayer of more than you realize, Tristan. We could not stand by when we had the power to aid you."

He stepped forward and embraced the petite warrior, a gesture which she shyly returned. He looked around and recognized Maura, the tiniest of the sister knights, and Colleen, and several others, the remnants of the brave company that had served him during the Darkwalker War. These female fighters of the Llewyrr had ridden chargers and carried silver lances then. Now they fought in furs and snowshoes, with longbow and sword. But always they battled with courage and consummate skill.

"My Lord King," said Brigit, bending at the waist in the slightest of bows. "The Sisters of Synnoria are at your service once again."

\* \* \* \* \*

The moorhound bounded in an ever-growing circle around Yazilliclick and Honkah-Fah-Snooei, stopping every several moments to shake more droplets of water from his shaggy coat.

"Why you know wolf?" asked the troll, looking suspiciously at the sprite.

"W-Wolf? He's no wolf. He's a dog—a dog! Like a blink dog, kind of, only he's b-bigger and he d-doesn't blink." Yazilliclick laughed at the notion of Canthus as a wolf. "He's m-my friend, and the f-friend of my friends, t-too!"

"Dog-friend?" The troll slowly absorbed the thought, and then his face brightened. "Dog-friend gots wine?"

"N-No! People gots—people *have* wine. The d-dog just g-goes with them—with them."

"Crud. We rest now." Honkah plopped himself on a fallen tree trunk and looked wistfully at Canthus and the gate. "I gots to go back to my guard gate."

"B-But we're g-guarding a g-gate here, aren't we—aren't

we? You're still a g-guardian troll. You j-just moved to a d-different gate, that's all!"

"Not my gate!"

"H-How often does anyone use y-your gate? Do people g-go through it a l-lot—a lot?"

"Sure! Just now, you did."

"I—I know. But how long before m-me?"

Honkah scratched his head, squinting his tiny eyes with the effort of his concentration. "Never."

"Well, someone j-just came through this g-gate, too. I bet it's even busier that yours. M-Maybe we should rest here and guard it—guard it! Then we can go find another g-gate, one that's even b-busier!"

The troll looked at him suspiciously but apparently could think of no effective rebuttal. He grunted and turned to stare at the earthen bank, as if expecting an invading army to pour through it in the next instant.

Canthus dropped and rolled in a field of flowers, squirming in delight. He displayed no curiosity or surprise about his transition from the depths of an icy torrent to this sunlit meadow. The moorhound sprang to his feet and bounded over to Yazilliclick, bumping the sprite with his nose and knocking him off the log.

"N-No, Canthus! I c-can't play now—now. I'm helping Honkah g-guard the g-gate!"

Across the meadow, the branches of a thick bush parted, and the head of a blink dog poked through, staring with interest at the trio. The dog, like all of its kind, had smooth brown fur, a pointed muzzle, and floppy ears that perked upward when, as now, the creature was attentive. The blink dog was about half the size of the moorhound.

The faerie dog suddenly teleported itself across the meadow, popping into sight right in front of Canthus. The moorhound barked sharply and leaped backward in surprise, then leaned toward the blink dog. The two canines sniffed each other tentatively, and then the blink dog popped out of sight, only to reappear across the meadow, with another of its kind beside it.

Canthus barked again, confused, then raced across the

meadow to once again sniff the other canines' noses, followed by a more intimate examination of each other. Abruptly both dogs of Faerie popped out of sight.

This time four of them appeared near the center of the meadow, and Canthus leaped over to them, his tail wagging playfully. The blink dogs, too, frolicked and rolled about the moorhound, and soon six of them had Canthus racing and chasing about the meadow.

Yazilliclick whooped with laughter at the dogs' antics, and even Honkah chuckled a bit before climbing gruffly to his feet. " 'Nuff rest! Show next gate now."

"O-Okay. C-C'mon, Canthus!" The moorhound ran to the sprite as Yazilliclick hovered in the air. They started off along a winding Faerie trail, following Honkah, the six blink dogs bounding and blinking along beside them.

\* \* \* \* \*

"This is the sign! The prophecy! Listen to me, men of the North, if you would heed your own salvation!" Taggar, aged cleric of Tempus, sprang onto the table like a young man. He banged a large serving spoon against a huge golden platter, ignoring the dents his blows inflicted on the precious plate.

The northmen in Grunnarch's great lodge, stunned by the events of the last few hours, looked on quietly, as if this uncharacteristic display was merely another piece of evidence that their world was falling to pieces around them.

And in a sense, perhaps it was. First there had been Grunnarch's declaration of a peace with one of their oldest and most bitter enemies. Then a great gleaming castle had sailed into the very harbor of the town, witnessed by all of them as they had poured forth to behold the miracle. It was a building finer than any existing in Norland, yet it sailed upon the water with the grace and speed of a sleek longship.

Third had come the message of the two people who had ridden the castle to Norland, the tall, proud young man and the plump, pretty maid. The Iron Keep had fallen! The settlements on the coast of Gwynneth had been razed!

And finally the message from the lips of the maid, who claimed to have heard it from a fire that had blazed even as the castle emerged from the sea. The next target of the army that had laid waste to Oman was Corwell, the very kingdom Grunnarch had so recently sworn to aid and defend!

Now the cleric stood atop a table and banged a spoon against a plate. Well, why not?

"Men of my lands, brave warriors of Norland, listen to me!" Grunnarch stood, his red hair seeming to blaze in the firelight. His eyes, too, blazed, and he fixed each of his followers with a commanding gaze. Taggar climbed stiffly down from the table and sat, satisfied that the king would explain the significance of the sign.

"This same cleric came to me two nights ago, in the presence of two chiefs, Urk Bearstooth and Eric Graybeard, who will vouch for my words, and gave me a prophecy. It was a prophecy direct from the lips of Tempus!" He held the rapt attention of every man in the room now. Tempus was not a kind god, but he was strong and fair and had long been the favorite of the men of the North. They could not but heed his advice.

"These are the words of Tempus, given before this council commenced: 'A messenger will arrive at the council, traveling not by foot or by mount, nor by ship. But he will arrive with the commands of Tempus upon his lips, and you must—you *must*—heed those words!'

"And now we are given to see this miracle, this edifice of stone that glides across the sea, and to hear the words of the one who has arrived during our council." Now Grunnarch lowered his voice, and an absolute hush fell over the hall.

"I shall take the *Northwind* to sea at first light, alone if I must, to heed the commands of Tempus. I sail to the aid of the king who saved my life when no good reason gave him cause to do so.

"And I go to atone for the evil we, the men of the North, have wrought upon these isles in the past year, to atone for the service we gave—albeit unknowingly—to the heart of evil itself, that came to us in the form of Thelgaar Ironhand. I shall confront the root of this evil and slay it, or I shall die trying. Do I sail alone, men of Norland?"

The walls shook, and the fires in the hearths blazed high from the force of the resounding chorus: "No!"

\* \* \* \* \*

Randolph slipped quietly through the gatehouse of Caer Corwell, thankful for the early darkness that concealed his movement from any watcher within the keep. He walked briskly down the castle road, meeting no one, and passed through the unguarded north gate of Corwell Town. He went immediately to the Inn of the Great Boar, passing from the chill darkness into a smoky warmth, from the silence to an atmosphere of quiet laughter and pleasant conversation.

Here his eyes quickly sought out Lord Mayor Dinsmore of Corwell Town and the lords Koart and Dynnatt.

"What is the meaning of this?" inquired Dynnatt as Randolph sat at a table. "Why the secrecy and subterfuge?"

None of them took notice of the obese stranger who sat at the next table, nor did they see the man lean closer to overhear their conversation. As he listened, the man's eyes narrowed to evil, hooded slits in his face.

"I wish we didn't have to meet like this," said Randolph. "Frankly, we need to talk without Pontswain present. I believe the kingdom is facing a very grave threat, and he prefers to lounge around, feasting and drinking like a king. He spends most of his time staring at the Crown of the Isles!"

The other men grunted in acknowledgment, not surprised by the description. "What is this threat you speak of?" asked the Lord Mayor.

Randolph described the message from the fisherman, informing the others that he had sent a fast boat to investigate. "But we might not hear anything until it's too late!"

"Indeed, that's Pontswain for you," grumbled Koart. "When we fought here last year, he held his company safe at home, as if his cantrev was the heart of the kingdom."

"And so he would again, except I believe he still wishes to take up residence in Corwell as our king. He would shed few tears if King Kendrick does not return from his quest."

"What do you suggest?" asked Dynnatt.

"Can you men muster your companies and prepare

them—quietly—to move to Corwell? I hope I'm wrong about this, but if we are attacked from the sea, we'll have precious little warning, and the town militia, together with the men of your two cantrevs, are all we could expect to have in place."

"The men won't like this . . . a winter muster," objected Koart. "And my company lost heavily fighting the Darkwalker."

"Indeed, as did all of ours." Randolph accepted the objection patiently. "I will do my best to see that your men are rewarded when the king returns, regardless of the outcome. But we must take some action."

"I agree." The Lord Mayor, with the most to lose in the event of a seaborne invasion, was the first to concur. It took several minutes of coaxing, and the promise of such reward as Randolph thought King Kendrick could manage, before the other two lords would accept.

"Very well. I thank you, good lords, for meeting me under such unusual circumstances, and I pray that my worries are groundless. Good evening." Randolph rose and bowed to the men before he left the inn. The three lords decided to enjoy a few more pitchers of ale before retiring.

Still none of them noticed the fat stranger, who had leaned back to his own table now, his cruel face twisted by a barrage of frustrations and schemes.

A most fortuitous meeting, this, Hobarth told himself. How in the Realms had Kendrick come to hold the Crown of the Isles? No matter, but the fact that he did put a major crimp in Hobarth's—and Bhaal's—plan. Hobarth had first experienced the crown when it had been held by the weakling, King Carrathal of Callidyrr, and he had no reason to suspect that its properties had weakened any in the hands of King Kendrick. Its property, actually, for the magical element of the crown only served one purpose so far as Hobarth knew.

It created an area of immunity around it. A *large* area of immunity.

When the crown had been held in Caer Callidyrr, Hobarth had been unable to work his clerical spells anywhere within the ample bounds of that vast fortress. Now, in the much smaller Caer Corwell, it would certainly protect that fortress against his castings. There would be no earthquake to tear down the castle walls here.

That is, unless the crown could somehow be removed. And here the plotting of the three lords and the captain had inadvertently provided Hobarth with a vehicle for accomplishing this.

The cleric got up heavily from his table and lumbered from the inn. He would find another, more private establishment and begin to work his plan. He sought out such a place—a quiet, tiny tavern tucked away on a darkened lane beside the waterfront. He entered and spotted a youth tending to some cleaning chores.

"Here, lad," he said, flipping the boy a gold coin and watching the youth's eyes widen in surprise and delight. "I would like you to do me a favor."

"Anything, your lordship!"

"Go up to the castle and find Lord Pontswain. Tell him that a man in town has a proposal for him—a mutually profitable proposition, you may call it. Ask if he would be good enough to meet me here at noon tomorrow to discuss it. Do you understand?"

The lad nodded eagerly.

"Go ahead, then. Be off with you!"

As the door slammed behind the departing youth, Hobarth sat down and accepted a large mug of ale from a barmaid. He felt very pleased with himself.

\* \* \* \* \*

"I found Avalon just after the storm struck. He was horribly wounded, but he lived."

"And he lives still?" Tristan held his breath.

"Yes." Brigit looked somber. "Though his days as a warhorse are over, he lives and grows healthy."

"Thank the goddess for that, at least. One of us thought dead, but alive instead—that is a welcome lightening of the burden of this quest."

"But how did you know we were here?" asked Robyn.

"We knew the desecration of the vale would not go unanswered, and when I found Avalon, we knew that you must be on the way. Then it was simply a matter of observing this flock of strange creatures, for we suspected they were following you, and making the deduction that you would head for the grove of the Great Druid. We planted ourselves upon that path and were proved correct when you came to us."

"You know of the grove? How fares it?" asked the druid.

"It has become an awful place, full of poison and death. The Moonwell itself is corrupt, turned dark and foul. The desolation throughout the vale starts there, spreading outward like a loathsome plague."

"Has it reached Synnoria?" Tristan tried to imagine the beautiful valley of the Llewyrr under the influence of the horrible desolation that surrounded them.

"Alas, you would not know Synnoria for the place you once saw—or heard, I should say." Brigit stopped abruptly, a catch in her voice, and tears welled within her deep brown eyes. "The rivers have ceased to run. Even the songs of the forest have died.

"Most of the Llewyrr have fled, leaving our valley to its fate. We have found temporary succor from our old rivals, the dwarves, who have helped see our people safely from the vale or have sheltered them in their underground fortresses."

Robyn's face drained of color, and Tristan, equally shocked, took her hand as he tried to imagine the magnitude of this disaster. He vividly recalled the sounds of Synnoria, so beautiful that they had all but driven him mad when the Llewyrr had escorted the companions through their valley during the Darkwalker War. They had been blindfolded during the passage because the Llewyrr had assured them that to look upon the beauty of the place would cause madness.

And now Synnoria, like Myrloch Vale, had fallen prey to the cancerous spread of darkness.

"This is the legacy of the Beast, Kazgoroth," sighed Brigit softly.

"No . . . this is the mark of the Beast's master," Robyn

answered bluntly. "But why must the most cherished places be the first ones to die?"

"Perhaps because true beauty is, by its very nature, frail," suggested Brigit.

"Beauty can be strong," argued Tavish, "but its very presence is abhorrent to the kind of evil that now confronts us. I think that is why these are the first places to fall."

"But they will not be the last, unless we prevail. We should get started on the last leg of this journey." Tristan looked at each of his companions, sharing their misery but silently urging their action.

The battlefield fell quickly out of sight as they entered the trees, once again making their way between the barren trunks of rotten oaks, hickories, and pines. Four of the sisters led the way, tromping a flattened path with their snowshoes, followed by Tristan and his companions, with Maura, Colleen, and Brigit, marching in a single file.

They moved in nearly total silence, surrounded by the soft scraping of clumps of snow falling among the dead branches. Winter's frosting grew steadily thicker on the ground.

Gentle, low hills rolled through the forest here, but the walking was easy. After a few minutes, their world had become a place of white snow and black tree trunks. The sifting flakes clouded the air and marked the limits of their vision.

Tristan's hopes rose rapidly with the arrival of the sisters. They were the finest fighters he had ever seen, and he still felt that this conflict would be resolved, in the end, through combat. They knew the vale and were equipped for this early winter in a way that he and his companions were not.

His hopes exploded with the thunderous rumble that shook the ground at his feet. He staggered backward and fell, but not before he saw a monstrous fissure erupt in the ground before him, swallowing the four sister knights who led the party. He saw the hole tear toward him, but something strong grabbed him by the scruff of the neck and pulled him to safety.

Green and red fountains of gas erupted from the fissure,

and the earth groaned as if the wound caused her physical pain. Rotten tree trunks leaned into the gap as the firmament that supported them fell away, slowly toppling into nothingness. Shrieks and cracks split the forest as other trees lost their limbs or toppled whole from the violent convulsions of the land.

Gasping and spitting to clear the traces of gas he had inhaled, Tristan looked up to see that it was Yak who had saved his life. He stood and stared, horrified, at the crevasse that had claimed the lives of four of the sisters. They hadn't had a chance!

The whirling snow settled around them, and at last they could see. But the confirmation of their eyes only deepened their sadness and heightened their sense of despair.

They faced an apparently bottomless fissure, more than a hundred feet wide. It stretched to the limits of sight to the left and to the right. In short, there appeared to be no way around it.

*　*　*　*　*

*The Darkwell bubbled and gurgled, pouring forth black smoke and thick, poisonous gases. Bhaal learned of the defeat of his flock as the surviving perytons came circling back to the well, and his rage caused deep cracks and gaping fissures to explode throughout the land, tearing still further at the wasteland of the vale.*

*Shantu crept to the edge of the black water, sensing his master's anger. The displacer beast crouched there, unmoving, for so he had been commanded. The perytons, too, shifted and flapped in agitation but remained around the well.*

*The body of the corrupted Genna Moonsinger, however, rose from the place where she had been sitting for many days and walked to the water's edge. Her eyes, flashing red, then fading to black, stared ahead at nothing. Then she heard her master's command and turned to leave. Retaining the form of the Great Druid's body, she disappeared into the forest to the south of the well.*

*Bhaal, meanwhile, used his rage to add form to his body.*

*The cord of substance connecting his presence here to his realm of Gehenna had now grown strong and unassailable. He was nearly ready to project himself beyond the Darkwell.*

*The form he had chosen for this projection was appropriate, given the nature of the Forgotten Realms. He would emerge from the well in the body of a man. But it would be no ordinary man. Instead, it would be a creature of awesome, looming size, and a visage terrible to behold.*

*And very soon now it would be ready to emerge.*

# ❧ 16 ❧

# BETRAYALS

Hobarth sighed in a moment of wistful regret. How simple this plan would be, he thought, if only he could cast the simple mage's spell allowing one to charm another person into performing those tasks the caster found useful or desirable. Instead, he was forced to resort to guile and trickery—effective tactics, to be sure, but so much more complicated.

In the next moment, he forgot his regrets. He would never exchange the spiritual depth and multi-planar accomplishments of his clerical skills for the cheap light and fire shows of the wizards. Indeed, he reminded himself—and Bhaal, should his master be listening—Hobarth had often before scorned the chicanery of his sorcerer allies, even while accepting and using their aid.

The cleric looked toward the door of the dingy inn as the hour approached noon. If the man, Pontswain, was true to the nature the lords in the Inn of the Great Boar had ascribed to him the previous night, Hobarth felt certain he would repond to his summons.

Indeed, he recognized the man as soon as he passed through the door of the inn. Lord Pontswain was handsome, with a luxurious spill of brown hair, but he had a tightness in his smile and a narrowness of gaze that told the cleric this certainly was the man for the task.

"My Lord Pontswain, would you care to join me?" The cleric rose and bowed humbly, gesturing to the vacant chair at his table. The man looked suspicious, but he came over and sat down. Good, thought the cleric, pleased. He fits the role perfectly!

"What do you want? My time is valuable, and I dislike these mysterious arrangements."

"Please forgive me. It would not be politic for me to come directly to the castle itself. You see, I am no friend of the Kendricks."

Pontswain's eyebrows raised at the admission, and he waited for the cleric to continue.

"This is no blood feud, I assure you, but years back the father of the current king, on a voyage to the Sword Coast, embarrassed my own father in quite a nasty scene. The details are far too unpleasant for me even to recount.

"Suffice to say that I desire to embarrass the son of that king, and I am willing to pay a handsome sum to do so. No one shall be hurt by this . . . prank, but it is hoped the king will be caused some discomfort."

"What is a 'handsome' sum?"

"You are interested, then?"

"Perhaps. Answer my question, man!"

"Gold . . . in the hundreds. Shall we say two hundred gold pieces upon agreeing to the deal, and an equal sum to be paid upon its completion?"

The lord could not conceal the flash of greed suddenly illuminating his eyes, though he tried to look as if he was carefully considering the offer. Hobarth suspected, correctly, that the sum exceeded the annual tax income that a cantrev lord on Corwell could expect to collect.

"And what do I have to do to collect this gold should I accept?"

"I understand your king has gained a proud symbol of his rank—a crown, or sceptre, or something. All you need do is remove it from his castle and take it to a place of hiding for a time. When he returns, he will be enraged to find it gone. You can arrange to have it returned some time in the future, as you wish. As I explained, I merely desire to cause him some momentary discomfort."

"Why did you seek me for this offer?"

Hobarth silently damned the man's curiosity. He had hoped the money alone would be enough to remove all doubts. "I have stayed in this town for several days. All around I see signs of slavish devotion to this upstart king, as if he is a god descended from the Outer Planes! You, on the other hand, have the reputation of being a free thinker, a man who is no man's lackey. Now answer; will you do this thing?"

Another suspicion lit the lord's eyes. "How do I know you do not wish to steal the crown for yourself?"

Hobarth shrugged. "Take it wherever you wish. I have no desire to see it. I simply want you to remove it from the castle."

"I know just the place," chuckled Pontswain, growing enthusiastic. In fact, he began to embellish the plan on his own. Perhaps the crown would not have to be returned for a very long time. . . . "I shall take it to my own cantrev, where I can be sure it will remain safe."

"Splendid," said the cleric, nodding. "That would be superb!"

"Now, about the gold . . ."

"Of course." Hobarth reached under the table for the sack he had claimed as his share from the plundering of the Iron Keep. He had barely more than two hundred gold, but that was of no matter. This fool would never collect the second payment. "Here. I suggest you take it somewhere private to count it."

Pontswain's eyes widened at the size of the pouch, and his hands trembled as he reached forward to sweep it into his hands. "Yes, of course. But I'm certain you'll have the correct amount, for I have not yet performed your task!" He seemed pleased with his clever deduction, but then his eyes clouded again.

"And where will you meet me with the second payment?"

"You say you will go to your cantrev. Why not there? But one other thing . . . you must do this task within the next two days."

"Two days! But I will need time to plan, to cover my tracks!"

Hobarth shrugged and reached for the sack. "Then I shall have to find someone else. . . ."

"No! Very well, in two days! Meet me at Cantrev

Pontswain four days from now." The lord described the road to his cantrev, which lay perhaps thirty miles away, along the southern shore of Corwell Firth. Hobarth listened patiently, nodding as if he would actually make the trip.

"Now, good luck to you. You'd best be off, before we are observed talking."

"Yes, yes, of course!" the lord replied, nodding and taking a furtive look around the empty inn. Only the unshaven inn-keeper shared the room with them, and he was busily scrubbing the bar. "Four days, then."

"Yes, four days." Hobarth smiled, Pontswain thought because of their arrangement. In reality, the cleric was con-templating the pleasant knowledge that, before four days passed, Caer Corwell would be a heap of rubble, joining the Iron Keep at the bottom of the sea.

\* \* \* \* \*

Once again black night descended around the compan-ions in Myrloch Vale. They were no closer to their destina-tion than they had been at the height of the day. All afternoon they had marched along the vast fissure, moving steadily eastward as they sought a place to cross. But the gap was too wide for even the tallest tree to bridge, seeming to mark an eternal scar across the face of the earth. Now, as darkness fell, they sought a place to make camp in the dead forest, surrounded by the towering proof of the potency of their foe.

The sudden loss of the four sister knights had quelled their rising optimism with brutal abruptness. The long afternoon's march had been glum and silent, aggravated by the frustrating knowledge that their objective lay only a day's march to the north, but every step they took moved them farther away.

Tristan saw Tavish stumble and lean weakly against the firbolg. The bard grew numb with fatigue, and he knew that she wouldn't be able to make it much farther. Only Yak's solid arm and apparently tireless muscles had kept her going this far.

"We'd better move back away from the fissure to camp,"

announced the king as the prepared to stop. "It could grow during the night."

"Very well." Brigit, now in the lead, agreed and turned toward the south. After another ten minutes, they judged themselves safely removed from the pit.

Robyn leaned against a tree and slowly sank to the ground. Her pale face seemed frozen in a look of bleak determination, but the redness in her eyes belied her apparent stoicism. Tristan pulled his tattered cape from his shoulders and spread it on the snow beside the tree. "Sit here. It'll help keep you dry," he said.

The other companions set about making camp in the snowy forest as Robyn moved to sit beside him. When she looked at him, he had never before seen such despair in her eyes.

"What's the use? I don't think we'll ever get there. We might as well turn around and go home!"

"You don't mean that. You can't! We've faced greater obstacles than this before, and we've always overcome them!"

"But I've always had the goddess beside me!" Robyn put her hands over her face so that Tristan could not see her weeping. "She's gone now . . . I know it! This blackness has killed more than the trees and the animals. It's killed the Earthmother herself!"

"Robyn, I know I've never fully understood your faith, but I have always trusted in it. Your faith is still the fiber that holds us all together, that compels us to go on! You may be right . . . perhaps the goddess is gone. But *we* aren't gone! I have seen you, even in the absence of the Earthmother, call a stream from the bare rocks and light a fire with no fuel that kept us all alive through a killing night!"

Tristan reached an arm out to Robyn, but she turned harshly away. The rejection struck through all the layers of his soul, knifing into his heart. In this, her moment of greatest despair, he was powerless to comfort her. He himself had destroyed the bond of trust that had once drawn them together.

He swore a silent, agonized oath. If only he could take back that blurry night in the castle, erase it from his memory, from hers! Tristan would do anything, he vowed, could he but right that wrong. But all this time, Robyn's back, trembling from cold or tears, mocked his good intent.

He recalled his own self-pity and how she had directed his thoughts away from his troubles to their combined hopes. He spoke softly to her, trying to do the same for her.

"You've said that the fourth scroll is the key to freeing the druids from their petrified forms. Well, there's no reason that scroll shouldn't work as well as the others. All we have to do is reach the grove, and I know we will do that!

"I don't know if you can believe me anymore, but I love you more than ever. If that love, whether you return it or not, can help you reach the end of this quest, please accept it. I ask nothing in return." Hesitantly Robyn looked into his eyes and smiled. At least, he thought it was a smile. Actually, it was more a faint twisting of her lips below her tear-stained cheeks and her reddened eyes, but he decided that it counted.

"Let's make camp," she said, very softly.

"Tomorrow we'll cross the fissure," he promised, "and that day, or the next—but soon—we will triumph!" He didn't explain how, and he was relieved that she didn't ask, for of course he didn't know the answer. Nevertheless, he believed in the truth of his words.

\* \* \* \* \*

The wind from the north blew fair, though the gray clouds threatened a winter gale. Even had a storm roared through the bay in full force, Grunnarch the Red would still have put to sea, so compelling was the combination of his own promise, the prophecy, and the miracle of this floating castle that had sailed to the wharf of his town.

That town lay far behind him now, and once again his horizon was defined by the rolling gray swells of the Sea of Moonshae. This time he did not sail alone, however. The bright sails of his countrymen blazed across the gray water, beneath the glowering sky, to all sides. Twenty proud long-ships sliced through the waves in an arrow-straight course to the south.

Before them, its proud spires knifing through the cloud-laden sky, sailed Caer Allisynn. The great stone edifice seemed to coast over the surface of the sea, calming a wide patch of heaving surface by its passage.

The Red King expected another ten ships to join him as they passed the southern tip of his island, for the lords of western Norland had ridden at full speed from the council to their own towns to raise their crews and prepare to put to sea. Then the thirty sleek warships of Norland would sail behind their king to go once again to war on Gwynneth. This time, however, they would fight with the Ffolk, not against them.

"It's a splendid sight, my lord." Koll, the young man from Gwynneth, joined the king in the prow. He had begged to accompany the expedition, and Grunnarch could not turn down such a courageous offer.

"And they will fight a splendid fight, to be sure! Can you wield an axe, lad, as well as you sail a castle?"

Koll grinned sheepishly. "I have yet to blood my blade, but I have been taught by the greatest fighters on the north coast."

"You speak bravely. I like that in a man!" Grunnarch paused, remembering the scene at the dock as they had prepared to sail. "Your woman, Gwen—she did not understand that war is a man's task?"

"No, sire. The Ffolk are odd that way. They allow their women to perform all manner of tasks best left to men. Perhaps that is why we have beaten them so many times."

The Red King looked sternly at the youth. "Never think that way, lad! With such overconfidence comes arrogance, and with arrogance comes failure. Besides, the last time we fought the Ffolk, it is we who were defeated."

Koll looked down, abashed. "I am sorry, my lord. I wished to make amends for the embarrassment she caused on the docks when she refused to leave the warriors. I fear that it was bad luck to have her dragged away like that."

"Bad luck, good luck. These things mean little. It is the courage in our hearts that counts for much, and the skill in our minds and our hands when we meet the foe.

"To that end, tell me what you know of the enemy that ravaged your coast."

Koll described the battle at Codsbay as he had seen it, including the fish-man that had climbed into their boat. He told of the destruction of the Iron Keep and the horde that had emerged from the sea to pour through the breach.

"It is as I feared . . . an enemy of great fighting strength coupled with supernatural might. We can only hope that the powers that watched over Corwell in the past retain their potency. If that can counter the supernatural, the blades of the North will surely overcome the fighting strength of the foe!"

Koll nodded, unsettled by the notion that they might need help to win this fight. He turned quietly and walked back to his bench in the open hull of the longship.

Neither he nor the Red King noticed the short, smooth-skinned sailor sitting quietly near the bow. The youth—for such the warrior must have been, as no beard grew from his pink and slightly plump face—looked down as Koll walked past. A soft hand, unusual for a man, went to the hilt of the sailor's shortsword, where its knuckles tightened in very warlike determination.

\* \* \* \* \*

Ysalla swiveled her bulging fish-eyes to look at the vast army floating and marching around her. The gleam of gold caught her eyes, here and there marking the presence of her priestesses. They marched in great adornment now, for the sacking of the Iron Keep had yielded treasure beyond her wildest imaginings.

Now the ranks of the sahuagin, hundreds strong, swam easily through the middle reaches of the gray sea, a hundred feet below the surface and an equal distance from the bottom. Below them, in vast numbers, marched the Dead of the Sea in a dull, plodding pace.

They had fought well, those corpses, though she had known they would. Unburdened by any of the emotional baggage of living warriors, this army could know no fear, nor despair, nor fatigue. They would follow the commands of the priestesses—commands which were, of course, the orders of Bhaal himself—unto and even beyond death. This made them an army mightier than any that could be mustered by the humans and other breathing creatures that would oppose them, for their power emanated from a dark and omnipresent god.

The army had marched through the Strait of the Leviathan in rapid time, never stopping for rest or sustenance. Now, as they entered the shallower regions of Corwell Firth, they turned their faces to the east. They would proceed along the bottom of the firth into gradually shallower water until they emerged from the sea on the very shore of Corwell Town.

There the cleric would be waiting to perform his magic, as he had at the Iron Keep. The human, Ysalla coldly acknowledged to herself, had proven most useful there. No doubt he would do so again.

And thus they would work the will of Bhaal.

\* \* \* \* \*

The fire crackled as the dead wood slowly burned to coals, spreading welcome warmth among the companions gathered around it. The little blaze flickered like their own hopes, surrounded by an all-encompassing blackness but refusing to die.

The group had trampled the snow flat over a small space in the woods, and now they sat in uneasy exhaustion. The night closed about them, as black and forbidding as ever, and seemed to warn away sleep.

The sisters had spread their heavy furs on the snow a short distance from the fire. Brigit and Colleen, however, now sat before the low flames. Tavish rested quietly opposite them, staring as if mesmerized at the dancing blaze. Yak squatted beside her, using her shortsword to carve a tree limb into a heavy, knob-ended club. Meanwhile, Pawldo worked arduously with his dagger and some long sticks, carving them into flat boards.

Robyn curled up on the far side of the blaze, with Newt sleeping on the druid's lap. Tristan sat beside her, using an old stump as a backrest. They all enjoyed each other's comradeship for a time without speaking.

The king remembered other fires, other camps during adventures that never, in retrospect, seemed so bleak and so painful as this one. He recalled the bristling fur of his great moorhound as Canthus slumbered beside a blaze, ignorant of the steaming hiss of his soaked fur. Or Daryth, leaning casually back in his bedroll, telling stories of Calimshan.

He thought of Yazilliclick, picturing the sprite arguing with Newt about some point of camping protocol. Always on those quests, those adventures, it seemed that hope had been high. Always the mission had been clear, the challenge clearly surmountable.

At least such was the way with his memory. But never before had they endured a cost such as this, and never had their hopes been so vague.

Gradually the moaning of the wind became more audible as it forced its way among the trees and across the snowy ground. The snowflakes that had been fluttering to earth all day began to fly in a diagonal direction, angling toward the south, until soon they raced past with the howling wind in an almost horizontal path.

Robyn shivered as she leaned back against Tristan's legs. He was grateful for the fur cape that Brigit had loaned them.

"What are you doing?" Robyn's question, to Pawldo, had an amused, lazy quality that reminded the king of a warm summer afternoon.

"I've been tromping around in this snow for too long, and I'm going to do something about it! I heard about these things once on a trip to Gnarhelm. They called 'em 'skis.' Well, I'm going to make me a pair, and I'll be the envy of all of us!"

Robyn laughed and Tristan looked on with interest. "What are they?" he asked.

"You put them on your feet, and they let you slide across the surface of the snow. They're like snowshoes, only better, because they slide."

"Yes, the Llewyrr have used skis." Brigit was watching the proceedings with interest. "But we prefer snowshoes for walking through a forest, though you will doubtless enjoy those if we have to go downhill!"

"I fear we'll have plenty of snow in either case," said Tristan. "I wonder how far we'll have to go."

"And I wonder what we'll find when we reach the grove." Robyn shivered again, perhaps not entirely from the cold. She had earlier explained to the sisters the waning of the goddess's powers and her fears that the Earthmother may already have expired.

"I accompanied a small band of the sisters there several weeks ago," said Colleen. "It was horribly scarred and changed."

"Like the vale?" Robyn gestured around them.

"Even worse. The trees here are dead, but there they have been split asunder by some terrible force. Even the high druid arches were smashed. Not a one was left standing."

Tristan wondered at Robyn's reaction to the news, remembering her earlier despair, but she sat up to question the knight further.

"What about the dead? There was a legion of skeletons and zombies, walking dead, attacking the place when I last saw it."

"There was no sign of them. Only the awful dark water at the heart of the grove, and the statues, like frozen people, around the well. I did not approach the water, though my three companions did. From where I stood, I could see that it was black, completely lifeless. . . ." Colleen paused, shaken by the memory. "The three sisters approached the pond, and there was a flash of blue light, like an explosion. And they were gone."

"I fled," the young Llewyrr woman admitted. She hung her head in shame as Brigit put a comforting hand upon her shoulder. "I ran until I could run no more." Colleen raised her head and looked square into Robyn's eyes.

"That is why I insisted upon coming along this time . . . to atone for my failure, my flight."

"You have nothing to atone for!" said the druid. "Because

you lived, you have provided us with news about what we may find there. It would have been foolish to sacrifice your life as well!"

"As I have told you also," said Brigit quietly, but Colleen angrily shook her head.

"The leader of our group, the one who took the others to the well, was my own mother! And the other two were my sisters!"

Tristan wondered how she could discuss the deaths of her family thus, with such apparent lack of emotion, but he sensed the rage and shame that burned within her. It was something that even the stoicism of her race could not completely hide. Now it blazed like fire from the depths of her wide brown eyes.

"What do you plan to do when we reach the well?" asked Brigit.

Robyn described the Scrolls of Arcanus, explaining how she had held back the mastery of stone spell to use in changing the statues back to flesh. "With all the druids of the grove free again, we will combine to drive back the darkness from the well."

"But if, as you fear, the goddess has perished, how will the druids accomplish this?" Brigit asked.

"Genna will know what to do. She is the key to all of this! I know that she still lives, if only we can reach her!"

"Yes, child, she does . . . and you have."

The voice, emerging from the blackness, shocked them into action. Tristan leaped to his feet, his sword a gleaming challenge in his hand. Brigit, too, whirled away from the fire and drew her weapon. Yak bellowed in surprise, dumping Tavish unceremoniously to the ground as he heaved himself to his feet.

Only Robyn remained calm, rising slowly and turning to the woods, an expression of bright hope on her face. "Genna? Is that you?"

The stocky figure of the Great Druid emerged from the darkness, and slowly Tristan relaxed. Genna's face, lined with wrinkles, regarded them from beneath a gray mop of unkempt hair. Robyn ran to her teacher and embraced her.

Then the young druid pulled back in surprise, searching Genna's face with concern.

"What is it, teacher? What's wrong?"

The Great Druid walked easily to the fireside and sat down. "I am sorry. I am not myself, and this awful darkness oppresses me. But it is good to find you, my dear. I knew you would not be far away."

A strange light gleamed in the Great Druid's eyes, but Robyn ascribed it to the reflection of the firelight. She sat beside Genna, suddenly alive with hope and optimism.

"Teacher, I have feared so! The goddess has been silent. My spells vanish, my powers are faint—and the earth itself seems to have died."

"The goddess lives, girl. My spells, my powers remain unaffected. Could it be that you have not been true to your faith?"

Robyn hung her head. "I have known doubt, and perhaps my will has been weak. I am sorry, teacher." Robyn took a deep breath and again looked at Genna. "But how did you escape? Are the other druids safe?"

"The tale of my escape is long, dark, and painful. It is best left for another time. The others are still . . . imprisoned. It is toward their succor that we must strive."

"Yes!" Robyn grew animated. "That is what we have been working toward! We have struggled against the darkness but always grow closer to the well. Now that you have joined us, I'm sure our mission will be successful!"

Genna asked about their experiences, nodding somberly as they described the desecration of the vale. She displayed no reaction as Robyn told her of the Scrolls of Arcanus and her hopes for the fourth scroll, the mastery of stone.

Tristan felt the party's spirits buoyed by the talk, enjoying the fact that none of them talked about their frustrations and sorrows. Instead, they focused on their hopes for a rapid conclusion to the quest. One by one, however, the companions fell silent. At last there was only the presence of the black night falling heavily and bearing their spirits down with it.

Genna looked away from the group, into the darkness of

the woods. Newt stirred restlessly and crawled onto Tristan's lap. He looked up at the Great Druid but said nothing.

And the stormy winds howled and the snowdrifts climbed higher.

\* \* \* \* \*

Randolph awakened uneasily, sitting up in his bed and staring nervously around his tiny room in Caer Corwell. Shaking his head to clear the cobwebs of sleep from his mind, he concluded that he was merely nervous.

The shutter banged in the window, and he heard the force of the winter storm raging outside. An omen? He wondered if this was the beginning of a storm of the same magnitude that had apparently ravaged the settlements to the north.

Wearily the captain of the guard stepped into his boots and threw a woolen shirt over his shoulders. It was still dark outside, but he knew that Gretta would already be at work in the kitchen.

He became more alert as he stepped into the corridor and descended the stairs into the Great Hall. Already the delightful aroma of frying bacon wafted forth from the kitchen, and he stepped through the door to find the plump cook tending a crowded cookstove.

"Good morning, sir!"

"How can you be so cheerful, Gretta? The sun hasn't even come up yet, and it's a beastly day outside to boot!" He tried to be gruff but couldn't help smiling in the face of her own robust good humor.

"Oh, and it'll be gettin' considerable colder, too, I'll wager. But my work keeps me in here by the warm fire, feedin' those more foolish types who walk the walls and stand in the gatehouse!"

"That explains it. Well, how about some food for one of those fools?"

She served him his usual massive plate of eggs and bacon, together with fresh cream, and he sat and ate very slowly, relishing each bite . . . or perhaps postponing the moment when he would have to go out into the weather.

"Odd about Lord Pontswain leaving like that," mentioned the cook as she brought him several slices of fresh bread.

His spoon stopped halfway to his mouth, and he looked at her in shock. "Leaving? Like what?"

"He didn't tell you? Come to think of it, he didn't exactly tell me either. I was tidying up, about to go to bed, when I found him in here loading food into a bag. Said he was leaving . . . that something had come up. The least he could have done was say good-bye!"

Randolph's indignation suddenly faded as he looked at the good side of the news. "This might work out pretty well. I'll be able to get things organized around here without having to fight him every step of—"

Randolph froze, a dull suspicion growing rapidly within him. Why had the lord left so suddenly and secretly? He had enjoyed his post here as temporary co-ruler, judging from the way he sat in the Great Hall, lording over everyone, staring covetously at the Crown of the Isles.

"Well, goodness!" declared Gretta, picking up the chair Randolph knocked over as he leaped from the table and burst through the door into the Great Hall.

She found him staring in slack-jawed shock at the mantle over the huge fireplace. She looked, too, for a moment not understanding his concern. Then she realized the difference and gasped at Pontswain's treachery.

The Crown of the Isles was gone!

\* \* \* \* \*

*Chauntea listened for the prayers of the one who wore her medallion, but they were not forthcoming. The druid still clung to the belief in her benign, but inescapably perished, goddess.*

Awaken! Heed my warning! *Chauntea tried to communicate with the woman, tried to tell her of the power she held in her Rose-in-Sun medallion, but Robyn of Gwynneth did not hear.*

*The goddess of farming and growth sensed another menace, the powerful presence of evil, near the medallion itself. It was a lurking, potent vileness, but well concealed. Even the druid did not suspect it.*

*Each of the scrolls, with the casting of their powerful spells, had brought the woman a little closer to this new goddess, but she had resisted the final steps, the decision of faith that could make her a powerful cleric of Chauntea.*

*But until the human made that decision, the deity would have to watch and wait.*

*And perhaps pray.*

# ❧ 17 ❧

# TEMPEST OF ICE AND FIRE

Storm winds howled through the night, and the snow raged across the lands in a blizzard of fury. The companions twisted and turned, sleeping little, brushing the snow from their furs to keep from being buried. Dawn brought no relief as the gray light seeped through the gale, illuminating a scene of shifting snowdrifts and frost.

Robyn pushed back the fur that covered her and felt the chill air against her face. Tristan stirred beside her, and she pulled close to him, reluctant to leave her principal source of warmth.

She felt the return of the dark despair she had known the previous evening. Genna's arrival had temporarily managed to raise the young druid's hopes, restoring her faith in the might of the great mother. She had prayed to the goddess for much of the night, concentrating intensely, desperately hoping for some kind of response. But there had been nothing.

Instead, her mind had whirled with visions of the redhaired vixen sprawled across Tristan's bed. The woman's musical laugh mocked her own pain and anger, and nightmare visions of despair and doom suddenly overwhelmed the druid's face. Robyn had twisted and turned in torment, wishing for the blissful protection of sleep.

All the while, she had known that the comfort of Tristan's warm embrace was right beside her, should she but choose to accept it. But all she could feel for him was hurt and betrayal, and so she turned away and huddled against the chill and didn't sleep.

Now the icy wind swirled about her, and stinging particles of snow chilled her skin every time they touched her face. She sat up and pulled her own cloak about her, though it did not insulate against the cold as well as the thick furs of the Llewyrr. Startled, Robyn saw Genna sitting alone in the blizzard, apparently unaffected by the cold.

"Didn't you sleep?" asked the young druid.

Her teacher shrugged. "A little. It seems time we were moving."

"To the well?" Genna made no response, and Robyn proceeded to tell her in more detail about the scrolls and her plan for freeing the druids from stone. She felt a moment of guilt, wondering if her teacher would berate her for using the scripts of one of the new gods, but Genna didn't appear to notice.

"We shall go the grove," said the Great Druid. "If this scroll will free the others, so be it, but we must be in the grove to face the . . . conclusion."

"Do you have enough power to control this storm, to ease our path?" asked Robyn, knowing that the Great Druid had often influenced the weather in the past, bringing rainfall to a parched valley or warming away the effects of a killing frost.

Genna looked at her in surprise, then rose and walked through the deep snow, away from the party. She was nearly out of sight in the swirling blizzard when Robyn saw her stop and raise her head to the sky. She spread her arms to her sides in the pose the younger druid had seen her use so often before when casting a potent spell.

Suddenly a searing blast of heat struck Robyn's face, and she instinctively slapped her hands over her eyes. A warmth like the inside of an oven surrounded her, and she felt the wind die away in that same instant. The snow on her cloak turned rapidly to water, and a fine drizzle began to fall from the trees, where the accumulated snow of the blizzard quickly melted.

"What—what happened?" Tristan stuck his head from beneath the fur, gasping for breath in the heat.

One by one, the others emerged from their sleeping shelters. "Am I dreaming?" Tavish demanded when confronted by the oppressive heat.

"It's a miracle!" Newt cried, buzzing happily among the trees. "Genna made it summertime again!"

"I don't remember any summer as warm as this!" Pawldo groaned, wiping sweat from his brow.

"Too hot!" grunted Yak.

Robyn stood amazed at this evidence of the Great Druid's vitality, and thus obviously the goddess's as well. The control weather spell that Robyn remembered had always changed the weather only to a degree, bringing rain from heavy clouds or slowing gale winds to a strong breeze. Yet here Genna had altered their entire environment from one extreme to the other.

Indeed, steam rose from the rapidly melting snow all around them. Genna returned to the group and stood calmly as they gathered their wet belongings. She offered no reaction to the continuing stream of remarks about the sudden dramatic change in weather.

"How is it that you can work such strong magic?" Robyn inquired wonderingly.

"Perhaps it is augmented by the changes in the vale. You see that my magic still works; that should be enough. Let's go now. It is time we were off."

Genna, Robyn, and the three sisters led the way as the companions broke camp and started back toward the fissure that blocked their way. Their camp, by now, had been reduced to a steamy patch of mud. All the snow had melted, pooling into water that soaked quickly into the barren ground.

"I don't know why I bothered making these!" Pawldo disgustedly threw his skis across his shoulder and started walking behind Tristan.

"Psst! Hey, Tristan!" Newt, in obvious agitation, popped into sight beside the king. His voice was an exaggerated whisper that certainly wouldn't carry more than a few hundred feet.

"What is it?"

"It's Genna. Something's different about her! I don't like

this one bit. You've got to tell Robyn!"

"What's different?" Tristan had never met the Great Druid before, but he had heard her described many times by Robyn. The young woman had portrayed her teacher as a warm, caring, and tender woman. "I had pictured somebody rather unlike her, I have to admit."

"I don't know what's different about her! I just know she's different. She's . . . *wrong* somehow, and we've got to warn Robyn!"

"I'll try to find a chance to. In the meantime, let's keep an eye on her. I'm sure Robyn would notice if something was really wrong."

Robyn marched steadily behind her teacher, who in turn followed Brigit, Colleen, and Maura. They walked silently, and the young druid felt the presence of Genna pushing the others along. The Great Druid seemed anxious to reach the well.

And indeed, why shouldn't she feel a powerful urgency? Had not Robyn herself been propelled by a similar urgency and tried to move her friends with the same compulsion? But still, the strange behavior of the Great Druid concerned her.

Then she thought of a possible explanation. She remembered the appearance of the druid Trahern at the grove some months earlier. He had borne with him an artifact of great evil, the Heart of Kazgoroth. The presence of that artifact in the grove had caused Genna's health to suffer and had altered the Great Druid's temperament to one of irascibility and anger.

Certainly she must be suffering even more from the total devastation and desecration of the vale. If the presence of a simple artifact had altered her personality, then it seemed quite logical that the destruction of all she considered sacred and holy would have an even greater effect.

But the power of this spell! Here, at least, was proof that Genna's faith sustained her, for only the imminent presence of a mighty deity could cause such a change in the natural order. The goddess *must* be alive!

Robyn noticed that their course took them across ground

that was again covered with deep snow, though it was rapidly melting. Behind them swirled a bluster of wet fog as cold air rolled across a patch of suddenly warmed ground. The magic, Robyn saw, created a bubble of warmth around them—around Genna, actually. It moved as she moved, and vanished as she left.

Soon the fissure yawned before them, and they turned to the east, following the edge of the crevasse in hopes of finding its end. They marched in silence. Tristan felt as though they walked through another world, a strange place of warm snow and ever-present death.

Suddenly the Great Druid halted. Robyn noticed that the fissure had narrowed to perhaps thirty feet in width, although farther along it soon widened again to the impassable barrier they had skirted for so long.

Tristan came up behind them. "What is it?"

"I don't know." Robyn turned to Genna. "Why did you stop here?"

"Be silent." The Great Druid held up her hand, an expression of intense concentration on her face. Robyn thought she saw something frightening in that look, but in another moment, Genna spoke. "We can cross here."

"How?" Tristan looked at the gap, its bottom lost somewhere in the depths, obscured by writhing gases.

"Wait here." Genna walked away from the group, continuing along the lip of the crevasse until she was nearly out of sight. Robyn could barely see her through the many tree trunks as the Great Druid turned toward the north and raised her arms.

Tristan stepped to Robyn's side and lowered his voice as the Great Druid stepped away from them. "Are you sure this is the same Genna Moonsinger you knew before?" he asked softly.

"Of course! Don't you think I'd recognize her?"

"Newt's worried. He told me he thinks she's changed somehow."

Robyn quickly explained her hypothesis explaining her teacher's cold nature. "Surely she's suffered enough! The least we can do is offer her our trust and support!"

The king persisted. "We have to be careful, that's all. We don't know what we're—"

"She doesn't need me to betray her now!" Robyn whirled on the king, her face growing white, her voice an intense whisper. "My doubts have already weakened my own faith! Don't ask me to challenge hers!"

Meanwhile, Genna chanted the words to her spell, ignoring the rest of the party. They watched expectantly, fearful and anxious about the result.

Suddenly the earth began to tremble, and two huge oaks toppled into the crevasse, their dead limbs straining skyward like fingers desperate to arrest the fall. Tristan seized Robyn's arm and pulled her back from the edge of the fissure. For a moment, he thought Genna had precipitated an earthquake that would dump them all to their doom, but the temblor eased quickly, except in the area directly before Genna Moonsinger.

The king watched in awe as the ground there twisted and bulged into an odd, misshapen mound of earth. The blob oozed slowly upward into a great pillar of soft mud. The pile loomed high over the druid's head, growing into a solid column of dirt.

An unnatural groaning rumbled through the air. The column shook and trembled as armlike appendages ripped themselves outward from the sides. Then one massive foot stepped free of the crater around it, and another leg pushed upward, twisting and stretching slowly as does a body kept too long in one position. When it was completely formed, it began to lumber toward the companions.

"*What . . . is . . . it?*" gasped Tavish. Yak growled in superstitious fear, brandishing the great club he carried.

"Wait! It's an elemental—an earth elemental." Robyn's voice was hushed. "Though I have never seen one so large or misshapen!"

The thing towered over the druid, more than twice the size of a large firbolg. Though it had humanlike limbs, at least in terms of their location, it bore little resemblance to any living creature. Its 'face' was a mass of clumpy dirt, marred by roots and sticks that emerged from it in all directions. Likewise its body and limbs were earthen, and pieces of it dropped away with each lumbering footstep. Each of its legs was as broad as a massive tree trunk.

The elemental stumbled like a hunchbacked giant as it approached, and the companions instinctively backed away. Meanwhile, Genna ignored them, walking briskly to the edge of the fissure. Then she gestured to the huge mass of earth, and slowly it returned to her side and bent over the chasm.

Tristan and Robyn watched in silent amazement as the monster leaned far over the lip, until slowly it toppled forward. With surprising alacrity, it reached out with its massive clublike hands and caught the other side of the fissure. finally it lay still, like a gigantic log stretching across the width of the gap.

"We can cross here." Genna gestured impatiently toward the elemental.

"Wait! What if it doesn't hold us?" Tristan stalled for a moment, not trusting the druid and fearful of a trap. He imagined Genna commanding the thing to dump them all into the pit as they crossed.

"It will. Hurry! We must reach the well."

Robyn stepped forward onto one of the thing's broad feet. She looked back in annoyance as the king reached out to grab her arm. "Let's at least use a rope for security!" He stared at the Great Druid as he made the suggestion. She merely shrugged and looked away.

"Here, Yak. Take this rope." Tristan uncoiled his line, binding one end firmly around his waist and handing the other to the firbolg. "Catch me if I fall!"

The king stepped onto the earth elemental, feeling his foot sink easily into the moist dirt of the creature's leg. He pulled it free and set down his other foot. The monstrous bridge seemed to be solid enough. It didn't sway perceptibly beneath his weight.

Tristan made the mistake of looking down once, and the yawning depth of the fissure, with the green gases writhing in its deepest reaches, caused a wave of dizziness to rush over him. He looked ahead and steadied himself, carefully taking the last few steps across the gap.

Once he stepped onto the other side of the fissure, he secured his line to the trunk of a dead oak, and the others followed in short order. Genna waited impatiently as the king untied and recoiled his rope.

"Now, forward!" Genna demanded. "Hurry!"

\* \* \* \* \*

Lord Mayor Dinsmore blinked wearily at the agitated rider outside his door. "What it is? Why did you awaken me?"

"Listen, man!" Randolph had precious little time for explanations. "The crown is gone. Pontswain has taken it. I've got to get it back before he reaches his own cantrev. Otherwise it'll take a battle to drive him out, and that's the last thing we need."

"Huh?" The mayor reluctantly came wide awake.

"I need you to continue the preparations in the town. Koart and Dynnatt should arrive today with their companies. Bivouac them in the town, as close together as possible. Remember, the threat is from the sea!" A sudden gust of wind swirled around him, driving snow down the back of his neck, and he pulled his cape tighter.

"Very well." The Lord Mayor looked at the storm, which had grown nearly to blizzard intensity. "Surely there can be no attack in this weather!"

"We cannot take that chance! You must do as I say. The kingdom depends on us! I don't know if this theft has anything to do with the menace to Corwell, but I suspect some kind of connection. Pontswain isn't fool enough to do something like this simply so he could keep the crown for a little while."

"Where can he have gone?"

"I suspect he's headed for his own cantrev. That's the only assumption I can make, though he could have gone anywhere. I intend to pursue him along the coast road."

"Good luck to you, Captain. May the goddess ride with you!"

Randolph nodded quickly in thanks as he turned his

speedy black gelding away from the lord's house. The horse sprang into the face of the storm, surefootedly trotting through the drifts that filled the streets leading out of Corwell Town.

"May the goddess watch over us all!" the captain murmured fervently to himself. He had a feeling they needed all the help they could get.

\* \* \* \* \*

Only four of the thirty longships remained visible. The others lay somewhere in the gray distance, obscured by the storm—or sunk. The full fury of the gale roared from the port beam now as the fleet made its sweeping turn to the east.

"We'll make the firth in another hour!" declared the Red King angrily, as if shouting at the storm would curb its fury. He knew that the sheltered waters of Corwell Firth would protect them from the raging storm, but how many of his ships would make it that far?

Even the vast form of the castle, riding beside them, could no longer quell the mountainous waves. Grunnarch never ceased to wonder at the sight. The huge structure did not bob or roll with the swell. Instead it rumbled implacidly forward, crashing through each wave with a force greater than the eternal ocean's.

There was one benefit of the storm: They had made the voyage from Norland to Gwynneth in record time. The longships had raced before the wind, riding the mountainous swells like ducklings in a torrent. Only the inherited skill and vast experience of the northern sailors had kept the entire fleet from destruction.

Finally the rough headlands of Corwell appeared off the port bow, and the mountainous waves shrank to the size of large hills. The snow continued to blow and the wind to howl, but the worst of the storm was past.

The longships closed ranks in these safer waters, and Grunnarch's spirits rose as more and more of the colored sails emerged from the haze.

The *Northwind* was soon surrounded by twenty-eight of

her sisters, and the Red King saw with a mixture of relief and sorrow that the storm had claimed one of his vessels. But only one.

And the morrow would bring them to the shores of Corwell itself.

\* \* \* \* \*

Pontswain had figured his plan carefully. He took into account the full night's start he would get by leaving in the evening, after the castle had retired. He carefully selected the fastest horse in the stable, to insure that even when pursuit developed, he could outdistance it. And he figured that, with a little luck, the disappearance of the crown would not be noticed immediately.

But he hadn't figured on this accursed storm raging off of the firth and making travel all but impossible. The wind rose and the snow assaulted him in the darkest hours of the night, well beyond Corwell Town but far from the protection of any settlement, or even farm, on the barren coastal moor.

The only shelter he could locate was this massive haystack that some herdsman had piled near the coast for the winter feeding of his stock. Now the weather forced him to take shelter here, staking the sleek mare to the leeward side of the stack while he himself burrowed into its depths to conserve what warmth he could.

At least, he consoled himself, the storm would make pursuit all but impossible. Besides, he had wandered far from the road in his efforts to find this makeshift shelter, and anyone who followed him would undoubtedly travel down the coast road. Pontswain reassured himself that he was perfectly safe.

In the darkness, he took the crown from the burlap sack where he had hidden it. Its diamond points seemed to shed sparkles of light, and the golden circlet felt warm to the touch. Thus comforted, clutching the crown to his breast, Pontswain fell asleep and waited for the storm to run its course.

\* \* \* \* \*

"More gates? We see most all gates already! Time to rest!" Honkah plopped onto a huge log, his arms crossed and a sullen expression darkening his features. His huge, hooked nose drooped forlornly, and even Yazilliclick could sense his fatigue.

"J-Just one more! Then we can r-rest some more—more. B-But if we f-find my friends, you can have wine when you r-rest!"

"No want wine. Want rest."

"P-Please? Just one more—one more?"

Canthus and the blink dogs lay on the ground panting, their pink tongues lolling downward from widespread, drooling jaws. Yazilliclick had to admit that the pace was grueling, but he felt that they were so close!

"Where's the n-next gate? I'll g-go myself—myself!"

Honkah looked down at the little sprite with a mixture of annoyance and surprise. With a groan, he lurched to his feet and started again through the pastoral woods of Faerie. "I show you. Alone, you just get lost."

The troll lumbered through yet another flower-studded meadow, his long limbs wobbling from his awkward gait. Once again Yazilliclick had to take to the air to keep up, while the dogs trotted along beside them. Every so often one or two of the blink dogs would teleport ahead of them and then lie down, panting easily as they waited for the others to catch up.

The troll reached the high bank of a crystalline brook and slid down the mossy embankment to splash into the water. It was only a foot or so deep, and Honkah made a great show of soaking each of his huge feet in the cool liquid, grunting with pleasure.

"Here gate." He chucked a thumb at the muddy bank, where an overhang of roots and bushes kept the dirt in perpetual shade. Here was the ubiquitous moss frame that the sprite was beginning to recognize as the distinguishing mark of the gates, or at least those gates that led to Myrloch Vale.

Canthus and the blink dogs leaped down the bank behind them, eagerly lapping up the sweet water and then collapsing on the bank of the little stream.

"W-Wait here." Yazilliclick ducked through the bank, feeling a momentary tingle as he stepped across the boundary between the planes.

A blast of frigid wind struck his face, and a swirling eddy of snow surrounded him. The howling of the storm drowned his voice as he called out, as loudly as he could, for his companions. He stayed for several minutes beside the huge snowdrift that marked the gate on the vale side, calling to Tristan, Robyn, and Newt, but he received no answer. Finally, dejected, he stepped back through the gate, unmindful of the sudden heat that washed over the gate in the second after he departed. Nor did he see the wind die or the snow begin to melt as the warmth grew to a sweltering heat.

"It's no use!" He sat on the edge of the stream, kicking the water with his feet in dejection, while Honkah looked at him sadly.

Canthus suddenly sprang to his feet, cocking his head to the side and staring at the gate. With a quick bark, he sprang at the embankment and passed through. Yapping in excitement, the blink dogs followed.

"Hey, w-wait—wait for me!" The sprite flew after the dogs, fearing he would lose his one link with his human companions.

Yazilliclick stopped short as he burst through the gate. Could this be the same place he had visited a scant minute earlier? Oppressive heat sweltered around him. Steam rose from the blanket of snow that incongruously covered the ground. The blink dogs stood together in a pack, confused, but Canthus leaped ahead, barking loudly.

The sprite heard a shout of joy and buzzed after the hound. He came around a huge tree trunk and bumped into a massive form. Looking up, he squealed in terror. "Help! Firbolg!"

Then he recognized the giant as the creature they had pulled from the tar pit. In the same instant, he saw Robyn and Tavish. Tristan, buried under the joyous bundle of fur that was his moorhound, rolled on the ground beside them.

"Yaz!" Newt buzzed to the sprite and gave him a toothy kiss. "I knew you were around somewhere! And you found Canthus! You're back! But where were you? How come you didn't take me along? What's the big idea, anyway? If this was supposed to be a joke, I don't think—"

"N-No, Newt, it wasn't a j-joke—a joke! I g-got lost, and this is the f-first time I could f-find you guys! And I f-found Canthus, and he f-found the b-blink dogs! Where are they, anyway?"

The sprite looked around, realizing that the faerie dogs had not followed Canthus to the companions. He saw one furry face poking around a tree trunk and gestured to the creature. Slowly the animal walked up to the sprite, but when Robyn made a move toward it, the dog blinked out of sight.

"They're always d-doing that—that! They're r-really nice dogs, though, and I think they l-like Canthus a l-lot. Maybe they'll c-come up to you in a minute." As he turned back to Robyn, Yazilliclick caught sight of another member of the party.

"G-Genna! How did y-you—did you get here? I'm so g-glad—so glad to see you! We th-thought something horrible had happened t-to you!"

"Yes, I know. Now we must be going!" urged Genna. "It is time to move on again!"

Tristan stood, clapping the sprite on the shoulder in greeting, his own eyes wet with tears. "You'll have to tell me how you did this," he said. "But thank you!"

"W-Wait!" cried Yazilliclick as the party turned again to their trail. "I'll be b-back in a minute, b-but I have to do something first—first. Does anyone have a b-bottle of wine?"

\* \* \* \* \*

Randolph slouched low in the saddle, wrapping his thick woolen cape as tightly around himself as possible. The storm howled off the firth with a vengeance, covering the moors and the road with snow. Indeed, as the drifts mounted and the horizon became a featureless white of blowing snow, the wind gave the captain his only bearing for direction.

The road had vanished beneath the snow, and the ground was a smooth surface of white. By keeping the storm to his right side, he hoped to maintain his southwesterly heading.

He lost track of how long he had been on the trail. The hour might have been early morning or noon. There was no way to tell from the bleak gray illumination.

Perhaps his course was laid by mere good fortune, or perhaps some benign power steered his hand through the blinding blizzard. In any event, the captain blinked his eyes and wiped the frost from his brow as he tried to identify the hulking shape emerging from the storm before him.

He judged correctly that it was just a haystack, but it was not until he passed it that he saw the dark form of a horse tethered beside the mound. In that instant, he knew that his search had ended.

Randolph leaped to the ground, drawing his longsword as he stepped into the scant shelter of the leeward side of the pile. He saw the cape of his quarry extending from beneath the straw, and for a moment, he wrestled with the temptation to drive his keen blade into the hay above it. He settled instead for a sharp kick.

Pontswain stumbled out into the storm, a look of utter shock on his handsome features. Before Randolph could speak, the lord drew his own sword, and only the captain's instinctive parry saved his throat from a deadly cut.

"Why?" grunted Randolph, striking aside Pontswain's thrust and settling back on guard. His eyes expressed a legion of scorn that could not be phrased into words.

"Don't be such a fool!" sneered the lord. Pontswain slashed savagely once, twice, and both times his blade clashed against the captain's steel.

"Your arrogance would be amusing, if you weren't so treacherous." Randolph held steady, watching his foe. "Did you really think you could steal the Crown of the Isles and escape like a thief in the night?"

"Your discovery and interference is trivial!" Pontswain sprang at the captain, slashing desperately, then suddenly stumbled back with a bleeding wound across his cheek.

"Now your arrogance *is* amusing!"

Randolph's blade slashed downward, meeting Pontswain's in a clash that was muffled by the fury of the storm. Again and again the weapons clashed as the two men fought slowly and awkwardly, impeded by their heavy winter garb.

Pontswain was the larger and stronger of the two, but Randolph possessed more skill with his weapon. At first the lord drove the captain back into the storm, and Randolph steadily gave ground, all the while analyzing his opponent's weaknesses. The snow clutched at his boots, threatening to trip him, but he retreated with care and precision.

At last the moment was right. Pontswain extended himself with a vicious slash, and in the split second before he recovered, the captain's blade slipped easily through his throat. The lord stumbled backward with a strangled gasp, his red blood spurting across the white snow and disappearing as quickly beneath fresh flakes.

Randolph wasted no time in checking his victim, for he felt a growing sense of urgency and danger. Even this amount of time away from Corwell, he feared, might prove disastrous. He reached into the haystack, located the golden artifact that he sought, and wrapped it in the same bag Pontswain had used to carry it away.

The body of his enemy had not yet grown cold as Randolph mounted his mare, taking the reins of Pontswain's steed in his hand, and started back through the storm toward Corwell Town.

*  *  *  *  *

Once again the companions camped in a muddy clearing in the woods, surrounded by desolation and darkness. The stifling heat of Genna's spell finally began to fade with nightfall. Though the snow around them still was melting, it did not fade away as quickly as it had earlier during the day's march.

I should feel relieved and confident, Tristan reminded himself. After all, Yazilliclick had returned, miraculously accompanied by Canthus. The great dog once again lay curled at his master's feet, breathing contentedly, not quite asleep. Still, the king felt a strong sense of foreboding.

They enjoyed Yaz's tale of his sojourn through Faerie. The six blink dogs had gradually overcome their shyness, though they rested some distance from the fire.

"Do you think we'll reach the grove tomorrow?" asked the king, idly scratching the moorhound's head.

"Yes, unless another fissure or tar pit or something blocks our way," Robyn replied quickly. "It can't be more than a couple of miles to the streambed south of Genna's grove."

"Yes," the Great Druid, lost somewhere in her own thoughts, agreed absently. She stared into the depths of their fire, ignoring the others for the most part. This, of course, was not unusual behavior from so solitary an individual as a Great Druid. The older members of the order were notoriously unsociable among people who did not share their faith and practices.

"And then you'll use the fourth scroll?" Tavish turned the conversation back to Robyn.

"Yes. From the way the others have worked, I'm certain it will do what we require—that is, allow the druids to return to flesh and blood. Our combined might should be enough to purify the well and resanctify the grove. After that, the healing of the land can begin."

As the others slowly drifted off to sleep, Tristan moved closer to Robyn's side. He reached out a tentative hand, but she did not take it.

"After tomorrow," he said softly, afraid of her response, "what will happen? What do you plan to do?"

For a moment, she looked at him, and the familiar smile played about her lips while her green eyes flashed a glimpse of the love he had once seen there.

But then the cold fire of anger erupted within her and a red haze fell across her vision, surprising Robyn herself with its intensity. She tried to look through the heat, to Tristan himself, but all she could see was the taunting vision of a red-haired woman. The image grew stronger, brighter, drowning everything else in her awareness.

"What does it matter?" she said roughly. "You have made your decision for yourself. Allow me to make mine!"

Even as she spoke, she cringed at the harshness of her words, the coldness of her voice. What was happening to her? She saw the pain clearly reflected in Tristan's face, and a part of her wanted to reach out and take him in her arms.

But the other part of her, the one that had spoken, would not allow this. And so she turned away from him, glaring into the fire as if she would quench it with an icy look.

Tristan could not muster the energy to curse, even inwardly. He slumped back against a tree stump, taking small consolation as Canthus nuzzled his hand. Idly he scratched the dog's ears, wondering what had become of the relationship he had once cherished. In truth, Robyn's answer had not surprised him, for it was quite in keeping with her manner of the last days. But why couldn't she forgive?

The black night offered no clue to an answer.

\* \* \* \* \*

*Bhaal pushed at the surface of the Darkwell with a broad and mighty hand. He saw the water ripple away from the pressure as it yielded to his physical form, and he knew that he would soon be ready to emerge.*

*He felt the power of long, tough sinews as monstrous muscles developed in the body that slowly coalesced around him. He began to smell and taste the water of the well through his own sensory organs, not through the supernatural awareness of his immortal form.*

*The cord connecting his center in the well to Gehenna remained strong. Now another cord—shorter but far more tough and able to cope with the threats of this physical world—grew from his body and connected it to the well. The cord would be invisible to those in the mortal world, but it would carry the essence of Bhaal's life and insure that even his physical body remained immortal.*

*Bhaal's was a body of gigantic size. Though manlike, with*

flowing hair and beard, it would tower over the mortals of the world. Its very presence would inspire fear and awe. Very soon now, it would walk the lands of the Forgotten Realms.

The god of murder sensed the approach of the humans, led by the corrupted form of the Great Druid, his servant. She served him well, indeed, bringing them nearer so that they might witness the explosion of Bhaal from the well. And in this same moment, they would know their doom.

# ❦ 18 ❦

# TO THE BLACK WATER

This would be the last day.

Robyn sensed this the moment she awakened. As on the previous morning, Genna sat nearby, motionless but awake and observant. With a quiet nod to her teacher, Robyn rose and made her way some distance into the woods. She noticed that the temperature, though still warm, did not have the sweltering nature of yesterday's oppressive weather.

Slowly, reverently, Robyn knelt on the muddy ground. She faced a blistered stump of an oak, surrounded by a brittle nest of dead, dried vines. Somehow this seemed an appropriate setting for her purpose.

The druid prayed to her goddess with all her vibrant, faithful heart. She begged for a word, some sort of a sign in return, to assure her of the great mother's presence. Robyn felt a sudden dread and wondered if the very fact of her asking confirmation of the goddess wasn't tantamount to doubting her existence. How could the mother honor such a request, when its very presence was proof of Robyn's lack of faith?

Barely suppressing a sob, Robyn looked to the sky, away from the inanimate representation of her deity. Even in her despair, she felt a strange tingle of vitality, an energy different than she had known. It was a potent feeling, frightening and mysterious.

Keenly aware of this odd sensation, Robyn rejoined her companions. Distracted, she broke fast and prepared for the march. Once she looked upon Tristan as he ate his bread, and the sight caused her a flash of pain. The hurt came from within her, as if from a hidden tumor rather than a physical wound.

She made a point not to look at the king again until he started toward the trail. Canthus paced watchfully by his master's side, and Robyn suddenly recalled a former feeling, of pride and love and desire as she watched him. But once again the image vanished in a vision of red hair and blind rage. Robyn choked back a gruff curse and turned away from Tristan, shaking.

What is doing this to me? she demanded of herself. The flare of rage had been so hateful, so unlike anything she had ever felt before this quest. It far superseded natural jealousy, and for a moment, Robyn wondered what made her anger so unnatural.

With a shake of her head, she touched the remaining Scroll of Arcanus, safe in the tube at her side. Genna started off in the lead, with Robyn following close behind. Tristan and the others fell into file behind.

The sultry heat of the tropics once again sweltered around them, melting the remaining snow and filling the air with steam. Robyn saw that the spell seemed to gain vitality as the druid moved, as if it thrived on the steady exertion of the Great Druid's body.

Genna set a demanding pace, and Robyn drove herself with equal determination. She felt the conclusion of her quest approaching and saw that the battle she had been forced to flee weeks earlier would soon be renewed and resolved.

The companions reached the stream bed that had once marked the southern boundary of the grove of the Great Druid. Now it was a barren ditch, choked with mud and rocky rubble. No water flowed here, nor had any snow accumulated in the stream bed. In fact, from here on into the grove, Robyn could see that the ground was bare. Either some source of heat had melted the snow on the ground, or the ravages of the storm had spared the area of the grove like the eye of a raging hurricane.

If the weather had avoided the grove, the destruction

wrought by the Darkwell had not. The formerly grand stands of oak, hickory and aspen, the once brilliant meadows and gardens, now stood withered under such an air of desolation as to make the rest of Myrloch Vale seem healthy by comparison.

Vines draped tree trunks, giving the woods a strangled look. Tendrils of mist writhed among the fallen forest giants, and the land itself seemed to writhe under the oppressive curse of death. But the land did not move, and only the gently drifting fog gave the earth a living effect.

The Great Druid appeared to take no notice of the change, striding boldly into the stream bed, stepping among the rocks and ignoring the clutching mud that sucked at her feet.

"Teacher, wait!" Robyn called out to Genna as she stepped into the stream bed herself, aware that the others had still not reached the border of the vale. Such had been the Great Druid's pace that the group now was stretched out over some distance. "Let the others catch up. We can approach the well together."

"Very well. But we must hurry."

Genna looked impatiently back at the trail as Tristan and Newt, followed by the dogs, came into view. A short time later, Yazilliclick buzzed from the woods, and then Tavish and Yak stepped into the open. Finally Brigit, Colleen, and Maura came cautiously forward in their role as guardians of the party's rear.

As soon as the others reached the north bank of the desolate streambed, Genna turned again, leading the group into the heart of the grove.

Robyn looked around them in shock, trying to recall the pastoral beauty of the druid's grove as it once had been. She looked at the mighty fir trunks, most of them now lying on the ground. The earth, once a rich black, was now a sickening brown that squished softly underfoot and gave rise to an overpowering stench of rot.

The sweltering heat of Genna's spell remained around them. Here it seemed more natural, for there was no evidence of the wintery blanket coating the rest of the vale.

Gaunt, skeletal branches of bushes and low trees seemed to reach out and clutch at the companions as they pushed through the woods. Robyn could see no trace of the pleasant paths and sunny walkways that had once curved gracefully among the forest giants.

Genna again hurried forward, and Robyn hastened to keep up. She froze in place with a gasp of dismay when the heart of the grove finally appeared among the twisted trunks before them.

Robyn would not have known the place by sight, though the palpable evil in the air around her confirmed that they had reached their destination. The ground around the well was barren of all plant life, a desolate expanse of muddy brown. She could plainly see the statues, nineteen of them now that Genna had escaped, frozen in place at the periphery of the water. Surrounding them had once been the proud stone arches, composed of two massive pillars and a heavy, flat crosspiece, erected by druids of a distant age. Now the crosspieces had fallen to ground and shattered, and most of the pillars had either been knocked down or leaned crazily against neighboring columns. Half the stones were buried in the oozing mud near the well, and the surfaces that were visible had become coated with a fetid, unhealthy scum.

Shallow craters covered the expanse of muck. Within several of these mud-rimmed holes, Robyn could see thick greenish slime, bubbling and seething like some ghastly stew. A wide fissure gaped in the ground along the west side of the clearing. Steaming gouts of gas erupted in many places along the fissure, often casting showers of mud as they did no. The spurts of gases combined to form a thin gray haze that hung constantly in the clearing, dimming the view of the skeletal trees on the opposite side.

Each breath of air seemed to burn the lungs of the companions. Robyn seemed frozen in a quandary of violent emotions. She wanted to turn and flee in heartstopping panic or to cry out her rage and attack with mindless ferocity. But attack what?

Stifling the desperate urge to scream, she stood still and

waited. Sweat popped from every pore on her body, and she shivered as the perspiration soaked her clothes.

The entire setting had been wracked by forces of incredible violence and power. Robyn took several deep breaths to calm herself before moving forward. As Genna marched ahead, Robyn felt Tristan step up to her side and sensed Pawldo, Tavish, and Yak close behind her. The blink dogs, in a racing pack led by Canthus, loped past them, cutting to the left in a wide circle around the well.

"Let's go," she whispered, again touching the reassuring warmth of the scroll at her side. Her eyes locked on the black water before them, and, unknown to her, a grimace of dark anger crossed Robyn's face.

Tristan held his sword before him, looking to the right and left for enemies he did not understand but nevertheless sensed awaited them. This place stank, and the very air made his flesh crawl. And what was there to fight? The statues stared back at him, as if mocking his mortal form. The king fixed his gaze on one of the stone forms after another, seeking some sign of movement or menace.

The companions emerged into the clearing around the well to the sudden flapping of wings, like geese struggling aloft from a small pond. But these "geese" had perverted antlers growing from their heads and the ghastly look of vile corruption. The deathbirds had been lurking among the shattered pillars around the well, but now they flew, their deadly antlers angling toward those who would threaten their master.

"Come on!" The king broke into a run, charging the flock even as the hideous creatures fought to gain altitude. He saw several arrows dart overhead, striking a pair of the monsters from the sky. The Sword of Cymrych Hugh compelled him, with a will of its own, to attack the things.

The ground shook beside him as Yak followed. Tristan heard, incongruous in the oppressive grove, the strident chords of Tavish's lute. Inexplicably, the notes brought a rush of ferocity to his heart, and he shouted an inarticulate challenge at the obscene flyers.

Pawldo advanced at his right, brandishing his sword. He

moved awkwardly, for his skis were strapped to his back. He had not used the things once during the long hike, but he remained reluctant to give up the products of his labor. Yak advanced at Tristan's left, the companions in line abreast to face the greatly reduced flock. Another shower of arrows rained overhead as the sisters and Yazilliclick maintained their deadly fire. The deathbirds dived, and the sword pulled the king from his feet as it thrust upward to cut the life from the leader of the flock.

Yak swung his heavy club and crushed one of the creatures in midair. The shattered body fell to earth as the firbolg turned on another deathbird, sending it veering madly away to avoid the knobby weapon.

"Tristan! Look out!" Robyn's voice, a desperate shout, suddenly jerked his attention back to the ground. He looked to his side, past Pawldo, to see a nightmare vision of death springing toward them, as if it charged straight from the lowest levels of the Abyss.

"What *is* that thing?" He whirled, the sword instinctively swiveling with him to face this new and much more serious threat. He sensed Yak crushing a deathbird above his head, but he could not tear his gaze from the black, hellish creature now lunging toward Pawldo.

Its eyes blazed a savage yellow, gleaming starkly against the midnight black of the creature's coat. Its long fangs drooled, and the two tentacles writhing from its shoulders reached like hungry snakes for the halfling's face. In that second, Tristan knew that this was the beast that had slain Daryth.

Pawldo swiveled, his skis swinging through a broad arc. The wooden boards passed right through the form of the drooling monster, but then they smashed into something solid, yet invisible, beyond the beast. The force of the blow knocked the halfling sideways, pushing him away from the snapping clamp of those horrid jaws.

Then Pawldo's body whipped into the air, and the king imagined him seized by one of those tentacles. With a dull thud, the halfling slammed back to earth and lay, utterly silent and motionless, beside the monster.

The creature crouched again, and this time Tristan sprang. He swung his sword through a vicious horizontal slash and felt it bite into flesh—but not where the monster appeared to be! Then he, too, stumbled backward, struck by an invisible tentacle that hurtled him to the ground. Once again his father's armor had saved him from a deep and slashing wound.

Tavish the bard stood entranced as the fight raged. The battlesong of the harpist was upon her, and her fingers flew across the strings. The words of an unknown song filled her heart, and though the lyrics made little sense as a story, they lifted the spirits of the Ffolk and urged them onward into battle.

Tavish watched the monsters attack, strumming with a fantastic intensity a tune and a rhythm born in her mind only as it was played. She felt the words erupt within her, whirling through her mind, and suddenly she sang. Her voice was a challenge to all the evil and blackness in the world, but especially to the dark power lurking before them, as she sang her message of hope and prayer for herself and her companions.

The lyrics of her song were incomplete, but now a tale began to take shape. She had no ending, for the song was a ballad, and the tale it told had not yet seen its conclusion. But Tavish felt herself swept along by the music, felt it raise the spirits of her companions, and so she challenged the darkness with growing courage and strength.

The deathbirds swirled in confused savagery, and several of them dove toward the bard. Tavish, caught in the rapture of her music, failed to see them coming.

But Robyn did. The druid let go of the scroll and momentarily attacked as a warrior, raising her scimitar into the air and slicing a wing from the leading deathbird. The monster's body crashed into the bard, knocking her to the ground, as Robyn whirled and cut another of the creatures from the sky before it could attack.

The lute fell from Tavish's hands and a black silence again settled over the clearing. The bard sat up awkwardly and saw the black panther-beast strike down Tristan as the king's weapon again struck at the empty air.

Not knowing why she did so, Tavish pulled forth the broken spectacles from the firbolg lair and fumbled to place them on her nose. She squinted toward the battle and immediately saw the beast in its true position, several feet to the side of the illusionary appearance.

Standing again, lifting her lute, Tavish cried out to the king. "There! To your left! There it is!" But then another of the deathbirds smashed into her face. A cruel antler tore at her cheek, and the glasses flew across the muddy ground. Tavish fell backward heavily, gasping for air and seeing the shadow of horned death looming over her.

Brigit and Maura nocked and fired their arrows with mechanical precision, while Colleen drew her sword and raced to Tristan's defense. One by one the silver missiles found targets in the flying creatures.

Brigit felt a great emptiness rise within her as the music ceased. She suddenly realized that, for a brief moment, the music had recalled memories of pristine Synnoria. The sister knight turned and saw Tavish on the ground, saw Robyn reach to strike one of the deathbirds with the now bloody scimitar.

But two more swept toward the prone bard, and Tavish squirmed awkwardly, too slow to get out of the way. Brigit dropped her bow and raced toward the fight, her own longsword extended.

None of the companions saw the displacer beast crouch, its yellow eyes gleaming, and slink along the ground. Genna pointed a finger, again unnoticed by the others, and the creature sprang toward Robyn's unarmed and unprotected back.

\*   \*   \*   \*   \*

Ysalla floated easily in the shallows, watching the great march below her. Hundreds and hundreds of the dead of the sea, preceded by the hulking corpses of the ogres, moved through the gap in the breakwater and approached the beaches at either side of Corwell Harbor.

The storm overhead clearly waned, though large breakers still smashed against the shore. The priestess could see no sign of sunlight through the thick clouds, and this pleased her. The Claws of the Deep could emerge from the water and fight and breathe among the air-breathing peoples, but they abhorred the light of the sun. This boded well for the coming battle, the priestess thought.

Sythissal, King of the Deep, drifted behind her, casually drawing a clawed hand along the ridges of her spine. She whirled on him, a hissing froth of bubbles exploding from her scaly maw.

Ysalla drew back her golden dagger and was on the verge of striking him for his insolence, but the sahuagin king floated breezily past. She understood the warning implicit in his gesture: Though the power of Bhaal had given her command of this great mass of undead creatures, the king had told her that he was her master, as well as lord of all the Claws of the Deep. Seething, she acknowledged the truth of his point.

But it would be *her* troops that would win this battle, she knew. Finally the mighty army had gathered into position for the attack, either inside the harbor or spread along the outer shores. It was time to move.

A dozen sahuagin, the yellow-scaled priestesses of Bhaal, ordered their legions forward. Lumbering but implacable, the undead emerged from the water. Ysalla surfaced, her proud spines breaking the water first like the dorsal fin of a monstrous shark. She saw that gray clouds glowered above and was pleased.

Everywhere around her the heads and bloated bodies of the dead of the sea emerged from the surf. To Ysalla, the sudden panic in the town was a powerful drug, and she knew that Sythissal's legions, too, would feed upon that fear. With steady, slow precision, the dead army marched to the shore and emerged from the water.

In the town, Hobarth watched the attack with unconcealed glee. From a room on the second floor of the inn, he faced the harbor. Now he stood at the window, observing the array of zombie troops before him. They advanced steadily along the wharf, clambering into the boats docked at the pier or struggling awkwardly up the steep seawall to shuffle along the docks. The Ffolk at the waterfront, in a mass outbreak of panic, turned and bolted for the central regions of the town.

Snow still floated gently from the sky, but the storm had passed. Now the white flurries drifted and eddied in the gentle breeze, in stark contrast to the brutal scene enacted on the ground.

To either side, Hobarth could see hundreds of undead outside the walls of Corwell Town. To the north, the grisly army shuffled forward against no resistance, sweeping along the edge of the town and cutting off retreat to the castle on its rocky knoll. Splendid! The Ffolk would be trapped in the town, and the castle could be dealt with later.

To the south, he saw the other wing of Ysalla's army. This segment turned toward the town as it came ashore, hammering at the gate and climbing, through sheer force of numbers, over the low wall and into the streets.

But what was this? Surprised, Hobarth looked down to see several hundred men, armed with swords and spears, carrying shields, gathering in the central square. Organized resistance! Hobarth picked out the figure of the town's Lord Mayor and realized that the militia had indeed been mustered.

He turned the other way upon hearing the screeching shrill of pipes and saw two more companies of men assembling in the streets. Some of the neighboring cantrev lords must have gathered their forces as well.

The cleric of Bhaal chuckled grimly as he observed these feeble preparations. He watched the three companies of the Ffolk, brave but doomed, gather together and move toward the waterfront. A bristling wall of spears advanced toward the first of the lumbering ogres. Hobarth saw several of the bloated creatures fall before the attack, though the others pressed mindlessly on. After all, the dead could know no fear.

But the living could. And Hobarth was determined to see that they did.

He called upon the might of his god, pulling a tiny scrap of insect larva from a pouch in his robe. He crushed it between his plump fingers, letting the dust swirl down to the street below as he summoned the might of his god to power his infernal casting.

Bhaal heard and answered. The dust of the insect larva suddenly blossomed and expanded, curling into a black cloud that began to flow through the streets of Corwell. Seeping and slithering forward, the cloud clung to the ground as it expanded. It probed alleys, filled yards, and slowly it took to life. The black cloud became a massive shroud of living insects, buzzing and humming in an infernal chorus.

Bees, wasps, locusts, hornets, savage biting flies, and a host of other insects filled the air and covered the streets. They flowed through the town with a nightmare hum. In the mass of their millions, they spelled horrible, painful death to anyone caught within their cloud.

The insect plague spread among the buildings and streets of Corwell Town, reaching forward with fingerlike tendrils to wrap around the men of the companies. First a few stragglers fell out of line, slapping and cursing the attack. Then the cloud gradually embraced them all, and the men broke and fled, unable to stand the supernatural attack.

And the legions of dead advanced through the town, unmolested.

\* \* \* \* \*

Tristan felt a shadow pass over him. He scrambled to his knees, instinctively keeping the Sword of Cymrych Hugh away from the mud. He saw the black monster spring toward Robyn as the young druid slashed at a deathbird, unaware of the horror approaching from behind.

"Robyn!" As the king screamed a warning, the words caught in his throat. He struggled to his feet, raging against the clutching mud, knowing he could never reach her in time.

Yak turned beside him, also too far away. Pawldo lay motionless; the three sister knights struggled with the remaining deathbirds; Tavish lay prone, struggling to rise

. . . none could help Robyn.

The displacer beast landed in a crouch, a low growl rumbling in its belly. Robyn spun and gasped in shock, staggering backward in the face of the horrible drooling visage. The beast crept forward, its tentacles flicking with deadly purpose.

Then it pounced. Desperately the woman dove to the side, sensing that the creature's balance was imperfect. She saw a deep wound in the monster's flank, a broken shaft of some kind protruding from it. It looked like a spear, only it was white.

One of the tentacles lashed across Robyn's legs, cutting her skin and knocking her to the ground. The monster twisted back toward her, and the druid saw the broken weapon that had been embedded in the creature's flank suddenly pop free from the wound. She lay helpless, watching the drooling fangs come closer, hearing the beast's deep, rumbling growls, smelling its fetid breath.

One, then another, and suddenly six four-footed creatures appeared before Robyn, snarling and yelping at the beast. The blink dogs, as a pack, lunged forward and snapped at the monster's flanks. They blinked in and out of sight at the front, sides, and rear of the beast.

Biting and snapping with surprising savagery, the dogs attacked the abominable cat-beast. The monster flew into a frenzy of rage, biting with its great teeth, slashing with its claws, and whipping its obscene tentacles at one after another of the nimble dogs.

Tristan started toward the melee, but then he saw Robyn starting to get up, apparently unhurt. Another deathbird soared at his face, and he quickly crouched into a defensive position.

"Get him, Canthus! Yippee!" shouted a shrill voice above the noise. The great moorhound raced across the field. Above him soared a tiny orange figure, shooting like an arrow toward the fight. "C'mon, you guys! Bite him! Chew his tail off!"

Canthus and Newt slashed into the fray, and suddenly the displacer beast whirled and lashed out from the center of the melee. Tristan saw the moorhound leap and snarl at the image of the beast, striking at the empty air. The blink dogs, conversely, snapped at no apparent foe, their teeth apparently closing on empty space, but as they pulled back, the image of the displacer beast snarled and shrieked in rage. The other-dimensional ability of the blink dogs apparently allowed them to see the displacer beast in its actual location.

As the fight raged, scarcely feet away from her, Robyn rose to her feet. She caught sight of the weapon that had fallen from the displacer beast's wound and picked it up. While she had at first thought it to be a spear, she now saw that it was an ivory horn.

With a dull feeling of shock, she recognized it. Kamerynn! Had he, too, succumbed to this savage presence? Was this horn all that remained of the proud unicorn that had saved her life, that had carried her into battle with the Beast? This shock, the proof of the death of the proudest child of the goddess Earthmother, now only strengthened Robyn's resolve. Grimly she tucked the horn into her belt and turned again to face the well.

Tavish at last found her glasses and stood beside Brigit and Maura. The two sisters had driven the flying predators back from the bard while she searched. Now Tavish again took up her lute.

A deathbird flapped toward Tristan, its antlers lowered. The sword of his ancestors surged forward, sinking into the monster's throat. The king flipped the limp creature to one side and started toward the melee again, only to see Robyn running toward him.

"The scroll! I've got to get to the statues!"

"Come with me!" He spun beside her and started toward the well. Yak and the sister knights continued to strike at the remaining deathbirds. Behind them, they could hear the roaring of the displacer beast, then the painful yelp of an injured blink dog.

Before them, Genna stood before the well, ignoring the battle raging behind her. She stood between two of the druid statues, staring at the black water. When Tristan and

Robyn joined her, she looked up suddenly, an expression of passionate hatred burning on her face. Robyn imagined the revulsion she must feel, confronted by this ultimate devastation.

"The scroll!" Genna demanded. "Now is the time!"

Robyn fumbled with the container as Tristan looked around frantically. The statue beside him was a white stone image of a middle-aged man. An uncanny look of brutal determination, etched in the stone, glared from his frozen face. In his hand was an upraised sickle.

Beyond him were others, men and woman, all dressed in the practical garb of the druids, all locked in positions of deadly combat. Armed with scythes, knives, staffs, poles, and a few heavy clubs, these druids had faced a nightmare army only to be imprisoned thus. He remembered Robyn's description of the miraculous white foam that had risen from the Moonwell, saving the druids from the disastrous climax of their battle.

If the scroll worked, if these statues once again became living druids, they would find themselves in the midst of another battle—against, Tristan suspected, an even mightier foe.

But could they save them now? He saw Robyn unroll the parchment, her hands shaking. Tristan saw the golden circlet, the Rose-in-Sun Medallion, glowing with an eager, hopeful aura.

Genna put out her hand, as if to steady Robyn's grip. The Great Druid's hand touched the scroll, and suddenly a blue light crackled through the air. Robyn recoiled from the druid's touch, her mouth wide in a soundless scream. Genna looked at her, her wrinkled face barren once again of any emotion.

Still the blue flame crackled and sizzled around them. Robyn remained immobile, her mouth wide, her eyes panic-stricken, full of disbelief and pain.

The parchment of the scroll burst into flame, and even Tristan could feel the heat from the fire. Now Robyn broke from her spell, screaming in terror, tumbling back against one of the statues to fall, sobbing, onto the ground. The flames consuming the parchment slowly faded, and the last of the Scrolls of Arcanus fluttered in useless ashes through the air, drifting on an eddy of wind to land in the black waters of the Darkwell.

\* \* \* \* \*

Randolph spurred his panting mount over the last rise before Corwell Town, thankful that the storm had diminished somewhat. A strong sense of urgency gripped him, and as he crested the low hill, he knew why.

He saw immediately that Corwell was under attack, and the attackers had come from the sea. He kicked the horse into a desperate gallop, and the animal gave its last strength to streak over the snow-covered moor, pounding frantically toward the town.

The captain could see a black haze, almost like smoke, hanging over the town. He saw warriors and women and children—indeed, the entire populace—fleeing from the city through its gates, or even over the walls. Then he heard the droning of the smoke, though he could still not believe its nature.

But as the horse staggered up to the town's south gate, he saw the tiny creatures that made up the cloud, and he instantly realized that powerful sorcery was at work.

"Rally 'round me, men of Corwell!" he cried, brandishing his sword among the crowd of fleeing warriors. He pulled hard on the reins, and somehow the tired horse found the strength to rear, pawing the air with its forehooves in a brazen challenge.

"To the attack!" Randolph leaped to the ground and started toward the narrow gate.

"Wait! You'll be killed!" Lord Mayor Dinsmore, among the fleeing warriors, pushed himself forward to the captain's side. "They have powerful sorcery! The enemy are not even alive! They're walking dead! Flight is the only hope!"

"Nonsense!" growled the captain. "We'll just have to kill them again! Follow me!"

He charged through the gate, heartened by the score or so of men who followed. More and more of the Ffolk saw his solitary advance and fell into rank, until the course of the rout had been reversed.

Randolph still carried the Crown of the Isles in the burlap sack, tied securely around his waist, but he gave the artifact no thought as he plunged into combat with a sea-bloated zombie. Nevertheless, the crown had a most pronounced effect as he moved onto the battlefield.

As the captain pushed into the city, the buzzing and biting insects of the plague began to fall dead in droves. A circle of immunity, with the captain at its heart, broke the effect of the spell in an ever-growing ring around him. Within minutes, not a single of the conjured insects remained in the air.

But the dead of the sea continued to advance. Even without the aid of dark magic, they far outnumbered the fighters of Corwell. Behind them, entering the town and spreading across the moors, came the horrible shapes of the sahuagin, merciless in their killing frenzy, savage in their pursuit of any human foe.

The Ffolk fought bravely, and their captain led them well. The men of Koart's and Dynnatt's companies rallied with the men of the town, but even together the humans were pushed back, and the dead and their masters claimed the town.

\* \* \* \* \*

Hobarth cursed the cruel fates that had given him the incompetent aid of Pontswain, for he understood exactly what had happened as his insect plague died away. Somehow the Crown of the Isles was back in Corwell. His powerful enchantments would be useless.

But that certainly did not mean the battle was lost. From his high vantage point, he watched the battle in the streets and saw the Ffolk driven from their town by the combined forces of the undead and the sahuagin. As the humans spilled onto the open moor, still more sahuagin emerged from the sea, seeking to cut them off from finding refuge in the castle.

As the cleric's gaze drifted across the waters of the firth, his jaw dropped in astonishment. What was that? For a moment, he thought he saw a mountain moving through the water. . . . Slowly the shape of a great castle became visible in the mist.

By all the dark gods, what could this mean? In another moment, the fleet of longships became clearly recognizable, gathered around the base of the floating fortress like ducklings around their mother. How was it possible that an edifice of stone and mortar, clearly a mass of tremendous weight, could move thus?

The castle seemed to ride lightly upon the waters of the firth. For a moment, the cleric felt a flash of panic as he imagined he saw a rank of supernatural archers or fire-spitting war machines arrayed along the floating parapet. But as the edifice drew closer, he saw that, to the best of his knowledge, the fortress was abandoned.

The cleric watched the fleet approach for several more minutes, counting more than two dozen ships, plus that mysterious fortress. Reinforcements for the Ffolk, to be sure, though he wondered why they would come from the men of the North.

But still the servant of Bhaal did not worry. Certainly their crews numbered little more than a thousand men or so, and that, he knew, would be insufficient to turn the tide. Even as he watched, a rank of sahuagin warriors turned to face the fresh attack from the sea.

The battle would still be won.

\* \* \* \* \*

"What have you done?" shouted the king, advancing toward the form of the Great Druid. Out of the corner of his eye, he saw Robyn, sprawled in the mud beside the Darkwell, look at her teacher with dull and horrified understanding. "You have betrayed us!"

"Betrayed?" Genna spoke in a flat tone, utterly devoid of feeling. "I serve my master faithfully."

Before Tristan's dumbfounded eyes, the sturdy figure of the middle-aged woman suddenly shifted, stretching and curving into the shape of a hulking bird. Its drooping head, bloodshot eyes gleaming, hung suspended from a crooked and malformed neck. A vulturelike beak snapped at him, and he stumbled back, almost too stunned to avoid the blow. Great black wings spread from the creature's sides, flapping slowly in an ominous gesture. Then the body shifted and wavered once more, becoming a shape burned into Tristan's memory at the homecoming feast. The king heard Robyn cry out in shock and pain as she, too, recognized the woman.

"You!" he gasped, seeing the spill of red hair and the fiery gleam in her eyes.

"It was you!" Robyn cried out beside him. Tristan couldn't tell whether it was in pain or in anger.

The young woman stared in shock at the metamorphosis of her teacher's body. Any semblance to Genna Moonsinger had completely disappeared. Slowly Robyn began to comprehend the corruption that had taken the Great Druid, culminating in the destruction of her scroll. Helplessly she looked to the ashes, already disappearing in the dark water, and then back to the red-haired face on the body before her.

That face twisted into the familiar sneer that had been the focus of Robyn's thoughts for so long. Once again hot rage burned within her, but this time the heat of her anger blazed toward this woman rather than Tristan.

And then the form shifted again, growing larger, looming over them and losing all semblance of humanity. The image of the redheaded woman vanished entirely, masked by a visage of black scales and red, gleaming eyes. It became a thing reptilian in nature, gigantic in stature. It became an enemy the king had slain once before.

"Kazgoroth!" The Sword of Cymrych Hugh sang a killing song in his hands . . . or was that the bard? He heard Tavish's ballad again, and his heart filled with hope, but it was a hope powered by an all-consuming rage.

"This time you *will* die!" he cried, advancing grimly toward the Beast. Its great tail lashed around the massive body, a heavy limb that could crush a human frame in an instant.

Tristan turned toward the tail, anticipating the source of the Beast's attack. His blade slashed out, and Kazgoroth reared backward, splashing into the water of the well and screaming its pain in an earthshaking bellow. The monster crouched now, hunching back. Good! It had learned to fear the sword! As the combatants paused momentarily, Tristan heard the fury of the fight behind him.

In the field, the blink dogs and Canthus still snapped at the displacer beast. Shantu bounded this way and that to avoid the sharp fangs of its attackers. Two of the blink dogs lay dead, paying the supreme price for their bravery, but the others, led by the huge moorhound, pursued the attack with increased savagery.

The blink dogs tore skin from the beast's flanks with each attack. One sank his teeth into a horned tentacle, and though the monster lashed the dog back and forth like a fish on a line, the tenacious canine held its grip. At that moment, one of the remaining dogs grabbed the other tentacle.

Canthus attacked savagely, like a creature born to kill. Often the great moorhound was confused by the monster's apparent location, but when the blink dogs managed to hold the creature at bay, the hound made a shrewd guess and lunged in, clamping his jaws over a place that seemed to be in midair.

Sharp fangs sank through skin, and Canthus felt the blood pounding through the monster's neck. And now the moorhound's jaws began to close more tightly.

Shantu twisted and writhed in the grip of the dogs. The monster slashed with its rear claws, disemboweling one blink dog. Its sharp front claws sank into the moorhound's flanks, raking the skin and the ribs underneath it. Still Canthus retained his grip, gradually closing off the air to the monster's brain. He felt something snap, then felt the spurt of warm blood as his jaws closed tighter. Slowly the struggles of the displacer beast lessened in intensity, and finally the creature lay still.

Tristan turned his full attention back to Kazgoroth as the Beast lumbered out of the well, lowering its head to charge. Robyn rolled away from the water, still on the muddy ground. She looked up at the creature, pleading with her eyes, seeking some sign of the existence of the druid she had revered, but there was nothing.

The Beast lashed out toward Tristan with one bony claw, and again the sword snicked forward. Kazgoroth reared up to its full height, pulling away from the deadly blade. Then its red eyes fell upon Robyn, still staring upward in shock and horror.

"Run!" Tristan cried a warning and leaped at the monster as it reached for Robyn with its foreclaws. The young druid finally stood, her back against one of the statues, and now she held her staff up before her. "Run!" he shouted again, lunging toward the beast to attack with his sword.

"Die!" she said quietly and threw the staff on the ground at Kazgoroth's feet.

The sudden explosion of crackling flame threw Tristan violently backward, knocking him to the ground. Robyn stumbled to his side and lifted him up. He saw that she was sobbing.

The flames exploded from the ground, a wall of fire such as the goddess granted to her faithful. But this spell came not from the power of the Earthmother, for that power was no more. It came instead from the plain ashwood staff. The shaft consumed itself in calling forth the heat from the bowels of the earth, the cleansing tongue of earthfire.

Kazgoroth felt the fire and shrieked, the explosion of sound carrying the agonies of a thousand planes of hell. The explosion of flames engulfed the creature to the top of its head, feeding on the Beast's flesh and bone. It was a flame of purity and light, and it blossomed in stark contrast to the darkness of the vale. For a long time, it held its shape, blazing against the sky, and when it faded, Kazgoroth the Beast was gone.

Behind Tristan, the cadence of Tavish's song reached a new crescendo. The bard struck chords of triumph and joy, with a martial beat that matched the pounding of the king's own heart.

"Mother!" Colleen's cry jerked Tristan's attention from the Darkwell. He saw the sister knight standing over the corpse of the last of the deathbirds, but her gaze was directed out over the field, to the shattered wood beyond the well.

"What is *that?*" cried Robyn, shocked and horrified at the apparition that emerged from those woods. It was quickly followed by two more.

"By the goddess, no!" Colleen shrieked her heartbreak in a cry that pierced straight to Tristan's heart, for now he understood. The three creatures had once been Sisters of Synnoria. That much was obvious from the scant wisps of blond hair that still clung to their torn and rotting scalps, and from their petite bodies. But now they shuffled forward with the mindless gait of the walking dead.

These were no zombies, however, no mere animated corpses that stumbled stupidly in obedience to a master's command. These were undead creatures of purpose. Their eyes glowed a charcoal red, hellishly fixed upon the sister knight who had once been sister or daughter in blood. But now Colleen was merely a potential victim, and the death knights advanced to the kill.

And at the same time, in the center of the Darkwell, the true horror began.

*　*　*　*　*

"To the shore!" Grunnarch's cry echoed throughout the fleet, and the longships veered sharply away from the battle at Corwell Town. In moments, they slid onto the sandy shore below Caer Corwell itself. The northmen leaped from their boats into the shallow water, then hurriedly pulled their longships high onto the shore.

The men of Norland surged along the gravelly beach, following the Red King toward the battle. Grunnarch had landed them some distance away from the fight to prevent the sahuagin from attacking his ships in the water, where the fish-men would have a decided advantage.

Now the northmen formed into a long line of hardened warriors, their axes raised high, spears thrust forward, helms gleaming even under the overcast skies. A roaring challenge rose from their throats as they thundered across the field.

Near Grunnarch, the slender and beardless Koll raised his voice in what he hoped was a fearful yell. This was a battle he would not run away from, he resolved. Nearby, but still unnoticed, the smooth-skinned warrior who had quietly joined the Red King's crew also advanced with the charge.

A lumbering mass of bloated ogres met the first rush of the northmen's assault. Their heavy clubs rose and fell, but they could withstand neither the ferocity nor the numbers of the determined attackers. As the ogres fell under the rush, a solid rank of sahuagin, more than a thousand strong and supported by a great marching mass of undead, turned to meet the charge.

The clash of metal against metal grew to a thunderous din, and the war cries of the northmen mingled with the hisses and shrieks of the sahuagin. Beside them, the Ffolk surged forward to join the fray, but the numbers of the living dead were simply too great. Gradually the armies of evil began to spread around the flanks of their human foes. Fighting bravely, among ever-growing piles of dead, Grunnarch and Randolph and the warriors who stood with them slowly fell back.

* * * * *

*Bhaal seethed and twisted below the surface of the Darkwell. He felt the death of Shantu, a cruel lance that pricked his pride. He knew the agony of Kazgoroth as the Beast died in consummate pain, consumed by the earth power it had sought so long to destroy.*

*Nevertheless, these setbacks only served to anger the murderous god, and in his rage, he became even more terrible. His body coalesced around him into a physical tool, though his soul remained encased in the protection of the well. Bhaal erupted upward, spilling the foul black water from his body as he rose higher and still higher into the air, feeling for the first time the air of the Forgotten Realms upon the flesh of his body.*

*First came the head, with its long, manelike shag of hair. The face, marked by a grimace of supernatural hatred, came next, followed by the monstrous torso with its muscular arms and legs. The god loomed higher and higher, towering over the humans and the firbolg, the broken druid* arches, and eventually over the blackened trees themselves.

As Bhaal exploded out of the water, towering above the combatants around the well, he strode to the shore and emerged from the water with the ease of a child splashing through a wading pool.

Bhaal's eyes glowed, hot coals sparking with the flames of hell itself. His fists, mountainous clubs of rocklike flesh, reached forth, eager to squeeze mortal bodies to death. His voice was the cry of primal evil, a thunderous bellow that resounded across the Realms, smashing trees, scattering birds, and sending shivers of fear down the spines of all who heard.

And then Bhaal moved to attack.

# ᴥ 19 ᴥ

# DEATH IN THE DARKWELL

Robyn recoiled instinctively, the sight of the god striking her like an explosion, driving her to her knees. She stared dumbstruck, frozen by a primeval, nameless terror. The ground shook, and she fell onto her face, helplessly quivering.

Colleen, next to the well, looked away from the undead creatures that had once been her family. She stared at the god rising above her, and then she, too, collapsed, lying senseless in the dark mud.

Yak bellowed plaintively, a cry of deep, primitive panic, then turned and lumbered off toward the woods, fleeing as rapidly as his trunklike legs could carry him. The blink dogs also ran, one by one blinking out of sight as they streaked toward the relative safety of the woods.

Even Canthus cringed, but the courageous moorhound would not desert his master. Instead, he crept forward, leaving the torn body of the displacer beast, and slinked toward Tristan's side.

Brigit and Maura had been advancing toward the well when the might of Bhaal exploded into reality. Brigit dropped her sword and stood staring in shock and fear. Maura, with a soft moan of despair, turned and fled toward the woods.

The pace of Tavish's ballad wavered as the bard struck her first discordant note. Then the song faded away entirely as Tavish stared, awestruck and disbelieving, at the abomination that reared before them.

Only Tristan moved of his own will, backing slowly away

from the well but holding his sword upraised before him like a shield. He stared at the god, feeling a deep and slow-burning rage, but he filtered his anger through a haze of calm detachment. This was the enemy. This was the goal they had expended so much to reach. Now he glared at the monstrous apparition, understanding the risks of attacking it but needing desperately to see this thing slain.

The power of the Sword of Cymrych Hugh surrounded him like an aura. The dark god seemed to recognize this power, for the giant's steps took it straight toward the king. Tristan knew that his atonement, and perhaps his death, was at hand.

The High King stared upward. He saw two horns protruding from the vast forehead, each longer than himself. With strange detachment, he looked full into the hate-wrenched face, distorted and leering. The giant form lumbered closer, splashing itself dry, and still the young king awaited it. Now Tristan felt ready for the fight to begin!

"Hey, Yaz! Get a look at this guy! I've *never*—Yaz? Where are you? Hey, come on back here! We've got more battling to do!" Newt buzzed above Shantu's body, calling to his friend, but the sprite, like so many others, had been overcome by terror at the dark god's appearance. Newt shrugged and buzzed toward the well, wondering what all the fuss was about. Sure, this fellow was big, but wasn't there a proverb about that, or something?

"*You!*" The voice of the god was a rumble like the deepest torment of a dying earth, shaking the ground and causing the very flesh to shiver. Tristan, sensing that the god spoke directly to him, paused as Bhaal advanced.

The god rose higher from the well, black water hissing around his waist and massive thighs. His legs, with more girth than the most monstrous tree, carried him in long, powerful strides toward the shore of the pond.

Toward Tristan Kendrick.

The Sword of Cymrych Hugh glowed with a silvery light, shining with a brilliance clearly visible even in the daylight. Unlike during the battles with the deathbirds and the owlbear, the sword did not compel the king to attack.

Instead, it floated easily in his hand, ready to respond to Tristan's own will.

Tristan looked up at the body of his foe, towering fully five times his own height. His highest blow could strike no farther than the giant's thigh, but the sword of his ancestor seemed to raise the young king's own stature, reinforcing his arm and his will. Yet how could human will match the might of this awesome and terrible god?

The giant form suddenly lunged, striking with a fist the size of a haystack. Instinctively Tristan raised his blade, knowing he would be crushed beneath that terrible blow should it strike him.

The god's fist met the Sword of Cymrych Hugh with a sound like a thunderclap. The king reeled back from the force of the blow, dazed by the blast of sound, but he still stood! And Bhaal, too, staggered back, shaking his massive head in shock and confusion.

Once again the giant form advanced. Tristan raised the sword high over his head, poised to parry another blow. A surge of hope flowed through him.

Robyn threw her hands over her ears as the thunder crashed beside her once more. She pressed her face flat against the soft mud as if she could burrow away from her fright. Ever so gradually she drove back the paralysis of fear that gripped her. Finally she twisted around to face the sky, and then her head spun dizzily as she sat up again.

Robyn's vision focused, and she saw, not the god battling the king, but the three undead Sisters of Synnoria advancing toward Colleen, who still lay prostrate in the mud. The ghastly forms, whose rotted flesh and strawlike tendrils of hair mocked the beauty of their victim, were almost upon her.

Robyn was unaware of the golden medallion, glowing with the pure light of divine power, as she started toward the three death knights. The nearest reached for Colleen's hair, sprawled like golden straw in the mud, as Robyn approached. Unconsciously guided by some deep and potent instinct, her hand went to the medallion. She felt the warmth of the talisman flow through her body, carrying words to her mouth.

"Go! I banish thee, in the name of Chauntea!"

She held the medallion high before her, and the golden light spilled like the rays of the midsummer sun, shining over the ghastly, rotten faces of the undead. It struck their eyes as a potent lance of virtue, searing their dead nerves and forcing them back.

The three dead knights raised their clawlike hands out before them, but they shrank away from the medallion and the woman who carried it. Robyn slowed to a walk, concentrating on the force of the medallion, using it to turn the undead from their intended victim. For each step she advanced, the death knights shrank back farther, until at last she reached Colleen's side.

Some distant part of Robyn's mind watched in amazement as she called upon the power of a new god. She knew that she had performed an act sacred to clerics of the new gods, for no druid could exert such a power over death itself! Genna herself had told her this.

Her mind balked at the implications as another thunderclap shook the clearing. She turned to see Tristan stagger beneath yet another blow from Bhaal's fist. The giant threw back his head and bellowed his own pain, for this time his blow had cost him a deep gash in his finger.

Robyn helped Colleen to her feet as the undead knights continued to back away from her. The young sister leaned weakly against her shoulder, trembling, and Robyn began to half-lead, half-carry her away from the black water.

\* \* \* \* \*

Chauntea blossomed to her full height and sang a song of hope and promise. Her plane, Elysium, the realm of ultimate good, resounded with the chorus, and power at last flowed freely from the goddess to her newest devotee. For Robyn had opened the floodgates of devotion with her use of the Rose-in-Sun Medallion. Chauntea's love flowed like a benign enchantment into the body of the young woman, once a druid but now forevermore a cleric.

Chauntea felt the warmth of Robyn's own love flowing

back to her in return, for the woman sensed the kinship between the goddess Earthmother, patron of nature and the wilds, and the goddess Chauntea, patron of growth and agriculture.

This goddess could not replace the druid spells that the great mother had given to Robyn. Those were gone forever. But in their place, she sent the divine blessing of clerical might: the power to turn away the dark forces of the walking dead, the power to cure grievous wounds, the power to bless her companions.

And the powers of new spells, different from the nature of the spells Robyn had once cast but certainly no less powerful. Now Robyn, Cleric of Chauntea, stepped to the side of her king to face the power of ultimate darkness.

\* \* \* \* \*

"I banish thee, in the name of Chauntea!"

Friar Nolan held his clerical talisman proudly before him, and the dead of the sea shrank back, covering their eyes with rotted, fleshless hands.

"Forward, for Corwell!" Randolph, beside the cleric, called out a challenge, and a dozen men of the Ffolk rushed after him. His longsword cut the throat of a surprised sahuagin before the monster could react to the flight of its undead allies.

Theirs was but a small island of victory in a vast sea of defeat. The bold friar's spell could turn only a dozen or so undead at a time, enough to give Randolph and his men a chance for a brief, limited counterattack, but that was all.

To all sides, across the moors, through the streets, and up the slopes of Corwell Knoll, the dead of the sea ranged freely, accompanied and prodded by their reptilian mistresses. The arrival of the northmen had provided brief moments of hope, but they, too, were being overwhelmed by the sheer numbers of the foe.

Grunnarch stood in the forefront of his warriors, his great battle-axe rising and falling with machinelike regularity, slashing the head from a sahuagin or slicing the legs from a zombie. All around him sprawled the grisly remains of his victims. Grunnarch, in turn, was also surrounded by the bodies of many of his own men. And body for body, he knew the battle could have but one outcome.

Near him fought young Koll, the flush of berserker rage upon him. His own sword was long since smashed to pieces on the heavy shield of a sahuagin war chief, but he had seized the monster and broken its neck with his bare hands. Then he had grabbed the creature's trident, which he now used to lay about himself with fanatical savagery.

Wading through ankle-deep gore, surrounded by a thundering cacophony of sound, the chaos of a life-and-death struggle, Koll became a true warrior of the North. He felt newly born as the berserker frenzy carried him to heights of ferocity he could never have imagined. His mind whirled with a thousand new sensations, and he knew that he was one of those rare men of the North truly born to fight.

But even such a frenzy could not, alone, carry the day against such a numerous foe. Koll's trident pierced the chests of two zombies at once, pressing them backward and then pinning the struggling corpses to the ground. With a roar more leonine than human, he seized an axe from a fallen warrior and began hacking with that.

In a matter of moments, he was down, tripped by the long haft of a sahuagin spear. Another fish-man leaped forward to slice his throat with its sharp teeth, but before the horrible jaws could close, the monster fell dead, slain by a single sword thrust.

Koll looked up, the frenzy falling from his eyes, to see a smooth-cheeked young warrior standing over him. The fighter wielded his sword with smooth skill, cutting another fish-man down and sending a zombie stumbling backward with a dangling leg. His rescuer was short but solid.

The warrior reached a hand down toward Koll, lifting him to his feet, and as he rose, the woolen hood fell from the head of his rescuer.

"Gwen!"

Her brown eyes smiled back at him, though her mouth remained fixed in a grimace of intensity. She thrust again, wielding her blade with deft precision. Koll quickly stood at her back, and together they fought against the onslaught of undead and reptiles.

"Women do not belong in battle!" she quoted, slaying another sahuagin.

"Perhaps I was wrong." He lopped the legs from a bloated undead ogre.

"Northmen women, perhaps!" She gasped and slashed. "But I am a daughter of the Ffolk!"

"A fact I will never again forget," he conceded, and then the clash of battle drowned out their voices.

\* \* \* \* \*

The thunderous smash of god's fist against man's artifact again wracked the clearing, but this time Tristan stumbled to one knee. His lungs strained for air as the fight steadily sapped his strength. Once again his blow had made a deep cut into the flesh of Bhaal's giant hand, but once again he watched the flesh close over the wound. In seconds, there was no sign the god had even suffered injury.

Tavish's song echoed across the field, and the king silently praised the courageous bard for regaining control after the first horrifying emergence of the god. The music flowed like fresh blood into his heart and through his limbs, but still the oppressive weight of the battle threatened to doom him.

Robyn suddenly appeared at his side, holding her scimitar awkwardly. She hacked at the god's great foot, bravely ignoring the looming crunch of Bhaal's blow. Only Tristan's lightning grab pulled her out from beneath the crushing fist.

"Go back!" he gasped. "This is my fight!"

"No! I have to—" Once again the god struck, this time kicking savagely at the woman. Tristan pushed her aside, absorbing the brunt of the blow against his ribs. He staggered to the side and landed with a low grunt.

"Now, go!" he groaned, springing to his feet as Bhaal lumbered forward. "You don't stand a chance against him! Without my sword, I wouldn't either."

Robyn saw the Sword of Cymrych Hugh seem to lift the

king through an acrobatic leap to strike a deep gash in the god's shin. She sprang backward, biting back her frustration as she realized that Tristan spoke the truth. But what could she do?

Tristan faced another attack, barely managing to dodge aside. His evasion cost him his balance, and once again he sprawled facedown in the mud. How long can I hold out? he wondered, forcing himself back to his feet.

As if in answer, Bhaal suddenly reached down and seized the statue of a druid. He twisted his mighty hands, and the white stone cracked into several pieces. Raising his hand, he hurled the head at Tristan.

Only the king's instant reaction saved him as he flicked the sword upward and deflected the missile. Next the god threw the torso, and this time the weight of the stone smashed him backward to sprawl on the ground.

Bhaal loomed over him, bringing a great foot forward to crush the life from his helpless victim, but suddenly a figure appeared beside Tristan. Her golden hair flashed with a brilliance like her silver blade as Brigit stepped in to slice at the swinging foot.

The god bellowed his rage as Tristan squirmed out of the way. Bhaal swung his huge hand toward the sister knight before Brigit recovered her guard. The crushing force of the blow knocked the warrior a dozen paces and left Brigit lying twisted and motionless in the thick mud on the shore of the Darkwell.

Tristan scrambled to his feet once more as Bhaal picked up another statue, and then a third, breaking them into pieces and hurling the fragments at the desperately twisting king. Tristan darted to the left, rolled to the right, leaped and ducked to avoid each missile. Somehow he succeeded, though the chunks of stone shattered against the ground or cut deep furrows in the sod all around him. He felt the earth itself shake under each impact.

Snarling, Canthus leaped at the giant feet of the god, but his fangs could do nothing to harm, or even distract, the monstrous opponent. Still he savaged the skin and ripped the flesh of the godly foe. Bhaal kicked at the dog and he sprang away. Then, as the giant turned his attention back to Tristan, the moorhound sprang once again and sank his fangs into Bhaal's flesh.

Tristan began to stagger with fatigue, the strain of his desperate evasion tactics threatening to drag him down. "By the legacy of Cymrych Hugh, give me strength!" The king whispered a desperate invocation, and sudden vitality flowed again through his veins. The sword glowed like a beacon before him, but the physical form of the god towered above him, above them all.

Bhaal again smashed a statue, but this time he hurled the pieces over the king and into the clearing beyond. Robyn dodged one that seemed directed at her, but another fragment of stone smashed into Tavish's chest, crushing the lute with a discordant twang. The bard flew backward, sprawling on the ground and gasping for breath.

Sobbing, Tavish sat up and looked at the shattered ruin of her instrument. Suddenly she pressed one hand to her face and realized that the spectacles had again fallen from her nose. The bard scrambled to her knees and desperately sought the crystal glasses on the muddy ground. Not knowing how else to help, Robyn joined her.

Bhaal smashed yet another statue, throwing the pieces at Tristan this time, but the king parried each with the blade, which moved more quickly than the eye could follow. He fought on pure instinct now, trusting the sword to parry blows that came too fast for his own reactions.

He saw an opening as the god bent to crush the last statue. Suddenly Tristan leaped forward and swung the Sword of Cymrych Hugh in a great slashing arc. He had never delivered a more powerful blow. His sword seemed to sing through the air with the speed of its flight, and the keen blade bit deep into the god's leg.

Bhaal roared in pain and rage, sinking to one knee as the wounded leg collapsed beneath him. Even as Tristan pulled back to strike another blow, however, the wound closed and the god again reared to his full height.

Robyn finally located the wire frames amid the trampled mud of the field. "Here . . . your spectacles!" Quickly she handed them to Tavish.

Frantically the bard wiped the mud from the glasses and perched them on her nose. One lens, the one that had been cracked, was gone entirely, smashed by the force of the god's blow. But the other one, smeared as it was, allowed her to see Bhaal in all his festering horror. She saw a body as raw as an open sore, surrounded in the black stuff of death. Only at the center of the body could she see a glow of vitality.

There, as Bhaal twisted away, she saw a curious thing. The pulsating might of the god's life force came to him through a long, silvery cord attached to the middle of his back! Tavish saw that the cord twisted its way down toward the Darkwell, winding its way across the surface of the water to touch a point near the middle of the well.

Surprised, she removed the glasses and saw simply the form of a giant beside the pond. Only when she placed the lens over her eye did she see the true vile nature of his body, and the cord that connected it to its soul, or life essence, or whatever source from which it drew its fiendish vitality.

"Come here!" she called to Robyn. "Can you see that?"

Tavish handed Robyn the spectacles, and she looked toward the giant figure. She saw past the king, past the form of the god, following with her eyes the silver cord leading to his root in the well. Quickly she moved closer to get a better view, stifling her revulsion, for she looked directly into the dark soul of Bhaal.

There in the middle of the well it floated, a pulsating bulb of dark evil. It glowed a hellish crimson, like liquid coal, as it slowly throbbed beneath the surface of the water. It looked much like a human heart, but huge and unmistakably perverted.

Gasping with strain, she at last turned away from the horrible beating of the great organ. The sight of the thing was an affront to her eyes, its image sending waves of disgust through her.

But at last, she thought, she may have discovered a way to harm the beast-god.

* * * * *

Grunnarch's arms grew numb with the strain of raising and lowering his axe. His valiant band of warriors had formed a great circle, their backs against the rocky knoll of Caer Corwell. Beside him fought the Ffolk in a similar circle, but from all sides pressed the tireless assault of their inhuman foes.

Finally Grunnarch's mighty strength failed, for just a moment. His axe became wedged in the skull of a great ogre zombie, and before he could pull it free, clawed hands scratched at his legs. Moist, rotten flesh fell from arms that seized his waist.

Undead hands ripped the axe from his hands and pulled his feet out from under him. A half-dozen zombies dragged the Red King from the circle of his men, and though the warriors of the north made a valiant rush to reclaim their king, the ranks of the enemy closed behind him, and Grunnarch the Red disappeared among the festering bodies of the dead of the sea.

* * * * *

Once again the powerful sword bit into the god's flesh, only to have the wound close behind it scarcely after the weapon was withdrawn. The thunderous explosion of sound had become almost routine as Tristan desperately strove to somehow defeat this thing.

"There's got to be a way!" gasped the king, whirling away and narrowly avoiding a crushing fist.

"There is! Bite him!" Newt popped into view beside the king and darted forward to sink his tiny sharp teeth into the god's calf. "Yuck!" The faerie dragon spat disgustedly, ignoring Bhaal's sudden swat, then popped out of sight once again.

"Tristan! We've found the secret! The glasses showed us the key!" Robyn once again appeared beside Tristan before the awesome giant. Breathlessly she described the vision that she and Tavish had seen through the glasses.

"We'll never harm the body out here, because its true soul

is in the well! That's the key!"

Bhaal pulled a huge tree trunk from the earth, ripping it free as a man might pluck a stalk of wheat. He swung the timber at the humans who stood before him. Once again Tristan raised his sword. The blade met the trunk solidly, and thunder smote their ears. The tree shattered to splinters, yet Tristan and the sword still stood.

"What can we do about it?" asked the king quickly.

"See if you can get to the shore. The god seems to try to keep us away from the well. Can you get past it?" Robyn once again slashed with her scimitar, ineffective as an attack but serving to attract the god's attention.

"I'll give it a try. Any plan is better than nothing!" Tristan darted to one side and tried to race past the towering form of the god, but Bhaal quickly stepped into his path, forcing the king back with a series of heavy blows, striving desperately to drive the man back from the Darkwell.

Robyn hacked at the god's heel with the scimitar, narrowly missing being kicked as Bhaal twisted toward her while still holding Tristan at bay. As she stumbled backward, her hand fell upon the ivory horn she had tucked into her belt— the horn of the unicorn, Kamerynn.

An idea born of desperation formed in her mind, and she dropped the scimitar and pulled out the horn. "I'm going to try something! Run to the well—now!"

Tristan didn't stop to question Robyn, though he wondered at her boldness as she dropped the silver weapon. He sprinted past the god's foot in a desperate race toward the Darkwell.

Bhaal spun on his other foot and lurched after the king, ignoring Robyn for a moment. She hefted the horn of Kamerynn high above her head like a javelin. Then she leaped to the side of Bhaal's foot as the god crouched to spring after Tristan. Putting all the force she could summon behind it and calling on the might of her newfound goddess to aid her blow, she drove the horn down toward the huge foot.

The unicorn's horn plunged through the skin and the flesh of the god's foot, through the bottom, and into the earth below. Like a huge nail, it anchored the foot to the ground.

Bhaal's bellow of rage shook the very depths of the earth, felling nearby trees and sending ripples across the water of the well. As the force of sound struck Tristan, he stumbled forward, struggling to regain his balance.

The physical body of Bhaal swayed precariously and crashed to the ground, its foot still firmly pinned by the horn. The earth itself trembled beneath the impact, and several more trees toppled to the ground. Tristan lost his footing and sprawled in the mud. Quickly he scrambled to his knees, holding his sword upraised, and for a moment, he thought he was free.

Suddenly a massive hand pinned him to the earth, driving the wind from his chest and threatening to crush his rib cage. He squirmed and managed to free his hands, including his sword, but then the massive fingers wrapped around him and lifted him from the ground. He groaned as the force of Bhaal's grip twisted his spine and slowly began to squeeze the life from him.

The links of his chain mail armor pressed into his skin, but the flexible armor seemed to absorb some of the crushing squeeze. Nonetheless, he could not draw a breath or move his torso or legs.

He looked desperately toward the well, a hundred feet away, as a red haze floated before his eyes. The black pool might have been a hundred miles distant, for all the good it did him. Through the mist he saw, or imagined, the crimson pulse of Bhaal's essence in the center of the well.

Pain exploded in Tristan's ears as the pressure of the blood pounding in his head grew to agonizing proportions. He tried to jab his blade into the hand that held him, but the angle made the attack impossible. He could only wave the weapon in the air fruitlessly, cursing this monstrous thing that was crushing the life out of him. He felt his consciousness rapidly slipping away.

Dimly he thought again of Robyn's message and pictured the soul of the god, so near yet so impossibly far. With his last strength, his lungs burning from lack of air, he threw his arm back and cast the Sword of Cymrych Hugh high into the air, toward the black water of the Darkwell.

The blade arched upward, spinning slowly, shining against the dark clouds that glowered overhead. Robyn froze, her heart pounding, as she saw the king's last desperate effort to save himself. Tavish held her breath as the weapon began its lazy descent. Still spinning, it seemed to tumble so slowly that time itself paused anxiously, waiting to see what would happen.

It became clear to them all that the sword would fall far short of the center of the well. It would not even reach the water. Tristan's awareness faded to black as he saw the sword drop inexorably toward the muddy shore. Robyn fought back a sob without success. Tavish sat, stupefied and devastated, on the ground.

Suddenly an orange shape popped into view, hovering in the air beside the falling sword. "Not here!" Newt grabbed the weapon in his forepaws, although the weight of the sword almost bore the faerie dragon to the earth.

"Over *here!*" Hovering awkwardly with the heavy weight, the dragon fluttered to the center of the Darkwell and dropped the sword.

The silver blade disappeared into the water with a soft splash, and for a moment nothing happened. Then the physical body of Bhaal cried out with a shriek of agony that made his thunderous roars throughout the battle seem almost silent. Robyn clapped her hands to her ears and fell backward, stunned.

The god's hand opened reflexively, and Tristan tumbled to the ground, unconscious. And then the flesh of the giant body began to shrivel and smoke, falling away from the bone in a hissing cloud of decay. Bhaal cried out again, a dull moan this time, and then the body vanished into a sizzling heap of gory sludge. Flowing into the well, the red liquid mass of Bhaal's flesh crackled with blue flame. Smoke erupted from the flesh, but the fire shed no heat.

The water of the Darkwell bubbled and seethed in a torment of agony as the blade struck deep into the god's unprotected soul. The bulb of his essence leaked ichor from a long gash where the Sword of Cymrych Hugh had sliced into it. Now the thing swirled through the water, torn asunder and rapidly spilling its power into the black water.

Explosions wracked the pond, casting curtains of steam and sludge into the surrounding air. The ground vibrated from a primordial wrenching, and gouts of steam and flame filled the sky.

Clouds of rancid smoke rose into the sky, destroying the Sword of Cymych Hugh with their venom, but at the same time driving the soul of Bhaal, writhing in torment, back from the Moonshaes, out of the Realms, and down through his dark gate.

\*　\*　\*　\*　\*

Grunnarch twisted and squirmed in the grasp of the dead, unable to break free. The zombies carried him through a throng of their own, but they did not kill him. Then the Red King learned why.

The animated corpses dumped him on the ground before a human, a living man in this sea of dead or reptilian enemies. The man was fat and ugly, his visage dominated by a cruel sneer that marked his bloated features.

Grunnarch struggled to rise, but the press of carrion behind him held him down.

"You are the king of the North," the man remarked calmly, as the zombies held back the raging king. Grunnarch spat toward him, but the spittle fell short.

"Spirited to the end, I see. I like that. My followers have brought you before me so that I may observe your death at close hand. Now I see that you shall make that a most pleasant experience."

Suddenly the fat man grasped his chest, a grimace of deep pain crossing his face. He moaned and staggered. At the same time, Grunnarch felt the grip of the zombies on his arms and legs weaken. With a surge of effort, the Red King broke free.

He did not notice the dead of the sea falling in legions all around him as the power of their god evaporated from the priestesses of the sahuagin.

He did see, however, the fear growing in the face of the man before him as Grunnarch closed his powerful hands about the cleric's neck. The Red King relished the growing awareness of impending death and the expression of despair in the man's eyes.

Something else glared hatefully from those eyes as well, though Grunnarch did not understand it. As Hobarth died, the cleric's last bitter thoughts were of his god. The cleric perished amid a horrible sense of betrayal, for here, in the hour of their ultimate victory, his god had forsaken him.

All across the field, the undead fell like twigs in the wind. The ogre corpses of the Scarlet Guard, the dead sailors of the sea, all were returned at last to the death that had been so cruelly interrupted. Without the power of Bhaal to animate them, the army disintegrated to so much carrion.

Now the Ffolk and the warriors of the North pressed forward, driving the sahuagin before them. The fish-men reeled in confusion, many of them turning on their priestesses in rage. The battle had been all but won with the legions of the dead beside them. Now it was sahuagin against human, and the numbers of the humans were as great as their own.

As one great, seething mass, the sahuagin turned toward the sea. They would fight no more for Bhaal.

\*　\*　\*　\*　\*

Robyn lifted her hand from Pawldo's head as the halfling's eyes blinked open.

"What—what happened? Where did they go?" Pawldo looked around, half afraid that the battle still raged. Finally he sat up, confused but relieved. Tristan, Colleen, and Tavish stayed with the halfling as Robyn hurried over to Brigit's still form on the shore of the pond.

The well was no longer dark, though neither could it be called a Moonwell. It lay placid now, simply a pond awaiting the cool ice of winter.

Robyn performed the same healing magic upon Brigit, and slowly the sister's eyes flickered open. She sensed, even before she sat up, that the vale around them was peaceful once again.

From the woods, Maura emerged, her eyes downcast. Colleen went to her companion and embraced her. The sister knight's shame at her flight was plainly visible, but no one censured her for it. They had all felt the same mind-numbing terror as Bhaal burst forth from the well. Yak and Yazilliclick soon followed the warrior into the clearing.

Tristan stepped to Robyn's side as she looked across the pond. "Your spells . . . how did you get them back?" he asked.

"These are new spells." Robyn looked wistful for a moment, then turned to the king with a soft smile. "I know I shall never have the old ones back, for the goddess is indeed dead. The Moonshaes are a mundane land now, like any other place in the Realms.

"But there are still gods to worship, benign and good gods. I have found one of those, and she has taken me to her heart. Together we will make this land grow again."

"And this is Chauntea?"

"Yes, she of the Rose-in-Sun sign." Robyn nodded at the well, then looked back at the king. "You, too, have lost something."

He looked toward the water, where the Sword of Cymrych Hugh had vanished forever. "It was a fitting end for the sword. I hope that its destruction also marks the end of my need for a weapon."

The king turned back to the black-haired woman beside him. "The beast is slain now, and the northmen . . . Grunnarch is a good man and a strong king. He and I will be allies, and our friendship will seal the peace between our peoples."

Robyn nodded. "With such a mixture of old and new, both the northmen and the Ffolk cannot help but prosper."

For a moment, thoughts of his past flooded Tristan's mind. He pictured his lifelong teacher, Arlen, killed in the first skirmish of the Darkwalker War. He recalled the sacrifice of the blacksmith, Gavin, saving Robyn as the Bloodriders stormed into Caer Corwell, but only at the cost of his own life. And all the others who had died during the war rooted in the bowels of a dark and hateful god.

"Is the god Bhaal truly dead?"

"I don't think so. I don't think we could possibly kill him, at least not here in our own world. But that is of little matter. The truth is that his power here has been broken, and so it shall remain for many generations."

The king thought for a moment of Daryth, and he knew that his pain would never vanish entirely. He said a silent prayer to his friend. Somehow, perhaps only because of his present sense of well-being, he felt a whisper of affection and forgiveness in Daryth's memory.

Then his mind came back to the present, and he smiled unconsciously. His shoulders had grown accustomed to bearing the weight of his chain mail, but now he unclasped the armor and shrugged free of it. He felt a delightful lightness of foot as the iron rings fell free.

Tristan looked awkwardly away from Robyn, disturbed by the warm glow in her green eyes. Then he looked back, hesitantly placing his arms upon her shoulders.

"I know I have hurt you, and we have seen the agent of this hurt today, in the body of your teacher and the Beast, Kazgoroth. Once I claimed to have been bewitched by her, but I know this isn't true. I simply made a mistake—an error in judgment that, because it has caused you such pain, I would do anything to take back. But I can't do that. All I can do is hope that you will be able to forgive me."

"I can," Robyn said simply, smiling. It was as if the weight of a great burden had been lifted from the king's shoulders. "The only bewitchment, I fear," Robyn went on, "was the anger in me that would not die. That anger was a poison as venomous as your infidelity, and lasting far longer. I believe that was her whole purpose in pursuing you, to break the bonds that hold us together.

"I owe you thanks that your love was deep enough to accept my anger, and still keep you by my side."

He swept her into his arms, kissing her warmly, and welcoming her returning embrace. A thought came to him as he remembered the calling of her druidic faith, when Robyn had been willing to serve her goddess as Great Druid, should such be the Earthmother's need.

"This new goddess . . . does she require . . . that is, must you remain chaste? Will you marry me?"

"I know nothing about that aspect of my new faith," Robyn said in mock seriousness, "but I promise not to ask until our children are grown."

\* \* \* \* \*

*The soul of Bhaal tumbled away from the well, down from the Moonshae Islands, out of the Forgotten Realms. The cord connecting the god to his home plane of Gehenna contracted violently, pulling his tortured and writhing form through the ether.*

*Thus Bhaal was ripped through the Outer Planes, past the bottomless pit of the Abyss, above the fiery levels of Hell, to be cast in defeat and impotence on the flaming mountainside that was his own world.*

*Here he lay in broken despair, scorned by other gods of evil who now far superseded him in might and influence, reviled by the gods of good who took great joy in his banishment. Motionless, Bhaal knew only suffering.*

*Thus he would lie for generations, as a forgotten god and a distant relic of the human past.*

# ✹ Epilogue ✹

They debated the merits of springtime but quickly decided to wed at the height of the Yule festivals. Friar Nolan performed the ceremony. A diamond ring bearing a stone of impressive size, a gift from Pawldo of Lowhill, symbolized their union.

The Great Hall of Caer Corwell overflowed with celebrators, and the party spilled into the courtyard, where great fires burned, holding winter's chill at bay.

Grunnarch and his northmen had stayed in Corwell, and they were joined by other guests from all over the isles: Lord Llewellyn and his own young bride, the Lady Fiona of Callidyrr; Lords Koart, Dynnatt, and Fergus from the cantrevs of Corwell; Brigit and a full complement of the Sisters of Synnoria; and the halflings of Lowhill. To a tumultuous welcome just prior to the ceremony, the dwarven chieftain Finellen arrived with a hundred of her doughty warriors.

The wedding itself was a simple ceremony, marred only by a minor incident as Newt surprised the guests with an illusion of a huge red dragon. They soon returned to the hall, and everything proceeded according to plan.

As winter closed in, Corwell bundled snugly against the world. Cheery fires glowed in every hearth, none more cheery than the blaze lighting the great fireplace of Caer Corwell. Once again the Ffolk sensed that their only enemies were natural ones, foes with which they had long coped successfully.

The great bulk of Caer Allisynn, the floating fortress,

stood at the shore of the firth throughout the winter, though heavy surf made access to the keep impossible. With the coming of spring, swimmers found the massive structure at rest firmly on the bottom.

The underwater exploration of the ancient building, smaller than Caer Corwell but more finely constructed, occupied the king for most of the summer, and the queen as well, until her pregnancy made such excursions dangerous. The relics of ancient glory, including volumes of lore from the time of Cymrych Hugh, would keep the bards and scribes busy for years.

The line of Kendricks received an addition in the autumn with the birth of the Princess Alicia. By late winter, yet another royal heir was expected.

Peace with the North became a fact of the land. The combined skills of the seafaring northmen and the craftsmanship of the Ffolk proved clearly useful to both peoples, and the recent military accomplishments of the Ffolk served as additional deterrence against any future raids.

The land itself did not change drastically. The blasted areas of Myrloch Vale gradually returned to normal. The fields continued to be worked with hoof and plow, but their area was considerably enlarged. The wild places grew smaller and fewer, though they still existed. The memory of the goddess remained with the land and the Ffolk, but the changing of eras had begun.

There were those, including the High King, who felt that perhaps this increased use of the land was not a bad thing, that perhaps it was merely the sign of fortuitous progress. Certainly this represented the view of the goddess Chauntea, and through her blessing came many years of bounty from the land.

And many healthy children to the Ffolk.

## THE AUTHOR

Douglas Niles is a Wisconsin native and former high school teacher who now writes and designs games for TSR, Inc. His game designs include THE HUNT FOR RED OCTOBER™, a boardgame based on Tom Clancy's novel of the same name, ONSLAUGHT™, DRAGONLANCE® adventure modules, and the ADVANCED DUNGEONS & DRAGONS® BATTLESYSTEM™ game, which won the 1985 H.G. Wells Award for best miniatures rules. He has written numerous interactive books and nearly two dozen role-playing modules. This is his third novel.

He lives in Delavan, Wisconsin, with his wife Chris, children Allison and David, and a 180-pound Saint Berlabrador named Yukon.

# ACKNOWLEDGMENTS

The creation of the Moonshae Trilogy has been a joyous task for the past few years, but it has not been mine alone. I am grateful for the opportunity to thank some of those who have contributed their energies.

Foremost has been the work of three talented editors who have helped shape the trilogy from its inception to its final form. Pat McGilligan, Mary Kirchoff, and Bill Larson have each provided invaluable aid and criticism to the books. Jim Ward has also been a source of wonderful ideas and (brutally) honest evaluations of manuscripts.

I owe thanks also to a team of British game designers, Graeme Morris, Phil Gallagher, and Jim Bambra. While the work we collaborated upon never came to be, some of its ingredients went on to become the Darkwalker.

Also to Jeff Grubb and Ed Greenwood, who found a place for my islands in the Forgotten Realms and made them welcome there.

And finally to Mike Cook and Lorraine Williams, for seeing these tales published.

Douglas Niles

# NOW ON YOUR HOME COMPUTER: ACTION
# AND ADVENTURE IN THE FORGOTTEN REALMS®!

# BUCK ROGERS
## BOOKS

# ARRIVAL

*Stories By Today's Hottest*
*Science Fiction Writers!*

Flint  Dille
Abigail  Irvine
M.S.  Murdock
Jerry  Oltion
Ulrike  O'Reilly
Robert  Sheckley

**A.D. 1995:** An American pilot flies a suicide mission against an enemy Space Defense Platform to save the world from nuclear war. Buck Rogers blasts his target and vanishes in a fiery blaze.

**A.D. 2456:** In the midst of this 25th century battle-field an artifact is discovered--one that is valuable enough to ignite a revolution. This artifact is none other than the perfectly preserved body of the 20th century hero, Buck Rogers.

# BUCK ROGERS
BOOKS

# THE MARTIAN WARS TRILOGY
## *M.S. Murdock*

*Rebellion 2456:* Buck Rogers joins NEO, a group of freedom fighters dedicated to ridding Earth of the Martian megacorporation RAM. NEO's goal is to gain enough of a following to destroy RAM's Earth Space Station. The outcome of that mission will determine the success of Earth's rebellion. Available in May 1989.

*Hammer of Mars:* Ignoring RAM threats and riding on the wave of NEO's recent victory, Buck Rogers travels to Venus to strike an alliance. Furious, RAM makes good on its threats and sends its massive armada against a defenseless Earth. Available in August 1989.

*Armageddon Off Vesta:* Martian troops speed to Earth in unprecedented numbers. Earth's survival depends on Buck's negotiations with Venus. But even as Venus considers offering aid to Earth, Mercury is poised to attack Venus. Relations among the inner planets have never been worse! Available in October 1989.

# DRAGONLANCE® *Preludes*

### *Darkness and Light*
Paul Thompson and Tonya Carter

*Darkness and Light* tells of the time Sturm and Kitiara spent traveling together before the fated meeting at the Inn of the Last Home. Accepting a ride on a gnomish flying vessel, they end up on Lunitari during a war. Eventually escaping, the two separate over ethics.

### *Kendermore*
Mary L. Kirchoff

A bounty hunter charges Tasslehoff Burrfoot with violating the kender laws of prearranged marriage. To ensure his return, Kendermore's council has his Uncle Trapspringer prisoner. Tas meets the last woolly mammoth and an alchemist who pickles one of everything, including kender!

### *Brothers Majere*

The origins of the brothers' love/hate relationship. Distraught over his ailing mother, Caramon reluctantly allows her to die. Unable to forgive his brother, or himself for his inability to help her, Raistlin agrees to pursue her last wish, an unwitting pawn in the struggle.

# NOW ON YOUR HOME COMPUTER: THE
# DRAGONLANCE® GAME WORLD COMES ALIVE!